THE
BLOOMSDAY
DEAD

ADRIAN McKINTY

SCRIBNER

NEW YORK   LONDON   TORONTO   SYDNEY

🜊

SCRIBNER
1230 Avenue of the Americas
New York, NY 10020

Copyright © 2007 by A. G. McKinty

SCRIBNER and design are trademarks of
Macmillan Library Reference USA, Inc., used under license
by Simon & Schuster, the publisher of this work.

For information about special discounts for bulk purchases,
please contact Simon & Schuster Special Sales:
1-800-456-6798 or business@simonandschuster.com

Text set in New Caledonia

Manufactured in the United States of America

10 9 8 7 6 5 4 3 2 1

Library of Congress Cataloging-in-Publication Data
McKinty, Adrian.
The Bloomsday dead / Adrian McKinty.
p. cm.
I. Title.
PS3563.C38322B55 2007
813'.54—dc22   2006050492

ISBN-13: 978-0-7432-6644-4
ISBN-10:   0-7432-6644-7

The only arms I allow myself to use: silence, exile and cunning.

—James Joyce, *Portrait of the Artist as a Young Man* (1916)

THE BLOOMSDAY DEAD

1: TELEMACHUS
(LIMA, PERU—JUNE 15, 6:00 A.M.)

S tate LY Plum P. Buck Mulligan." Hector handed me this message on the cliffs at Miraflores.

I set the binoculars on the wall, took the note, and put it in my pocket. Hector was watching my face to see if there was annoyance or even dread in my eyes, but I was giving nothing away.

The sun was rising over the Andes, turning the Pacific a pinkish blue. The sky to the east was a long golden gray and in the west the Southern Cross and the moon had set into the sea.

I thanked Hector with a nod and put my sunglasses on.

Wild lilacs were growing among the cacti and a warm breeze was blowing through the poplars. There was, as yet, no traffic and normally it would be peaceful up here. Just the cliffs and the beach and the whole of the sleeping city behind me. Fog burning off the headland and a few early-morning dog walkers demonstrating that Latin love for miniature poodles and Lhasas.

"Lovely, isn't it?" I said in English.

Hector shook his head uncomprehendingly.

I smiled, watched the usual dazzling collection of seabirds rising on the thermals off the cliffs. Occasionally you'd see an albatross or a peregrine falcon and rarer still sometimes a lost condor or two.

The smell of orange blossom and oleander.

"Lima has a bad rap, but I like it," I said in Spanish.

Especially this time of day before the two-stroke motors and the diesel engines and the coal fires really got going. Hector nodded, pleased with the remark and happy that he'd found me before I retired to bed. He knew that after the night shift I liked to come here with a cup of coffee. Last week I came to watch the first transit of Venus in living memory but mostly it was either to do some amateur ornithology or, he suspected, to stare through the binocs at the pretty surfer girls catching the big rolling breakers at the meeting of the continent and the ocean.

Today about a dozen early surfers, all of them in their teens, wearing full wet suits, booties, and gloves. Half of them female, a new feature of the scene in the city. None of them looked like Kit, the surfer girl I'd been forced to kill in Maine a long time ago, but they all reminded me of her—I mean, that's the sort of thing you never get over.

I sipped the coffee, frowned at the sound of a power drill. This particular morning, much to my annoyance, it was not quiet up here. There were a score of grips and roadies building the set for a free concert by the Indian Chiefs. They were working with un-Peruvian noise and diligence and it didn't surprise me at all to see that their supervisor was an Australian.

Hector blinked at me in that obvious way of his, to prod me into action.

"Thanks for the note, Hector, you go on home," I said.

"Is everything ok, boss?" he asked.

"No, but I'll take care of it," I responded.

Hector nodded. He was still only a kid. I'd been training him for about three months and he didn't look at all uncomfortable in the suit and tie that I'd bought for him. I'd taught Hector to be polite, calm, well mannered and now he could be employed as a bouncer anywhere in the world. I'm sure the customers at the Lima Miraflores Hilton had no idea that Hector lived in a house he had built himself in the *pueblos jóvenes* slums to the east of here, where the walls were corrugated metal sheets, where water came from a stand pipe and sewage ran in the street. Displaced from his shanty, Hector appeared elegant, poised, and aristocratic. The marriage of a conquistador bloodline with Inca royalty. And he was smart and he had compassion. He was an ideal lieutenant. He couldn't be more than twenty-one or twenty-two; he'd go far, probably have my job in five or six years.

"It seems a bit early for this kind of nonsense," he said with a resigned shake of the head. He was talking about the contents of the note.

"It's either very early or very late," I agreed.

"Are you sure you don't want me to deal with it, I don't mind," Hector said with another look of sympathy.

He knew I'd had a rough night of it. A kid from Sweden had taken an overdose and I'd had to see him to the hospital, then I kicked some whores out of the lobby, and then we'd dealt with an elderly American couple who claimed they couldn't breathe in the polluted air and wanted an oxygen machine. Later today the Japanese ambassador to Peru was coming for an informal breakfast talk on the possibility of extraditing disgraced Peruvian ex-president Fujimori from his bolt hole in Tokyo. The talks wouldn't go anywhere but it was good for all parties to be seen looking for a solution. Good for the hotel especially. The ambassador had his own security people, but we didn't need a disturbance wrecking the tranquility of the visit.

"No, I'll fix it, Hector, you can go on home," I said.

Hector nodded, walked back across the street to change into his jeans and T-shirt for the scooter ride to the slums. He'd been on the night shift, too, and was bound to be tired.

The surfers were doing lazy cutbacks and the sun was inching over those high, dry mountains that someday I'd go and visit. A blind man had recently climbed Everest, so surely I, a man challenged merely with an artificial foot, could hike the Inca Trail to Machu Picchu.

I took a big swig of the coffee and set down the cup.

A few schoolgirls had come by to see if the roadies could give them backstage passes to the Chiefs; the roadies had none to give away but they chatted up the girls anyway.

"Get your backs into it, you dago bastards," the Australian foreman barked. Without the note drawing me away to business I might have gone over and smacked that bugger for spoiling my meditations.

I looked at the message. It was easy enough to decipher.

In stateroom LY (that is, the fiftieth floor, suite Y), a Plum (in other words, a drunk American) named Mr. P. Buck was creating a Mulligan (i.e., a disturbance). The codes had been established by the previous head of security at the Miraflores Hilton, an avid golfer. At some point

I was going to drop the references to Mulligans, Eagles, Birdies, and the like. But I'd only been here for a few months and there were other, more pressing priorities.

I sighed, crumpled the note in disgust, and threw it in the nearest garbage can.

A drunk American, probably fighting with a prostitute.

P. Buck—I wondered if R.E.M. were in town, the guitarist was called Peter Buck and had once been arrested and acquitted of being drunk and disorderly on a British Airways flight. I shook my head. If an American rock star had been staying at my hotel, I would have known about it before now. Still, Peter Buck was one of my heroes and I crossed the street with a heightened level of expectation.

The hotel was new, tall, gleaming with glass and curved stainless steel—like something Frank Gehry might have come up with on a bad day.

Tinco, the nervous Ecuadorean night manager, grabbed me at the double doors.

"I heard," I said before he could open his mouth.

"Stateroom LY, hurry, please, we have the Japanese ambassador arriving this morning," he said, grasping his hands in front of him in a pleading gesture.

"I know," I said. "Don't worry, relax, I'll take care of it."

"One of the girls has complained," he said, looking sadly at the floor.

"Which girls? The hookers?"

"The maid. She's very young."

He wanted me to come up with a solution before I'd even assessed what the problem was.

"Ok, I'll send her away for a week and when she comes back you give her a raise and we'll keep an eye on her to see if she keeps her mouth shut. Got it?"

Tinco nodded. I yawned and headed for the bank of elevators.

Usually I showered and went to bed now and slept until two or three in the afternoon, when the older, tradition-bound Peruvians were getting up from their siestas. And like I say, it had been a tedious, tiring night and I was looking forward to some shut-eye.

Hopefully, this wouldn't take too long.

I pressed the P button and the lift sped me up to the penthouses on the fiftieth floor. It was a boast of the hotel that it was one of the tallest buildings in South America but even the express elevators seemed to take forever.

I took the time to adjust my appearance in the mirror.

My hair was in the crew cut of an Israeli commando, dirty blond, but recently I'd noticed a couple of gray strands around the ears. I hadn't had a chance to shave, and I looked a little rougher than usual, though the Peruvian sun had done much to erase the obvious Paddy pallor in my features. I'd do.

The elevator doors clicked.

I checked guns one and two, hitched down the bottom of my trousers, drank the rest of my coffee. I turned left and strolled toward room LY.

The sound of fighting coming down the hall. No, not fighting, someone smashing things up.

So he hadn't got himself exhausted just yet.

I hastened my pace.

Nice up here. Plush golden carpets, paintings of the Andes and Indian women in bowler hats. Fresh flowers, views up and down the foggy coast.

I turned the corner. There was a maid I didn't know and Tony, one of my boys, standing patiently at the stateroom's entrance. Tony smiled at me and jerked his thumb through the door.

"How bad is it?" I asked.

"Not bad, he's trashed the room, but he hasn't hurt himself yet," Tony said.

"He alone?"

"He's alone and lonely. He tried to grab Angelika here," Tony said. "She doesn't speak Spanish so good; she didn't know what he wanted."

Angelika nodded. She was a flat-faced Indian girl, probably just in from the highlands. I pulled out my wallet and removed ten twenty-dollar bills. I gave them to Angelika and said to Tony, "Tell her she didn't see anything, nothing happened here."

Tony nodded and told her the same thing in Quechua, the Indian language of the mountains.

Angelika took the money, seemed very pleased, and curtsied to me.

"She can take the rest of the week off," I said. "Maybe have a little vacation." I gave her five more Andrew Jacksons.

"*Muchas gracias,* Señor Forsignyo," Angelika said.

"It's nothing, I'm sorry this had to happen to you," I said and Tony translated.

I gave her my empty coffee mug and said *"Yusulipayki,"* the only word I knew in Quechua. She thanked me in return and shuffled off down the corridor. She'd be ok. The crashing continued from inside the room.

"He keeps saying that he's not happy," Tony said.

"Nobody's bloody happy."

"No. Except my dog," Tony said.

"Hey, it isn't Peter Buck, the rock star, is it?" I asked.

"Peter Buck? Which group is he a member of?"

"R.E.M."

"This one I am not very familiar with," Tony admitted. "But the gentleman is fifty or perhaps sixty years old, bald and fat, he does not look like a rock star to me."

"Maybe it's Van Morrison," I said, took a deep breath, and barged into the room.

                                   ✿   ✿   ✿

I rode the elevator down to the seventh floor and walked along the corridor to my corner room. Here the carpets were less plush and the pictures on the wall were prints. But it was still nice.

The business hadn't taken long.

I'd forced Mr. Buck to sit down on the bed and we'd talked. Apparently, the maid had refused to have sex with him even though he'd offered her good money. While I sympathized, Tony slipped a Mickey into a gin and tonic that knocked the bastard out. The cleaning service would fix his room while he dozed. Probably wouldn't remember a thing about it until he got a five-thousand-dollar extra on his hotel bill.

Still, as incidents go, not one to write home about.

I found the key card and opened my door.

The room was dark. I yawned again. I wouldn't even turn the light on. Straight ahead past the sofa and the boom box, a left turn into the bedroom. Go to sleep, wake up, and have some eggs with steak.

"Señor Michael Forsythe?" a voice asked from the sofa.

"¿Qué?" I said.

The lights came on.

"Do not move."

There was a man behind me. I could see in the reflection of the mirrored dresser that he was pointing a 9mm at my head. Slightly redundant since the man sitting on the sofa held a pump-action shotgun. They were both dressed in shiny gangster-fabulous suits. They spoke Spanish with northern accents. Colombian, I would have guessed, but that just might be prejudice on my part.

"You are Michael Forsythe?" asked the one with the 9mm.

"No, amigo," I said. "Don't know who that is."

"You are Michael Forsythe," he said again, but this time it wasn't a question.

The one with the shotgun motioned for me to put my hands up and the other one frisked my upper body, removing my obvious gun, my binoculars and wallet. They looked at the photo on my ID.

"It's him," Shotgun said.

The two men backed away from me. I stood with my hands over my head for a moment.

"Ok, what do we do now?" I wondered.

"We wait."

One of the gunmen sat down on the sofa while the other motioned me into the center of the room.

"Kneel on the floor with your hands over your head," Shotgun said, flashing a crooked smile in my direction.

"Are you going to kill me?" I asked.

"Quite possibly," the one with the shotgun said, which, if nothing else, was an interesting answer. Not an imminent threat of death anyway.

"Well, I hate to spoil your little plans and I know you guys don't like surprises, so you should know that if I don't call the front desk and tell them I cleaned up that disturbance on the fiftieth floor they are going to send a couple of guys up here looking for me."

The two men glanced at one other and conferred in low tones. Nine-millimeter brought me the phone.

"Call them. Let them know you are going to bed and do not wish to be disturbed," he said.

I took the phone.

"Of course, if you say anything to warn them or anything we do not like we will kill you immediately. Those are our instructions," Shotgun added.

"Shoot first, eh?" I said.

"Yes."

I picked up the phone, dialed the front desk and got through to Tinco.

"Tinco. I took care of the problem on the fiftieth. Tell Hector that he can go home, I don't want to go bird-watching this morning, I already saw an eagle. Got that? Ok, I'm going to go to bed."

I hung up the phone and looked at the two men. They seemed satisfied. If Hector hadn't left, he'd be up here in five minutes. Eagle was the call sign for major security alert.

I stood for a moment and the men motioned me to kneel again. All the tiredness had left me now and I was ready to raise holy hell if I got the chance. But the men were cautious. Keeping themselves well away from a sudden spin kick or a roll and punch. By the time I was halfway through either of those moves, I'd be dead. I scanned them. Skinny, young, but not that young. Experienced looking. This was not their first hit. Both in their late twenties or early thirties. The one with the shotgun was slightly older, slightly yellower, his hair greased back over a bald spot. Both had an odd burn mark above their knuckles. Some kind of gangster tattoo. I'd seen similar ones before. They were representing. Unlikely they were freelance. Unlikely they were amateurs.

"How long do we wait?" I asked, but before either could answer, the younger one's cell phone rang. He flipped it open and put it to his ear.

"It's him," he said in English. "It's definitely him. What do you want us to do?"

The person on the phone said something. The two men stood, leveled their weapons. I closed my eyes expecting instant death, but then opened them again—if death was coming I wanted to meet it head-on. And besides, I had a little ace in the hole that those two goons didn't know about. Maybe take one of the bastards with me. That arrogant son of a bitch with the shotgun, perhaps.

But they weren't killing me, they were adjusting themselves. The client wanted to speak to me first. The man with the 9mm gave me the phone. His eyes were expressionless. Cold.

"It's for you," he said with a sneer.

"Hola," I said.

"Michael," Bridget replied.

I recognized her voice immediately. I staggered a little and the man with the pistol had to steady me.

"You," I muttered, unable to articulate anything more.

"Michael, if you're taking this call it means that a man is pointing a gun at your head," Bridget said.

"He is," I agreed.

"He's been instructed to kill you," Bridget said.

"Aye, I gathered that."

"I mean business," Bridget said.

I knew she did. A year ago, in March 2003, when the U.S. Army was rolling into Baghdad and most people had other things on their minds, she'd sent a team of five assassins to get me at my hiding place in Los Angeles. A nasty little crew, but they'd screwed it up and I'd taken care of them. Still, I knew she'd come for me again. Honor demanded it. I had killed her fiancé, the mob boss Darkey White, and I had turned state's evidence against all my old pals. A killer and a traitor. Bridget wanted me dead, even if all that had taken place in 1992—twelve goddamn years ago. You had to admire her tenacity.

After LA I had skipped town, getting a job here in Lima as head of security at the Miraflores Hilton.

I had thought that I'd be safe for a while. I liked the place, I liked the people, I could have maybe established a wee home here permanently, settled down, a family. A nice local girl. A couple of cute kids. You could get a house overlooking the ocean for a pittance.

Now those plans were dead. Bridget was going to taunt me and her boys were going to pop me. And if Hector came running through the door, they'd have him too, poor bastard.

"I want you to listen to me, Michael," Bridget said.

"I'm listening."

"You better not try anything, these men are trained professionals."

"Oh, professionals, eh? Oh, my goodness. I am keeking my whips," I groaned, attempting bravado.

"Michael, you worthless shit, shut up and listen to me," Bridget said.

"If the nuns could hear you talk like that," I mocked.

"I am dead serious."

"I know, Bridget, but you should have come here yourself, I would have liked to have seen you one last time," I said.

"For a decade I've been trying to kill you, and, believe me, if something hadn't come up, I would have come there and I would have watched them torture you with arc-welding gear until you were begging me for death. But, like I say, something terrible has happened."

"Go on," I said.

"My daughter, Siobhan, she's gone missing," Bridget said.

I had no idea that Bridget had a daughter. It was a new one on me; she must have a boyfriend or maybe even a husband in her life now. Well, bully for her. I guess she wasn't holding a candle out for yours truly.

"Where are you, in New York?" I asked.

"Belfast, I'm in Belfast, Northern Ireland. She's been missing for three days. I am worried sick. She's only eleven years old, Michael."

"What? Eleven?" I said hesitantly.

"Eleven," Bridget confirmed.

"She's Darkey's kid?" I asked, making an intuitive leap.

"Yes."

This information was another shocker. Bloody hell. So she had been pregnant the night I'd smacked her and knocked her unconscious and then killed her old man. In mitigation she had been trying to shoot me, but still, I'd hit a pregnant woman and I'd murdered the little girl's da in cold blood. What a charmer I was and no mistake.

"Where do I come in?" I asked.

"I want you to find her, Michael. You know Belfast like nobody else, you have the contacts, you can ask around. I need you, Michael, and by God you owe me."

"Well, that's debatable, love," I said. "Darkey kind of got on my bad side. I'd say the score's pretty even."

"This isn't a request, Michael. If you don't tell my boys the stop command they are going to kill you."

Not just playing the tough nut, she was the tough nut. She'd changed a lot, but that side of her was always there if I'd been smart enough to see it. I smiled to myself. Hmmm. What would she look like after all these years?

"I do as you say, or I'm toast," I said.

"Either you are going to be dead or they are going to accompany you to the airport and then fly with you to Dublin to make sure you take the flight. And then I'm going to meet all three of you at the Europa Hotel in Belfast. And if you don't find Siobhan I'm going to shoot you myself," Bridget intoned with clinical, controlled malice.

"Just to be clear, certain death, or near certain death, are the two choices," I said.

Bridget sighed with impatience. And suddenly I saw her on the other end of the line. Older, yes, but still the curves, the red hair, the alabaster skin, those not quite human eyes. Always a bit of an unearthly quality about my Bridge, as if she'd come from that part of the west of Ireland where the people had supposedly descended from the union of elves and men.

"Michael, I could have had them kill you right now. I've known where you are for two weeks now. We were planning the hit, but then this came up."

"How did you find me this time, Bridget?"

"We heard you went to South America, we put the feelers out. Money opens a lot of doors."

I grimaced. I really was getting careless in my decrepitude. Should have dyed my hair or grown a mustache; just because I was on another continent I thought I was safe.

"Why should I trust you?" I asked.

"If you don't, you're dead. If you try anything, you're dead. If you mess with me in any way at all, you're dead. These are hundred-thousand-a-hit Colombian ice men. They're good at what they do, they're younger than you and better than you. I've told them to take no chances on the possibility of you escaping. I'd rather have you dead and useless, than alive and on the run."

"So I've no alternative," I said.

"None."

I stared at the two badass Colombians, shook my head, dismissed the possibility of a play—any move would bring forth their bad side. And also, it looked now like Hector wasn't coming. So what choice did I have?

"What choice do I have? You win, Bridget, I'll do it," I said.

Bridget groaned with relief, which told me that the daughter thing maybe wasn't a scam. That maybe she wasn't acting. Meryl Streep would be hard pressed to convey that much information in a groan.

"What do I tell the goons?"

"You say this: 'The pussy begs you not to shoot him,'" Bridget said.

"You're not just making all this up to humiliate me before you kill me?" I asked.

"You'll know about that one second after you say it. Get on that plane. Meet me in Belfast. It pains me to say it but I need your help, you traitor, stool-pigeon piece of shit."

The line went dead.

"And I love you, too, sweetie," I said and placed the phone on the floor.

"She hung up," I explained.

"Ok, now we kill you," Shotgun said.

"Wait a minute, Pablo, me old mate. She said that I was to say 'The pussy begs you not to shoot him.'"

Shotgun considered for a second, fought back a look of frustration, put down his weapon.

"Shit. I was looking forward to doing you. The head of hotel security in his own hotel. That would have added to our prestige," he said.

The man with the 9mm looked at his boss.

"Now we're not going to do it?" he asked.

His partner shook his head. Reluctantly, he put the 9mm in a shoulder holster.

"We're all flying to Europe, no?" I said.

"Yes. You have five minutes to pack and then we're going to the airport, I have a car waiting."

Shotgun threw an airline ticket at me. I examined it. British Airways first class direct from Lima to New York, Aer Lingus first class from New York to Dublin.

Commercial jets, not private ones. Dear, oh, dear. Bridget's little cock-up. You can't railroad someone from Peru to Ireland using commercial flights. Who did she think she was dealing with? She should have coughed up the money for a Learjet.

"The plan is if I don't cooperate you'll kill me?" I asked Shotgun.

"That's right," he replied.

"The two of you and the one of me."

"Yeah. Hurry and get packed."

"You'll kill me?"

"If necessary. Yes."

"Like to see you attempt that on a plane that's going to JFK," I said.

I was just trying to test his limits, make him a bit eggy, but I saw immediately that I had blundered. This was a mistake. His brow furrowed. I'd really made him think about this whole rotten assignment. About the obvious flaw in the arrangements. Goddammit, I had to get him back on track.

"Not that I'll be a problem. I won't cause you any trouble, I want to leave this bloody town anyway. Yeah, we'll go to New York and then Ireland," I said hastily.

But the atmosphere in the room had changed. The seismic shift had happened and Shotgun was thinking along different lines now.

"No, no, you are right, Forsythe. We will have too much trouble with you. The pay is the same either way," he said. "Step back, Rique."

Rique saw that Shotgun was going to kill me.

"What are you going to tell her?" Rique asked.

"We had to kill him. He tried to escape. It was him or us," Shotgun said.

Rique nodded.

"Now wait a minute. This isn't what Bridget wants, this isn't what she's paying you for. She wants you to take me to Ireland," I said desperately.

Rique lifted the 9mm.

It was typical of me to let my big mouth get me into trouble. Bloody typical. And where was that eejit Hector? Halfway home? God save us, there was only one way out now.

I fell to my knees and started to beg for mercy in evangelical Spanish. I invoked the mother of Jesus and the Virgin of Guadalupe (who I think are the same person but I'm no expert).

"Please, please, please, don't kill me, you're not supposed to, you're not supposed to, in the name of the Father and the Son and the . . ."

And as I begged, I leaned forward, let my hand run down my trousers, and removed the tiny three-shot .22 pistol that I kept there for just such an emergency. My ace in the hole. In South America it was considered cowardly to strap a gun around your ankle. That was something a *puta* would do.

Better a live *puta* than a dead hero.

"You are going to die, Irish pig," Shotgun said.

"Yeah, you're right, tough guy, but not today," I said, tumbling from my kneeling posture into a forward roll that carried me over the hardwood floor, while at the same time grabbing the gun from my ankle holster and shooting the chatty bastard in the neck. He fell forward, frothy, arterial blood spewing from a mortal wound.

I scrambled to the side and Rique fired twice with the 9mm, hitting the piece of carpet where I'd been a tenth of a second ago. I dived behind the sofa and took two shots of my own, missing the dodgy bugger both times. Shit. That was the end of my little gun. Had to move fast now. I tossed the weapon and picked the boom box off the floor and threw it at him. It missed, exploded into the wall, spewing CDs, batteries, and sparks.

Rique shot again, sending a bullet into the ceiling above my head. I hurled a vase and then a small glass coffee table.

The door opened.

Hector came in.

"Thank God, over here, mate," I said.

Rique yelled at Hector: "He's unarmed. Shoot him."

Hector pulled out his revolver.

"You said I wouldn't be involved," Hector muttered.

Rique turned to lecture him.

"Do as you are told, and . . ." Rique began.

I picked up my favorite leather armchair and ran at Rique. It was studded leather with a metal back, so it might afford some protection.

I charged the bastard, hoping he wouldn't have sense enough to shoot me in the legs.

But Rique was flustered by all the things happening at once. He fired off the rest of his clip into the leather chair before I smashed into him, driving him backward into the tinted plate-glass window. My Irish was up and my momentum easily took out the thick safety glass.

Chair and assassin smashed through the window and tumbled through the early-morning air onto the car park below. I was lucky I didn't fall out after them. I scrambled to a dead stop, but I didn't even pause to admire my luck or watch Rique smash to pieces on the hood of the Japanese ambassador's limousine, which, rather inconveniently, had just pulled up outside. Instead I strode across the room and grabbed the gun out of Hector's hand. He was dazed and bleeding from a cut on his fingertip he'd somehow managed to acquire when he'd taken his pistol out.

I pistol-whipped him across the face and kicked his legs from under him. He collapsed to the floor.

"Hector, Hector, Hector," I said with disappointment.

"I'm sorry, so sorry," Hector said, his eyes filling with tears. I checked the revolver, saw that it was loaded, cleaned, ready.

"Hector, you realize this is going to have to go on your résumé," I told him.

"Oh, please don't hurt me, they said they would kill my family, they said—"

I put the gun in his mouth and rattled it around his teeth.

"Save it, mate, they already told me, you came to them, you sought them out. What was the finder's fee?"

"I don't know what you're talking about, I love you, boss, I don't know what—"

Clicking the hammer back is such a cliché in these situations, but in my experience it is a shortcut to the truth.

I clicked the hammer back.

"Ten thousand dollars," he said.

"Damn it, Hector, if you needed the money I would have loaned it to you."

"I wanted to earn it."

"There are better ways," I muttered.

"You would know," Hector said petulantly, making a move for the knife he kept in his pocket. That wasn't going to happen twice in the same hotel room. I kicked his arms apart, so that he was spread-eagled on the floor. I took the gun out of his mouth and placed it a couple of inches from his forehead.

"You are one disloyal asshole," I told him without much passion.

He closed his sad brown eyes.

"No more disloyal than you," he said.

"There's a difference," I explained. "I did it to save my skin, you did it for the goddamn money."

"What are you going to do to me?"

"I'm going to salvage your honor, my friend," I said.

Hector understood. He blinked away the tears, flinched.

I pulled the trigger, blowing off the top part of his head, his blood and brains spraying over me.

I placed Hector's gun in the dead assassin's hand, I put the three-shot .22 in Hector's bloody paw.

I poured myself a whisky, picked up the phone, and called down to the front desk.

"Oh, my God, Hector saved my life, he's dying, he's dying, get help up here quick," I said and hung up.

It didn't take long for me to see flashing lights racing along the seafront. They'd send the paramilitary police for this one and I'm sure Bridget would have a plan B as per usual. Time to skip.

I stood, stretched, drank the whisky.

And as the stench of a slaughterhouse rose and the cold sea air blew in through the smashed window and the blood of both bodies pooled into the imitation Persian rugs, I washed my hands in the bathroom sink, grabbed my shoulder bag, packed, and got ready to run again.

2: SIREN
(NEW YORK—JUNE 15, 4:00 P.M.)

The inquiries of the Peruvian police would take days. I didn't have days. My cover was blown. I was screwed if I stayed in this country. I ran them a story that the two characters from Colombia had come into my room with guns and started asking all sorts of questions about the Japanese ambassador, Hector arrived, pushed one out the window and shot the other while taking a mortal wound himself.

The story would work if they wanted it to work. They had uncovered an assassination plot and a local boy was the hero.

I told them I was registered under the United States Witness Protection Program and now I had to fly the coop on the first flight out. They weren't down with that at all. But they also didn't want to mess with the FBI.

A signed statement, a videotaped statement, a fake contact address later, and I was all set to go.

It was too late to get a reservation now, but I didn't need to beg the airlines. I had a perfectly good ticket on the flight to New York. Bridget's ticket. And from New York I could go anywhere in the world.

It wasn't exactly the safest thing to do, but it was convenient.

The downside was obvious. Almost certainly she'd find out about the Lima fuckup and she'd quickly organize someone to meet my plane at JFK. They'd have my photo and maybe a threatening look or two but it wouldn't matter a tuppeny shite because in New York I'd have the good old *federales* rendezvous with me and I'd disappear once again into the black hole of the WPP. Aye, and this time I'd go the full De Niro. Gain twenty pounds, dye my hair, move to bloody China.

I checked in, boarded the plane, found my seat, relaxed. The movie they were playing was *O Brother, Where Art Thou?* which I'd already seen, so, there was nothing else for it but to tilt my chair back as far as it would go and try to get in an hour or two of kip. But even in first class that was practically impossible. You don't come down from a gun battle just like that. I read *Peruvian Golfer* until it was chow time. A pretty stewardess gave me a dozen options and I picked the eggs and she brought me scrambled ones that tasted almost like eggs. We started chatting and one thing led to another and she gave me her phone number in the Bronx and if it had been Manhattan I might have kept it.

We flew over Panama, the western edge of Cuba, the land of Johnny Reb, and touched down at JFK a few minutes early. As soon as the wheels squealed I called up Dan Connolly in the FBI. He wasn't at his desk, so I dialed his cell phone and left a message.

"Dan, it's Michael F., I'm in the shit again. I know it's a chore but I'm going to need someone to meet me at International Arrivals of the British Airways terminal in JFK. I just touched down. I'll wait as long as it takes. You can reach me on the cell."

I hung up, found my U.S. passport, went through immigration, and forgot totally about the coca leaves in my shoulder bag. I panicked that customs was going to pull me over, but it didn't, and I walked into the arrivals hall. Waited.

Tens of thousands of people. New York City just out through the doors. But there was no way I was leaving the airport without my escort from the feds.

Bridget, if she was smart, would have a couple of guys on me right now. Not that they could do anything in here. She had wasted her chance again. And she nearly had me going there with that cock-and-bull story about the kid. For the more I thought about it, the more I realized it was impossible that Bridget could have an eleven-year-old child. I would have heard, somebody would have told me. I mean, for Christ's sake, I'd seen her in court when I'd been accusing Darkey's confederates. She wasn't in the dock, but I'd spotted her in the public gallery in that black suit of hers, giving me the evil eye. No way she'd just given birth. And besides, Darkey didn't want kids. He told me and Sunshine that he'd adopt a hardworking Asian boy when he was in his sixties. It was a joke, but I didn't see Bridget defying him by not taking her birth-control pills.

No way.

I was hungry and bored. I sauntered over to Hudson News and bought the *Times, Daily News,* and *Post,* joined the line of carbohydrate lovers at Au Bon Pain. I ordered a big coffee, cheese Danish, sat down, and enjoyed reading the press in English for a change.

Did the Tuesday crossword and scoped the crowd to see if I could spy out Bridget's men. But the place was far too hectic. Maybe she'd be on the ball, maybe not, it didn't matter.

Au Bon Pain was getting crowded and a German couple with a baby annexed the free seats at my table. I got up and looked for another hangout.

At the end of the terminal sat one of those fake pubs which seemed as good a location as any for a long wait. I walked to the City Arms, ordered a Sam Adams. My cell phone rang when I'd drunk my beer and was thinking of popping for another.

"Where are you now, Forsythe?" Dan asked.

"No hello?"

"Where are you?"

"JFK."

"What are you doing there? You can be acquired at JFK," Dan said.

"Acquired? Acquired? You wanna watch it, mate. You're beginning to sound like the FBI manual."

"Shanghaied, kidnapped, lifted, whatever you want. You were never supposed to come back to New York," Dan insisted.

I hadn't been to the city in seven years, not since our days in the FBI field office in Queens.

"I had a ticket, it was first class, seemed a shame not to use it. Besides, I had to get out of Lima. Bridget, God rest her big bum, sent two Colombian assassins to blow my brains out."

"I read about it on the wire. You handled it in your usual low-key way, didn't you? You know the story is on CNN."

"Is it? Well, it can't be helped," I said cheerfully.

Dan muttered some inaudible obscenity that involved my mother.

"Michael, like I say, we have talked about New York. You're not supposed to come here, ever."

"As if they are going to *acquire* me in the middle of the most heavily policed airport in the Western Hemisphere. Get real. This isn't Al Qaeda, these guys need an exit strategy after a hit. Wouldn't get twenty feet in here."

"Well, I'm glad you seem ok about it. I'm not. Where exactly are you?"

"I'm in the City Arms in the BA terminal."

"Can you hang tight for about half an hour? I'll have a couple of guys come over there and meet you. I can't get down there in person at the moment. But I'll see you later today."

"Ok, do I know the guys?"

"You don't. Uhm, let me see, ok. They'll ask you if you think the Jets have a chance next year, to which you'll reply—"

"I don't want to talk about the Jets," I interrupted. "Ask me a baseball question. I can do baseball."

"You don't need to know the sport, Michael, you just have to say what I tell you to say."

"I don't want to do a question about the goddamn New York Jets. I want to do a baseball question. I know baseball," I protested.

"Jesus. It doesn't matter what the sport is."

"Of course it does, I'm not going to walk up to someone and say 'So who do you like in the curling world championships? They say the ice is fast this year.' Right bloody giveaway that would be."

Dan laughed and then sighed.

"You know, Michael, sometimes I wish you weren't so good at staying alive. Sometimes, I wish . . ."

"Better leave that thought unsaid. Joe Namath, he plays for the Jets, right?"

"Thirty years ago."

"Ok, forget him. They can ask me what I think about the dodgy Yankees pitching rotation. And I'll say: 'I don't think it stacks up against the Sox,' how about that?"

"Fine, whatever you like. I'll take care of it."

"Thanks, Dan."

"All right, hang tight. Sending some people to pull you out of yet another jam."

"You love me really, I can tell," I said.

I closed the phone, grinned. What Dan didn't realize was that if you've been fighting for your life a few hours earlier you can afford to be a bit bloody glib.

I got some lunch, a heretical Irish stew that contained peas and sweet corn.

Went to the bog, washed my face, ordered a Bloody Mary, sat with my back to the wall, decided to check out the señoritas. New York was a paradise after four months in Lima. Not that the Peruvian girls weren't attractive but there it was mere variations on a theme whereas here it was the choral symphony. Coeds, redheads, blondes, business-women, stewardesses, cops, women soldiers, and on the far side of the bar two skanks straight out of a Snoop Dogg video trying to tease a Hasidic man by kissing in front of him. The man, me, and about fifty-two hundred other people trying not to look. Blond hair, long legs, white stilettos, pretty faces. Russian. Touching each other on the ass and toying with each other's hair. You didn't get that in Lima either.

"New York City," I said with appreciation.

Next to the Hasid a goofy-looking character seemed to spot me. He gave a half wave, walked over quickly, and plonked himself down in the seat directly in front of me. It panicked me for a second. Sort of thing I'd do. Have a couple of hookers do a big distraction and send the guy in while my dick was doing the thinking for me.

He didn't have a scary vibe at all, though, and I relaxed a little as I looked him up and down. He was wearing a grin a decibel or two quieter than his ensemble of Hawaiian shirt, shorts, purple sandals, fanny pack, and bicycle messenger bag. Twenty-five or twenty-six, blond hair, goatee. Reasonably good-looking. He wasn't carrying a piece and he wasn't interested in the hussies, which meant he was either a homosexual, or part of their team, or he really wanted to talk to me.

"Hey, you're in my view," I said.

"Mr. Forsythe?" he asked in a serious FBI way.

"No."

"Mr. Forsythe, am I glad to see you. You look a little bit different from the photograph. A little bit older."

"Aye, well, you're no picnic yourself. You ever hear the expression sartorially challenged?"

His eyes glazed over.

"What are you talking about?" he asked.

"What am I talking about? What are *you* talking about? Aren't you supposed to ask me about the Yankees? Don't they teach you anything?"

Before he could answer, a cold feeling went down my spine. This wasn't Dan's man. I pushed my chair back from the table and looked him in the eyes.

"You're not with the feds," I said.

"No, no, not at all," he said with a little laugh. "What gave you that idea?"

"Who are you? Are you Bridget's?"

"Yes. I work for Ms. Callaghan. I was told to meet you off your flight. I was instructed to ask you if you are going to continue on to Dublin."

"You must be joking. Continue on to Dublin? So Bridget can torture me, with, what was it, arc-welding gear? You must be out of your mind. Nah, I'm just going to sit tight here, wait till my good buddies in the FBI show up, go off with them. Easy. And if you want to try anything here and now with a couple of hundred witnesses around, dozens of plainclothes cops, you go ahead. See how far you bloody get."

"No. You don't understand. I am not muscle, Mr. Forsythe, I am an attorney, I work for Ms. Callaghan. Please excuse the way I look, I was on my way to Puerto Rico, actually. But I was told to wait here to talk to you."

"You're an attorney? Pull the other one, pal, it has bells on. Keep away from me," I said.

"I am an attorney, Mr. Forsythe, and I do work for Ms. Callaghan. I have a message to convey to you," he said.

Still keeping my distance from him and watching his hands, I set down my coffee cup and snapped my fingers.

"Let me see some goddamn ID," I demanded.

"Certainly."

He reached in the pocket of his shorts and removed a wallet. He showed me a bar association card, a Columbia law library card, a driver's license, and a membership in the Princeton Club.

"Ok, sonny, first of all, what exactly did they tell you about me and how did you know what flight I was on?" I demanded.

"They told me that since I was going to JFK, could I meet flight 223 from Lima, Peru, and find a Michael Forsythe. They faxed me your picture. Unfortunately, I had to go the bathroom briefly, and typically that was the moment that you, well . . . of course that was the precise moment when you came through. I had a sign made with your name on it, do you want to see the sign?"

I gazed daggers. He continued: "Ok, no sign, forget the sign, ok, so anyway I went out into the arrivals hall and I thought I'd lost you, but, you see, I knew you were Irish, so I thought to myself, why don't I check the pub and anyway I—"

"Yeah, if I'd been black you would have checked the watermelon stand? Enough of your nonsense, what's the goddamn message?" I asked.

He rummaged in the bicycle messenger bag and brought out a fax sheet. He unfolded it and began reading: "It's from Mr. Moran, do you know Mr. Moran?" he asked.

"No, I don't know Mr. Moran, read me the bloody message before I really lose my patience."

"Ms. Callaghan apologizes for her heavy-handed behavior of this morning. She says that she urgently needs your help and she would like to speak to you again," he said, producing a cell phone from his bike bag and placing it on the table.

"What's the deal here? Is it going to blow up as soon as you walk off?" I inquired.

"Uh, no, it's just a phone. She wants to talk to you," he said.

"Bridget wants to talk to me? Ok, fine, I got some time. But I'll call her on my phone. You ever hear of ricin nerve-toxin poison? One touch of it and you're toast. For all I know you're wearing some sort of protective lubrication on your hands, that phone is coated in poison, and I'm about to be topped like they did with that Bulgarian."

The kid looked at me to see if I was taking the piss out of him, which, if truth be told, I half was.

"Why don't you just give me her number, if you're legit I'll call her on the phone," I said.

He gave me the number without any fuss at all. A Belfast listing. I dialed it.

"Hello, Europa Hotel," a voice answered.

"Yeah, I need Bridget Callaghan, she says she's staying there."

"One moment, please."

"Hello?" Bridget said.

"Nice try, sister," I said. "I didn't bite last time, I won't bite this time, took care of your delightful emissaries," I said.

"Yes, Michael, I heard about your exploits. In fact, I saw the results of your shenanigans on BBC World. For God's sake, they weren't there to kill you. Don't you believe me? I need your help."

"Aye, they weren't there to kill me, that's why they pulled out their guns and told me to make my peace with the Lord."

I looked at the lawyer and put my hand over the receiver.

"Are you getting an earful of all of this? Make yourself scarce for a minute."

"I'll sit over there until you need me," he said, moving to an adjacent table.

"They weren't supposed to hurt you, Michael," Bridget insisted.

I laughed out loud.

"Oh, Bridget, the times we had, you make me smile, and I suppose the men in Los Angeles last year wanted to take me to a surprise party in Malibu."

"No, they were there to kill you. They were there to kill you and cut your fucking head off and bring it to me. But the two men today were there to make sure you flew to Ireland. My daughter has gone missing and I need your help. For God's sake, I'm a mother and my only child has vanished. I need your help, Michael," she said, her voice trembling.

I looked at the phone. I found her very affecting. She was good. She nearly had me convinced. All she had to do was squirt a few and I'd be on my way to the Emerald Isle and certain death.

"Honey, look, it's been great talking to you and it was very clever of you to find me twice in one day. But this time I'm out of your life forever. I'm going to India, wearing a turban, opening a pawnshop in

Bombay, so adios, Bridget, my love. And I'll give you this wee warning, honey: my patience has its limits. This game can go two ways. Try this one more time and if I find you're still after me, I'm coming for you, understand? Be a lot harder for you to conceal your movements than it will be for me to conceal mine. I've had twelve years of practice."

"Are you threatening me?"

"Aye. I am."

"Michael, first off, you are no position to fucking threaten me. Second off, I'm not trying to con you or scam you. Everything I said was completely true," she said.

"I am sure it was. Right back to 'I love you' and 'Let's run away together.' Bridget, it's been terrific having this chat. Do keep in touch. Do think about what I've said. Hate to have to kill ya some night like I did with your boyfriend back in the day. But I will if you keep on my case. And now I have to go, love, got a couple of *federales* coming to meet me and give me a lift downtown. So I wouldn't try anything."

"Don't go, Michael, don't go, listen to me, just listen. Everything I said was true. My daughter, Siobhan, has gone missing in Belfast. We were over here on a trip, we come here every summer. We were in Belfast. On Saturday she went for a walk, she didn't come back to the hotel. She said she was going to get a milk shake but no one at the milk shake place saw her. Michael, she has completely disappeared. The police are looking for her, you can call up their tip line if you don't believe me. 01232-PSNI-TIP. Please, Michael, I want you on board. I am losing my mind, I've got every single person I know helping me here. The police, everyone. Please, I'm willing to let bygones be bygones. Wipe the slate clean, if you would just come and help. I know you're good at being you and you're better than anyone I know. I'm not trying to flatter you, Michael, but you're the best I've ever met. This is your town, you can find her, I know you can. Please come. Please."

And now she did start to cry. She cried and cried.

I could feel the tide shifting under my feet. I blinked. And I fought against it, but it didn't help and now I did believe her.

Shit.

What an eejit I was.

"Don't cry, Bridget, please don't cry," I said.

The sobbing continued for another minute.

"Ok, enough, I'll come," I said.

Bridget blew her nose. Sniffled.

"I love her. She's my whole universe, Michael."

"I understand. I'm sure she's fine. Kids run away sometimes. Especially at that age. It's a mother-daughter thing more than likely. Don't worry about her. We'll get her."

"Thank you, Michael. That man who contacted you will give you fifteen thousand dollars for expenses and a ticket to Dublin. The plane goes in an hour, you better hurry if you're going to catch it," Bridget said.

"I'll be calling that tip line, I need to confirm this. What did you say her legal name was?" I asked.

"Siobhan Callaghan. Eleven, nearly twelve years old. The spit of her ma."

"Heartbreaker, in other words."

"She's my whole life, Michael, I want you to help me."

"Ok, if it's kosher, I'll be on the plane. Bridget, I got to warn you, I don't respond well to heavy stuff; if you have goons waiting to meet me in Ireland, I'll kill them and you'll never hear from me again. And if it's a trick, I'll make sure you go down. I'm getting mighty tired of this."

"Thank you, Michael. It's not a trick. I hate you. I hate your guts. But I need you. I'm pulling out all the stops."

"Ok."

She hung up. I motioned the kid to come over.

"Ok, dickwad, you got some money for me," I said.

"Mr. Forsythe, I have been instructed to give you this envelope containing fifteen thousand dollars and a confirmation for your Aer Lingus ticket to Dublin on the five-fifteen flight this evening."

"Take out the money and put a few bills in your mouth."

"Why my mouth?"

"Didn't I tell you about the nerve toxin? If they've poisoned the money, I want it to kill you first."

The kid hesitated, as if considering the possibility that someone had indeed spiked the dough. He put the first two bills in his mouth with no ill effect.

"Ok, now, the thirteenth bill and the last five."

He did those as well, again without keeling over or spitting blood.

"This may seem crazy to you but you never know with Bridget. She's smart. Now do the same with the airline ticket and then piss off out of my life and go back to your *vida loca*."

"Can I get a receipt for the money?" he asked.

"A receipt? Oh, I see. Of course. You're worried I'll take the money and just fuck away off with it. Well, I'll let you in on a little secret, that's precisely what I'm going to do," I said.

"Ms. Callaghan believes you will not do that. However, Mr. Moran has instructed me—"

"He's instructed you, has he?"

"Yes, he has. I am to ask politely but I am not to coerce you in any way," he said.

"You think you could coerce me if you really needed to?"

"Um, well, it isn't really my department," he said.

"No, I didn't think so."

He nodded, stood.

"Good luck, Mr. Forsythe," he said.

I watched him walk out of the airport and hail a cab. I counted the money. Fifteen large, sure enough. And I could have it for free. But there was that other thing she said. She would "wipe the slate clean" if I helped her.

Wipe the slate clean.

Now that was an attractive proposition. My body ached from the exhaustion of it all. Dodging her and her minions. Twelve years I'd been on the run from the New York Irish mob. Since Christmas Eve 1992. Now Bridget claimed she was willing to forgive it all. Forgive me killing Darkey, forgive me selling Darkey's boys down the river. Why?

There were really only two possibilities.

One, that this was all a trap, an elaborate hoax to get me to come to Ireland.

Two, she really did have a daughter who had gone missing and like any concerned parent she was at the end of her tether. If I were a betting man, I'd have gone for one.

But you never knew. I sipped the dregs of my beer.

"How do you think the Red Sox rotation will match up against the opposition this year," a voice said.

I looked up.

A tall, blond storm trooper of a man, in a wide blue business suit. A clone behind him with dark hair.

"Can't you cocksuckers get anything right?" I said. "Yankees' rotation and I'm supposed to mention the— Oh, forget it, take a seat, there's been a slight change of plans. . . ."

❊   ❊   ❊

When his lads phoned Dan and told him that I was heading for Dublin, Dan said he wouldn't allow me to go until he spoke to me in the flesh. I told him I'd miss my plane, so Dan told the DHS that he needed a background check of every passenger on the Aer Lingus flight to Dublin.

"That'll hold the bastards up for an hour or so," Dan said while he drove in from an "important conference," which in fact was almost certainly a golf course in Westchester.

He arrived about thirty minutes later in navy slacks, white shirt, and red Kangol beret. I hadn't seen him in person for a long time. He was a nice guy, going places with the bureau. An administrator, not a field man. He wouldn't be in witness protection forever. Although twelve years could seem like it. Tall, bald, but good-looking and very affable. I liked him. He sat down at my table and ordered a lime juice for himself and another beer for me. The agents got up and slipped into the background.

Dan had known me since '93, when the FBI had offered me that first deal to rat out Darkey's organization. He'd helped me in '97 when the bureau and MI6 had had me infiltrate an IRA splinter group in Massachusetts and he'd cleaned up that ugly situation last year when Bridget had sent her men to Los Angeles. We'd been through a lot together and we shook hands with genuine affection.

"Michael, first thing I have to say is I'm sorry I didn't meet you off the plane, I thought we'd have a couple of days and I was right in the middle of, well, to be honest, I was right in the middle of a foursome at the country club."

"Aye. That's ok. Makes me happy to see that you're golfing in the middle of a workday. That's what our taxpayers' money goes on."

"Since when did you ever pay taxes?" he asked.

"Sales tax."

"Ok, so what's this I hear about you wanting to fly to Dublin?"

"I talked to Bridget. Her daughter's gone missing and she wants my help to find her. She's willing to wipe the slate clean."

Dan smiled.

"It's a trap, don't you see that?" he said without inflection.

"Does she have a daughter?" I asked.

"She does."

"Is it Darkey's kid?"

"It is," he said flatly.

"How come I never knew about this?"

Dan looked embarrassed.

"Why would you need to know? Bridget never took the stand, even as a witness, so it never came out in court. Furthermore, it was information we did not wish to share with you because we didn't think it was important," Dan said. It was an answer filled with weasel words.

"You didn't want me to know she was pregnant when I killed her fiancé and rolled up her fiancé's gang; you thought it might throw me a bit, didn't you?"

"It wasn't relevant, Michael, it still isn't," Dan insisted.

"It's relevant. While I was waiting for you, I called up the police in Belfast. Bridget did indeed file a missing persons report three days ago."

"That doesn't mean anything. It could still be a setup. The kid could be in the room with her right now," Dan said.

"I know."

"Michael, come on, we'll go to Midtown, get you in a nice hotel, maybe the Plaza. Take it easy for a few days and then we'll send you somewhere new."

"Dan, that's precisely it. I'm tired of this. Tired of running. Tired of moving to new cities. I want to check this out, if there's any possibility that this could be real I want to investigate."

"Big mistake," Dan said, shaking his head.

"I don't think so."

Dan sighed. "Let me remind you who we're talking about here," he said. "After you helped put the rest of Darkey's crew behind bars, Bridget was off the scene for a while. She wasn't a natural successor to Darkey White. There were at least two other candidates Duffy could have put in charge of Upper Manhattan and Riverdale. He wasn't a sentimentalist. He didn't owe her a goddamn thing. Bridget made her own way to the top. Murdered her way up. She started with next to nothing. Not even Darkey's name, remember. She got a few loyal men, she took out the opposition without a second—"

I didn't want to hear this right now.

"I read the papers," I interrupted.

"James Hanratty, shot on the way back from his sister's wedding. Pat Kavanagh, shot in front of his wife and two kids. Miles Nagobaleen, pushed in front of a subway train. This isn't the girl you used to know, Michael. She's ruthless. When Duffy died someone ordered the murder of Duffy's brother the very same night, so he was out of the picture too. We suspect she's ordered at least three hits in the last year, not counting the ones on you. I mean, come on, Michael. Why do you think the Boston mob stays out of New York? They're scared of her. And they're right to be."

"She's a killer," I said, trying to sound blasé.

"No, Michael, more than that. She's the general behind the killers."

"She's also a mother," I said.

Dan took a sip of my beer, put the bottle back on the table, shook his head. His eyes were sad, he knew he wasn't going to convince me.

"We can't look after you outside United States jurisdiction," he said.

"Dan, I'm not that bad at looking after myself, as you well know."

"Michael, if you go to Ireland, there's nothing I can do to protect you."

"I realize that."

"If we lose you, it'll be a black eye for the whole program, a huge setback. It'll discourage other potential informants. It won't be good for anyone."

"Least of all me."

"Least of all you, exactly."

Dan looked at me for a long time. He leaned back with a big exaggerated sigh.

"But you're set on going, aren't you?" he said finally.

I tapped the passport on the table.

"Don't worry, Dan, they won't harm me now I'm an American citizen," I said.

Dan shook his head, for him this was not an occasion for levity.

"There's nothing I can say?" he said sadly.

"No."

Dan motioned for one of the agents to come over. He told him something I couldn't catch and the agent sloped off.

"What was that all about?" I asked.

"I'm going to get some paperwork faxed over. I'll want you to sign a release ending your relationship with the WPP. If you're killed by Bridget Callaghan or one of her employees, or meet with any kind of accident while you're there, I want us off the hook. I'll want us to be able to say that you did this strictly against my advice and that you were no longer a member of the WPP."

I nodded. He was right. There was no point kicking up a stink about it. He ordered two more Sam Adams, getting one for himself this time. We clinked the bottles together.

"Ok, so tell me everything you know about the daughter," I asked.

"Her name is Siobhan, it's spelled with a *b*, pronounced Sha-vawn, but there's a *b* in there somewhere."

"Christ, I'm Irish, I know how to spell Siobhan."

"Ok, we believe it's Darkey's kid. I think she must be about eleven or twelve. She went to private school in Manhattan. A good student. Pretty girl, takes after her mother, not Darkey, thank God. Only child, but she has a lot of cousins. . . . And, uhh, well, I'm afraid that's about all I know."

"You think Bridget is the type of person to use her daughter in a ploy to get me?"

"I don't, frankly, but nothing would surprise me."

"How often does Bridget go to Belfast?"

"I have no idea. I do have other cases, you know. I heard something about a home in Donegal, wherever that is."

"It's in the west. But that would make sense. Ok. That's fine."

We talked for a couple of minutes and Dan stood up. One of the goons was coming back with a bunch of forms.

"Here come those faxes. Let me get you dinner at the executive club. Airline food is getting worse and worse," Dan said

"Aer Lingus never hit the culinary high notes to start with," I said. Dan smiled and put his arm around me and we left for what I'm sure Dan thought was something of a last supper.

✿   ✿   ✿

The flight was full and overbooked. Aer Lingus offered me two first-class tickets and a thousand dollars to fly tomorrow. But I wanted to go now.

There was a festive air to the check-in crowd and it made me wonder if there was some holiday or event taking place that I didn't know about. A wealthy-looking, trim, educated crowd, so it wasn't some drinking binge or the hurling final. It wasn't the Olympics, but I did know that the Tour de France sometimes went out of country. Perhaps that was it. The Tour de France was having an Irish leg this year.

I got a window seat and they brought me champagne and gave me a copy of *Ulysses,* which was strange.

"Don't you do movies anymore, love?" I asked the stewardess.

"Sorry?"

"Like I know Aer Lingus is a bit backward but most of the other airlines have films, and computer games and stuff like that. Giving someone a brick-size book for a six-hour flight is pretty lame," I said.

"No, that's just a complimentary copy, we have a dozen films for you to watch, sir," she said, raised her eyebrows, and walked off to deal with a less obtuse passenger.

The woman next to me had heard the conversation. She obviously had enough dough to be flying first but she looked like a retired English teacher from central casting. Aran sweater, granny glasses, sensible shoes. I supposed she was about sixty.

"I take it, young man, that you're not flying to Dublin for the festivities," she said in a patrician accent.

"No, I'm just going home. What festivities?"

"You don't know what day it is tomorrow?"

"Aye, it's Wednesday."

"No, no, no, it's Bloomsday. June 16, 2004. It's the hundredth Bloomsday," she said, doing little to disguise her contempt for my ignorance.

"Flower festival, is it?" I asked.

"What?"

"Bloomsday is some sort of flower festival?"

"Good God, no, not that kind of bloom. Leopold Bloom. You haven't read *Ulysses* then?" she asked, holding up her complimentary copy.

"How could I? Only just got it."

"Previously," she said with a touch of exasperation.

"No, I haven't. I heard it was a dirty book," I said and took a swig of my champagne. The woman's thin lips thinned even more.

"It is most certainly not. It is the greatest work of literature of the last or perhaps of any other century."

"Aye, that's what people say about *Moby Dick*, too. I wouldn't read that either, it must be filthy with that title," I said and smiled at a sudden remembrance of a time, years ago, when I dragged an old pal of mine called Scotchy to visit Melville's grave in the Bronx. A used-car dealer we knew had refused to pay the increased protection money and we were there in the dead of night breaking the windows and slashing the tires of every third vehicle on his lot. Woodlawn Cemetery was just next door and of course Scotch and I had both read *Billy Budd* for school. Scotchy cracked up when he saw that the author of *Moby Dick* had pussy willows growing on his grave.

And of course like every other Mick in the world, I'd tried to read *Ulysses* a couple of times.

"And tomorrow is when the book was published, is it?" I asked for the entertainment value.

"Tomorrow, June 16, is when Leopold Bloom spent the day walking around Dublin in the book."

"Leopold Bloom. Something to do with Mel Brooks, right? Hope there's going to be singing."

The woman shook her head impatiently.

"It's really when Joyce met Nora Barnacle. There will be a big parade and lots of festivities," the woman said, and bored with my ignorance, turned away.

I swallowed a gag about Nora Barnacle and the Little Mermaid and examined the book. Joyce looked chic in eye patch and bow tie. I put it in the seat pocket in front of me. Not really my cup of tea and I only hoped that the festivities wouldn't impede a successful navigation through Dublin to Connolly Station and the train to Belfast. Still, if this was as big a deal as the old lady was saying, the traffic would be coming south, not north, and I'd have no bother getting to my home city.

And, who knew, maybe Bridget would be waiting there with open arms. Maybe I'd ask around my old haunts and we'd find darling Siobhan together. Maybe all would be forgiven and tonight I could sleep easily for the first time in a dozen years.

I smiled. Sure. Shut-eye, though, was going to be essential whatever happened. I swallowed an Ambien, finished another glass of champagne, turned off the light, and closed the window shade.

The pill took about fifteen minutes to kick in.

The sky darkened, the stars came out, the 777 raced east to greet the dawn.

I pulled the blanket around me and drifted into a chemical sleep.

The Atlantic, heaving silent and black five miles below us; and I dreamed of it, of words and things, of whale boats, barnacles, eye-patched Irish men, Leopold Bloom in and out of Dublin pubs, Starbuck and Scotchy and Siobhan, all of them missing, and Ishmael's rescuer, the devious cruising *Rachel*, seeking out *her* lost children, but only finding another orphan.

3: OXEN OF THE SUN
(DUBLIN—JUNE 16, 4:15 A.M.)

The fucking coca leaves. Perfectly legal in Peru, useful for calming nausea and helping you get through the night shift. Really quite benign. You stick a couple in your cheek, they slowly dissolve, and you're set. Almost impossible to refine cocaine from the leaves in their dried form and completely impossible with the tiny amount I had left in my backpack. But even so, most western governments had declared them illegal controlled substances.

The dog stopped barking.

"I'd loike ye ta come wit me, sur," the customs agent said. I hadn't heard that hardcore North Dublin accent in a long time and I could barely understand the man. The words were there but it was like hearing Anglo-Saxon or being aurally dyslexic. It took me a while to process what he'd said.

"Of course," I said after a long pause.

I accompanied him into an antechamber.

"Look, I know why the dog is going crazy, I've got these coca leaves in my pack, the dog probably thinks they're cocaine."

"Iz zat so, sur?"

"Aye it is."

"Yaar fra America?"

"No, originally I'm from Belfast. I work in America now. Well, Peru. It's complicated. . . . Until yesterday I was the head of security at the Miraflores Hilton in Lima. We used to take the leaves for the night shift."

The customs agent found the bag of coca leaves and sniffed them. He was an older gentleman, fifties or sixties, a shock of white hair, dead capillary nose, ruddy cheeks, chubby body squeezed into a faded white shirt. The sort of desperate character who would like nothing more than to fuck someone over at four in the morning. It looked bad. If the authorities were feeling ungenerous I knew that this could be seen as an attempt to smuggle coke into Ireland. I could be looking at jail time.

"What ya doin in Oirland?"

"I've come to help an old girlfriend of mine. Her daughter has gone missing and she's really cracking up and I've come to support her and maybe help find the girl."

"What's hur neem?"

"Bridget Callaghan."

He didn't mean to show a reaction but he did. His eyes widened slightly. He knew who she was.

"What's yur neem?"

"Michael Forsythe."

"Ok. Did ye breeng anyting else illegal?"

"No," I said and turned out my pockets. The customs agent went through my stuff anyway. He noted the fifteen thousand dollars of Bridget's money and a couple of grand of my own there too. He stared at me for a moment and his eyes drifted back to the cash.

It gave me an idea. I toyed with it, dismissed it, floated it again.

But this was the situation. If they arrested me, it would take me a couple of days to hit bail, and the wee lassie could be dead, or in the Hare Krishnas, or a member of a biker gang, or taking drugs in some dingy flat, long before I could be of any assistance. Once again I'd be bloody straight into Bridget's bad books. Michael the traitor, Michael the fuckup. And to overegg that custard Bridget or anyone else then would have an excellent opportunity of killing me while I waited on remand in an Irish jail.

That was option 1.

But there was always option 2.

What about it then? Just looking at him, I knew he wasn't going to let me go with a stiff talking to. I was too old and he was too old for that. Aye, it would have to be the other way.

His greedy eyes on the money.

Bringing in a few harmless leaves was no big deal but attempting to bribe a government official could get me seriously fucked. If he took it badly, he'd report me and they'd throw the book at me. I could be facing years, not months; also, there was no way he could ignore it. He might be irked. Beyond irked. Seriously pissed off. "Some Yank scumbag comes in here attempting to bribe me with his wad of cash. I'll bloody do you, mate."

Yeah, but . . .

I was a friend of Bridget Callaghan and he'd heard of her. Maybe even was a little afraid of her. Jesus, it was a lot to weigh in my mind.

"Why don't ya teek a seat and I'll inform ye of yer rights," the man said and I could more or less follow him completely now.

I sat down. Now or never.

Every year *The Economist* publishes a table of the countries whose public officials are amenable to bribery. Denmark is always near the bottom of the table, the very least subornable in the world. Try to talk your way out of a traffic ticket in Copenhagen and they'll bung you in the slammer. India is at the top with the most corrupt officials. It's not even really seen as corruption out there, it's just the way business gets done. Now where did Ireland fit in on the scale? I tried to remember. Somewhere between Britain and America on the lower part of the page.

I gave the agent the final once-over. An old whiskey-breathed sad sack, who clearly hated work, me, himself. He might just respond to the right level of incentive program.

"I'm really sorry this had to happen; I use the coca leaves for purely medicinal purposes, they're not illegal in Peru, I forgot they were in my bag. Of course, it's no excuse. Is there any way I can pay an on-the-spot fine and get out of here? Bridget Callaghan is expecting me."

The man regarded me closely. He looked at the fifteen thousand dollars in bills sitting on the table. He closed his eyes.

He was thinking about it.

Good.

"De ye have a contact for Miss Callaghan?" he asked.

"I do," I said and gave him Bridget's phone number in the Belfast Europa.

"Jus a moment," he said, took away my passport, and left the room.

He hadn't given me his name. He hadn't told me where he was going. I sat down on the chair. Waited.

Twenty minutes later he came back.

"You're who ye say ye are. I have a great deal of respect for Miss Callaghan. The fine'll be about two thousand dollars, that's the equivalent to the euros," he said, and involuntarily licked his lips in anticipation.

"I'd like my passport back," I said.

He gave me the passport and took the coca leaves and threw them in a garbage can behind him. I counted out two thousand dollars, gave them to him.

I wondered if he had indeed called Bridget at the Europa. It would have woken her up, but more than that, it would have alerted her that I was back in the country. I'd have to be on my toes.

Then again, he didn't seem the type to call. He was just killing twenty minutes out there, making me sweat while he thought it over. He could really do what he liked. It was four in the bloody morning. There were no other customs inspectors on.

I was pleased with myself. A good guess on my part. Two thousand was about the right price for this unimaginative, pathetic, small-time shitehawke.

"Thanks very much," I said. "I won't let it happen again."

I repacked my bag, patted the dog, left the customs office, and walked through the Green Channel.

My trials, however, weren't over just yet.

A man from the department of agriculture.

"Did you visit any zoos in America?"

"No."

"Farms?"

"No."

"Agricultural research stations?"

"No."

An assassin entering the country was one thing, but the prospect of diseased feed or potato blight or another mad cow epidemic sent the Irish around the bend.

"Have you ever had occasion to eat squirrel, flying squirrel, capybara, or other rodents?" he asked.

I rolled my eyes and answered all the stupid questions.

Another half hour of officialdom and when I was done finally I went to the bathroom, washed my face, walked out of the airport and into my first Irish day in a very long time.

❀   ❀   ❀

Buses had taken away most of the passengers from my plane and the rest had gotten the few remaining taxis. A typical charming summer's morning in Ireland. A cold, gray sky and a freezing wind skewering in from the Irish Sea. I shivered in my thin leather jacket, Stanley work boots, and jeans. I didn't even have a hat. At least the sun was already coming up. June 16 marks the earliest sunrise in the northern hemisphere and there would be light now until close to midnight since it was the week of the summer solstice. I went to the taxi rank. Only one car lurking over there. A black, slightly beat-up, Mercedes. The cabbie drove over and stopped the car beside me. I hopped in the back.

"Connolly Station," I said.

"The station it is," the driver said, and after that encounter with the customs agent I could understand the accent completely now. It just took you a minute or two to get back in the game. Ireland has about three or four major regional accents. Some of them very hard to follow. In Northern Ireland I can put a man within twenty miles of his hometown and in the south fifty. Or at least I could before my long years of exile.

The driver looked at me in the mirror, switched off the engine, turned around.

"That'll be twenty euros, is that all right?" he said.

"Sure . . . but I've only got dollars, ok?"

He shook his head.

"I don't take dollars."

I swore inwardly. Another Irish subtlety I'd forgotten. Don't give details when you don't have to.

"Come on, mate, just get going," I said.

"I don't take dollars, you'll have to get change," the taxi man insisted.

"You don't take dollars at all, never?"

"No, I could lose me license."

"Come on, do me a favor. I'll give you fifty bucks if you just get cracking," I said.

"You're going to have to get change, pal, euros, or else you'll be walking where ya want to go," the driver said, getting somewhat hot under the collar. I looked at him in the mirror. He was about my age, wearing a Manchester United beanie hat and a thick sweater with reindeer on it. Big build, fat, frothy lips, the skin tone of a granite statue. A Dublin accent, but a hint of the north in it too.

I was about to give the bastard a piece of my mind but then stopped, unclenched my fists, and found a place of inner tranquility.

"Ok, mate, I'll get the bloody euros," I said through the window and smiled reassuringly at him. He didn't smile back. He seemed nervous. He wiped tiny beads of sweat off his forehead. Interesting, but I didn't have the time to probe the inner psychology of a cabbie, I was freezing out here. I sprinted back to the overhang outside the terminal. I asked a pair of cops where I could change money.

"Inside couple of bureaus de change, Eire Bank's got a better rate than National," one said.

"And a prettier girl," his partner added.

I found the two bureaus de change and headed for the National Bank. Old habit: whatever a peeler says, play safe and do the opposite.

I gave the girl three thousand dollars. She gave me back two thousand four hundred and ninety euros.

"Happy Bloomsday," she said.

"Thanks, happy Bloom to you, too, love."

I walked back out to the taxis. The driver was on his cell phone. He hung up hurriedly when he saw me, gave me a big fake smile.

"Ok, mate, where to? Connolly?" the driver asked.

"I haven't been here in a while, is it Connolly Station where you get the trains to Belfast?"

"It is too now, and is that where you want to go?"

"No, I was just asking that to make small talk. Come on, let's get out of here," I said, once again betraying my irritation.

"Connolly Station it is," the driver said, and I knew he was going to take the most expensive route that he bloody could.

Streets.

Trees.

Cars.

Dublin is a city I don't know well. Drop me a few blocks from O'Connell Street and I'm banjaxed. I can get you to Trinity and St. Pat's and a brothel opposite the Four Courts but that's about it. It's not my town at all. When I lived in Belfast I'd be down about twice a year for a rugby match. Don't think I've ever stayed overnight. Lot of beggars about back then, now it's yuppies with cell phones and PDAs.

Dubliners have changed quite a bit. Nowadays they're increasingly like Londoners. Cosmopolitan, busy, cheeky. They think just because they know where to get a decent pint of Guinness or a half-decent cup of coffee that this gives them the right to put on airs. I suppose they're arrogant because they live in a nice town. Good new statues, new architecture, and a really lovely Georgian zone near Trinity. Belfast, by contrast, is a bloody disaster area. The old ugliness from before the war, the 1970s bomb-damage ugliness, the 1990s rebuilding ugliness. Belfast never makes *Lonely Planet*'s list of most beautiful cities. Still, salt of the earth. Scotchy used to say, "Scratch a Dubliner and underneath you'll find a snob; scratch a man from Belfast and he'll punch you in the face for taking liberties."

Anyway, I don't know Dublin, so it wasn't until I saw that the cabbie was driving over a Liffey River bridge that I began to get suspicious.

Dublin Airport is in the north of the city.

Connolly Station, as far as I remembered, is also in the north of the city. Certainly north of the Liffey. Driving from the airport to Connolly should not for any reason involve crossing the river.

I reexamined the driver. Scars on his hands. Big guy, bruiser, you would have thought. Slow, but you wouldn't want to mess with him. Knock your block off, he would.

No, I didn't like him at all.

And now that I checked out the cab, I began to notice a few odd things as well.

There was no meter, but that wasn't so unusual, a lot of minicabs in Dublin didn't have meters, same with gypsy cabs in New York. But there was no glass partition between the driver and me. No credit card machine, no identity card hanging from his mirror, and he had no sticker allowing him into airport parking.

In fact, there was nothing in the cab that looked like a cab at all.

A wee moment of interior monologue: *Michael, don't be so paranoid. He's just a working stiff. He's not out to get you. The whole world doesn't revolve around you and your fucking problems. You know what the word* solipsism *means? Well, look it up in the dictionary, you eejit.*

Aye, but then again who exactly had the driver been on the phone with that he was so fucking anxious to hang up on when I came back? And further on that point, why send me away in the first place unless it was to make a call? Of course he could take dollars. Everybody took dollars, especially when it was off the books.

I tried to peer through the window to figure out where we were. The last of the night had been more or less banished but it was hard to see now through the morning mist. Vague buildings went past, but there were no landmarks, not that I could have recognized the landmarks anyway. Maybe St. Patrick's Cathedral and Trinity College, but anything else would have left me none the wiser.

"Do you have a cigarette?" I asked the driver, for something to say.

"I do not. I have given up. Since my birthday. Over a month now."

"Good for you, it's a filthy habit," I agreed.

"Aye, well, for me the encouragement was the pubs, you know," the driver said.

"What?"

"The pubs, you know, the ban," he said.

"They banned smoking in Irish pubs? Hadn't heard."

"Every pub in the south. No smoking anywhere; I was opposed, but it's a good thing, I see that now, helped me quit. Social thing, out with your mates. I notice the difference when I go up to Belfast, Jesus, the smoke would knock you out."

"You go up to Belfast often?" I asked in a completely neutral voice.

"Aye, now and again. Business, you know?"

"What sort of business, what's your line?"

"Oh, nothing you would be interested in. The taxi business, that's it. Stuff to do with that. You know how it is."

I did not know how it was. The taxi business, in Belfast? The more he talked the more I didn't like this little scenario.

"Are we near the station?" I asked.

"Not too far now, I'll have you there for the first Enterprise train. Think that goes off at six o'clock. You'll have time to get your breakfast and get a paper and a seat. You should reserve your seat, though, it's very popular. Faster, too, just a couple of hours and you'll be in Central Station in Belfast. It's great. Really quick now that the Provos have stopped bombing the line," the driver said rapidly.

"What's your name if you don't mind me asking?" I said.

"Padraig Lugh. But it's funny, you know, nobody ever calls me Paddy or Pad or anything like that, everybody always calls me Padraig."

"Do you want them to call you Paddy?"

"No, I do not. I like Padraig."

"How do you spell that last name?" I asked, wondering if it was fake.

"L-u-g-h. He's the old Irish sun god, you know."

"I know," I said.

"And what's your name?" he asked.

"Name's Michael," I said slowly, not liking his curiosity.

"Pleased to meet you, Michael," Padraig said and put his hand behind his head for me to shake.

I shook it. It was cold, clammy, trembling.

Jesus, was Padraig a player? It couldn't be coincidence if he was. Maybe they were waiting for me. Maybe the customs guy had tipped them off and told his mates that he would hold me just long enough for them to get there. Maybe Paddy had been on the phone to them. Sent me back in to get euros just to confirm my ID.

Or maybe he was just an ordinary driver with a touch of palsy, taking me on the magical mystery tour to bump up his fare.

I let go of his hand.

"It's nice to meet you, too, Padraig. Listen, I was wondering, I couldn't help noticing that we'd crossed over the Liffey."

"Aye, we did, too," Padraig agreed with a sigh.

"Isn't Connolly Station on the other side of the river?"

"Do you know the city well at all now?"

"Not really," I admitted.

"Well, I'll tell you, it's actually quicker for me to scoot over the bridge and skip along the south side and skip back than it would be for me to try to get through all the construction around the Abbey and the station and the Customs House, you know."

"Oh sure, I wasn't impugning your abilities as a driver. Not at all. I was only asking," I said a little apologetically.

"It's all right. Listen, I take taxis when I'm abroad and I'm always wondering if the bloody driver is ripping me off," Padraig said with a laugh and turned around to reassure me. He seemed hurt and I felt embarrassed now.

No. Padraig wasn't an assassin or a goon or a player. He was just a cabbie taking me on the quickest route to the station.

Well, that's what happens when you've spent twelve years on the run. You've got a Ph.D. in suspicion. It helps you stay alive but it doesn't do much for interpersonal contacts.

I frowned.

Aye.

And wasn't that the heart of everything.

The reason I was here. Not for Bridget. For me. Since 1992 I hadn't had a relationship that lasted more than six months. It wasn't the fact that I had to lie to every woman I met. It was more the nagging distrust that would creep in between her and me. A slow imploding destruction. They could always tell I had secrets. I was suspicious of everything they did. It put the mustard in the chocolate cake. Lies, lies, and more lies. You couldn't build anything on that. And I'd never been tempted to tell anyone the truth. That I was a wanted man. That I had killed a mob boss and the FBI had cut me a deal to keep me out of jail. That I'd killed six more people in Maine and Massachusetts, two of them women. How could you tell someone that? Especially someone you loved? You'd be putting her in danger. Jeopardizing her life. You could never share, you must always dissemble. Aye, and it would continue to be that way. The way things had to be. Living in shadows, always on guard, always a skeptic.

Like being in the Masons without the social contacts or the aprons.

"So you can't smoke in any bars at all? What about clubs?" I asked, for something to say.

"Clubs, I don't know, I am not a member of any clubs, to tell you the truth now."

"They're probably exempt," I said.

"Aye, well, it's a pity you're leaving for Belfast; if the weather stays nice there's going to be quite the shindig in Dub today."

"Yeah, I heard about that, Bloomsday, right, something to do with James Joyce?"

"Aye, you're right. I haven't read the book meself. I'm not a big reader. And I'm not likely to be now. I just got satellite, you know. Four hundred channels, powerful stuff. Who would want to read with all that carry-on. And bejesus, have you seen the length of that book? But a lot of famous people are coming to town. I heard Gwyneth Paltrow was staying at the Gresham."

"Gwyneth Paltrow?"

"That's what I heard, she's big into literature like, and I think she's Irish way back, so she is."

"Who else is going to be here?"

"Oh, I don't know. Liam Neeson, I think, people like that. You know, famous people."

"Who's the most famous person you ever had in your taxi?" I asked, trying to see if he really was a taxi driver.

"I have had all of U2."

"Nice guys?" I asked.

"Great. Great guys. Really great. Wonderful lads. . . . Hate that Bono, though. Can't stand him. Lecturing all of us to give money to Africa, while he, an Irish artist for all love, has never paid a fucking red cent in tax in his life and, I might add, whose personal fortune could clear the debts of about twenty of the poorest countries in the world. Fucker."

"Stiffed you on a tip, huh?" I guessed.

"No, not really, could have been better, though; anyway, this was back when I had my own cab, you know, when I was doing it for a living. Back in the 1980s. Had all the boys in here at one time or another," the driver said and in the mirror I caught a wistful look on his face.

Back when he had his own cab? Back when he did this for a living? So what exactly was he doing now?

He wasn't a taxi driver anymore. Now my antennae were really up, and I wasn't too surprised when he said:

"Shite, do you feel that? Oh, do you feel that? Ah, Jayzus."

"Feel what?"

"The bump, boom, boom, boomp."

"I don't feel anything."

He turned with a leery smile of broken yellow choppers. Slight nervous twitch to the eye.

"Aye, it looks like we got a flat on the left front. You probably can't feel it back there. Would you mind if I just got out and checked? Station is only five minutes away, but I don't want to fuck the wheels."

I tensed.

The car slowed.

"Just be two secs to take a look at it," he said.

Christ, I had been right the whole time. A plot. There *was* something rotten in Denmark.

The car stopped.

"Don't mind if I go out?" he asked.

"Sure, go, you can check the tire," I said.

He opened the door, left it open.

I looked out the window and I knew it was a play. We were definitely somewhere near the docks or the water in the east of the city, south of the Liffey. A warehouse district. I couldn't tell exactly where, because I didn't know and also because the fog had reduced the visibility to about forty or fifty feet. But no houses, anyway, no cars. The perfect place for a hit.

I readied myself. What was he going to do? Get out of the car, pull out a piece, and shoot me through the window? If it wasn't his car, sure, why not? Maybe he'd hijacked it last night. And what was I going to do? I didn't know yet. Have to figure it out very soon.

I watched him carefully. He bent down to check the tire. His hands were hanging by his sides. He knelt down again. Here it comes, I thought. I put my fingers on the far door handle, ready to slide out backward, get up, and sprint off into the fog as best I could.

Aye, that would be the move. Turn the handle, push the door, roll, and run.

It would depend upon how good a shot he'd be and what his shooter was.

Padraig stood, smiled at me.

"Shite, there's something wedged between the tire and the rim, you couldn't just give us a wee hand there, could you?" he said.

"I can't, sorry, I have a business meeting, don't want to get my hands all dirty," I said with an apologetic look.

"No, no, you won't have to touch anything. I'll just need you to hold the torch while I try and see what's wedged in there. I'll get it from the boot."

I didn't see how I could say no to that. Gingerly, I opened the door, edged out of the car, keeping the vehicle between him and me. He popped the trunk and removed a flashlight. Turned it on.

"Come on round, I'll need you to hold this for me," he said. "I'll knock a couple of bucks off the fare."

"I thought you didn't take dollars," I said.

"Euros, I'll knock a couple of euros off," he corrected himself with a laugh.

"What do you want me to do?"

"You just hold the light. I can't see under the rim. I'll bang whatever's there out with this," he said, holding up a tire iron and giving me another wonderful welcoming Irish smile.

So you want me to bend down and hold the flashlight, meanwhile you stand beside me with a fucking tire iron and thump it repeatedly into my skull. I don't think so, mate.

"Something stuck in the wheel rim, eh?" I asked.

"Aye."

"Let's get the light on it," I said. "Oh, I see it, there it is," and as he bent down to take a look I smacked the flashlight onto the top of his head and rammed it backward into his nose. Blood squirted, cartilage broke.

"That enough goddamn light for you?" I said.

I went to kick him but the blows to the head had hardly dented that thick skull. He swung the tire iron at me. It crashed into the Mercedes, scraping a big chunk out of the door.

In the *Book of Five Rings* and other Chinese manuals of martial arts, there's a maxim that says: "If there's a big bastard with a tire iron trying to murder you and you're armed with only a flashlight, a good option is to fucking leg it."

I legged it.

I ran straight for the dense bank of fog farther down the street. I got about ten paces before he rugby tackled me to the ground. Jesus. For a big guy he sure could move. He was holding me around the legs. I stuck my thumb in his right eye socket and gouged and he let go of me and screamed. He lashed out with the tire iron but I slid out of the way as it came crashing down on the pavement with a nasty discordant clanging noise. I got to my feet but the strapping around my prosthesis had come undone. It would take a minute to fix it. A minute, a thousand years, no difference in this situation.

I leaped on his back and put my arm around his throat and squeezed. He somehow managed to stand up with me on top of him and then he staggered and fell deliberately backward in an attempt to crush me underneath him. I let go of his throat and pushed him away. He grabbed me by my leather jacket, threw me violently to the street, lost his balance, fell down, and bounced to his feet again like Gene Kelly on crack.

Something flashed and I saw that now he had a knife in his left hand and the tire iron in the other.

"Bloody attack me, would you? I'll kill you for that, you bastard," he said.

"Jesus, me attack you? You were going to brain me," I said, breathing hard.

"I wasn't going near you," he said, gasping.

"What did you say?" I asked.

"I wasn't going near you."

"What are you saying? You weren't going to attack me?" I asked.

"Hell, no, what are you talking about?"

"Are you saying this is all a misunderstanding? I thought you were about to beat me to death," I said incredulously.

"What the fook would I do that for?" the cabbie asked.

"I thought you were a hit man," I said, my voice becoming a little less disbelieving.

"A hit man, Jesus Christ, have you some imagination. I wanted to check me tires."

"Oh, shit," I said and groaned. That was my problem all over—I knew how to go from zero to a hundred, but I didn't know how to dial it down.

"Shit is right, I'll be taking you to the Garda, me bucko. I think you broke my nose. Sue you, I will, and I'll press charges."

"Jesus, I'm really sorry, mate, I read the situation all wrong. Usually I get it right but this time—"

"Save it for the judge. Don't know what your problem is. You better wait in the Beemer, we have some haggling to do if you don't want me to call the peelers," the big man said, getting his breath back and turning away from me. That was all I needed to hear. I readied myself.

He began walking back to the car.

I ran at him and drop-kicked him in the back. He went down hard with a crash. The tire iron slipped out of his hand and he rolled around fast and lashed out with the knife. I was so close it caught me in the stomach, tearing my leather jacket and T-shirt and gouging a four-inch slash below my belly button.

I held my hand over the wound, blood pouring out between my fingers, and reeled for a quarter of a second, gathered my wits, grabbed the tire iron, and smashed it into his head so fast he didn't have time to get a protective arm up. I thumped him on the temple and behind the ear. And again. And again.

I kicked the knife out of his hand.

Blood was everywhere, his skull was cracked, synaptic fluid oozing out onto his face.

"Why?" he said and gave me a look of such confusion that I thought, is it possible that I'm wrong?

I sank to one knee.

"What did you say?"

He looked at me with desperation.

"Why?" he whispered almost inaudibly.

I leaned next to him. Doubt took over. I cradled his head. His eyes were blinking fast, his body shaking. I had made a terrible mistake.

"You called your car a Beemer, and it's a Merc. How could you forget the make of your own car? I thought you'd hijacked it."

"Christ," he said.

I set down his head and got to my feet.

"Help, can anybody help?" I managed to shout, but there was no one around. I knelt down again.

"I'm sorry," I said to Padraig.

His face was a mess, his skull smashed in. If he didn't get assistance he'd be in serious trouble. Blood on the brain, coma, death.

I had really cocked up this time.

His hand reached up and he pulled me close.

He was barely there, about to pass out, almost choking from the blood in his mouth.

"You fuck . . . Forsythe . . ." he said weakly.

One second. Two. Three.

"How do you know my name?" I asked.

"Fucking kill you . . . Forsythe," he mumbled, his voice trailing away.

His eyes closed and he fell into the black pit of unconsciousness.

I stood, nodded.

Well, well, well.

He was an assassin. No other way he could have known my name. Son of a bitch. I had been right.

Finish the bastard off? Nah. Wasn't worth it.

But, oh Jesus, Bridget. What were you playing at? It didn't make any sense. Didn't she realize I'd get the first flight out now?

Blackness at the edges of my eyes.

I fell down onto the street.

I examined my belly. Losing blood. The gash wasn't deep, but I didn't like the look of it.

Blinked.

Stumbled.

Got up again.

The fog was lifting but I couldn't see any houses or pedestrians or passing cars. I went to the Mercedes and got in. He'd left the key. I started the car and drove it about half a mile, anywhere, just to get away.

Pulled it into an alley. Passed out. Woke.

Blood flowing through my fingertips. Oozing, not pouring. Looked in the car for anything to do first aid. Nothing.

Opened the door. A swaying pavement, houses.

A sign said we were on Holles Street, which was near Marrion Square. Miles from Connolly. The cabbie'd had no intention of taking me to the train station. He was heading for the docks the whole time.

His job was supposed to be to lift me or kill me. But it was still puzzling. He had no gun. Why not? And why only one of him? And if it was a purely random shakedown how in the name of Jehovah did he know my name?

I grabbed my backpack, opened it, swallowed a couple of Percocet, got out of the car, popped the trunk.

Washer fluid, oil, spare tire, rags, assorted tools, big roll of duct tape. Do the job. I took off my T-shirt, ripped a rag in half, poured on the washer fluid, cleaned the wound.

Jesus.

Ride that pain.

I dried my belly with another rag, used a third as a bandage, and wrapped it on with four good turns of duct tape. Do for now.

Had to go, cops would be on me, needed to get some *agua*.

In a minute. In a minute.

I got back in the car, closed my eyes, and the blackness came and I was gone again.

4: CIRCE
(DUBLIN—JUNE 16, 9:15 A.M.)

A sliver of moon. A lemon sky. Morning drawing a breath across the window. Bridget's hair spread out over the white sheets in a gossamer bloom of vermilion and gold.

She's asleep on the pillow next to me. Eyes closed, mouth open.

The fan's on, but I can still hear the phone ringing in the other room.

It can only be Scotchy, so I'm letting it go.

A smell of honeysuckle. The faint murmur of the city. Sunflowers poking up through the bottom of the fire escape.

Her body is so still and white and beautiful it could be carved from Botticino marble.

It can only be Scotchy telling me to meet him at the airport. We're flying down to Florida for a funeral. Darkey's there already, which is why we've got this night together. Our only night together.

Her breathing becomes more shallow. Her eyelids flutter.

"What's that noise?" she mumbles.

"Nothing, go back to sleep."

She yawns.

"What are you doing?" she asks.

"Watching you."

"Get the phone, Michael. It might be important."

"It's never important."

"Get the phone," she insists.

"It's Scotchy, it's nothing," I tell her.

She shakes her head in disgust. Out of all the boys in Darkey's crew, it's Scotchy she hates the most. Something about that feral weasel-faced wee hood. He's never made a pass at her, nothing like that, he wouldn't dare cross Darkey, it's more his unfathomable unpleasant mind and that sleekit, native cunning. You could tell that under all that bigmouthed bluster there was something darker going on. Put the wind up anybody.

The phone gets louder.

"Just get it. Could be Andy," she says.

"Ok," I say. I take her hand, kiss it, then stand. I slide off the mattress, open the bedroom door.

Suddenly she wakes fully, looks at me with those deep green eyes. I wait to see if she's going to say anything but she doesn't. I walk into the living room. The phone's fallen under the sofa. I move a roach trap, grab it.

"No. Wait. Don't get it," she says urgently, almost in panic. "Don't get it. Don't get it. You're right, let it go. Come here instead."

But it's too late. I've already picked up the handset and heard Scotchy's nasal intake of breath before he speaks.

"Hello."

"LaGuardia, one hour, Bruce," Scotchy says. "Hurry up."

"My name's not Bruce," I tell him for the thousandth time.

"One hour. Hurry up."

I put the phone down. Bridget sighs. Yes, it's too late. . . .

Lima.

But there was no ocean. And the sky was the wrong color. Eggshell rather than deep blue.

What was going on?

Ask Hector, he'll tell me.

"Hector. Hector."

Uhhh.

Where was my cell phone? I tried to sit, but an awful scrabbling pain took my breath away. I was in a car. A street sign said "Holles Street Maternity Next Left."

Holles Street, Dublin?

It all came back. Hector was toast. I'd shot him in the head. I'd thrown an assassin out the window and I'd killed his partner with an upside-down .22 shot in his throat.

A woman in a blue dress was staring at me.

"Are you all right, love?" she asked.

I got out of the car. Out, into the morning with no idea where I was going, or what in the name of God I was going to do next. Sunlight. Cirrus clouds. Nothing Irish about the day, but I knew it was definitely Dublin because the Liffey was a presence beyond the gray forms of the buildings. A smell off it that reminded me of gasoline. I couldn't see it, but I could sense it was there, sluggish, like some dead thing on what was already a deadly morning. The lovely Liffey moving along effluent into the tidal basin, coating the pylons, bridges, and the wee blind alleys on the water's edge. And there definitely was a stink from off it. If not petrol, diesel. Enough that I could tell. Dublin. Aye. That's right.

There were stars in front of my eyes, as if my retina had become detached. I blinked for half a minute and the stars vanished.

I walked away from the car.

Only just in time.

Two men pulled up in a Ford Sierra, got out, and headed for the Mercedes.

Your average eejit might have thought, Ah, couple of car thieves.

But not me. Their suits were crumpled and dirty. Even from here they stank of fags and coffee. What man, who wore a suit, got this dirty this early?

Bloody cops or I'm a Chinaman.

"Morning," one of them shouted across the street to me, with no love at all in the greeting and sleekit peeler eyes.

I nodded in reply and then thought better of it.

"Lavly day, innit?" I said in estuary English.

In about five minutes they'd have a warrant out for me. Why not have them thinking I was a Cockney?

Backpack was still in there, but my IDs and cash were in my jacket. Screw it. I hobbled down the street, and when I was out of sight I ran as best as I could with a duct-tape bandage, sore foot, artificial foot, jetlag, painkillers, possible detached retina, sleeping pill, and no idea where I was going.

I was wrong about the five minutes.

It couldn't have been more than two.

"Hey, you," the cops yelled. "Stop."

I had about a couple of hundred yards on them. Even with my handicaps, if I couldn't lose them in rush hour in a busy city like Dublin I deserved to be bloody caught.

I turned a corner and found that I was at Trinity College.

Excellent.

I ran in through the gates and chucked myself into a seething mass of students, visitors, and other extras in my little scene.

Total chaos.

Even more chaos than usual, which meant that a big party of tourists had just arrived, or that it was exam time, or graduation.

"What's the *craic*?" I asked a forlorn girl who was looking everywhere for her friends.

"It's the parade," she said and pointed to a corner of the quad where a big disorganized line had formed and was filing out into the street. I saw then that it was part of the Bloom thing. The kids were all dressed in Edwardian gear, some were riding old-fashioned bicycles, and there was even a horse-drawn omnibus pulling drunken members of a rugby team.

As good a place as any.

I joined the procession just as the two peels arrived at the college gates. One of them still had his cigarette in his mouth. Jesus, didn't they want to catch me? Let go your fag, you cheap Mick flatfoot.

They were both around twenty years older than me. Just about the right age to be thoroughly beaten down by the system, cynical and fed up. Maybe a couple of younger coppers would have stopped everyone from leaving Trinity, called in assistance, created a huge palaver. Not these characters. The parade wove its way past them without either lifting a finger. But even so, no point being a bloody fool about it. I snatched the flat cap off one kid's head, threaded my way through the crowd, tripped another kid, and ripped the Edwardian jacket off his back as he fell down.

"Jesus," he said, but whether that was followed by anything else, I don't know because I had taken three steps to the side and four back.

I pulled the Edwardian coat over my leather jacket, put on the flat cap.

I followed the kids out of Trinity and into the road.

Nice.

Now I was in a parade of a couple of hundred similarly dressed and high-spirited students heading for O'Connell Street. Like to see them find me now.

We marched merrily away from Trinity and turned north.

I wasn't that familiar with *Ulysses* but it was an easy assumption that a lot of the weans were dressed as characters from the book. There were barbers, undertakers, bookies, priests, nuns, all of them in old-timey gear and most so cute you could forgive them for being young, exuberant, and irritating. And besides, they'd saved my hide.

Some of them were drinking and I got passed a can of Guinness, which I took gratefully.

"Cheers, mate," I said.

"Sure, 'tis no problem," a girl said. She had red cheeks and brown hair and was dressed as a tarty maid.

I took a large swig of the Guinness. Its effect was restorative.

"Are you for going to the party, young sir?" she asked in bad Edwardian. She was about nineteen or twenty and came from somewhere in County Kerry.

"Alas, fair lady, I have no time for such an enchanting offer," I said. "I'm pressed by agents of the Castle."

"Maybe another time," she said and clinked her can of alcohol-free beer into mine. And maybe I would another time, but now I had to get out of town. It had been a staggeringly difficult twenty-four hours and what I needed more than anything was a place to gather my wits and lie low.

I knew no one in Dublin and I figured that all the old safe houses and chop joints I used to hang out in were probably gone. But seeing the Kerry girl dressed like that had given me an idea.

Back in my day, running with the teen rackets in 1990 Belfast, Chopper Clonfert used to take us lads to a whorehouse near the Four Courts on one of the north quays of the Liffey. It primarily catered to lawyers and civil servants but Chopper worked big time for the rackets and he was the Belfast rep. So the girls, without too much feeling of resentment, would let us have a freebie. If it was still there (and this was nearly fifteen years ago), it might be a good place to bolt to for a while. I couldn't use Chopper's name to get in (Chopper had long since turned legit) but I could just pose as an ordinary client. With my long coat, flat cap, and haggard demeanor, I did look a bit like a crappy Dublin family-services lawyer or something.

Aye, the beginnings of a plan.

Go there, get my bearings, clean up. Maybe see to this wound. Anyway, I needed to be gone from the madding crowd and it was probably not a good idea to walk around too much longer in a blood-stained T-shirt.

Also I wanted to call Bridget from a quiet spot. I needed to know what the score was. Hopefully, her tone of voice would tell me. Had the cabbie been hers? Had he been anybody's? Had I hallucinated or misremembered him saying my name? Bridget wouldn't have all the answers but she'd have some of them.

And with that solved, it would make the next step clearer. Had to get out of Dublin. But whether I had to get out of Ireland, too, was the big question.

The cops didn't worry me; if the cabbie lived he wouldn't talk and if he died there'd be another gangland murder along tomorrow to occupy their limited attention span. In my eyes the Garda Síochána was only a notch or two above the Irish Army and, as an ex-member of the British Army, I had nothing but contempt for that body. Any squaddie worth his salt would join the Irish Guards in London; any peeler up to scuds would get into one of the big metropolitan police forces across the water. Irish coppers and soldiers were second-rate.

But complacency is also one of the byways on the road to ruin. I would have to put my contempt on the back burner and play it bloody safe.

"Are you a lecturer?" the girl finally plucked up the courage to ask.

"No, no, not really," I told her.

"Are you a mature student?"

"Yeah, you could say that, I'm always learning," I replied.

"Well, I think that's great, it's wonderful to go back to university at your age, education is very important."

"Shit, how old do you think I am?"

"Forty?" she suggested.

Well, Jesus, let's see how you look after a knife fight, love.

"Ach, I'm barely in my thirties," I said. "Just been partying all night, that's all."

"What are you studying?" she asked, but before I could make something up, we'd arrived at the O'Connell Street Bridge and a scene of complete bedlam. This parade was clearly not part of the official Bloomsday festivities and the cops were totally unprepared. Traffic was still trying to come off the quays and up the street and the parade wanted to head north onto O'Connell Street.

Buses, cars, trucks, bicyclists, and pedestrians had formed an ugly confused mess right in the center of the city. Some of the students were getting restless. They began shouting at the peels and chanting. Baffled tourists were getting separated from their tour groups, taxi drivers were yelling, the cops were flailing about uselessly waiting for instruction. It was all fine by me. The more disorder the better.

"Honey, I must be off," I told the girl.

She held my sleeve.

"Are you not going on to Jury's?"

"I can't, sorry," I said. "I have to go, really, it's like I said, I'm on the run from Johnny law."

She reached into her tart handbag looking for something. She tipped it upside down and out dropped a big hippy Volkswagen key chain. I picked it up and gave it to her. By this time she had found what she was searching for—a piece of card with a Dublin telephone number on it.

"It's my cell. Give me a call if you're not doing anything later," she said.

"I will, if I don't get lifted," I said.

"Riorden," she said and offered me her hand.

"Brian," I said and slipped away from her and the rest of the students. I dipped under the boom mike of a BBC camera crew, escaped a video unit from RTE television, and just about avoided being knocked into a bus by one of the old geezers from *60 Minutes*.

I walked west and at a green phone booth took a look back for tails.

Nobody after me at all. I'd lost the cops and they'd lost me. Excellent.

Lost them. Now part two of the plan. The Four Courts. Where the hell were they?

Somewhere on the water.

I stopped a man in jeans and a Joyce T-shirt.

"Excuse me, you don't happen to know whereabouts the Four Courts are? I know it's around here somewhere, but I can't quite remember."

"Oh, my goodness. I am frightfully sorry, but I have no idea," he said with an English accent.

The next woman:

"*Weiss nicht.* I live here, but I do not know. Four Courts? I haff a map of ze whole city in—"

And it took me six more people until I found a Dubliner. You wouldn't have seen that in the old days either. People immigrating *to* Dublin.

The native, though, told me it was piss easy, just follow the river and I couldn't miss it.

I followed the river and didn't miss it.

The big domed gray legal building right on the water. Barristers, judges, solicitors, clients all milling about the front.

"This is the Four Courts, isn't it?" I asked a solicitor having a smoke.

"'Tis indeed," he said. "Do you need a lawyer?"

"Nah, but could I bum a cigarette?"

He lit me a ciggy and I sat down on the steps. Everything was hurting. The fag helped a bit.

I could think.

Now that I'd found the Four Courts, I had to search my memory to locate where the brothel had been. It was certainly on this side of the water. And it was pretty close by because I remember Bobby Fullerton seeing his brief at the Chinese restaurant, which was right next to the brothel.

Hmmm.

It seemed simple enough. And although I'm not a negative individual, I had to admit that the chances of all those things still being there after all this time seemed unlikely.

I got up, began walking, turned left, followed the quay, and my heart sank. It became immediately apparent that everything I remembered about these streets had utterly changed. Where there had been seedy pawnshops, tobacconists, and greasy diners, now there were Internet cafés, Gap stores, and of course Starbucks, where they make you bloody queue twice. Never get away with that in Belfast, I hoped.

I walked down a side street that looked familiar, went halfway along it, stopped, came back to the quay. Tried another left, a second left, a third, tried a right, but now I was utterly baffled and well lost in the alleys and back streets. All of them gentrified, painted, scrubbed, new windows, window treatments. The Dubs had even started putting up blue plaques like you saw in London. "Handel slept here," "Wilde lived here," that kind of malarkey. And no ragamuffin children or beggars. I suppose now if you wanted to know what the Dublin alleys looked like when this was my stamping ground you'd have to go to a seedy *hutong* in Beijing or a back street in Bombay.

But then, suddenly, with Beijing on my mind, I spotted two Chinese guys carrying a pole of pink dangling ducks. I followed them. Down one street, up another. They stopped outside a restaurant, fumbled for a set of keys, and went in.

Ahh. I stepped back. Was this the same place?

Yeah. Bloody hell.

Completely different now, of course. Before, a concrete bunker with grilles over the window and a heavy iron door. Now, tinted plate glass, plush tables, a lilac paint job, and a big new sign. Still, something about it rang a bell. And if this was the restaurant the brothel was the house immediately to the left. A three-story Georgian affair, with the blinds pulled down.

No blue plaque announcing "Brendan Behan bonked here," but you never knew, it might still be the same establishment. Someone had sandblasted the brick front, removed the old wooden window frames, and put in air-conditioning vents. Back in the day the front door had been a low-key brown, as befitted a whorehouse. Now it was a bright blue with a gold knocker and letter box.

I went up the steps, knocked.

Waited.

Probably a firm of insurance agents in here now.

I knocked again.

The door was opened by a beautiful hard-faced blonde with vampiric eyes. Skin the color of driven snow and slightly Asiatic features. She was wearing a tight silk see-through black sweater, black miniskirt, and knee-length leather boots. Certainly not an Irish girl, and if she was in the insurance business it could only have been for Satan, fiddling the actuarial tables on potential soul sellers.

"Yes?" she said in an imperious Russian accent.

"I'm here for a little R and R, is this the right place?"

"Perhaps. Would you like to come in?" she said.

"Aye, I would at that."

"Please, follow me."

I went in.

There exists a school of thought which holds that madams in brothels, bordellos, and whorehouses are endowed with wisdom, taste, and a singular ability for understanding human nature. I have no idea where this notion sprang from, but in my experience madams are about as wise and sensible as the average giggly third-grade teacher. And as for taste, not in the brothels I've been in. The proprietor of the Four Courts whorehouse was no exception. Her tastes ran to cliché and old-world decadence. The blinds were drawn and the fake Tiffany lamps were exuding a dull-yellow depressing glow that made you wonder if they were trying to conceal the merchandise. Incense burning in a corner smelled of dead cat, and once you'd adjusted to the dim surroundings, you saw that the elegant blue door on the outside was in contrast to the bright reds, golds, chandeliers, paintings of eagles, and classical figurines in a look that seemed to be a cross between antebellum New Orleans and the Reich chancellory.

"My name is Lara," the Russian girl lied.

"Aye, and I'm Doctor Zhivago. Listen, I need to speak to the woman of the house, if you don't mind; I've got a couple of questions," I said.

"We cater to all tastes."

"Aye, I'm sure you do, but all I need is a quiet room, where I can have a shower and gather my thoughts, no fuss; I'll pay top dollar, and if someone would be so good as to bring me a cup of tea, I would love it."

"It is three hundred euros for one girl, for one half hour, it might be extra for, uh, your particular, uh, needs," she said, looking at me as if I were the biggest pervert who had walked in in months, God alone knew what I wanted to do with the girl and the tea.

"Yeah, I don't need a girl. I just need a quiet room. Tell the boss."

The Russian motioned for me to sit down on a leather chair. An Albanian cleaning woman started vacuuming the rugs. Lara went off and came back with an older conservatively dressed Irish woman in a black wig and ivory glasses. She sat down opposite.

I offered the three hundred euros. She refused to accept it.

"Ye can't stay here, if that's what you're thinking. This is a respectable house, whatever you've done, this isn't a place for fugitives," she said, blowing my whole madam-smart-as-a-third-grade-teacher theory out of the water.

"I don't know what you're talking about," I said.

"No, of course not, that's why you're dripping blood on me leather seat and you're wearing someone else's coat."

"Ok, there's no need to be hasty. But you're right, I need a place to lie low until I can figure how I can get out of town. I won't be any trouble."

"You won't be any trouble cos you won't be here. Get the fuck out, before I get the help to throw you out," she said. "And we wouldn't want your pretty face more beat up than it already is."

"I'm working for Bridget Callaghan," I said—the only card I had, and not mentioning, of course, that there was more than a possibility that lovely Bridget was trying to bloody kill me.

"Are you now?" she said, batting not an eye. "And who might that be?"

"The head of the fucking Irish mob in New York City, as if you didn't know," I said with menace.

She shook her head slightly. Took a small intake of breath.

"Ok, ok. Keep your voice down for one thing; this is a respectable house, so it is. And so what? Even if you do work for her, what's that to me? You sitting there on the run from the Guards, frightening me girls."

"I'll tell you what it is to you, love. It's bloody this. If Bridget hears that you wouldn't help me, that you said there was no room at the inn when I was in a tight spot, you better fucking have fire insurance."

She was going to say something, stopped herself, smiled, nodded. This was a hooker with a heart of brass. She knew what was what. She gave me a final once-over to see if she believed me. Apparently she did.

"What's your name?" she asked.

"Michael Forsythe."

Her eyebrows raised a fraction, but she recovered quickly and asked me another question: "You worked for Bridget Callaghan a long time?"

"We go back a long, long way."

"And would you be able to prove that if it was necessary?"

"I would. Listen, love, I just got into town. I've already had a fucking lot to deal with, I just need a hour to get my bloody head straight."

The madam sighed and got to her feet.

"It's more or less an empty house at the moment," she said to herself.

"You'll let me have a room?"

"Ok, ok, we'll see what we can do. I suppose you're here to help with the missing wee girl?"

"You heard about that?"

"Oh aye, it's big news in certain quarters."

"Is it?" I asked, for information.

"It is indeed now."

"What do you know about it?"

"Well, my first thought was that the lassie—Siobhan, is it?—must have run off, because no one in Ireland would dare to have lifted Bridget Callaghan's wean. But I'll tell you this, I'm not so sure now, that pop music nowadays, it's all about drugs, one of those heroin fiends could have taken her off the street to his drug den. Let me tell you. I certainly don't allow drug users in my establishment. Anything could happen."

"Very wise."

"You say your name is Michael Forsythe?" she asked a little slyly.

"That's right. That mean anything to you?"

"No, no, not at all. Yeah, shame about the wee girl. But it happened in Belfast and, sure, Belfast is crazy like. I don't know what's going on up there. The lines aren't set yet, not like down here. Dublin's a lot more civilized, you know what's what. Anyway, enough of the chitchat, get you a room. What do you want in your tea?"

"I'll take milk and sugar," I said.

The woman made a movement to a man I'd only just noticed lurking in deep shadow by the grandfather clock. He shimmered out of the foyer.

"Follow me."

I had trouble getting up, so she helped me to my feet and led me down the corridor and into a side room. She unlocked the door and we entered.

Another decor change from the way I remembered these rooms. Cheap and cheerful in my day, now fussy Victorian: a four-poster bed hung with silky drapes, pictures of ballerinas and puppies lost in string, chintzy mirrors, clocks, sinister-looking china dolls. I couldn't have imagined a worse room in which to try to get an erection and fuck a stranger. But maybe the girls were so bloody great it didn't matter what the interior decoration was like.

"You can take a shower and I'll have someone go out and buy you a change of clothes. Thirty-two trouser and a large for a shirt, is it? Aye, looks like it. Well now, ok. And do you need a girl on the house?"

"No."

"Fine, I'll bring you clothes and let you get on with things. You can freshen up and get your shite together, but you can't stay long. You certainly can't stay over. If the Guards are looking for you, for anything serious, I don't need it coming near my house."

"I understand, I'll be out of here within the hour. Oh, and if you could bring me a needle and a strong piece of thread, that would help too."

She nodded, left the room. I lay down on the bed and began

pulling off my clothes. I checked the straps around my artificial foot; sometimes you got chafing on the stump, but everything looked ok. I put it back on. A knock at the door.

"Who is it?" I asked.

"Lara, with your tea," she said.

I opened the door extremely cautiously, in case of trouble, but it was nothing more invidious than the gray-eyed hooker with a teapot on a tray. Behind her, in the corridor, a man wearing a pig nose was naked, on all fours, being led by another Russian girl dressed domina-trix-fashion in leathers and spiked boots. Probably the chief justice of Ireland, the chief constable of Dublin, someone like that.

"Will that be all now, sir?" Lara said, having rehearsed the phrase to sound like an Irish girl.

"If someone could get me a T-shirt, it would be great. This one's ruined."

"Very well," she said and closed the door behind her.

I drank some tea and ate a couple of the chocolate biscuits that came with it. They'd also provided that needle and thread. I started running the shower to get the hot water warmed up.

I picked the phone up from the bedside table. I found Bridget's number at the Europa.

Well, this was it. Your last chance, my dear. She'd have to be pretty bloody convincing. Fool me once, shame on you; fool me twice . . .

I dialed the Europa Hotel, got through to her room.

"Who's this?" a man asked.

"Who's this?" I asked.

"Moran."

"I want to speak to Bridget, this is Michael Forsythe," I said.

"Hold on," the man said with cold anger.

"Michael, are you in Belfast?" Bridget asked urgently.

"Am I hell. I'm not in the grave, anyway."

"What are you talking about?"

"Despite your best efforts I am still walking the same planet Earth as you," I said.

"Michael, I don't have time for this, come to the point," Bridget muttered impatiently.

"Honestly, this is getting very tiresome," I said.

"Tiresome for me, too. What are you talking about?" Bridget yelled.

"Your boy tried to kill me, as if you didn't know," I said.

"What boy?"

"Your boy, the cab driver. Surprise, surprise, he knew my name and he tried to fucking kill me."

Bridget considered the information. Her breathing became shorter and she sounded irritated.

"Michael, I don't know what is going on. If someone tried to kill you, it was nothing to do with me."

"Bridget, I know you're playing. Do you think I am that stupid?" I said, a half-rhetorical, half-real query.

"Michael, believe me, I don't know what you're talking about. I didn't send anyone to kill you. Why would I do that when I could have killed you in Peru?"

Fair point.

"You didn't send someone to the airport to meet me?"

"No."

I leaned back in the leather chair, tapped the phone against my forehead. Just exactly how good was she? Was she good enough to send two hit teams at me in two days, fail in both the hits, and still convince me that she wasn't trying to knock me off?

"Bridget, I know it was you, I—" I tried to say but Bridget cut me off.

"Listen to me, you worthless shit. You killed my fiancé and I'm giving you a chance to fucking balance the ledger. My daughter's gone missing. Do you understand? I don't know what the fuck you've been doing in Dublin, I don't care. I need your help. The most precious thing in the world to me is Siobhan. Not you or what you've been up to, you son of a bitch. I don't have the time to talk to you anymore. I'll be in the Europa, you'll either come or you won't, it's up to you. You are not my concern right now. Ok? I have a million things to do, so I have to go. Hell with you, Michael, useless as fucking usual."

She hung up.

I listened to the dial tone and then the recorded operator told me to put the phone down. Jesus. Where did that leave me? It was back to the original question. Was she good enough to hit me and still make me come to her in Belfast?

I groaned, put my head in my hands.

She was.

What was happening to me? What kind of an idiot had I become? Was my judgment going? Either that or a possibility that was worse. Maybe I really didn't buy it, maybe I didn't believe her at all. I didn't believe her but I wanted to go to Belfast anyway. I was being drawn to her even though I knew it would bring death. I wanted to see her this one last time whatever the cost.

Was that what was going on?

I shrugged. Nah. It wasn't as complicated as that. I simply believed her. She was telling the truth. What was happening to me had nothing to do with her. It was a coincidence. I had more than one enemy in the world, after all, and maybe I had several in Ireland. And by now, my presence was known about and advertised.

I removed the duct tape, took my trousers off, and climbed into the shower.

Quick shower. Quick dry.

I wrapped the towel around me and sat on the end of the bed. I ripped off a piece of pillowcase, dipped the needle in the hot tea, and double threaded it. I grabbed the flesh on either side of my knife wound. Easy does it. I pushed the needle through the epidermis, threaded it over the wound, drove it through the skin on the other side of the cut. I repeated the procedure five times in a crisscross pattern and gently pulled the stitches tight. When the wound was together, I tied off the thread, wiped away the blood, applied a bit of pillowcase as a bandage, and rewrapped the duct tape around the whole thing.

I spent a while recovering from the waves of pain and then I started dressing.

There was a knock outside. Ah, Lara with the T-shirt. I pulled on my trousers and opened the door.

Not Lara. A six-foot-four bald guy with a goatee, a black suit, narrow slits for eyes, and a six-shot .38 revolver in his meaty paw.

"What the fuck is all this?" I asked. "The lady of the house and I have an arrangement."

"Are you Michael Forsythe?" he asked in a Belfast accent.

If I hadn't learned in the last ten years, certainly the last two days had taught me the inefficacy of answering to that name.

"Who are you?" I asked.

"Oh, you don't need to know who I am. Put your hands on your head and make like a fucking statue. One move and there's a bullet in that bandage in your gut."

I put my hands over my head. The man rummaged through my things and found my passport. That wouldn't help him. I was called Brian O'Nolan on that. Still, he looked at the picture and at me and compared it with a mental picture.

"I think it is you," he said rhetorically. "The foot too, bit of a give-away."

"You want to tell me what this is all about?" I asked.

"No, I want you to put these on," he said and threw me a pair of handcuffs. I let them drop on the floor.

"And if I don't?"

"Just put on the cuffs," he said.

"Bridget sent you?"

He didn't offer any information, but perhaps that was a tell in a very slight shake of the head.

"I won't put the cuffs on unless you tell me what's going to happen after I do."

"You'll be going on a journey, see some old pals. Now put the cuffs on. You'll be fucking sorry if you don't, it's all the same to me."

"Did the madam tell you I was here?"

"Yeah, she did, now get those things on," he yelled.

"At least let me get dressed first."

He thought about it for a second.

"Ok. No funny stuff or I'll top ya."

I put on my clothes, taxing his patience with my Stanley boots. I picked up the handcuffs. Standard cop jobs. I placed one over my wrist and casually tilted my arm so he couldn't see exactly what I was doing, and closed the cuff about halfway. I tugged the metal between my finger and thumb to show him that it was locked. The man seemed satisfied. Of course it wasn't locked at all. I put the second loop over my other wrist and closed it, this time all the way. I held my hands in front of me with the big gap on the right side, underneath my wrist where he couldn't see it. If he had any brains he'd kick me in the balls, kneel on me, put the gun in my face, and make sure the handcuffs were really bloody tight.

But he was a trusting son of a bitch and either not very good at this or was under orders to go softy softly with me.

"You walk ahead of me, we'll wait downstairs, there'll be a car along in a couple of minutes."

"Where are we going?"

"Doesn't concern you."

"The Garda is looking for me. You can't just take me away, they'll spot you in a second."

"Aye, heard about that. How long have you been in the city? About four hours? And they already have a photofit of you up on the telly for attempted murder. Nice work. But don't you worry about the Garda, mate, we know all the ins and outs of this town, believe me."

"Where we going?" I tried again.

"North," he said ominously.

So it was Bridget.

I walked along the oak-paneled corridor and into the foyer. It had been cleared of girls, clients in pig noses, and Albanian cleaning ladies.

He was behind me. I looked at our reflections in the polished oak. He was following me about four feet back.

I wriggled out of the right handcuff. A tiny clinking sound, but he couldn't see what I was doing.

I wouldn't have long to make my move. A car was coming. Presumably with more men inside.

Three steps led down from the hallway into the foyer.

It would have to be now.

I tripped and fell down the steps, keeping my hands in front and landing on what looked like my unprotected face.

"Jesus," the man said and ran over to help. He transferred the revolver from his right to his left hand and pulled me up by the hair. I let him lift me six inches off the ground then I made a grab for the gun. My left hand found his wrist, I stuck my knuckle into the pressure point an inch below his life line.

He screamed, his grip loosened, and I grabbed the pistol. He threw a punch at me with his right, missed, smacked his fist into the hardwood floor. I kicked his legs and he fell on top of me. He landed with a two-hundred-pound crash on my back, crushing the air out of my lungs and nearly opening my stitches.

Painfully I rolled to the side just as he was drawing back a big fist to smash into my face, but there wasn't going to be a fight. I wriggled my arm free, held the gun out horizontally, and pulled the trigger. A bullet caught him in the armpit. He screamed and writhed, and I pushed him off. And as he made a desperate lunge for the gun, I shot him in the shoulder. The second bullet knocked him on his spine.

I stood up and backed well away from him.

"Who do you work for?" I asked.

Through one of the brothel windows I could see that a red Range Rover had pulled up outside. Men getting out. Bollocks. No time for twenty questions.

"Ammo," I said.

He pointed to his jacket pocket. I reached in and pulled out a bag full of assorted .38 shells. Old, new; still, they would do the job.

"Handcuff key?"

"Other pocket."

I reached in and took out the key.

"Don't kill me," he pleaded.

"This is your lucky day, pal," I said and ran back up the foyer steps and along the corridor, kicking open doors until I found a room with a girl inside.

Mousy little brunette taking a break.

"Is there a back way out of here?" I asked her.

"What?"

I put the gun on her forehead.

"Is there a back way out of here?" I asked again.

❀   ❀   ❀

Running. Those stars again. My eyes were definitely fucked up. Couldn't see properly. I rubbed them. Big red birds sitting around a black mark in the road. As I got close they turned into kids in Man. United shirts.

I looked back.

No one behind me.

"Over here, mister," a voice said, and a tiny hand tugged me down a narrow lane. Dogs barking. Papers. Cardboard boxes. Beer cans. Bottles. Narrow streets. An outdoor toilet. Smell of bacon fat. Curtains of gray slate, yards of washing.

"This way," the voice said.

Finally I stopped seeing the stars. But Jesus, I'd have to get to a doctor for that.

We went into a court between some back-to-backs and then across a yard full of burned-out cars. In front of us was an open space where a block of flats had once stood and now was derelict. Kids playing in the cement, women talking. Caravans. Trailer homes.

"You're safe now, mister," the voice said. The kid was a boy of about thirteen. A dark-haired wee mucker with a scar on his face below the ear. He was wearing a patched sweater, dirty plimsolls, and trousers miles too big for him. Clearly he was a Gypsy kid, or a *traveler*, if you wanted to be politically correct about it.

"Who ya running from? The poliss?" the kid asked when he saw that I had my breath back.

"Sort of."

"Aye, thought so. I just seen this eejit running and I thought the poliss are after him. That's why I done come after ya, show ya a wee route."

"Thanks."

The kid looked at the handcuff still attached to my left wrist. It was also still holding a silenced revolver, but the boy didn't give a shit about the gun.

"Did ya make a break for it? Outta the car?"

"Aye. Sure," I said. I found the key, took the handcuffs off, and gave them to him.

"Did ya have that key made? How did ya get out of those things?" he asked.

"You ever heard of Houdini?"

"Nope."

I drank in air, safetied the pistol, and shoved it down the front of my trousers.

"Ya want me to get ya a drink or something?" the kid asked.

"No. Thanks."

"Are ya heading back?"

"Yes."

"Where to?"

"Belfast," I found myself saying. "I'm going to Belfast to get some answers."

The boy was looking at me funny now. Squinting as the sun came out and then smirking as it went back behind the clouds. I stretched my shoulders where they hurt and reached in my pocket. I found a twenty-euro note.

"Buy yourself some candy," I said.

"I will," the kid said, with a trace of ungracious defiance, as if he was just begging me to tell him to say thank you, in which case he would be ready to tell me to fuck away off. But I wasn't falling for it. I looked at the wee lad and found myself breaking into a grin.

"Have you any brothers or sisters?" I asked.

"Jesus, you've no idea, mister."

"Give them a share of the candy."

"I will," the kid promised.

"Give you another twenty if you could russle me up a T-shirt, this one's fucked."

The kid nodded, walked across the waste ground, walked into the nearest caravan, came out with a black Led Zeppelin T-shirt. A man appeared and said something to the kid and pointed at me. The kid replied, nodded. Brought me the T-shirt. I put it on.

"What did that man want?" I asked.

"Nothing. He was just telling me there was two men who came after ya, looking for ya, loike, asking questions."

"What did he say to them?"

The kid grinned.

"Nobody saw anything or anybody."

"Ok. Good. Which way back into the city center?"

"Down to the right. All the way down the hill."

I left the boy and walked down the hill, past boarded-up houses and a few scary-looking hoods keeping watch at the corners. This was the heart of a bad area (interestingly, just behind the façade of new Dublin) and I walked fast to get out of it, but not so quickly that I would attract attention. If they thought I was an undercover cop or a rival hood I'd be approached at gunpoint, bundled into a van, and taken somewhere to be interrogated. Take me bloody hours to get out of it.

At the bottom of the hill I came to a bus station and then I saw some familiar street signs.

I was near the river again.

Belfast, I'd told the kid. And Belfast it would be.

The peelers.

Oh, they'd send a couple of beat cops to the exit points. Avoid the train station, avoid the bus station, avoid the airport, but there was no way the Garda could control cars leaving the city, not these days. Dublin was a big, modern commuter city with a thousand roads in and out.

Piss easy, steal a car, drive out of town. Shit, hire a car. They didn't know who I was. Get my credit card, dial Hertz.

I found a quiet nook and took out my cell phone.

I called up every car-hire place in County Dublin but in every one the story was the same: "We're all out of cars, there's a big festival in Dublin to do with James Joyce. You'll have no problem tomorrow, but not today."

So, it was either thieve a vehicle or risk the bus or train stations. I really could chance the latter two. I didn't have much respect for the Garda's ability to apprehend someone even if they did have a photofit. But then again maybe that would be pushing my luck just too far.

As for the first option. There were hundreds of cars parked right here in the street, but who knew what fuckwit would miss his vehicle fifteen minutes from now, call the cops, and then they'd circulate the license plate and some keen motorcyle cop would lift me. What then? Shoot an unarmed Garda Síochána just trying to do his duty?

Nah. I had another idea. I found the card in my trouser pocket. I phoned the number.

"Hello," I said when I got connected.

"I can't hear you."

"Hey, it's me, the old geezer from the parade."

"Oh, you, where did you go?" Riorden asked.

"Hey, let me ask you something, have you got a car, a Volkswagen?"

"Yeah, I do, a Volkswagen Beetle. One of the new ones. Why do you want to know?"

"Uh, I don't. Just checking. Friend of mine wants to buy a car, he really likes Volkswagens, that's all. You're not in the market to sell it?"

"Is that why you called me up?"

"No, you got me. It's only an excuse, I wanted to see you again and I couldn't think of a reason for calling you. Where are you?"

"We're still at Jury's, do you know it?"

"Aye, I know it."

Twenty minutes later I walked into Jury's. A party was in full swing. It was a nice June day, the international media were in town, term was winding down. What more excuse did you need for celebration?

In any case it was packed with students. Standing room only and there wasn't much room to stand. Two hundred dead easy if someone shouted "Fire."

I found the girl talking to an enormous black-haired English rugby player in an Aran sweater. She was on lemonade, but he was half wasted and thought his luck was in. I waited till she took a bathroom break before I approached him.

"Fuck off, Hercules, the lady is spoken for," I said with menace.

"Are you talking to me?" the rugby player asked.

"No, I'm talking to the midget who works you by remote control, now fuck away off before we test the adage, the bigger they are . . ."

"You've got to be pulling my leg?" he said.

"No. I'm not pulling your fucking leg. I'm not climbing up your fucking beanstalk to steal your magic beans either. I'm telling you to fuck away off before I get upset."

"Jesus, are you looking for trouble?" he persisted.

"Believe me, I don't have to go looking. I'll count to ten and you better be out of here, this lady is spoken for."

"You picked the wrong guy to start a fight with," he maintained.

As I began my countdown, he clenched his fists.

"One, two, three, four," I counted and kneed him right in the nut sack. He sank to the floor and as he tumbled I grabbed him by the hair and smacked my fist twice into his face. He wilted, wobbled, fell. I checked to see if anyone had spotted my assault on a brother student, but everyone was drunk, exuberant, not paying attention and I was a fast wee turd when occasion arose.

"Lend a hand here, Nigel can't hold his drink," I shouted and pushed the big guy's head backward onto the concrete floor.

A couple of his mates, looking round for the first time, saw that their pal was out for the count and ran to help him. Just then the girl came out of the toilet.

"Your boyfriend can't take his drink," I said.

"He's not my boyfriend," the girl said, looking to see that he wasn't dead, but not much beyond that.

"Good, you deserve better," I said.

"Who are you?" she asked, exasperated.

I bit my lip.

I was going to romance her but suddenly, from out of nowhere, I was fed up with this story. I wanted to expedite matters. I wanted to bring things to the goddamn climax. There wasn't time for an hour or two's worth of bullshit.

"You want the truth?" I asked.

"Yeah?"

"I'm a police officer, I'm undercover. Inspector Brian O'Nolan. Dublin CID. I know you don't want to hear this in the middle of a party but someone broke into your car," I said deadpan.

"Someone broke into my car?" she said, horrified.

"That's right. We ran the plate, your name and number came up and I thought, Jesus, that's a coincidence, I was talking to that wee lassie this morning."

"Is that why you asked about it on the phone?"

"Aye, but I hate to tell people bad news on the phone. Thought I'd come in person. Come on. We'd like you to ID the vehicle and drive it to the nearest station for us, if you don't mind."

"Jesus, I'm glad I gave you my number," she said, happy enough to buy the story without a heartbeat.

"Come on, let's go ID the car."

Five minutes later and we were at a small parking lot near Trinity. I deflected easily the many "You don't look like a cop" or "You have a bit of an American accent" questions, reassured her that her car was relatively unharmed, and asked her a couple of details about her habits, friends, and teachers to see if she would be missed.

"There's the car," she said, pointing to a blue Volkswagen. "Shite. It looks ok from here."

I checked the street.

There were people about but no one paying us any particular attention. We walked to the vehicle.

She looked at me with first a puzzled and then a suspicious expression playing across her pretty face.

"No one broke into the car," she said.

"Don't scream or I'll fucking shoot you," I said, taking out the revolver and shoving it into her ribs.

"Are you serious?" she asked, wondering, no doubt, if this was all some nasty practical joke.

"Aye."

"W-what do you want?" she asked, a little bit more frightened this time.

"Well, I want your car, but you'll have to come with me, because I don't want you reporting me and I'm not feeling well enough to drive."

"You must be kidding," she said, her big eyes widening in terror. Her chest heaving up and down. It was not unattractive. I pushed the gun farther into her body.

"No joke, love. Now unlock the fucking car and get in."

"You wouldn't kill me in broad daylight."

"I fucking would," I said savagely.

This was the turning point for her.

"I don't want to get shot. I'm, I'm . . . I'm pregnant," she said and began to sob.

It threw me for a second, but only for a second.

"You listen to me, honey. You're going to live till you're a hundred and twenty years old. You're going to be popping champagne corks in the year 2100 and you're going to be here when the aliens show up with all their videos of Jesus and Alexander the Great. Either that, or you're going to be fucking dead with a bullet in your skull, thirty seconds from now. Your call. And if you die, the bairn dies too."

She composed herself a little, looked at me, stared at the gun.

"What do you want?" she asked.

"We're going to get in your car and you're going to drive me to Belfast and you're going to drive back down to Dublin and never bloody mention this to anybody. Now enough yakking, get in the fucking car and drive."

5: PENELOPE
(BELFAST—JUNE 16, 1:35 P.M.)

Dublin in the rearview mirror. At last. The girl stinking of fear, sweating, not speaking, but that was ok. The journey was only two hours now that the Irish government had gotten millions from the European Structural Fund and finally built a couple of decent roads.

She was a competent driver even with a maniac kidnapper pointing a gun at her. She drove carefully and fast. It was all good. We had a full tank of petrol and in the backseat there was even a water bottle and a packet of biscuits. I ate the biscuits, offered her one, but she refused, giving me a look of utter scorn. I liked that.

The run was quick, easy, and straightforward until we hit Drogheda.

Here things were bollocksed because of a traffic jam on the bypass; the cops were diverting people into the center of town and over the Boyne Bridge. We were moving very slowly and there were about a dozen Garda milling about uselessly. I knew she wouldn't try anything but I had to remind her.

"Honey, just because you see a lot of cops and the traffic's slow, don't think of being a hero. You make one bolt for that door and I'll fucking plug ya. And don't think I wouldn't just because I like you. I've killed more people in the last twenty-four hours than you'll kill in this and in your next half-dozen incarnations on planet Earth."

"I believe you. You seem like a bastard," she said bravely.

"Aye, well, we'll all live through this and it'll be something you can tell your wean about."

"Don't think I'd tell her anything about the likes of you."

"You'd be surprised how I can grow on people. Seriously. Peruvians, Colombians, Russians, Americans, I make friends wherever I go."

We drove over the Boyne Bridge.

The river seemed clean and Drogheda looked better than I'd ever seen it. Prosperity suited the Republic of Ireland. There were new signs up all over the town pointing to Tara, Newgrange, the Battle of the Boyne, and other wonders of County Meath.

"Ever been to Newgrange?" I asked.

"No."

"Should go. Fascinating."

She said nothing. We drove on for a while. The silence was irritating.

"What you studying at Trinity?" I asked.

"French," she said, reluctant to give me any information.

"French. Old mate of mine studied French at NYU. Sunshine. He was quite the character. He was always quoting the *Flowers of Evil* guy."

"Baudelaire, and it's *Fleurs du Mal*," she said with condescension.

"Yeah, well, had a bit of a sticky end, did Sunshine, although it wasn't totally unjustified," I said to myself.

The girl stole a look in my direction.

"Is that what you do? Terrorize women and hurt people?" she asked.

I shook my head.

"I try not to hurt anybody. But sometimes, when needs arise, you have to step on a few toes," I explained.

"Aren't you worried about the consequences?" she said.

"What consequences?" I replied, genuinely puzzled.

"Hell," she said.

I laughed.

"Of course. We're in Ireland. Hell. No. I don't think about hell. There is no hell. Hell is a place in Norway, halfway between Bergen and the Arctic Circle," I said and popped a digestive biscuit in my mouth.

"Don't you believe the Bible?"

"Fairy stories. I suppose they don't teach you Darwin in the Republic of Ireland."

"Of course they do, it's not Iran."

"But you don't believe him?"

"I don't see how believing in Darwin and the Bible is mutually exclusive."

"It is. I mean, do the bacteria in your stomach go to heaven when they die? Eight hundred million years ago, we were those bacteria. It's just silly."

She slunk into silence, nodded to herself in the rearview mirror. Whatever else happened today, at least she and me were going to go to different places, even if she was an unwed mother-to-be. Still, all this talk hadn't been good for me. Morbid thoughts of eternal punishment weren't the things I needed to have floating through my mind when every mile was bringing me closer to Belfast.

"Is Baudelaire your favorite?" I asked.

She pursed her lips, shook her head.

"Montaigne," she said.

"Go on, give us a burst."

"No."

"Go on, humor the guy who has a pistol pointed at your kidneys."

She thought for a moment and turned to face me.

"I'll make you a deal," she said.

"Ok, I'm listening."

"I'll give you a Montaigne quote if you do something for me."

"Ok."

"That thing is really making me frightened. Really frightened. If you put the gun away, I promise I won't try anything. I'll drop you off in Belfast without any fuss or problems at all."

I put the revolver in my pocket. No one could refuse such a reasonable request.

"Now the other part of the deal. Let's hear what that Montaigne fella has to say," I said.

"Je veux que la mort me trouve plantant mes choux."

"Very apt, I'm sure," I said, although the only word I understood was *death*.

We got through Drogheda and a bypass skirted us around Dundalk. The border to Northern Ireland, which had once been a big deal with army, police, helicopters, road blocks, razor wire, mines was now only apparent in the roadside markings which changed from yellow to white. We were in Northern Ireland a good couple of miles before I even noticed that.

"We're in the north," I said, surprised.

"Yes," she said.

"I thought we'd have to bluff our way through a checkpoint, or at least customs," I muttered.

"They got rid of all that years ago," she said with quiet contempt.

We drove through the Mourne Mountains: bleak stony slopes, bereft of trees, people, and even sheep. Next Newry and Portadown—two nasty wee shiteholes unloved by God, the residents, and everyone else. Shit-colored housing estates where men went to the pub, women raised the kids, the TV was always on, and if it wasn't chips for dinner there would be hell to pay.

Marsh on our left and right.

A few planes landing at the airport. An army helicopter. Ugly cottages and redbrick homes and I knew we were closing inexorably on the city.

"I've never been to Belfast," the girl said. Her first words in fifty miles.

"You haven't missed out on much."

"Maybe you should let me out. I'll only get us lost."

"I'll tell you where to go when we're close enough."

And as we came up the motorway, I began to smell the city. Rain, sea, bog, that burnt aroma of peat, tobacco, and car exhaust.

The sky was gray. It got colder.

Then the landmarks.

A place where I'd had a car accident.

A Protestant mural for the Ulster Volunteer Force. A Catholic mural for the Hunger Strikers.

Milltown Cemetery, where a madman had run amok at an IRA funeral, throwing hand grenades. The city hospital, so ugly Prince Charles had been flown in especially to denounce it.

She turned off for the city center. Close enough.

"You can stop the car, just go in anywhere along here."

She slowed the car and pulled in off the hard shoulder. Got a little bit of a panic attack, started hyperventilating. No doubt the possibility flitted through her mind that I was going to kill her now.

She was looking for an escape route, for witnesses. But the traffic was fast moving and the shoulder was deserted.

I reassured her anyway.

"Take it easy. We're parting company. I'm not going to touch you," I said.

She nodded nervously.

"You really pregnant or were you lying to save your skin?" I asked.

"I'm pregnant. Three months," she said with a blush.

"The dad know?"

"He knows, but he doesn't want to know."

"Your parents?"

"Of course not."

"Keeping it?"

"Think so."

"Either way you'll need some dough. Take this," I said, giving her almost all the money I had in my wallet. Easily ten or eleven grand.

"You can't give me this," she said, aghast.

"Oh, I can, it's not stolen or anything, but don't tell anyone."

"But you can't give me all this money," she protested.

"Yes, I can. I'm an eccentric millionaire. That's just the sort of thing I do."

She hesitated still, but I forced it on her. I gave her a look that communicated how impolitic it would be to refuse. She took it word-lessly.

"You see that roundabout up ahead?"

She nodded.

"I said, do you see the roundabout?"

"I do."

"Ok. These are the rules. You turn round right now and you head to Dublin and you don't stop once until you're there. You park your car in your space and you go about your life as if nothing had happened. You tell no one what transpired here today."

"I understand."

"Good. Now go back to your existence. You had to cross the line into my life for a while. But it's over now. Good luck with the kid. If your folks don't dig it, I'd say fuck 'em all, go to London and present yourself at social services. They'll give you a flat and that dough will tide you over."

She nodded silently.

She opened her mouth to say something, changed her mind, and then finally asked it: "What's your name?" she managed in a whisper.

"Michael," I said.

"Wasn't there a Michel in the Bible, a woman?"

"I don't know," I admitted.

"It would be a pretty name for a girl," she mused.

"Aye."

I got out of the car and walked away.

She sat there frozen for a second.

"Drive," I said.

She nodded, put the car in first, stalled it, restarted it, got it going, and headed for the rotary. She exited the roundabout and sped down the other side of the dual carriageway. And I stood there and almost wistfully watched the car take her back into the land of civilized people.

❊   ❊   ❊

Sunshine in Dublin. Rain in Belfast. How could it be otherwise? Each place within the city colonized by the greasy empire of Belfast rain. Every timber, stone, neck, collar, bare head and arm. The dull East Ulster rain that was born conjoined with oil and diesel fumes and tinged with salt and soot. Arriving in broad horizontal sheets, as part of the fabric as the city hall or the lough or the furnaces in Harland and Wolff.

I breathed deep. That air redolent with violence and blood. And everywhere the reminders of six years of sectarian cold war, thirty years of low-level civil war, eight hundred years of unceasing, boiling trouble and strife.

They say the air over Jerusalem is thick with prayers, and Dublin might have its fair share of storytellers, but this is where the real bullshit artists live. The air over this town is thick with lies. Thousands of prisoners have been released under the cease-fire agreements—thousands of gunmen walking these streets, making up a past, a false narrative of peace and tranquility.

Until the seventeenth century it didn't even exist on the maps. It was drained from the mudflats and named in Irish for a river, the Farset, which has since been culverted over and is now part of the sewage system.

Ahh, Belfast.

You gotta love it.

I walked down Great Victoria Street to the Europa Hotel. The last time I'd seen this place, all the windows within half a mile had been blown out by a thousand-pound bomb. The Crown Bar was destroyed, Robinsons Bar was still smoldering, and the Unionist Party headquarters was a hole in the sidewalk.

Bill Clinton had been to Belfast three times since then. George W. Bush had come during the mopping-up phase of the Iraq war. With American help, Tony Blair and Irish Prime Minister Bertie Ahern had brought a peace deal between the Protestants and Catholics. A shaky peace deal with many ups and downs, but a peace deal nonetheless. Cease-fires had been declared and all the paramilitary prisoners had been released, and although the two sides hadn't come to a final agreement, at least they were still talking. There were dissidents on both wings, but there hadn't been a serious terrorist bombing in Belfast in six years. Enough time for McDonald's and Burger King to destroy the local food franchises and for real estate developers to go nuts in virgin territory.

The gleaming new Europa, though, was taking no chances. They had a security guard in a booth at the car park and metal detectors installed just inside the double doors.

Metal detectors.

I considered my options for a moment.

I didn't want to give up my weapon. Gunless in Belfast was like being gunless in Dodge. Next to the Europa there was a Boots chemist.

I entered, hunted around for things that might be useful, and finally purchased a pack of Ziploc bags. I went across the street to the rebuilt Crown Bar. I avoided the temptation to buy a pint and hustled back to the toilets, found a cubicle. I took out the gun and placed it in one of the Ziploc bags. I squeezed all the air out and sealed the bag. I put this bag upside down in another Ziploc bag and sealed it and then put the two bags inside a third bag and sealed it as well. The shells were already in a bag but I didn't like the look of it. I sealed them up in Ziplocs. I took the top off the toilet tank and placed the gun inside. It floated for a second and then sank to the bottom of the cistern. Well, maybe it would be ok. I remembered reading that in Vietnam the soldiers had protected their M16s with condoms, so perhaps this would work. I chucked in the .38 rounds and they floated.

I closed the tank, exited the pub, waited for a break in the traffic, recrossed Great Victoria Street. Went through the double doors and the metal detector.

The Europa was like any other soulless, dreary corporate hotel, except they were playing up the Irish touches: green trimmings, fresh shamrock plants on the coffee tables, a couple of framed Jack B. Yeats paintings, and spotty, unhealthy-looking people behind reception.

The piped music was the slow movement from Beethoven's Seventh, which, although not Irish, certainly was depressing enough to create a Belfast ambience.

"Hi," I said.

"Good morning, sir, welcome to the Europa Hotel, Belfast's premier city-center hotel, featuring a full range of services and a new Atkins-friendly cuisine," the receptionist said. A very young brown-haired kid with a gold earring and a slight West Belfast lisp.

"I have an appointment to see Bridget Callaghan," I said.

"The presidential suite. I'll announce you," he said.

"Don't announce me."

"I have to."

"No, no, I'm an old friend, I'll just head on up there."

"Mr. Moran doesn't allow anyone up to the presidential suite without being announced first."

I didn't want to press the point, so I gave him my name and stood there while he made his call.

"Hello, this is reception, I'd like to speak to Mr. Moran. . . . Yes, Mr. Moran, this is Sebastian at reception, there's a, uh, gentleman to see Ms. Callaghan, a Michael Forsythe, shall I send him up? . . . Yes, he's alone. . . . Certainly."

He hung up the phone and nodded at me.

"You can go up. It's the top floor."

"Thanks."

I went to the bank of elevators, pressed the up button, and while I waited I admired the plate-glass windows I had helped put in twelve years ago.

The doors dinged.

Two long-haired goons in tailored suits were standing inside the lift. Definitely Yanks, since both looked like rejects from Arena Football or the World Wrestling Federation. One was an ugly-looking white guy, the other an angry thick-necked black man.

"Moran?" I asked the white guy.

"Forsythe?" he asked me.

"Aye," I said, wondering yet again if there would ever be an occasion when I'd be happy to answer that question.

"Dave wants to see you. You better get in the elevator," he said.

"I'm here to see Bridget."

"Everyone who wants to see Ms. Callaghan sees Dave first."

"Ok."

"Can we pat you down?" he asked.

They did a fast, efficient search, found nothing. We all got inside the lift. The white guy pressed the button for the top floor. The black dude gave me the skunk eye.

"Are you eyeballing me?" he said in a completely aggressive manner. It took me aback. Jesus, who did Bridget have working for her these days? Hotheads? Eejits? Not wonder they couldn't do something as simple as killing a traitor like me.

"Yeah, I am eyeballing you. You look like Barry Bonds on anger-management day. Have you ever noticed that your neck is actually bigger than your head?"

The black guy made a move, but the lift opened on the top floor. With the men on either side of me, I walked to a door just off the presidential suite. They knocked and waited.

"Enter," another American voice said.

We went in. The blinds were pulled down in a huge room that

stank of cigarette smoke. A fat little character wearing a wrinkled red shirt, sitting in a leather chair, poring over documents. He stood. He was about forty, looked about fifty, balding, a leathery expression, evil slits for eyes. I had the feeling that I had seen him before.

"We meet at last, Forsythe. Finally. You fucker," he said in a Nassau County honk that was so contaminated with fury he was barely able to get the words out.

"You have the better of me, who are you?" I replied.

"You know how many times I've dreamed of this moment," he said more to himself than me.

"Who the fuck are you?" I asked again.

"You bastard, Forsythe. A nod to these two guys and they'll take you to the roof and throw you the fuck off," he said, grinding his fist into his hand. An unconscious gesture, but it reminded me so much of other little nut jobs—Napoleon, Caesar, Hitler—I couldn't help but suppress a laugh. I sat down in the leather chair opposite him. It was an empty threat. If he was going to top me he would have done it instead of blabbing about it. I smiled.

"You're wasting my valuable time," I said. "I'm here to see Bridget Callaghan."

The man stared at me and gestured to the two goons.

"You can go," he told them. I turned and waved.

"See ya. Have fun bench pressing each other," I said. They left without responding.

I looked at the man.

"Ok, so who are you?" I asked.

"We've met before," he said.

"Have we? I don't remember. Just tell me your goddamn name."

"David Moran. Bob Moran was my brother," he said with grim satisfaction.

I nodded. Yeah. We had met before. And now I understood. I'd killed Big Bob Moran at his house in Oyster Bay, Long Island. Big Bob had been the henchman for Darkey White. He had set me up in Mexico, implicated me in a drugs buy, and gotten me thrown in a Mexican prison, where three of my crew had died. If any fucker on this Earth deserved to die it was Big Bob Moran. I had killed him and in twelve years I had shed not a tear or had one moment of remorse for what I'd done. If Bob's brother worked for Bridget, so be it. I understood his point of view. You had to pay for blood, no matter if that blood was as vile a concoction as the one that you'd find in the late Big Bob.

"Bob had it coming," I told Moran.

"We all have it coming," Moran said.

"I don't want to start anything with you, I'm here to help Bridget, what's done is done as far as I'm concerned. It's past. Over. Dead."

"Somebody famous once said, 'The past is never dead, it's not even past,'" he added.

"Christ, you're quite the little book of aphorisms, aren't you," I said, and gave him my best irritating cheeky grin.

His knuckles went white with fury. His eyes closed. I could see his skin turning the color of his tracksuit. Then after a quarter of a minute, his breathing mellowed and he calmed himself.

"Not only did you kill Bob, but you ratted out the whole operation. A murderer and a fucking rat."

"Well, you seem to have done ok for yourself," I said, looking around the room.

"You have no idea how hard it was. You left her with nothing. Just contacts and brains. We had to struggle every day for the first few years."

"Cry me a river. Where is she?"

"What you did, Forsythe. You should be ten times dead by now," he said.

"But as you can see, I'm as large as life. And, I'll tell you, if it's a choice between death or listening to you slabbering away all afternoon, I'll take the former."

He shook his head, rubbed his hands over his chin.

"You're alive because of Siobhan. You're alive because of her, although I for one will never forget that you robbed that girl of her father. Darkey White."

"Darkey had it coming most of all," I said deadpan.

"In the olden times they would cut out traitors' hearts and burn them in front of them while they were still alive," Moran said coldly.

"History expert, are you, too? As well as the Oxford book of quotations."

"You listen to me, Forsythe. If I had my way, I guarantee you, you wouldn't leave this room in one piece," Moran said.

"You're boring me and you're wasting my time. I don't quite know what you do for Bridget but I'm here to help find her daughter. If you killed me Bridget would fucking top you; you're doing me no favors, so don't threaten me again, pal, or I'm outta here and you can explain that to your boss," I told the fat fuck.

He was going to say something else, but he bit his tongue. It gave me a chance to get in a question or two of my own.

"And I suppose it's you then, in your ham-fisted way, that's been trying to kill me since I got into Dublin," I said coolly.

A flicker of surprise flitted across his features. He didn't need to say anything. He'd told me.

"What are you talking about?"

"Two hit men, two separate hits, one of them a taxi driver, one got me in a brothel. The second hit was more interesting because the madam informed on me, so the word must have gone out somehow."

"We haven't been trying to kill you. Bridget, for whatever reason, thinks you can help find Siobhan."

"And you haven't taken an independent initiative?"

His teeth glinted, he shook his head.

"We've been ordered not to lay a finger on you."

"Well, that's good," I said.

"I want you dead. There's a lot of us who work for Bridget that want you dead. But not yet."

"Ok."

"But let me give you a heads-up, Forsythe. More of a heads-up than you ever gave Bob. Things have changed radically just in the last hour."

"What do you mean?"

"A note was delivered to the hotel from the scumbags who're holding Siobhan. They went ten million dollars by midnight tonight. A third cash, two-thirds international bearer bonds. If they don't get it, they say they're going to kill her."

"Was the note genuine? How do you know it's not just bullshit?"

"There was a lock of hair in the envelope, the cops have taken the note, hair, and envelope for DNA testing. Bridget thinks it's Siobhan's hair, but she can't be sure."

"What does the DNA say?"

"That won't be ready until tomorrow afternoon."

"So you've no choice, you've got to raise the ten million."

Moran nodded grimly.

"The note said that they would call with details sometime between nine and midnight. We're supposed to wait at the Arthur Street police station because they're going to want specific street closures from the police."

"Jesus, how long was this note? Have you got a copy?"

"The police have it. That was it. No details. Just the hair, raise the money, await further instructions," Moran said, sounding tired.

"Can you raise the money?"

He nodded.

"The guy who delivered it?"

"Left it at reception, wearing motorcycle leathers and a helmet. Only said 'Message for Bridget Callaghan.'"

"Belfast accent?"

"Apparently so. . . . But that's neither here nor there, Forsythe. You see that now, right? This changes things."

I shook my head.

"I don't see how this changes anything for me," I said.

"Before the girl was missing, maybe she'd run away, now we know she's been kidnapped."

"That doesn't affect my job, what I'm here to do," I said.

"Yeah, it does. The deadline. Midnight tonight. Either way, if we get Siobhan back at midnight or they kill her, fair warning, pal, I'm coming after you whether Bridget gives me the ok or not."

He rubbed his hand into his fist again, barely able to contain his hatred for me. I had killed his useless brother and he was going to get me. Bob, who never even fucking mentioned David, or, if he had, he certainly wasn't a big part of his life. Over the years David had probably blown Bob up into a heroic and sentimental figure. It was pathetic, really. But I had to reassure him that his little fucking revenge-murder scheme would come to naught.

"Don't worry, mate, if those fuckers kill Siobhan, Bridget'll get me long before you do."

He nodded, got to his feet.

"We understand each other then," he said.

"We do."

I stood too.

"I'll take you to her. Please, go gentle, she's at her wits' end," he said.

He led me out of the room and along the corridor to a big set of double doors. He knocked and we entered the presidential suite at last. Belfast spread out before me through the rainy windows. Black Mountain, Divis Mountain, new hotels, new offices, and the River Lagan slaking its way through the mudflats. From up here, you could see down the gray lough to Kilroot and maybe all the way to Scotland.

It was more like a command center than a hotel room. There were several burly-looking guys, a police officer in uniform, a detective, a girl carrying a water bottle, a man with a—

And there she was.

After all this time.

The most attractive woman I had seen in a decade. The most attractive woman I had ever seen.

Devastating still.

Bridget. Beyond rhetoric. Beyond words. Describing the shades of green and blue that her eyes took on in different moods could fill the book.

And, yes, she was a woman now, not a girl.

Her hair, the subtlest of copper tints. Her skin like pages from the New Testament. Her body placed on Earth by Lucifer's minions to ruin marriages, to start fights, to cause accidents, to send four young men to their deaths in Mexico.

Think Deneuve around the time of *Belle de Jour*. Kelly in *High Noon*. Ekberg in *La Dolce Vita*. Beautiful, almost a little too beautiful. Blondes, but the redheads I could mention wouldn't come close. Bette Davis, maybe, but Kidman, give me a break.

Bridget was thirty now. At the height of her powers. Every man in the room looking at her. It was impossible not to.

The eyes of a martyr, the lips of a killer, dangerous curves.

You'd run traffic lights on Fifth Avenue to get a glimpse of her. You'd propose to her on the subway.

Her black skirt was quiet elegance. Her low-heeled shoes simplicity itself. The sort of simpleness that cost fifty thousand dollars. The sort of elegance that kept Vera Wang up all night, sewing the thing by hand.

Bridget.

Where have you been all these years?

I never knew how empty I felt until this moment.

The sum multiplied by zero, the shaken Etch A Sketch, the black hole radiating itself to nothingness.

A void, a nonplace.

Oh, Bridget.

She saw me. She turned. She'd been crying.

She came across the room in slow motion.

The sun went behind a cloud.

She opened her mouth.

"Michael," she said.

❃   ❃   ❃

The room had been cleared. Bridget was sitting at one end of the sofa. I was sitting at the other.

Her hands folded on her lap. Her face drained of color. Her eyes ashen and restrained. She looked knackered. I could tell she hadn't slept in four nights. She had refused the pills they had no doubt offered her.

She was sitting forward on the sofa, her bum barely on the leather cushion.

A maid brought a pot of green tea with one cup.

She closed her tired eyes, wiped the tear-clotted lashes, mouthed "thank you" to the maid, who couldn't leave fast enough.

There'd been no hello, no apologies. Just a hand gesture and everyone had fled. She sat, I sat.

She sipped the tea.

We both waited for the other to begin.

Bridget broke first.

"Michael, I know there's a lot of history between us . . ." she began, her voice trailing off into the silence.

"You don't even need to say it," I said.

"I do. It's not that I don't want to talk about it. I have a lot of things I want to tell you, there's a lot of things I want to ask you. But not now. I don't want to hear your reasons for what you did. I know you have reasons and I know you believe in them. But I don't want this to be about you and me. I called you in because of Siobhan. I only want to talk about her."

Her breasts heaved under her silk sweater.

So this was how it was going to be.

What was it Dan had told me? This woman is a killer, a general, an archmanipulator.

I looked at those big hooded eyelids. I don't recall what color they used to be but now they were as dark as soot. They didn't tell me anything.

I'd go careful.

"Bridget, I completely agree. I don't want to talk about the past. I'm sure you did what you thought was right and I did what I thought was right. Let's leave it there," I said, not believing a bloody word of it. There were no two sides to this case. Darkey had brought his death upon himself.

Bridget nodded, breathed out. This was the first difficult hurdle dealt with. There was an awkward silence. She seemed almost too exhausted to continue now. How much was act and how much was real?

"You've come a long way," I said, thinking of Dan's list of corpses; of those frozen faces I'd seen in the newspaper. Any one of them could have been me. And what had Moran said? "We had to struggle in the early years." I'll bet you did. You got your hands dirty. You personally.

I waited for her reply, but instead she looked at me briefly, turned away, and chose not to answer.

A different approach.

"I didn't even know you had a baby," I said.

"The FBI didn't tell you?"

"No."

Bridget was shocked.

"Well, they knew. It wasn't a secret. The DA knew. The feds knew."

"No one told me. I didn't notice it in the press, although I avoided reading the press as much as possible."

"Well, that was me. I insisted that we didn't mention her. I wanted to keep her name out of the news. My lawyers wanted to use my baby to hurt your credibility. You know, 'We're supposed to believe this man who robbed a girl of her father,' that kind of argument. But I didn't want Siobhan's name mentioned at all."

Bridget wasn't aware that she was making me angry. I'd thought we weren't going to talk about the past. I thought we weren't going to go down that road because, hell, honey, I could give as good as I got in that department.

"Why?" I asked.

"I want Siobhan to have as normal an existence as possible, Michael. I don't want her name connected to a murder trial. I don't want her photo in the papers, ever, unless she's winning the Nobel Prize."

Bridget paused here. It was a laugh break, and although it didn't make me laugh, it touched me a little that she was at least trying to be civil. I smiled.

"No, Michael, I didn't want her connected with that mess. Especially when she was just a little baby. She's my girl, Michael, and I love her. No one has a right to publish her picture or use her in a court case."

"I understand that."

"So you really didn't know?" she asked with a look of skepticism.

"No. No one told me. I suppose they didn't want me to feel guilty and retract my testimony," I said.

"You must have seen that I'd put on some weight after the birth when I came to the trial," she said, still with a touch of doubt.

"I didn't notice. You were sitting at the back most days."

She nodded.

"Maybe not that much weight. I wasn't nursing anyway. My sister, Anne, in Seattle looked after Siobhan for the first couple of years, while all the unpleasantness was going on. While everything settled down. Perhaps that's why . . . Perhaps I missed something there, some bond, maybe that's the reason we fight so much. . . ." Bridget said, her voice guttering into a guilty silence.

"And I'm not sure I would have done what I did that December night if I'd known you were pregnant," I just about stopped myself from saying.

"Well, all I can say, Michael, is that she's a blessing. She's my whole life. There is nothing I wouldn't do to get her back," Bridget said.

"And that's why I'm here and still alive," I said.

"That's why you're here," she agreed, her tone of voice eager, anxious.

I could tell that she was itching to be done with the formalities, to talk about her missing daughter. She was already a little impatient with me. That's what happened when you were surrounded by yesmen. When you could click your fingers to get what you wanted. And that's also what happened when you were the general, up above the action, away from the kill box, away from the rifle sight. You got impatient, you got sloppy, you let your guard down.

And she'd been bloodied now and that not only was bad but it looked bad too.

You should be careful about showing your vulnerable side.

Do you ever cry in front of Moran back there? I wouldn't. Weakness kills you, Bridget. Word gets around. It's a vicious circle. And the more you're fucked, the more you look fucked and the more you are fucked. Moran won't tell you that. Sure, he seems to care and he probably does care about you and Siobhan, but everyone has another persona and he can't forget that if you fall, he rises. And then there's me. What I want. This isn't just about you. I need my goddamn guarantee.

"Look me in the eye and tell me that if I find Siobhan you'll never go after me again. I need you to say it and I need you to look at me," I said.

She put down her cup. Pushed the hair from her face.

"I gave you my word that if you find Siobhan, I will wipe the slate and make sure everyone knows it's wiped."

She offered me her hand and I shook. There was no spark between us and her hand withdrew.

I believed her. At least that was the thought in her mind at the present moment. It would be the best I could ever get.

"I'm . . ." but I couldn't finish the thought. She had unsettled me with that touch.

Bridget sipped her tea. I had nothing to do with my hands. They were fidgeting nervously. I sat on them. She remembered her manners.

"Thank you for coming, Michael. It must have taken some courage," she said.

"You're welcome, Bridget."

"Moran didn't want me to ask you, but his men have turned up nothing. And the police have drawn a blank too. You were the only one I could think of. You lived here. You were born here and you know the city. You know the rackets."

"I do, Bridget, you did right calling me. It was the right thing to do."

She bit her lip, wiped tears from her eyes.

"Do you really think you can find her? Do you think you can help?"

"Do you still want me to look into it?"

"What do you mean?"

"In light of the current developments?"

"Oh God, yeah, that could be a crank, it could be anything. We won't know a thing until we get that phone call. There was the hair, Michael, but I'll tell you the truth, I can't be a hundred percent sure it was hers. . . . Everyone probably thinks I'm a terrible parent," she said, angry at herself for being unable to tell what no mother could tell.

"No, no," I said. "You're not."

She shook her head, sobbed, internally beating herself up over that and a million other things that proved she was the worst ma in the world.

"Anyway, yes, I want you to do what you can, despite this new stuff," she said.

"Well, Bridget, in that case I can tell you this. If Siobhan is in Belfast, I'll find her. I promise, I'll find her. I know this city like the back of my hand. I have contacts in the police, in the Protestant paramilitaries, in the Catholic paramilitaries. I even have an old pal who's a rising politician. If anyone can find her, it's me."

She seemed reassured a little. She wiped her cheeks.

"Why don't you tell me what happened? Why were you in Belfast in the first place?" I asked.

"We come here every year. My grandparents were from Ulster. We usually spend a day in Belfast and then we go to Donegal; I bought a house out there. It's nice. It's on the beach, Siobhan loves it. It's not like the Hamptons. It's totally isolated. We have horses."

"So you were in Belfast just for the day?"

"No, this year was a little different. This year I had some business to take care of. We were going to be here for a week and then we were supposed to go to Donegal for another week."

"What was the business?"

"I don't think that's relevant," Bridget said curtly. Her tone of voice changing, her eyes narrowing, her persona falling back into business mode. Wary, hostile, sure of herself.

"I'll decide what's relevant," I said. I had to remind her that this was my conversation, not hers. I was not one of her employees.

She took another sip from her cup.

"Would you like some tea?" she asked to defuse the tension.

"No, thanks."

She crossed her legs, rested her hands in her lap.

"Bridget, you're going to have to trust me. What was the business you were doing here?"

She sighed, looked at me for a half minute.

"It's really not important."

"Tell me anyway."

"Well, um, ok. This was a bit of a one-off thing. Not drugs, not guns, not passports. Believe me, I've looked into it."

"Just tell me anyway, Bridget."

"Ok. Fine. Have you heard of a thing called outsourcing?"

"No."

"It's where they take American jobs and send them to countries where it's cheaper to do business. A lot of services are moving abroad. You know, dial-up help for computers and things like that. India is a very popular place, but so's Ireland. It's got a young, well-educated workforce who'll take half the pay of kids in America. On this particular trip, I came with the president of our technical services union. I was in town to sign some contracts, making sure all those Irish jobs from American companies were properly unionized."

"And that those unions were your unions. Right?" I said.

She nodded.

"That was the main thing, few other items, some other minor business. It all went very smoothly, I assure you."

I shook my head.

"You're bound to have made enemies. Could one of your, um, business associates have arranged to have Siobhan kidnapped?"

Bridget laughed. And for a moment the weeping mother left and the general came back.

"No chance. No chance at all. No one would fuck with me. No one who knew anything about me would touch my daughter. I'd burn their eyes out with a blowtorch. That's why I thought she was safe, Michael; I'm well known in this town. I checked that angle out, anyway. Moran looked into it, as did the cops. There's been zero paramilitary involvement. I talked to all my business partners. The heads of all the factions. I brought them up here. No one knows anything."

"Are you sure about that?"

"I'm sure."

"Ten million is a big incentive."

"Ten million is nothing, Michael. We're talking about trade between Ireland and America that's worth billions."

"I know, but remember this is Belfast."

"Moran's boys have been on it round the clock. The police, too."

"Ok, so just to be clear, you guys don't think there's a paramilitary involvement in any of this?"

"No. I really don't think so. The head of the IRA and the head of the UDA assured me that they knew nothing about her disappearance; and until we got this note, we all thought she had just run away."

"Ok. I'll check it out, regardless," I said almost to myself.

"I'd expect you to."

"How long have you actually been in Belfast?" I asked.

"We got here last Thursday, Thursday the tenth. We were supposed to be here six days. We were supposed to be going to Donegal today. I had a lot arranged. A lot to take care of and then we were going to spend a nice week doing nothing. I wanted to celebrate and chill out after taking care of business here and getting good news from Peru about y—"

"Me," I said, finishing her thought.

She nodded, this time without embarrassment.

"Ok, so when did Siobhan disappear?"

"Saturday. We'd been fighting all morning and—"

"Fighting?" I interrupted.

"Yes, fighting. She wanted to go to Donegal. She didn't want to be here. She was bored. But there was no way I was going to let her have the run of that house on her own. She was screaming at me. She said that I treated her like a baby. That I didn't love her."

I nodded sympathetically.

"She said she felt like a prisoner here in the hotel," Bridget said.

"What happened then?"

"She stormed out of the room."

"And then?"

"I caught her at the elevator. I asked her where she thought she was going."

"What did she say?"

"She said she was going to the Malt Shop to get a drink, a milk shake."

"You let her go?" I asked.

"It's just a few blocks from here. She'd gone a couple of times before. I thought it would let her cool off. It's been so tedious for her here. And besides, I think there was a boy she'd seen or something."

"What boy?"

"One time we went for breakfast there was a boy there, she told me she thought he was cute."

"You get a good look at him?" I asked.

Bridget shook her head.

"Excuse me for a moment, Michael, my head is killing me," she said. She picked up the phone and said, "I need some aspirin, please."

In a few seconds the white guy from the elevator came in with aspirin. She took two, gave him the bottle back, and he left. She swallowed the pills, looked at me.

"Where were we?" she asked.

"She went to the Malt Shop. Maybe she was meeting that boy?"

"I don't know about that. It's just one of those places where kids hang out."

"Did you tell the police about the boy?"

"Of course."

"Ok, so she went to this Malt Shop, what time at?"

"I don't know, it was the morning, maybe around eleven."

"What happened next?"

"She didn't come back," Bridget said, fighting back tears.

"What did you do?"

"Michael, she begged me not to have Ryan follow her, she said it made her feel like she was being watched all the time. She made me promise, and I told Moran to call him off. If he'd been watching her, maybe . . ."

"It might have made no difference," I said trying to be reassuring.

She sighed. It was interesting watching her move between these aspects of herself. Between the mother, the businesswoman, the mob boss. Was she aware that her voice changed pitch, that her head lowered when she was talking about Siobhan?

I gave her a moment to embrace all those feelings of guilt and loss, and then I continued.

"Back to Saturday, what happened next?" I asked.

"I waited a few hours, and I sent a couple of my boys down to fetch her, but she wasn't there and no one had seen her."

"And then what?"

"I called the cops. They came immediately. They said that she had probably just run away and she'd be back before dark. But she didn't come back, so they sent a team of detectives out looking for her. She didn't come back all night."

"Has she ever run away before?"

Bridget closed her eyes.

"One time in the city, she skipped school and didn't come back until ten o'clock."

"Why did she run away that time?"

"Oh, it was the stupidest thing, the school was having a trip to the Galápagos."

"The Galápagos?" I said surprised.

"It's a fancy school."

"Sorry, please continue."

"Well, we made a deal and I said she could go if she maintained a B average, and she hates math and she got a D in math, and I said she couldn't go."

"You're pretty hard-core," I said, but with a smile to show that I approved of her setting limits, since both of us could have done with some when we were that age.

"No," she said to herself. "You can never win."

"What exactly happened on that occasion in New York?"

"She called me from school on her cell and she said that this was the last day to sign up for the trip and what was I going to do about it. I told her that we had discussed this and she wasn't going. So she said 'I hate you,' and she hung up the phone and she didn't come back from school. She left a message on the machine that she was running away, she was taking a bus from Penn Station. I went crazy. I got everyone who worked for me down to Penn Station, dozens of guys, I called the police, I called Greyhound, but she'd never even gone there. She'd spent the whole day in Washington Square Park playing chess with all those crazy people down there. And then she'd gone to some café and called her friend Sue, and told her she was running away, and Sue told her that I was frantic and she should go home."

"She came home after that?"

"Yeah, she came home at about ten o'clock."

"Did she call Sue this time? Did she call anybody?"

"No. She didn't make any calls on her cell that day. And the police told me that according to Verizon that was very unusual."

"How many calls did she make on a normal day?"

"About a dozen."

"And none on the day she disappeared?"

"No."

"Hmmm."

"What does it sound like to you?"

"I don't know," I said, although the lack of phone calls scared me. That made it sound a bit premeditated. That boy had told her not to call anyone in case she got cold feet. It seemed to make it more likely that the boy was the agent for the kidnappers. Either that or he'd planned to run off with her, or rape her, or whatever, and then he'd found out who she was and panicked. Perhaps killed her and faked that note to throw the police off the scent.

I took a pad from the writing desk, grabbed a hotel pen.

"You better tell me details."

"Like what?"

"For starters, everything you remember about the boy."

"You think the boy might be involved?"

"Describe him."

"I didn't even really look at him. A teenager, I thought, red hair, thin."

"Distinguishing marks, tattoos?"

"I didn't get a good look. He came behind our table to get a salt shaker. I couldn't see him, but Siobhan's eyes were all over him and, well . . ."

"Well what?"

"I thought maybe he smelled a bit," she said dismissively.

"What do you mean?"

"There was a smell off him, you know, a funky teenage smell."

"What kind of a smell?"

"I don't know, Michael, I'm not even sure it was him behind me."

"What kind of a smell?" I insisted.

"Jesus, I don't know, aftershave, pot, spot cream, I don't know."

"Pot?"

"I don't know, Michael."

"When was this? When did you see him?"

"On Friday morning, I took her to the Malt Shop for a pancake breakfast. She'd been there on her own the previous day to get a milk shake, and before she'd said something like 'There's a boy who's always there that I like, I think he's really cute.'"

"So she'd mentioned him several times before or just that once?"

"I've been so busy, Michael, she could have, but I don't really remember."

"That's ok. But you saw him on Friday?"

"Yes."

"Working there?"

"No."

"Just hanging out?"

"Having a milk shake."

"What was he wearing?"

"I honestly can't recall," she said.

"Bridget, think," I insisted.

"I don't remember, I didn't pay him any attention. I had a lot on my mind. She's too young to have crushes on boys, so I didn't take it seriously. Maybe a black sweatshirt."

"Anything on it? Logos? Letters?"

"I don't know, I'm not even sure about the color. There could be a bird or something."

"What type of bird?"

"I don't know. I really don't know."

"Ok. Did she speak to the boy on the Friday?"

"No."

"How did you know that that was the boy she'd been talking about?"

"She was looking at him and I asked her if that was the boy she thought was cute and she told me to mind my own business, but I could tell."

"So you don't actually know that the redheaded boy in the black sweatshirt was the one she'd been talking about."

"She didn't actually say it, but I think that was him."

"And you didn't get a good look at him?"

"Not really. I couldn't even do a sketch for the police."

"That's ok. And then you perhaps smelled pot on him?"

"Maybe."

"What is this Malt Shop?"

"It's a place a few blocks from here. It's one of those diners, one of those nostalgia places. It's full of kids. There were cars outside. Siobhan went there her first day here, I think she saw an ad for it on TV. She dragged me there on Friday and we had pancakes and a couple of malted milk shakes."

"Siobhan liked it there?"

"She really liked it, it was full of boys. She went there a few times, maybe to practice flirting or something, who knows."

"Flirting at her age?"

"Yeah, I know. Not even a teenager yet. I shouldn't have let her go. I've no excuses. I was trying to do too much in too short a time, Michael. She was bored here in the hotel and it was only a few blocks away."

"How often did she go there on her own?"

Bridget said nothing, started to cry a little. I passed her the box of Kleenex. She took a tissue, whispered a thank-you. And again I thought this is what happened to you when you thought yourself invulnerable. When you'd been at the top too long.

"How many times did she go there in total?"

"I don't know. The place wasn't here the last time we were in Belfast. We went there for breakfast on Friday. She had been there on Thursday. She went back Friday afternoon. And then she went there on Saturday. Or at least she said she was going there on Saturday. The police have been there and asked questions already. No one even remembers her. I sent my boys to ask around, and they can be pretty intimidating, but no one seems to recall her or that red-haired boy. It's a very busy place. It's a whole scene. I suppose he wasn't a regular either."

"But Siobhan said she'd seen the boy a couple of times. It sounds like he *was* a regular there," I suggested.

"Well, no one remembered him."

"The cops went down there?"

"Yeah, they brought a photo of Siobhan to show around, but no one had noticed her. Michael, I'm not sure that that's where she really went. I really have no idea."

"Do you have another photograph of her?"

Bridget nodded.

"Could I have it, please? I'm going to need it."

Bridget walked across the room, grabbed her handbag, took out a purse, removed a Polaroid, gave it to me. I examined the girl.

She was pretty with coppery blond hair and big green eyes. She had none of Darkey's coloring or his pug nose. All her looks came from Bridget. Rosy cheeks and a charming, happy smile which suggested that she got the joke. In the photo she was wearing a blue dress with flowers around the collar.

"That's from a few months ago," Bridget said.

I nodded, shaken from my reverie.

"Is this what she was wearing when she went missing?" I asked.

Bridget smiled.

"God, no, you can never get her into anything formal. On Christmas when she visits her grandma, that's about the only time she'll wear a dress."

"So what *was* she wearing?"

"Blue jeans and white Adidas sneakers and an Abercrombie sweat-shirt with a hood."

"What color was the sweatshirt?"

"Bright yellow."

"That's good, that's pretty distinctive," I said, trying to give her some crumb of comfort.

"That's what the cops said too, but they drew a blank."

"Well, we'll see. I'll ask around."

"Thank you," she said sweetly.

"Did she have any other friends or family here?"

"No."

Bridget lit herself a cigarette, brushed the hair back from her face. I couldn't think of any more questions. I had a lot to be going on with. I could get cracking right now. But I was reluctant to leave her. I didn't want to go so soon after being deprived of her presence all these years.

"Is that enough?" she asked.

I nodded.

Bridget stood.

"Wait a minute, Bridget, let me ask you something."

She turned, leaned unsteadily against a table.

"What?"

"Bridget, I'm going to do my very best to find Siobhan, but I need to know that I can trust you. I was attacked in Dublin by two men. I talked to Moran and he said it was nothing to do with him or you. Is that the truth?"

Bridget shook her head.

"Michael, I don't know anything about that. I sent those men to kill you in Lima but by the time the op was on, Siobhan had gone missing, my men had found nothing, and the police were clueless. I thought you might be able to help where they couldn't. I called the assassins off. I don't know who tried to hit you in Dublin, but it was nothing to do with me. I promise."

I didn't need to reflect on it for a while. I believed her.

"Ok," I said. "I'll do my best. I'll do more than my best. I'll bring your daughter back," I said.

Bridget wrote something on a piece of paper. She handed it to me.

She touched the side of my palm. Her fingertips were cold. I shuddered involuntarily. I smelled her hair and the sweat on her body. I felt her breath.

"Two phone numbers," she said.

I looked at the note.

"The top one is my cell, the bottom one is Moran's."

"Ok, I'll call in periodically," I said.

I put the note in my jacket pocket.

"What are you going to do now?" I asked.

"I'm going to raise ten million dollars and I'm going to go to the police station and wait for them to call."

"So you don't think that was a crank note?"

"I don't know, Michael, but what else can I do?"

"Aye."

"What are you going to do now?" she asked.

"I'm going to take this photograph and go down to the Malt Shop and ask some questions."

She leaned heavily on the table. She looked, for a moment, like she was going to fall forward into my arms.

"Thank you," she muttered softly.

"Thank you, Bridget," I said stupidly.

I stood and looked out the window.

"Ok, there's the bat signal, I have to go," I said.

She grinned weakly and turned to me. Our eyes locked longer than was strictly necessary.

"Good luck, Michael."

She didn't offer me her hand. I didn't offer mine. We continued to stare at each other. But then she nodded. The interview was done. I turned on my heel and walked out of the room.

Moran and a couple of heavies were waiting outside the door. Moran stopped me.

"Are you filled in?" he asked.

"I am."

"I hope you can help, Michael, I mean that sincerely. Siobhan's the priority."

I nodded.

"But remember what we talked about," he said quietly.

I didn't reply. I walked quickly through the length of the suite, turned into the corridor, and pressed the button for the ground floor. I was glad to be getting away from these people.

"Goodbye, Mr. Forsythe. Have a great day," Sebastian said.

"I have other plans," I said and walked out of the hotel.

6: THE RAT'S NEST
(BELFAST—JUNE 16, 2:15 P.M.)

I exited the Europa Hotel, ran across Great Victoria Street, and juked into the Crown Bar. It was packed full of civil servants finishing their lunchtime pints, desperately trying to think of a reason for not going back to work. In the 1980s they might have called in a bomb scare, but you couldn't have gotten away with that in Belfast nowadays.

I went to the bog, locked the cubicle door, retrieved my .38 and the bag of shells.

I checked the gun. Dry as bone. I'd have to write Ziploc a letter and let them know how useful their product was at keeping water away from firearms. I loaded the weapon and shoved it my pocket.

When I came out of the toilet, I saw one of Bridget's goons sitting casually at the bar, smoking a cigarette.

Moran had obviously put a tail on me so I would be easier to find and kill when the midnight deadline came and went.

He would be the first order of business. I pulled the fire alarm next to the toilet and in the ensuing chaos sat next to him at the bar.

"I want to talk to you. Come with me to the snug," I said.

He was a young guy, early twenties, easily intimidated.

"Listen, I don't want to cause any—"

"The snug, over here."

We walked over to one of the large enclosed booths while the barman assured everyone that the alarm had gone off by accident and told the customers to resume their seats. But still, it was pretty noisy and in a sec it wouldn't be, so as soon I closed the snug door, I grabbed an empty Guinness bottle from the table and smashed it over the tail's head. He slumped over and I laid him on the floor. With some care I removed the glass from his scalp and put him in the recovery position. He'd be right as rain in half an hour. I searched him for guns but all he had was a flick knife—what the hell was he going to do with that? I opened the snug door, walked quickly through the bar, slipped out the side entrance, turned right on Great Victoria, and headed south toward Bradbury Place and the Malt Shop.

The streets were packed. Shoppers, walkers, students, skateboarders, and a new phenomenon, Eastern Europeans begging with wooden bowls and makeshift signs that said "Please Help." I gave them a few quid and hurried on. The first edition of the *Belfast Telegraph* had just been printed and about every fifty feet a newsboy was standing on a bunch of papers yelling "Telleyo, telleyo."

The headline was "Hospital Cash Crisis." I scanned the paper, nothing about Bridget or Siobhan, and I wondered if the peelers had asked for a news blackout. By the time of the third edition, some of the havoc I had wrought would be the lead story and cover photograph. But that was in a couple of hours. Not quite yet.

I binned the paper and started looking for the Malt Shop.

I was pretty familiar with this district, but there were new buildings up, old buildings gone. Nice restaurants, fancy cars. And despite my predictions, a plague of Starbucks. The big change was how differently people dressed from when I'd last been here in 1992. Back then half the men would have been in jackets and ties, the rest would have worn button shirts, and all the old-timers wouldn't have been caught dead outside in anything less than a three-piece tweed suit and flat cap. Now everyone was dressed in casual wear: bright floppy T-shirts, shorts, sandals, cargo pants and the number of football shirts was staggering. Manchester United, Glasgow Rangers, and Glasgow Celtic being the most common. The women, too, were dressed down in baggy jeans and T-shirts and a lot of them were wearing Real Madrid football shirts, which at first I thought was some kind of solidarity thing with the bombing back in March but then I noticed that the shirts all had David Beckham's number.

The final status symbol worn by a good chunk of the under-thirty population was a New York Yankees baseball cap. Cheap airfares, weak dollar, any mug could go to New York these days.

Still, it wasn't all bad.

Two o'clock is quitting time for a lot of schools. And I'd like to find the man who isn't moved by hordes of beautiful seventeen- and eighteen-year-old sixth-formers striding toward the train station in short skirts, patent leather shoes, white shirts, and ties.

I couldn't go farther down the street because the cops had blocked off the road for a march and "historical pageant" by a small group of Independent Apprentice Boys who were reenacting a scene from the siege of Derry. The IAB were in full regalia, sweating in the humidity. Dark suits, black ties, black bowler hats, and orange-colored sashes. The scene was the famous one where the Protestant apprentice boys locked the gates of Derry to stop the Catholic armies from capturing the city—an actual historical event that had happened over three hundred years ago. I had never heard of the reenactment being performed in Belfast before. They'd probably gotten a cultural grant from the European Community. The "Boys" were actually forty- and fifty-year-old men with beer guts, bad mustaches, and hair so unkempt Vidal Sassoon would have broken down and wept. They were all obviously the worse for drink. The Catholic army this afternoon was an intoxicated man in a green sweater with a pikestaff.

"You're not getting in," one of the Boys was saying to him.

"Aye, no fucking way," said the other.

"We're shutting the gates," a third managed between belches.

The man in the green sweater did not seem that put out. Right in front of me, another of the Apprentice Boys climbed on top of a parked car and began stamping on the roof. It had an Irish Republic license plate and the Boy was obviously under the impression that it, too, was a representative of King James's Catholic army. A peeler went over and told him to get down. The peeler was old, fat, and bored. He tapped his service revolver once and the Boy, spooked, got off the roof.

"Right, that's it, I think you're all through," an inspector shouted and waved for the other coppers to reopen the streets. They began lifting the yellow tape.

"Black bastards," the other Boys yelled in protest. "Black bastard" not a comment on race but rather on the policemen's very dark green uniform, which appeared black. Indeed, in Northern Ireland the small number of foreign immigrants gave the wannabe racist scant opportunities. There was a sizable Chinese community, although racists tended to ignore them for fear that each one was a potential Bruce Lee who would kick their shit in.

The Boys refused to get off the street and the peels had to send in the riot police. While I waited to get going, I asked one of the schoolgirls if she knew where the Malt Shop was—a pretty brunette who looked as if she had never been exposed to sunshine in her life.

"Aye," she said, looking to make sure her friends weren't too far away. "You're going the right direction but it's on the other side of the street, just past the Ulster Bank."

"Thanks very much."

"No problem, although I tell ya, I wouldn't go in there if I were you," she said, her big brown eyes blinking slowly.

"Why's that?"

"You a tourist? Are you from America?"

"No, well, sort of, I am from out of town," I admitted.

"If you want a milk shake go to McDonald's, that place is a bit dodgy," the girl said.

"Is it now? Like what? Drugs?"

"I don't know. If you go looking for drugs you find them anywhere. 'Course they still do good milk shakes like."

"Well, thanks for the tip."

"I could do with a milk shake myself," she said with something close to a giggle.

"Love, if I was ten years younger, had slept, was untroubled by heavies, and not trying to solve a missing person's case before midnight, I would be honored to buy you a milk shake, but as it is . . ." I said, shrugged apologetically, saw the street was finally cleared, and hurried in the direction of the Ulster Bank.

I was down on the Golden Mile now.

Belfast was mostly a nineteenth-century phenomenon, a side effect of a booming linen industry, docks, and shipyard. Its population had increased tenfold in less than a hundred years. Catholics flooding

to certain sectors of the town, Protestants to others; and it has remained a segregated city. Prod and RC sections as clearly delineated
as the black and white neighborhoods of Boston or Detroit. East
Belfast: almost entirely Protestant. West Belfast, divided between a
Protestant ghetto along the Shankill Road and a Catholic ghetto
along the Falls Road. Impossible to wander into the wrong neighborhood by mistake. The Shankill Road bedecked with murals depicting
various Protestant heroes, usually in the primary colors of red, white,
and blue. The Falls Road had murals showing Catholic heroes, in
green, white, and gold. The exception, however, was South Belfast.
The area I was walking in right now. This part of the city was where
the university district met the commercial heart. This was middle-
and upper-class Belfast. Houses were more attractive, the streets
were wider, trees didn't get ripped to be turned into kindling around
bonfire time and there were a lot of students, couples, and young
people. Here there were no Protestant or Catholic bars. No murals,
no flags, and little sectarianism.

But even so, you'd be kidding yourself if you thought the paramilitaries let these businesses thrive without interference. The Malt Shop
would certainly be no exception.

"That must be it," I said to myself as I caught a glimpse, three
blocks ahead, of a miraculously unvandalized 1958 pink Cadillac that
had been turned into an outside eating booth.

I jogged to the café with a feeling of urgency. Outside, three other
cars that had been converted into tables. Another Caddy, a red Ford
Thunderbird, and a distinctly anachronistic De Lorean. Despite the
intermittent drizzle, all were packed.

I went in.

A large fifties-style diner, with a soda fountain, waiters on rollers
skates, Buddy Holly on the jukebox, and other artifacts from the
hazily misremembered days of the Eisenhower administration. The
menu was standard diner fare with the occasional Ulster speciality
such as deep-fried Mars bars served in a piece of soda bread. Completely bunged full of weans, enjoying malts and milk shakes.

A waitress in a nylon polka-dot dress and dreadlocks skated up
to me.

"Help you?"

I took out the picture of Siobhan.

"I'm looking for this girl. She was seen with one of the regulars in here. Skinny ginger-haired kid. Ring any bells?"

The girl groaned. Clearly this wasn't the first or even the second time someone had come by asking these questions. Bridget's boys, the police, Bridget's boys again, and the police again.

Well, they weren't me.

"Listen, love, this is bloody serious, have you seen this girl?" I asked with an intimidating burr.

She shook her head.

"You'll want to see the manager," she said.

"Eventually," I said. "I'll show the photo around first."

"You're not allowed to bother the customers," she said.

"Says who?"

There were at least three dozen people in the Malt Shop, not one over twenty-five. I showed them the photo, asked about the mysterious redheaded kid, but no one had seen a bloody thing. I tried my hand with the waiters and the dudes behind the counter, but again all I drew were blank expressions.

This in itself was a wee bit suspicious.

Nobody said, "Oh aye, she looks a bit familiar" or "A kid with red hair, aye, there's a lot of kids with red hair" or "I think I might have seen her, did she have a wee dog?"

None of the usual stuff.

I mean, I know that Belfast people are very good at keeping their mouths shut, seeing nothing, and minding their own business. That's why they had to replace jury trials with secret three-judge courts— no witnesses wanted to testify in front of twelve strangers and no juries wanted to convict terrorists who would come seeking revenge. And I know that Ireland has a well-established and long-standing culture of silence going back at least to the horror of informers during the 1798 Rebellion. But this was different. This was deeper. This was like everyone had been schooled. This was like the word had gone out.

And what had Bridget said? He had smelled of pot. And what the schoolgirl just told me? This place is druggie central. Aye, I could see that now. The paramilitaries ran this particular establishment with a grip of iron. There were probably a couple in here right at this very moment.

I sat down and ordered a malt.

The place began filling up with more schoolkids and students. A couple of cops came in, were given free malteds, and sat slurping them in the window seat. Useless wankers.

I found Dreadlocks again.

"Ok, love, go get the manager, I'll talk to him now," I said.

"He's in a meeting."

My eyes narrowed.

"Go get the manager," I said very quietly.

"Ok," she said.

The manager: twenty-one years old at the most, thin, greased black hair, earring, a zigzag line of stubble from his sideburns to his chin.

He sat down at my table.

"Are you another policeman?" he asked in a Dublin accent.

"What's that on your face, you forget to shave?" I asked, to start the conversation on the wrong foot.

"It's called style," he said.

"Is that how they're spelling shite these days? Seen this girl?" I asked, showing him the photograph.

"I've told you all before, I haven't seen her."

"Let me tell you something, fuckface. You might have fooled Bridget Callaghan's boys because they're from out of town, you might have fooled the peelers because they don't want to know. But I know this place is a clearinghouse for pot, I also know you're protected by the paramilitaries, and I also know you've seen this girl."

He said nothing, stared at the floor.

"You've seen her and you've seen her with a ginger-bap kid and you are fucking going to tell me the name of that boy."

The manager looked at me.

He bit his lip, scratched at his bad skin. I saw that I was right. He wasn't going to win any poker hands anytime soon. He had seen her. And he did know the name of the boy. And what's more, he wanted to tell me all about it. He hesitated, opened and closed his mouth. Dried the froth from his lips.

He'd changed his mind. He couldn't afford to tell me. He didn't know me from Adam.

"He's a wee hood, drug dealer, and a girl's life is at stake. You must know who he is," I barked.

"I don't know who he is, and I've never seen the girl," he said, and his eyes flitted around the café to see if anyone was watching him.

I had to raise the stakes.

I took out the .38 and set it on the table.

"Listen to me, I'm not someone to be fucked with," I said.

"You better put that gun away, there's a couple of cops over at the window," the manager said.

"I seen them. And if I have to, I'll fucking kill them, too. I need to find this girl," I said.

The color remaining in his face drained away. But he was caught between the devil he knew and a new one with a gun. He took a drink of water, made his call.

"Listen, I'm telling you, I never saw the girl, and I never seen that boy everybody's talking about. You can ask anybody in here. They'll all say the same."

"I have asked everybody in here and they all have said the same, which is bloody suspicious. Who are you all afraid of?"

"Nobody."

"Who runs this place?"

"I'm the manager."

"No, who really runs it. Who are you paying off to?"

"I don't know what you're talking about."

"I'm talking about the man that you pay protection money to every week, I'm talking about the man that makes you let him sell drugs on your fine premises here."

He shook his head.

"Was he just dealing pot or was it stronger stuff too?" I asked.

"I don't know. If kids are buying marijuana it's nothing to do with me," he said. I tapped the table. Well, at least that was one thing confirmed.

"Look, I'm very busy, I have to go," the manager said, starting to get up.

"Sit the fuck down. Do you know who Bridget Callaghan is?"

He nodded, sat.

"Do you know what she'll do to you if she finds out that you're preventing her from getting her daughter back in one piece?"

He nodded again.

"I mean, this is Bridget Callaghan I'm talking about here," I said.

He was sweating, shaking, scared, but even so he was more frightened of them than he was of me, even with the promise of Bridget's wrath and a .38 sitting right here on the table.

I scoped the joint.

The place was stuffed to the brim with school boys and girls. The two cops. I really couldn't shoot the fucker. I couldn't actually put the gun to his head and order him to speak. The only thing to do would be to wait until he closed up shop and get the son of a bitch on the way home.

"What time you finish up here?"

"We're open to midnight."

"You stay till midnight?" I asked.

"Yeah," he replied sensibly.

"Listen, is there any way we could talk in a back room or in private somewhere?" I attempted. Get him back there, show him the meaning of fear.

"Uh, no, I can't do that, sorry," he said.

"I'll give you one more chance: the name of the boy or the name of the person you pay off to."

"I've told you, I don't know."

One of the cops walked past on his way to the bathroom. I put the gun in my jacket pocket.

"Are we done?" the manager asked.

If I'd more time I could work on him. But I didn't. I stood.

"You haven't heard the last of me," I told him.

I turned on my heel and walked out of the Malt Shop onto Bradbury Place.

"Shit," I said. Christ on a bike. I'd thought that I could succeed where the cops and Bridget had failed. Instead I'd bollocksed it up. Run into a brick wall.

I leaned against the window.

And I hadn't exactly told Bridget the truth either.

I wasn't connected. I wasn't tuned in. I didn't know people. Sure, I'd run with the teen rackets back in the early nineties, but that was a long time ago. I hadn't kept track of any of those useless fucks.

I bummed a cigarette off a passing student and sat down in the Ford Thunderbird. What the hell was I going to do now? I took a couple of drags on the ciggy and threw it away. Nodded to myself. Aye, there was nothing else for it. I wasn't connected, but I knew a man who was. I had only one card up my sleeve, but that card was a wild one-eyed jack.

Chopper Clonfert owed me a favor.

*　*　*

Back when we were both teenagers, Chopper and I had collaborated on a massive smuggling operation across the border between Northern and Southern Ireland. Petrol, butter, cows, booze moved north; condoms, birth control pills, banned videos, and sometimes the same cows moved south. It was a more innocent time, when the paramilitaries weren't keen on drugs and the cops didn't exactly rate cattle rustling as high on their list of priorities. But even so, it was still a risky operation. You had to move product through a number of territories, and for the sake of good business you needed a truce among all the separate gangs and factions.

One wet Saturday night, Chopper and I got lifted driving a lorry load of whisky. I was just a kid, so the Garda Síochána didn't even cuff me, but they worked Chopper over and threw him in the back of a van. He could have done five years for smuggling, but lucky for him, I wandered to the back of the lorry, broke a bottle of hundred proof, threw in a lit cigarette, and ran like hell.

Classed as a fuckup by the Guards and with virtually no evidence, Chopper pled guilty to importing without a licence, got six months and was out in four. Of course, by that time I was in the army and then I went to America and I hadn't seen him since. But I read things about him on the BBC. I had followed his career. Nowadays he no longer called himself Chopper.

Now he was a Northern Ireland assemblyman, a Belfast City councillor, and one of the rising stars of the Independent Republican Party. Indeed, he was tipped as a potential leader and was almost certain to become an MP at next year's election.

Garrett Clonfert. Né Chopper.

The one villain in Belfast I knew was still in the game.

He had to be, because you don't get to become an IRP councillor without having murdered your way through your rivals. Hard for an outsider to keep track of the fissiparous alphabet soup of Irish politics, and even I had trouble sometimes, but I did know that IRP was an offshoot of Republican Sinn Fein, who were themselves a radical offshoot of Provisional Sinn Fein, itself a breakaway of official Sinn Fein. IRP was by far the nastiest of the lot. It had renounced the IRA cease-fire of 1997 as a perfidious betrayal. Its military wing had planted a dozen bombs since 1998, pre-9/11 they had praised Osama bin Laden as an anticolonialist freedom fighter, and they were linked with ETA, the PLO, and the Italian Red Brigades. It didn't fill me with glee to have to go begging for help from my old pal Chopper, but realistically he was my only hope.

A quick scan of the phone book. A ten-minute walk from the Malt Shop.

Councillor Clonfert's offices were in a new glass-and-steel building off the Ormeau Road, near the BBC.

The entire ground floor was an IRP "advice center" for his constituents. There were a couple of hard men looking for work as well as some genuine local people there to complain about the drains, the trash collection, and the noisy neighbors. The place was painted a blushed shade of rehab-facility pink. There were posters of smiling children, of all races, holding hands. Embroidered along an entire wall was a Bayeux-style tapestry, also either done by children or mentally challenged adults, depicting scenes of daily life in Ireland. Scenes that were frozen in time about 1927. Sheep farmers, dairy farmers, fishermen. And above these scenes of mythical rural idyll was emblazoned the baffling IRP motto: "Peace, Power, Prosperity."

I found a receptionist whose name tag said she was called Doreen. Older broad with a poisonous expression and a blond Partonesque wig.

"Doreen, I'd like to speak to Garrett, please. I'm an old friend of his. Name's Michael Forsythe."

"Councillor Clonfert is on a conference call with Brussels at the moment," Doreen said with a hateful smile. "If you wouldn't mind taking a seat, I'll see—"

I interrupted.

"Doreen, I don't mean to be rude but this is extremely urgent. Could you please tell him that Michael Forsythe wants to see him."

Doreen looked across at the two heavies who were sitting on a sofa reading the Keira Knightley issue of *Vanity Fair*.

"Listen, Doreen, there's no need to get your goons involved. I'm not a troublemaker. Please, just call up Garrett and I'll guarantee you he'll want to see me," I said quietly.

Doreen picked up her telephone and turned away from me. She spoke very quietly.

"I'm so sorry, Councillor Clonfert, but there's a gentleman here to see you, he's says it's very urgent. He says his name is Michael Forsythe, I can get Richard to see him off the . . . Oh, ok. Ok. I'll send him right in."

Doreen looked at me with a bit more respect.

"Mr. Forsythe, you take the door behind me and then it's the first door on your left. I'll buzz you in," she said.

She pressed a button on her desk and the massive armored door behind her swung open. Garrett would have needed this level of additional security because you never knew who might try and kill him. Because I seemed to be an old friend, she'd hadn't got the two ganches to pat me down.

That might be handy.

Outside Garrett's office there was a poster of pasty-faced Irish weans standing on Blackpool Pier with the words "Vote Clonfert: A Bridge to the Future" underneath. Might have been nice if the photographer had used an actual bridge.

To catch him off guard, I tried to open Garrett's door without knocking but the handle didn't turn.

"Who is it?" he yelled from inside.

"Michael Forsythe," I said.

"It is you. Wait a second, Michael, and I'll buzz you in."

The door buzzed. The handle turned.

He was sitting at a large oak desk in a massive office. Behind him, through an enormous window, I could see the BBC building and cloudy Belfast.

Leather chairs, a leather sofa. Computers and a stereo playing Radio 3. Art prints on the wall: a Gauguin full of naked Polynesian girls and the detail from Klimt's *Three Ages of Woman* that cuts out the old broad. On one side of his desk a photograph of Councillor Clonfert getting lost in a three-way hug with Senator Ted Kennedy and Congressman Peter King at the unveiling of the Irish famine memorial in New York City. On the other side a photo of Garrett with an attractive younger woman and a little girl.

Garrett stood and offered me his hand. He had put on weight since last I'd seen him, but he looked good. Late thirties, sandy hair, smooth cheeks, and warm open eyes and smile. He was wearing an Italian tailored silk suit in a fetching shade of burgundy. It was flashy for Belfast, and a canary yellow silk tie didn't help tone him down.

"Michael Forsythe, as I live and breathe," he said.

"Chopper Clonfert," I said.

We shook hands.

"Sit down, sit down. Cigar? They're very good," he said.

"No, thanks."

"Michael Forsythe, Michael Forsythe. You're a bit of a legend, aren't you?"

"Nah, not really. You're the star, Garrett. Councillor, assemblyman—I'm very impressed."

"Yeah, well, I'm just doing my bit for the people. A life of service turned out to be my calling."

"Very good of you, I'm sure."

His eyes went glassy as he remembered the old days.

"Jesus, Michael Forsythe. I haven't seen you since way back. Boy, oh boy, I couldn't believe it when I heard you'd joined the British army. I'm glad you got out and I didn't have to kill you," he said with a big laugh.

"Maybe I would have killed you."

Garrett laughed again.

"Oh, don't worry, you don't have to brag, I know all about you, Michael. I heard about your exploits in America."

"What ya hear?"

"You killed Darkey White over money. That's the story on the street."

"It's close enough," I said.

"What are you doing with yourself these days? Maybe I got the wrong end of the stick, but I'd been led to believe that you were living a secret identity, in the witness protection program," Garrett said.

"Aye."

"I heard you were in Australia."

"No, I wasn't. . . . Listen, Garrett, I'd love to talk about old times and your rise to fame and fortune, but I came here because I need your help."

Garrett's smile disappeared from his face.

"You need my help?" he said suspiciously.

"Yeah."

"Michael, um, these days I have to keep within the letter of the law, I'm running for parliament and—"

"Garrett, it's nothing illegal. I'm working for Bridget Callaghan, her wee girl—"

"I know. Her wee girl ran away with some fella and she's been doing her nut, sending her boys everywhere looking for her. I know all about it."

"Aye. Well, her boys have drawn a blank and the cops have been fucking useless and now they've received a ransom demand."

Garrett nodded slowly.

"Have they now? So she's been kidnapped."

"That's what it looks like."

"I heard she ran off. Maybe she staged it to get her ma's money."

I was getting a little impatient with this.

"Garrett, regardless of how it happened, I'm trying to find her and I'd like you to help me."

Garrett pushed his chair back on the rollers, creating a psychological and physical distance between us. You didn't need to be a head shrinker to read those signs.

"You owe me a favor, Chopper," I said.

He laughed.

"A favor? What the fuck are you talking about?"

"For the van full of nicked whisky. If I hadn't torched it, blown it the fuck up, you would have done five years for that."

Garrett shook his head.

"No way, Michael. I would have bought my way out of that one. I would have done what I done, no matter if you'd torched that van or not. Stop kidding yourself, mate. I don't owe you a fucking thing."

I closed my eyes. Seethed. This was the wrong thing to say to me on the day I'd had.

"Take that cigar now," I said.

Garrett opened a box on the table, took out two cigars, cut the end off, lit them both, and passed one to me.

"Michael, let's go get some lunch. I'm happy to see you, let's talk about what you're about and what you've been up to. It's fascinating that you're actually working for the woman who, I heard, had a million-fucking-dollar contract on ya. I mean, for Jesus' sake."

I puffed on the cigar. An expensive Cuban. Way above a councilman's salary.

"Garrett, I don't want to threaten you—" I began again.

Garrett laughed.

"You. Threaten me? Whose town do you think this is? Aye, I know who she is and I seen her goons about, but let me tell you, this isn't the fucking Big Apple. Don't even try to go down that road. Don't embarrass yourself. Would you walk into Palermo and start mouthing off about Bridget Callaghan? Well, don't walk in here and try the same thing."

"Garrett, it wouldn't just be her. You wouldn't want the IRA after you, would ya?"

"The IRA, Michael, is on cease-fire. Come on, enough of this talk, you're spoiling what could be a nice reunion between old pals."

"Hear me out, Garrett, all I want to know is the name of the gangster who owns the Malt Shop on Bradbury Place. That's all, just a fucking name. Fucking manager was too afeared to tell me, but I know you know. You'd have to know."

Garrett nodded. He did know. He knew all the underbosses in his territory.

"Why is that name so important to you?" he asked.

"The Malt Shop is where Siobhan Callaghan met the boy she dis-

appeared with. The boy was reeking of pot. A drug dealer. He has to
be connected. He'd have to get permission to deal there and whoever gave him that permission will know who he is and where he
lives."

Garrett rubbed his chin, slowly shook his head.

"I'm sorry, Michael, I can't help you, I don't want to rock the boat.
If they ever found that I had told someone who—"

"I've got a .38 in my pocket," I interrupted.

"I'll pretend you didn't say that, Michael. The intercom has been
on the whole time you've been in here. I know you're joking, but I
wouldn't want my boys rushing in and fucking shooting you by mistake. That would be an ugly thing to happen to the prospective MP
for West Belfast. Even with the whole IRP behind me, it would hurt
my campaign," he said jovially.

I was angry now.

"'Peace, Power, Prosperity,' my arse."

"Michael, all those things are important. We're bringing people together. We are taking power from the old archetypes committed to a
past full of hate. We're building a new society here."

"Chopper, don't come the politician with me, don't get ideas above
your station. You are what you've always been, a small-time fucking
hood. Ignorant hood, too," I said.

He forced his laugh harder.

"Ignorant. How so? Oh, do enlighten me, rat exile from abroad,"
he said, not at all nonplussed.

"I know where you come from, mate, even if your constituents
have forgotten. I know you are in an ugly fucking business and if your
boys rush in, well and good, let them do their worst, you'll be dead before the door handle turns," I said, pulling out the revolver and pointing it at his head.

"Put that away, you're making a fool of yourself."

"Aye, well, better a breathing fool than a dead fucker."

"You'd never get out of here alive."

"Shoot my way out."

"You wouldn't dare kill me. Your life wouldn't be worth tuppence."

"Who owns the Malt Shop on Bradbury Place?"

"Michael, forget it, what do you care about some missing wee tart."

A knock at the door.

"Is there a problem, Councillor Clonfert?" a voice asked.

Chopper looked at me quizzically. He was right. If I laid a finger on him, his boys would top me. There was no angle in killing him and Chopper was certainly brave enough to see me blink first.

We regarded each other for a half minute, and then for the second time in an hour I put the gun away, my bluff called, my threat useless.

"There's no problem, Peter. Mr. Forsythe here was just leaving," Chopper said.

Aye, the son of a bitch knew I wouldn't kill him. He knew I couldn't kill him. But everyone has a weakness. I got to my feet.

"Well, Garrett, you can keep your cigars, I suppose I'll he heading on."

Garrett stood too.

"Michael, it's always interesting being with you. So over the top. So old school. You should have gone into the theater," he said, and offered me his hand again. I shook it and winked at him.

"You're a brave man, Chopper, should have know better than to threaten you."

"Aye," Garrett said, pleased with himself.

I hesitated, thought for a moment, nodded at the photograph of him with his wife and child.

"Although if I were you, I'd put a couple of bodyguards on that wee girl of yours and keep them there for at least ten years, that's how long Bridget waited till she hit me. She's patient."

"What did you say?"

"You heard me, Garrett," I said, and began walking for the door.

"Bridget Callaghan wouldn't dare come after my family," he said, his face completely at odds with his words.

"Nah, not your family. Just your wee girl, she's old school too, eye for eye, tooth for tooth, dead daughter for dead daughter."

Garrett let me walk two more paces. He hit the intercom button on his desk, turning it off to give him privacy.

"Sit down," he said in a whisper.

"I think I'll stand."

"What would you tell Bridget?"

"When her daughter turns up dead, I'll tell her that you're the one that stopped me from saving Siobhan and that you have a lovely wee girl yourself."

This was the chink in his armor. He paled and sweat appeared on his forehead. He looked at me with the cold hate that comes from the mingling of shame and fear.

"Seamus Deasey. It's his turf. If it's a drug place, they're paying off to him."

"Where would I find him?"

"He's in the fucking book."

"I need to find him right now."

"He might be in the Rat's Nest."

"What's that?"

"It's a pub on Valencia Street."

"Where?"

"Off the Falls Road."

"Bad area?"

"Bad fucking area."

"Ok. Take it easy, Garrett." I threw the lit cigar onto his carpet, stamped it out.

"Aye, don't hurry back, Forsythe, and remember, not everyone you'll meet is as mellow and well adjusted as me."

I left the office. Nodded to Doreen. Not the happiest of reunions. But at least I had a name. It was something to go on. Chopper hadn't been lying. He was tough as old boots, but he couldn't be tough for everyone. Shouldn't have put up that Klimt of the ma and bairn, not that with the old family photo too. That was overdoing it. Wouldn't have thought to get you from that direction, Chopper. Did you forget, it was you, mate, who told me long ago to hide your weakness, your vulnerabilities. You don't display them for all the world to see.

Nah.

I exited the advice center.

Out into the street.

Checked for tails.

It was a brisk fifteen-minute walk to the Falls Road. I'd do it in ten.

❊   ❊   ❊

The Falls Road.

You know why I don't like it?

Because there is still evil in this town.

I can sense it.

In the pavement, in the fold of tenebrous color, in the eclipse of shapes.

I can sense it because I helped make it.

I feel its presence, its power.

From Saint Patrick to the Vikings, Ireland had five centuries of peace. Never before nor after. That time ripped apart literally in a Norse blood eagle of ribs and axe-cleaved hearts. And ever since we've had the creature with us. Our shadow, our watcher, our tormentor, our instigator. It sleeps. It dreams. But it's still here. Coiled. Hungry. A stalking monster of revenge and memory. It moves and weaves. Slipping sideways, backwards, but always moving, driven by malcontent. Its greatest reign, the Troubles. And I suppose some might say that it's not sleeping, it's dying. It's possible, but it's too soon to tell. Certainly, on the surface, we are in the time of no more war. Terrorism doesn't happen in Ireland nowadays. America, the Middle East, Russia, across the water, those are the hot spots. No radical Muslim sleeper agents here, and Ulster has an uneasy peace.

But the evil waits. Biding its time. It moves the clouds, it stirs the breeze.

Whispering with a voice so delicate that it will throw a switch on a circuit board. Click—and a breath of a wire shifts into a new and more significant alignment. A minuscule voltage disappears from a battery and jolts into a doughnut ring of industrial detonator. Viper quick, the Semtex expands a millionfold into a couple of bags of fertilizer or roughly two hundred pounds of ammonium nitrate, homemade, stomach-churning, disemboweling explosive. A chain reaction and the fertilizer rips through a police station, or the floor of someone's car, or into a bag of sharpened roofing nails.

Ulster had a thousand of these bombings in twenty years.

And the force behind them is still here. Unknown, undefinable. Waiting, watching, under the death murals of the Hunger Strikers, Mother Ireland, and the IRA. Tourists come and take photographs of these giant wall paintings, but I know that those are armed men on the street corners. Ex-cons with walkie-talkie phones. Bookies' runners wearing sneakers. Drug dealers in shell suits. Weans in the ubiquitous Yankees hats.

All along the Falls Road. This dingy terrace of redbricked houses. This heartland of the IRA.

Aye.

I turn down Valencia Street.

The Rat's Nest.

A pokey corner pub, with grilles on the window and homemade speed bumps on the road outside to stop terrorists from the other side driving past and hurling petrol bombs.

I pause outside.

Take a breath.

Sniff the air.

Heavy thoughts, Michael.

Heavy and a little prescient.

But don't worry, you needn't fear the random Semtex bomb, the mobile phone ignition system, those roofing nails.

You just look out for bullets and the odd grenade.

You just look out.

I shake the cobwebs from my head, compose myself, and walk into the bar. . . .

Seen one paramilitary pub, seen 'em all.

Low ceilings, blacked-out windows, pool table, dartboard. All male, all hoods, waiting around for something to do. Imagine an old-fashioned western. The piano player stops and everybody turns around, the villain looks up from the card table, and the doc says it's probably best that you leave. No piano player, no poker, no friendly doc but an identical vibe. I strode to the counter.

"Are you lost?" the barman asked.

"No. I'm looking for Seamus Deasey."

The young barman said nothing.

A pause.

A cold, elongated silence. I knew Deasey was looking at me.

I turned.

Six men walking over from a booth next to the pool table. All of them in jeans, T-shirts, and shit-kicking boots.

"I'm Deasey," Seamus said. He was the shortest of the six. Shaved head, pug face, long arms, boxer's nose. In fact, he looked like a middleweight who could have been good but just wasn't tall enough. Two of his mates were bringing over their pool cues. I stepped away from the bar in case the keep cold-clocked me from behind with a hurling stick.

"What the fuck do you want?" Deasey asked.

I let him get four paces away and as fast as a cat on vet-visit day I pulled out the .38-caliber revolver, extended my arm completely, and pointed the gun at Deasey's broken nose. This was the third time I'd threatened someone with a bullet in the brain since arriving in Belfast, but this time I decided I was not fucking backing down.

Deasey didn't react but his mates produced assorted hand cannons, shiny pimp pistols, and other flashy pieces of shite that would kill me just as good as a proper gun.

"You know who I am?" I said.

Deasey smiled, unafraid.

"Should I?"

"I'm Michael Forsythe. You might have heard of me, I killed Darkey White in America."

Deasey nodded.

"Aye, I heard of you. You're the rat Bridget Callaghan's been looking for."

"Aye, well, times have changed. Bridget Callaghan needs my help to find her missing wean. She's called me to look for Siobhan. The last place she was seen was the Malt Shop with a ginger-haired kid. It's one of your places and that's why I've come to see you."

"Great fucking story. You're a regular raconteur," Deasey said and winked at his mates, who dutifully chuckled.

"I want to know the name of the kid that met her in the Malt Shop," I said, and nodded the gun at him.

Some of his buds made a move but Deasey stopped them. He didn't want them screwing up and getting him killed. But even so, he didn't look in the least freaked by the revolver.

"I suppose you believe your own hype, Forsythe," he said.

"I have hype? I didn't even know I had hype."

"They say you're un-fucking-killable," Deasey said.

"Is that what *they* say?"

"Aye, *they* do. They say you need a fucking army to take the man who topped Darkey White. Well, I've got news for you, Forsythe. Take a gander about ye. This is a fucking army. Every person in this place works for me."

I looked around the bar at the assorted ne'er-do-wells, killers, probationed terrorists, and murderers released under the Good Friday Agreement.

"I'm not here for trouble," I said slowly.

Deasey laughed.

"Funny way of showing it."

"I just need your help. I need the name of that kid," I said.

"First of all, Forsythe, how in the name of fuck would I know the name of any kid that goes to the fucking Malt Shop on Bradbury Place. That's not exactly my kind of joint."

"Listen, Deasey, I don't have the time. I know you didn't want to tell the police, but if you don't tell me I'll bloody shoot you."

"I don't know who told you to come here, but you've put yourself in big-time shit."

"The Malt Shop is your place. Chopper Clonfert told me that. The kid's one of your dealers. Now, I know he wasn't acting under your orders when he went after the girl. You would never have been allowed to kidnap Bridget Callaghan's daughter in Belfast. The IRA do not want a war with her and the whole of the fucking Irish mob in America. But the kid was working for you and I wouldn't want it to get back to Bridget that you were implicated."

"Is that supposed to be a threat?"

"No, this fucking .38 pointed at your head is supposed to be a threat."

"I had nothing to do with the disappearance of Bridget Callaghan's wean. And I don't fucking know anybody who has."

"Deasey, just tell me the lad's name and I'll get out of here."

"I'm telling you nothing, Forsythe," he said, cool as mustard.

"Deasey, you must have been born stupid. When I tell Bridget you're working with the kidnappers—"

Deasey interrupted as much to reassure his own men as me.

"You're not listening, Forsythe. I don't know anything about any fucking kidnapping. You said yourself no fucking hood in Belfast would kidnap Bridget Callaghan's wean. And you're right. There's too much spread coming in from the States. There's no percentage in it, see? It wouldn't be good for business. You are barking up the wrong tree. Now get the fuck out of here and count your lucky stars you caught me in a good mood today."

I sighed with impatience.

"Deasey, I'm not leaving until you tell me that kid's name. Red-headed wee lad, dealer in your bar. You know who I'm talking about. I know you know. You better fucking tell me."

"Or you'll what?"

"I'll fucking top you."

"You'll be dead before I hit the fucking floor," Deasey observed.

"Aye. More than likely. We'll both die because of some piece-of-shit pot dealer who helped lift Siobhan Callaghan," I said.

One of the boys could take it no more and swung his pool cue at me. I shot him in the stomach. Someone else shot at me, missed, and almost killed the barman behind me. I rushed Deasey, shoved the .38 against his throat, and cocked the hammer.

"Tell your boys to be cool," I screamed.

Silence, except for the gangster on the floor crawling about in agony.

"Cool it, lads, fucking cool it," Deasey demanded.

I could feel his garlicky beer breath on my face. Nervous doglike pants.

Belly shot began weeping, retching. A .38-slug stomach wound from this range could easily kill someone.

"Aaah, help me, aaah," he groaned, the smell of blood and guts permeating the room like frying onions.

"Better get him to the Royal," I suggested.

"Do it," Deasey said. "He's dying."

Two of the hoods picked up their fallen comrade and carried him outside.

"How did it come to this?" I asked.

Deasey was tense: shallows breaths, sweat, touch of the trembles.

"I didn't have anything to do with taking that girl," he said in a hoarse whisper, the fight gone from him now. The blood having brought home the very real danger that I posed.

"I know, Deasey, I'm not saying you did. But one of your boys did. Pot dealer in the Malt Shop. Skinny. All I want is his fucking name. You owe him fucking nothing anyway, and he's implicated you in a piece of serious fucking shit."

"Aye," Deasey said.

"You know who I'm talking about, don't ya?" I said, and dragged the revolver up along his face and rested it on his temple. It moved easily through his sweat.

"I know who you're talking about," Deasey admitted finally.

"That's right. You're going to give me his name and address, and he better be there when I call because if he gets tipped off between now and then—"

"Enough threats. Bridget Callaghan doesn't scare me."

"You shouldn't be worried about her. You should be worried about me. You know how much damage your skull will do to my gun if I pull this trigger at point-blank range?"

"No."

"None at all."

It was a tough spot for Deasey. If he told me the name and address he would lose face in front of his men. But if he didn't tell me, perhaps I was the sort of person who might just be mental enough to blow his fucking head off. I'd just shot one of his pals a minute ago. He might be next.

"I don't know his address. I really don't. I could find out but it would take some hours. If you give me a number I'll call you up with—"

"Now, now, Deasey, up until now we've been honest with each other. I wanted to know the kid's name, you didn't want to tell me. Let's keep it on the level."

The revolver's barrel was turning his skin blue.

"Barry, he lives on a boat on the Lagan path, called the *Ginger Bap*, that's all I know. I don't keep track of every fucking shithead pot dealer in my employ."

"Barry?"

"Barry," Deasey confirmed.

I turned to Deasey's crew.

"Ok now, lads, Deasey and me are going to walk outside. The first character I see pop his noggin out gets it between the fucking eyes and the next bullet's for Deasey himself. So I'd stay in here if I were you. Now everybody drop your guns and go behind the bar."

No one moved.

"Do it," Deasey said.

The gangsters put down their firearms and shuffled behind the tiny bar.

Still holding the gun to his temple, I walked Deasey to the door. To exit, I would have to turn my back on them. I turned, pushed open the doors. For a split second I was exposed. The hairs on my neck stood up. But no one was going to attempt to be a hero. We made it out into the street.

"Thanks for the information about Barry," I said.

"Somehow I don't think it's going to do you any fucking good," he said with a thin smile.

"We'll see."

I removed the gun from his temple and stepped away from him.

"I hope you've got life insurance, because after this little display your loved ones are going to need it. Not that a rat informer has any loved ones," Deasey said.

"Turn round," I said.

He turned.

I cracked the butt of the .38 into the back of his head and let him collapse on the sidewalk.

I legged it as fast as I could down the hill. Kept running down the Falls Road and didn't stop until I was safe in the center of Belfast again.

"Where's the Lagan path?" I asked a passerby.

He told me, I caught my breath, winced as the slash across my gut decided to become very painful, and headed east for my encounter with Barry and a possible rescue of Siobhan.

Walking.

Jogging.

Running . . .

I wasn't worried about Deasey's threat.

If he was big talk, then it was all just bullshit. And if he was going to try and do something, well, he could fucking take a number and join the queue. Me and the evil had it sussed. He was small fry. I was Michael Forsythe.

Let them add to the legend. Let them believe it. Let them tell it.

He survived twelve years on the run and at least three hits. He lost a foot, escaped from a Mexican prison, and destroyed the empire of Darkey White.

He isn't someone to be fucked with. He's a ghost, a bogeyman.

They say that when he was conceived the good fairy was on sabbatical. They say that when he was born vultures perched themselves on the houses of his enemies.

7: THE WANDERING ROCKS (BELFAST—JUNE 16, 4:00 P.M.)

The Lagan poised between tides. A break in the clouds. The sun at the very head of Belfast Lough. The daylight nearing its apogee. This is the only time of year and the only time of day that Belfast can take on a Mediterranean aspect, and then just for a moment. Waders on the muddy riverbank. Bees among the bankside flowers. Irises, wild roses, bluebells pushing up through dandelion and grass. Red dust from the Sahara falling on the apartment balconies. A turquoise cast to the sky—a deep blue that seems to make a noise like sighing. No one stirs. Birds. An egret preening itself on an ocher roof tile. Starlings on drooping telegraph wires. Seagulls following the customs boat. An entire duma of Arctic terns waiting in the glasslike trees for the tide to sink a little more.

And then a hazy disturbance over the water.

It's ending now.

In a minute, gray clouds will rush in to fill the vacuum. The prevailing westerlies will banish that Saharan breeze and Belfast will become again the dour northern town of bricks, slate, and tarmacadam.

But let's be Zen and appreciate the last few seconds of the golden light.

This is all new. There was no Lagan path when I lived here.

And it's with some feeling of astonishment that I walk past the gleaming apartment buildings, condo complexes, and town houses.

Parapets, shutters, classical façades, in shades of coral and sun-faded white. Big windows that want to embrace the river and the city, rather than repel it. Someone made a fortune on the peace dividend around here. This used to be a scary towpath where street gangs would rule the day and the homeless would sleep at night. Filth, rusting shopping carts, and burned-out cars were the only ornaments for the choked water that was filled habitually with diesel and chemical pollutants.

But in the 1970s and '80s terrorism and unemployment closed the shipyards and engineering works that ran along the river. The factories were gutted, the heavy machinery stripped and sent to Seoul. A decade of neglect and then the IRA cease-fire and the UDA cease-fire. The peace process. Millions from the United States and Europe for regeneration and suddenly this stretch of water must have seemed like a good investment. Clear out the factories, clean the river, make a nice Laganside path, build homes for yuppies.

And I quite like what they've done with it. Even when the sun is finally suffocated by a black cloud and it starts to drizzle. A different feeling here from old Belfast. The people who live in these apartments travel. They go places and they bring back tasteful souvenirs from the Algarve and Andalucía. Olive oil containers, spice racks, expensive wine. They know black people, they know gay people. They know who Yo-Yo Ma is. They think Vivaldi is vulgar and they are in love with Janáček.

Easy to look down on people like that. But hopefully they're the future. Eventually the tenements and back-to-backs will disappear. And along with them the parochialism, the subordination of women, the mistrust of outsiders, the hatred for the other side. It might take a hundred years and a civil war but if these people are the vector of things to come, the evil will wither away and Belfast will be like any other dull, wet northern European city. And if I for one live to see it, I won't shed a fucking tear. . . .

Game face on. I turned a bend in the river and saw the beginning of the long line of houseboats. Attractive converted barges that were tied up along the river. Some long and thin like coal boats, others squat, with an extra story on top. Most well maintained, decorated with flowers, all reasonably seaworthy. There were about two dozen of them moored behind one another stretching for about a quarter of a mile. They weren't the famous teak houseboats of the Vale of Kash-mir, but they weren't the stinking old hulks that I was expecting.

I walked past a couple and stopped at the first one that had some-one on deck. A young man wearing yellow shorts and a purple rain-coat. He was patting a golden retriever and reading a book with the title *Evolution: The Fossils Say No!*

The breeze turned. I shivered and felt the cold on my stitches.

"Excuse me, I'm looking for the *Ginger Bap*," I said, zipping my leather jacket over the Zeppelin T-shirt.

He looked up from the book. He had sleekit eyes and was practi-cally a skinhead, but I figured he couldn't be that bad because of his canine and sartorial choices.

At least that was my assumption until he said, "Why, what are they to you?" with more than a bit of hostility.

"They're nothing to me, I was looking for them."

"Didn't catch your name."

"Michael Forsythe. What's your name, if you don't mind me fuck-ing asking," I said with a wee tone in my voice.

"Donald . . . Did you say Constable Michael Forsythe?"

"No."

"Are you not with the police?"

"No."

He put down the book, his eyes closed, and he shook his head as if he didn't quite believe me.

"Well, listen, to tell you the truth, I was thinking of calling the po-lice, so I was," he confided.

"Why was that?" I asked.

"There's a smell coming from their boat, something awful, so it is."

"Which one is it?"

"It's the next one along. Down there, so it is, just right ahead of ya."

I looked to where he was pointing. One of the larger boats. A high-sided, flat-bottomed cabin cruiser that had been moored there for some time by the look of the slime on either side of the fenders. It was shipshape but there were bits of paper and leaves sticking against the safety rail.

"Robby noticed something was up first yesterday and then I twigged the smell this morning," Donald said.

"I take it Robby's your dog," I said.

"Aye, he is," he said, offering no more information.

"What happened that got Robby so upset?" I asked.

Donald's natural Belfast reticence and his desire to get this off his chest conflicted inside him for a few seconds but eventually the latter won out.

"Well, it was pretty scary. Lying in me bed. I don't know what time it was. Maybe three or four in the morning. Robby starts growling and I tell him to shut up, but he keeps carrying on and I get worried. So I look around the boat and go up on deck and check the ropes and have a wee shoofty about, so I do."

"What ya see?" I asked.

"Nothing. Everything's normal."

"Ok, go on," I said.

"Well, Robby's whimpering now and I don't know what's going on, I comfort him and he goes back to sleep right. But it creeps me out and I don't sleep too easy."

"And then what?"

"Well, I got up yesterday and I went into the Tech and came back last night, everything seemed fine, except that Robby was a wee bit out of sorts the whole day, but he does that sometimes, didn't really think too much about it. But by this morning first thing when I woke up I started smelling the stink, so I did."

"From the *Ginger Bap*?"

"Aye."

"Did you go over there?"

Donald's eyes narrowed and he wiped his mouth. He wondered if he really should be talking this much to a perfect stranger. I smiled in the most friendly way I could. A smile that often has the unintentional side effect of scaring the bejesus out of people.

"Aye, I did go over. I said, 'Barry, open up,' but there was no answer."

"Did you go on board?"

"No, I did not, it's a strict rule around here, you don't go on other people's boats without permission. No way."

"What did you do then?"

"Are you sure you're not a peeler?" Donald asked suspiciously.

"I'm not a peeler, but I'm working for the peelers, so it would probably be in your best interests to answer my questions."

"Look, I'm not causing trouble. I have never caused any trouble in my life, if you don't count trouble at football matches and you'd be hard pressed to avoid a spot of bother at them Old Firm games cos they are—"

"Donald, please, what did you do next?" I interrupted.

"Nothing. I didn't do anything. I just minded my own business," he said.

"Ok, probably very wise. Now, do me a favor, Donald, tell me about Barry."

"What do you want to know?"

"Does he live there alone?"

"Nah, he lives with his mate."

"Who's his mate?"

"I don't know, student from Scotland or something. Barry's an art student at Tech. Photography and shite like that. Other bloke's in the same racket, I think. Almost everybody on these boats are students of some sort. I'm at the Tech myself. This is spillover accommodation. I don't mind it."

"So Barry must be at least sixteen if he's at the Tech?" I asked.

"Barry? Probably near eighteen, thereabouts. You could say he looks a good bit younger, though."

I nodded. It all seemed correct so far, but I had to be sure it was the right guy.

"What exactly does he look like?" I asked.

"I don't know, average looking, I suppose."

"What color was his hair?"

"What does his boat say?" Donald answered sarcastically. I looked at the *Ginger Bap*.

"Ginger hair. He's a redhead," I said.

"Aye, he has a ponytail."

"Does he have a black sweatshirt with a bird on it?" I asked.

"Aye. Owls Football Team. Wee tiny owl. Black, dark blue, something like that."

"You ever see Barry with a girl?"

"Oh, aye, them boys are a couple of jack the lads. Wee lasses in there left and right, so they are."

"Did you see a girl going in there in the last couple of days?" I asked.

"The last couple of days? Well, for a start, I haven't seen Barry at all for two days. But before that, I think I just seen him and the Jock. No wee girls."

"Maybe you heard a girl's voice or noticed anything unusual?"

"No girl and nothing unusual until yesterday morning," he said.

"At around three in the morning, right?

"Right."

"The two boys normally come back that late?"

"Nah, the bars close at twelve, so they're there pretty sharpish after that, so they are."

I nodded, touched the .38 in my jacket pocket. If what had happened was what I thought had happened, I wouldn't be needing the gun but you never knew.

"Ok, Donald, thanks very much," I said.

"Are you going over there?"

"Aye."

"Do you think there's something wrong?"

"Yeah, I do," I said without emotion.

"What do you want me to do?"

"I want you to sit tight and do nothing for the moment."

"Do you think there's been an accident or something? Maybe they left their gas on," Donald suggested.

"Well, we'll see."

"I'll go with you," Donald offered.

"No."

"It's my neighborly and civic duty, so it is," Donald said, annoying me now.

"No, you stay here. If you want to become a good citizen, you just go back to your novel and take it easy," I said.

I walked quickly to the *Ginger Bap*.

When I got closer I saw that the vessel was listing slightly. Obviously you needed to pump the bilges every couple of days and obviously no one had worked the bilges for at least the last twenty-four hours.

And of course there was the smell. The unmistakable stench of death.

I suppose that's what Deasey meant when he said the information wouldn't do me any good. And Donald was probably right about the timing too. The bloody dog had heard something with its dog ears. Something it hadn't liked. Whatever had occurred had taken place yesterday in the wee hours.

I stepped on the side of the deck. The boat rocked slightly. The plastic fenders squeaked against the quay. I leaned on the safety rail and pulled myself on board. I found the door to the main cabin. I turned the handle. Locked. I examined it closer; no, not locked, jammed. Whoever had done this had exited the boat and jammed the lock shut with a line of wire shoved between the bolt and the side. Either of the two boys would have had the key so it wasn't them.

It was just a piece-of-shit wee bolt that gave after one kick from my Stanley boot. I pulled the hatch open.

The smell hit me. Putrefaction. Either someone was dead down below or a freezer full of meat was rotting. I gagged and stood back.

Donald's dog started to bark.

"What's going on?" Donald called over.

"Do you have a phone?" I shouted back.

"Aye."

"You better call for an ambulance. Not the cops, not yet," I said, and stepped inside. I held my T-shirt over my nose and took out the .38. There was plenty of light in the upper cabin and not a trace of disorder. Tidy cupboards, an empty bottle of Jack Daniel's. A table with two half-full coffee cups on either side of it. The *Belfast Telegraph* from June 13 next to one cup and beside the other a magazine called *Panties Panties Panties* with a cover photo of a jaded Chinese woman wearing neither panties nor anything else.

Just then the boat groaned in the water. Instinctively I called out: "Is there anybody here?"

Of course there was no reply. I looked into the coffee cups. The boys had been up, drinking coffee to keep themselves awake. They'd been expecting someone. And that someone had arrived.

I held the T-shirt to my nose and pulled open the door that presumably led to the lower cabins. A ladder that went into the dark hole.

"Hello?" I tried again.

I stepped onto the ladder and kept the .38 in front of me. It wasn't Bristol fashion but I was ex-army, not a navy ponce, so I descended the ladder facing forward with the gun out—just in case there were any surprises. A passing barge made the boat rock and the door closed behind me, leaving me in complete darkness. I wasn't bloody having that. Whatever was down here I wanted to fucking see it. The curtains had been pulled over the rectangular portholes.

I stepped off the final rung, crossed the room, and tugged the curtains back.

Sunlight streamed in.

The cabin looked disturbed, but it hadn't been ransacked. There had been no fight. The foldaway beds on either side of the central walkway were unmade and there were clothes on the floor. There were books and a clothesline pegged with black-and-white photographs. Crappy photographs of trees, mountains, small children, and bits of rubbish on the sidewalk. Also a galley, a CD player, and a set of CDs hanging on a stand.

The smell was even stronger down here.

Two doors.

One behind the stairs that led to the bilges and the engine; and a door at the end of the cabin that went to the heads and the rest of the boat. My hunch told me it was the forward door and as I approached I saw that there was a sticky residue leaking out underneath.

No, not leaking, it had leaked yesterday morning. Now it was just rotting.

"Aye," I said sadly.

Carefully I pushed open the door with the .38.

Blood everywhere in a narrow corridor. On the wooden cabin floor, on the walls, even on the ceiling. I bent down and touched it, tasted it. Dry, brownish, and stale. At least a day old. A door to my left that was marked "WC."

I eased it open.

This, presumably, was the Scottish student.

A good-looking blond-haired boy about twenty-one or twenty-two still wearing his pajamas. His hands were coarsely bound behind his back with a dressing-gown tie. He'd been shot twice in the head. The first bullet in the back of the neck had killed him. After he'd fallen dead into the shower unit, they'd shot him again right down on the top of his skull just to be sure. They'd done it with a nasty big-caliber weapon. If I hadn't known for a fact that they'd used a silencer, I would have guessed a pump-action shotgun because the kid's face was hanging off his head and his brains, blood, and bits of skull were everywhere over the tiny bathroom.

I nodded, walked back into the hall, put away the .38. No one was alive in here. They'd seen to that. Execution style.

The forward cabin.

A body wedged against the door. Carefully I nudged it ajar.

A broken mirror, bloody bedsheets, and a redheaded girl sprawled facedown on the floor with her throat cut.

"Oh, my God, Siobhan," I said.

My legs weakened.

I bent down, gently turned her over.

It wasn't her.

It was a boy. A slender youth with hippie-length red hair. His forehead had been smashed in with a heavy object, a baseball bat or a hammer. They'd done this several times and then they'd cut his throat.

This was Barry, without a doubt.

I stood.

"Poor wee fuck, should have stuck to your photos and your small-time Mary Jane," I said to myself.

I searched the rest of the forward cabin but there were no more bodies. And the guys who had done this wouldn't have left any evidence.

I stepped over Barry's corpse, avoided looking at the dead Scot, and did a scout of the central cabin. Finally I went to that back door and checked the bilges and the engine room.

She wasn't here. No Siobhan.

Not even a trace of her.

I climbed the ladder and closed the cabin door. I opened the window and sat down at the boys' table.

Barry's job had been to win her confidence and get her out of the center of town. But he hadn't been the one that had lifted her. I doubted that she'd ever even been here. He'd charmed her, won her over, walked her away from the bright lights and the cops and Bridget's goons. Down some alley and then the real kidnappers had bundled her into a van.

They let Barry go home with his dough and then they'd come after him to make sure he kept his fucking mouth shut.

"Well, that's that."

I almost took a sip of two-day-old coffee to get the taste of blood out of my mouth.

I had to be a hundred-percent positive before I left. . . .

I braved the stench and went back downstairs, doing a final and complete search just to be sure, but there were no smugglers' bulkheads or secret compartments or hidey-holes filled with kidnapped girls.

But she wasn't here. She'd never been here. That wasn't the plan.

Two bodies, buckets of blood, flies.

A complete dead end. No goddamn pun intended.

I sighed, climbed out onto the deck, took a deep breath.

"Fantastic," I said, and to add to my joy, now the cops were coming. Four of them. Waddling along the Lagan path without a care in the world, chatting away.

Have to deal with those bastards and that will eat up a lot of precious time. That eejit called the peelers even after I told him.

"Shit," I muttered and ducked back inside the boat. Maybe there was a way of avoiding them. Could I make it off the vessel without being seen? The peelers arrived at Donald's boat. The dog began barking. Donald pointed at the *Ginger Bap*.

"Damn."

No, there was no way out.

Not unless I jumped into the Lagan and swam for it and then they'd think I was involved and probably plug me.

Reluctantly, I climbed back out onto the deck and I waved at the cops to pedal their slow arses over here and get things bloody moving.

❋   ❋   ❋

Four cops, one a woman. The lead with a big graying Zapata mustache. All of them in shirtsleeves, but only the lass wearing her bulletproof vest. Nice-looking bit of stuff too, from this distance. Pert nose, cute figure, and blond hair almost hidden under her hat.

"Who are you?" the lead copper yells at me as if I'm a football hooligan messing about on the terraces.

I pick up a forget-me-not that has floated onto the deck. I sniff it.

"Get off that boat," he shouts.

I do not reply. I don't respond well to hectoring. Especially not from a bloody cop. Let the bastard come over and talk to me like a civilized person.

"Hey, did you fucking hear me there, pal?" Zapata tries again.

I hope he sees my ironic grin. I mean, I know two people have been murdered and it's a pretty serious situation. But even so there's no need for coarseness or incivility.

In my day the police had been called the Royal Ulster Constabulary and were a largely white male Protestant force. After the Patten Report their name had been changed first to the Northern Ireland Police Service, which had an unfortunate acronym, and then to the Police Service of Northern Ireland. Supposedly, now they are less white, less male, less Prod, and more responsive to the public.

Old habits, however, clearly die hard.

I sit down on the deck and dangle my legs over the side.

I'd be smoking if I had a cigarette.

The lead cop decides to pretend I'm not there. That's how his authority will survive my disobedience of his direct order. I see it as a small victory for the general public. Bloody cops. I lean my head back against the cabin behind me.

Blink.

And then there's something I miss.

The stiffening of the air. A sudden tension. Violent thoughts leaking into the atmosphere.

For the last ten years I've been a wanted man. Hyperaware. Able to take in everything within my field of vision. Able to siphon out the chatter from the real data. Able to see what is relevant and what is not. Whether people are potential threats or harmless individuals going about their lives. Unlike Bridget, I haven't had bodyguards, armored cars, lackeys. It has kept me cautious, suspicious, paranoid. It has kept me alive. I'm always looking for the assassin carrying the handgun under the bunch of flowers.

Bridget, however, has changed things.

She has given me an escape from that kind of thinking. Away from that life: if you find Siobhan the slate is wiped. You're clean. Safe.

The killers will be withdrawn. You don't have to sit next to the wall at the back of the bar. You don't have to count the exits and memorize them. You don't have to move house every single year. You can live like a normal man again.

An attractive proposition.

It would be nice to sit outside in a café, it would be nice to day-dream, to let people come and go.

And with these thoughts ebbing into my consciousness, it could be that my guard has fallen a little. The promise of that. That little chink of hope.

And perhaps that's why I don't see the van drive up an alley be-tween the apartment complexes. Maybe that's why I don't notice the two men in ski masks getting slowly out.

The chugging of a river barge, birds, clouds, footsteps. Feedback through the police radios.

A midge lands on me and begins sucking my blood.

My mind preparing the talking points. I'm a private investigator working for Bridget Callaghan. I got a tip-off about a man called Barry who lived on a boat called the *Ginger Bap*. I came here to check him out, the lock on the cabin was already broken, so I went down and I found these bodies. I told Donnie over there to call you guys. Don't worry, I'm a professional, I didn't touch a thing.

Aye, that'll do.

As they come closer, the air is so inert I can hear their entire te-dious cop conversation. Zapata is talking about the decline of modern music.

"All just a beat and a backing track. No bloody talent needed for that. I remember when you could actually hear tunes and there were decent lyrics."

"What are you going on about, there are A1 bands about these days, so there are. Fact is, you never listen to anything but the bloody

Beatles. Love me bloody do, for Chrissake," one of the other cops replies.

"Load of shite; tell ya, boy, I know more about it than you and your Downtown Radio country special. Garth Brooks and all that oul shite."

The midge continues sucking my arm. Only the female of the biting species of midge eat blood. They need fats and protein to make eggs. Sperm is cheap. I let her get on with it. The cops are nearly over.

I stand.

"You were talking about rap a minute ago. Now what are you whittering on about? You should listen to modern stuff sometime, PJ Harvey or the White Stripes."

"Same oul balls."

"Gentlemen, please," the woman says, mocking them.

"I used to be in a band, drummer in a three-piece," the peeler who hasn't spoken yet begins, but before anyone can say anything more, the rocket-propelled grenade aimed at me explodes ten feet short of the boat, right in front of the four cops.

Disastrous noise.

A clenched light-cone warning a second before the hail.

I literally hit the deck.

Talk, invective, all sucked away and burned in the air, like a record scraping off.

A civilian would perhaps have been killed by the explosion. The cops, even lulled as they are, still have a fast reaction-response time. The white flash of the blast gives them an instant to get down. An instant, it is hardly quantifiable. The time it takes for me in free fall to clatter to the wood. Three of the cops even get hands up to their faces before the shock wave rains debris and fire over their bodies and blows out four pairs of eardrums. The monstrous sound is metal twisting and advanced chemical morphology. An ammonia flare of Soviet-made fire, a smell like chaff igniting.

The shock wave rocks the boat and slides me across the deck right onto the port side.

The guy that fired the RPG on the embankment sees that he's short and hurriedly begins to load another grenade. And now I notice him, when it's too bloody late. And there's a comrade next to him with some kind of heavy machine gun.

The grenade attached, the shooter gets down on one knee and aims at the boat, at me, not at the cops. So this isn't an attack on the peelers by the IRA or a Republican faction, this a hit on yours truly.

The grenade launches, flies through the air in an instant, and hits the stern of the *Ginger Bap*.

A terrifying rip of noise and flame, the entire fiberglass rear of the boat exploding into pieces. This time I'm not quite so lucky. I'm thrown against the safety rail on the starboard side, the metal supports scouring into my back, the plastic rail gouging into my shoulder. I lie there stunned for a second and then I'm drenched in burning fiberglass.

I lose consciousness for a moment.

Blackness.

Pain.

Light.

Fingers. Arms. Pelvis. Stomach. Chest. Shoulder blades. Neck and head.

Motion? Yes.

A verb. Yes. A verb in my mouth.

Lips back. Tongue spit. Air migrating through my voice box. "Help."

I try to sit up. I brush the burning embers off my body.

The peelers are hit too. Kevlar flak jackets kindling in the afternoon air. Hair and skin burning. Blood pouring out onto the swept street from unspecified multiple wounds. The blast echoing off the embankment like timpani fading diminuendo.

"Jesus Christ Almighty," I mutter in disbelief. "What the—"

A crater where the rear hull of the boat had been and a rain of fragments.

I'm alive. Singed, but in one piece. The boat is sinking. The RPG man is preparing his third grenade.

Get overboard, Michael.

I try to move. Stuck. Pinned. Huge chunks of what looks like the cabin roof lying on my legs. I start pushing them off.

Look up.

The RPG man: still trying to load the grenade. The coppers: the first hit got them bad. It seems to me, though, that no one is actually dead. At least not yet. One of the boys has lost his shoe and by the looks of it a couple of toes. White-hot pieces of shrapnel embedded in the others—wound marks on their arms and legs. All of them yelling. Shouting into their radios. The young policewoman screaming about her shoulder. Something red sticking out of her uniform. Their words melded together in a patter of confusion. Crackled voices speaking back, telling them help is on the way.

The woman cop's hat floats down among the smoldering flakes of metal confetti and lands burning on the deck, where other fragments have been dumped by the explosion.

In the split second between grenade launches and while I'm attempting to get the cabin roof off my legs I'm oddly fascinated by her. With her hat gone she looks like a person now. Her bob of yellow hair lying in a divot of rainwater, a scarlet trail oozing into the blond from a laceration on her scalp. She's dazed and flailing, but now she's doing the only sensible thing of the five of us.

She's going for her gun.

What a damn fine idea.

I stop kicking the cabin roof and pull out the .38. I level it with a steady hand and take a shot at the grenade launcher.

He's fifty yards off and it looks like I'm not even going to be close, but at least I won't be alone. Blondie, with blood in her eyes and a hurt hand, somehow gets to a kneeling position and starts shooting her Glock 9mm semiautomatic.

"Die, you fuckers, die," she screams.

She fires nine shots, I fire six, all of them missing.

We start to reload.

"Get here, right now," Blondie barks into her radio, while slotting another clip into the Glock. One of the front peelers, with gray hair and nearest the boat, has clearly been flash-blinded, standing up, staggering in front of me with his hands over his eyes. I nearly shoot him by accident, but neither Blondie nor I have hit anything and now RPG man has got the third grenade in the bloody launcher.

I put him between the sights.

One round, two rounds, three rounds, six rounds. Every one a miss.

Flip chamber, punch ejector, reload out of the bag in my pocket.

Blondie has her 9mm ready. She holds it in both hands, patiently squeezes the trigger, and hits the van next to RPG man just as he fires the weapon. It makes him jump, the grenade arcs high into the air and drops harmlessly into the Lagan without even exploding.

The boat is tilting backward now, beginning to founder. We're inclined thirty degrees off the vertical and the roof fragments start sliding off my legs by themselves. Help them with a kick and a shove.

Obviously that's it for the grenades because RPG man turns to his mate and starts taking ammo from a box. His buddy is a skinny figure, but he must be strong because I see that what he's holding is an old army-issue general-purpose machine gun. A GPMG or Jimpy, as we used to call 'em back in the service—an ugly belt-fed weapon that makes up in punch for what it loses in accuracy. Two-man operation. One shoots, the other feeds the belt. 7.62-millimeter slugs that'll come at you at 550 rounds a minute.

These boys don't have much experience with it because it takes them a long time to clear the breach. But then they do and when it gets going the Jimpy sings as bullets flow through the belt and spray over the embankment, the path, the river, and the boat. The shots random at first but gradually zeroing on the sinking *Ginger Bap*.

Shell casings pumping out of the gun and fast-moving rounds tearing up the tarmac.

"Shit."

You're supposed to fire it from a tripod but these guys have clearly seen too many 'Nam movies, where the old M60 got used in close-order action.

I stop reloading and lie down flat on the deck.

Jimpy rounds slicing into the *Bap*'s hull like a BB into butter.

Only way out, over the side.

I crawl backward for the safety rail and know that I'm not going to make it.

But I don't need to. Blondie has her wits about her. She's not fazed. One knee, balanced, two hands, aiming very carefully at the shooter. She fires off four shots, all four hitting the machine gunner in the chest, killing him instantly.

His partner yells something, picks up the Jimpy, and tries to fire it single-handed. No chance. He burns himself on the stock and in the afternoon murk I watch the tracer sailing harmlessly overhead like fireflies on the river.

A one-sided gun battle ensues.

The hood can't work the machine gun and I'm shooting at him, Blondie's shooting at him, and finally beside her Zapata pulls out an enormous Model 500 Smith & Wesson .50-caliber handgun. His bullets cross the dead ground toward the machine gunner in huge resounding whomps that would put the fear of God into anyone who wasn't shooting back from an Apache helicopter.

A third cop joins the fray lying on his back firing with his left hand, his shots wild, but it's all more than enough to draw the machine gunner's attention away from me for good.

"Fucking pigs," he screams and tries to lower the Jimpy sufficiently to get an angle on the peelers.

He doesn't know what he's doing, and even if he did, he can't handle a gun like that by himself. In desperation he crouches low, balancing the gun on his knee, but the inevitable overheating happens, the weapon seizes and instantly bucks away from him.

He pulls out a revolver, shoots off a couple of slugs, drops the gun, runs for the van.

"Come back, you son of a bitch," the policewoman yells, fires the last round in her clip and it bloody hits him, knocking him to the ground.

Good on ya, love.

"Cease fire," Zapata yells.

And the silence is worse than the noise.

A dozen car alarms, ducks clacking, coppers moaning. Above us an army observation helicopter that has seen the whole thing. It's unarmed, so it's not as if they could have helped but even so, bastards.

I take it all in in a split second: The flash-blinded peeler sitting down, Blondie and Zapata looking for a tourniquet for their other colleague, way down the river a police Land Rover tearing along the Lagan path, and up on the embankment RPG man getting awkwardly to his feet and making a shambling run for it.

Time for me to go.

❖   ❖   ❖

No point pissing about. The boat with a forty-five-degree list that was rapidly becoming a right angle. I crawled across the deck to the edge of the rail. The .38 slipped out of my hand and clattered down toward the cabin. Almost vertical now. Foolish to go after it. I'd be in for a dunking or worse. I climbed through the safety rail, sat on the edge of the *Ginger Bap,* and, like a big white rat, jumped off the sinking ship and landed on one of the fenders.

I pulled myself up onto the Lagan path, walked over to the coppers. "Everybody ok?"

Zapata was sitting up. The woman standing. The others in agony, shrapnel making them feel like they were pincushions. I didn't see anyone dying, though. I bent down to adjust the straps on my prosthesis.

"Who the fuck are you?" Zapata asked.

"I'm from America. FBI. Going after that guy," I said.

"What guy?"

"The guy who fired the RPG is hit but he's running," I had to explain so they didn't bloody shoot at me when I legged it.

That was all I had to say. Zapata nodded, bought it.

"Just for the record, I think they were trying to kill me, not you. You were merely in the wrong place at the wrong time," I said and ran up the embankment after Mr. RPG.

I stopped for a quarter of a second at the place where they'd done the hit. The Jimpy was seething, the van was peppered with bullet holes and had two flat tires. A blood trail led down the alley. I was right, Blondie had hit him. A goddamn markswoman, that lass. She had killed the Jimpy guy and plugged this character, too.

In other circumstances, I would have gone back and proposed.

I followed the trail behind the first of the condo buildings, lost it on the pavement, and found it at a rusting yellow trash compactor where he'd paused for a second, leaning on it, getting a breather and revealing his position with his bloody paws.

He'd turned left and continued running along this street, which was parallel to the Lagan.

Worried me. If he kept going straight, eventually this road led out of these bankside condo developments and into a feeder road for the city. Once he was on that he could lose himself in the crowds.

He had a big lead, but he was hit bad and I was angry.

The blood drops closer now.

He was moving slower.

Two feet between drops.

Then one foot.

Then six inches.

I was near. I turned a corner. The trail led between two large apartment buildings and abruptly stopped.

Had he climbed into a getaway car? No way. They had come in that damn van and the van was still parked along the embankment.

I scanned the alley.

Concrete walls. No doors leading into the apartment buildings and no obvious hiding places like trash bins or a skip. I ran to the end of the street.

A field, a piece of waste ground, and one of the main roads.

Shit. I'd bloody lost him? It didn't make sense. Who brings two getaway cars to a hit?

I searched the alley again.

The condo complexes on either side of the alley were identical three-story-high apartment buildings with balconies. No doors on the ground-floor flats, and the windows that I could see were closed.

People don't just vanish.

Maybe he'd taken a moment, patched himself up, and run to the waste ground. I sprinted to the bottom of the alley again, but there appeared to be no one in that featureless cinder track. He could be hiding under a bunch of newspapers or garbage, but I didn't think so. He was back here somewhere.

I examined the ground-floor apartment windows and saw that not only were they not open, but they didn't open.

The only other possibility was that he might just have had the strength to climb up onto one of the second-floor balconies. I went to the nearest one and examined it closely. Nothing. The next one.

And what was that? A speck of red on the balcony rail. I smiled. Blood. Fresh blood.

With a heroic effort of will he had somehow climbed up there. Bullet wound or no bullet wound. I stepped back and surveyed the balcony. The door to the apartment was shut. I couldn't tell if it was locked but I guessed it was. The lights were off and no one was home, and if you lived on the second floor it would probably be sensible to lock the balcony door.

My hunch was that he was still crouching up there, lying behind the concrete balcony walls, breathing hard, listening to me, hoping that eventually I would give it up as a bad job and piss off home.

"I'll give you five seconds to stand up and then I'm throwing the hand grenade onto that balcony. Five, four, three, two—"

He stood.

He'd lost the ski mask. Bald guy, forties, gray face, gut. One of the old-timers. Reliable, he was rusty with the RPG, but it hadn't been the first time he'd fired the weapon. I'm sure he'd knocked over quite a few Land Rovers in his time. His hair was singed from the back flare on the weapon and his denim jacket at the shoulder was ripped open. I faked holding the grenade in my hand.

"Get those hands up," I said.

He put his hands over his head.

"Get down from there," I ordered.

"I can't get down, I'm hurt," he whined.

"All right, I've had enough of you, try to kill me, would ya. I'll blow your fucking head off."

"Wait, wait, wait."

Gingerly, he tested his weight on the balcony rail. He leaned his stomach on the edge, toppled over, and dropped to the ground. I saw now that the woman peeler had hit him on the buttocks or lower back. It was, in fact, only a glancing wound, but still, he'd been a moving target, a good hundred feet away, got to give her credit.

And yeah, he'd really messed up his shoulder from firing the rocket-propelled grenade. Torn jacket, lot of blood.

He tried to stand, so I belted him on the side of the face. He skidded into a wall and fell down sideways into a gutter. An empty revolver tumbled out of his inside jacket pocket. As luck would have it, a .38. See, that's why you get a PC over a Mac. They're shitty, but the bastards are everywhere.

I picked up the revolver, checked the chamber—seemed clean enough. I pulled six rounds out of my pocket and loaded the gun. I waggled it at him.

"Ok, now we talk," I said.

Two stories up a man opened a window in one of the yuppie flats and looked out.

"What the bloody hell is going on down there?" he shouted in a Scottish accent.

"He's trying to kill me," the RPG man said.

"You say another word and you're a dead man," I muttered sotto voce and then to the yuppie: "Michael Forsythe, CID, this man has just attacked four police officers, I'm arresting him."

"Perhaps I could see your identification?" the canny Scot demanded.

I pointed the gun at him.

"Get the fuck back in your fucking flat before I arrest you for obstruction of justice. If you're nervous, mate, call the bloody cops," I shouted back. He ducked his head inside and closed the window.

I turned the gun on RPG again.

"Ok, you, on your knees, hands behind your head. One move and it's tea and crumpets with Beelzebub."

He knelt. I did a quick pat down. I took the wallet from his back pocket. Five hundred quid and a driving license that said he was called Jimmy Walker. I kept the money and put the wallet back in his pocket.

I squatted down next to Jimmy, smiled at him, and smacked him in the ear with the butt of my revolver. He hit the ground.

"God," he screamed.

"Who do you work for?" I demanded.

He kept his trap shut. I kicked him in the wound on his arse.

"Jesus Christ," he gasped.

"Who do you work for?" I asked again.

"I work for Body O'Neill."

"Who's that?"

"Bloody hell, where are you from?"

"Who is it?"

"Commander Belfast Brigade IRA," Jimmy said.

"You weren't going for the cops, were you? It was me, wasn't it?"

"Of course it was you," he said.

"Why me? Why the hit? What did I ever do to Body O'Neill?"

"I don't know. I do what I'm told."

"What did O'Neill say I'd done?"

"I don't fucking know. We were told to hit you, that's all."

"Why an RPG, bit excessive, no?"

"O'Neill said you were hard to fucking kill, he said you were slippery. He told us that we had to use overwhelming force. Sammy said you were the guy who had killed Darkey White years ago and had survived a couple of hits. He said we should fire a bloody antitank rocket at ya. See you survive that. Then we got the idea of the RPG."

"Who's Sammy?"

"My partner."

"On the Jimpy?"

"Aye, is he—"

"The woman cop killed him. When did you get the order to hit me? Last night?"

"Are you joking? Like forty-five minutes ago," he said, surprised.

"What did they tell you?"

"They said you were going to be at this boat called the *Ginger Bap,* one of the Lagan boats. Said we had to do it right now."

"And Sammy and you had access to an RPG?"

"Yeah, Sammy and me learned how to fire one years back in Libya. We set it up when we saw you on the boat, but we nearly called it off because of the cops."

"Aye. Cops'll think you tried to hit them, won't they? You may have jeopardized the entire fucking cease-fire. Well done."

"We weren't breaking the cease-fire, we were just trying to top you, you bastard," he said defensively.

I sighed, shook my head. I would have liked to have killed him but as a public service I was going to have to let him live. If I shot the fucker then the peelers and the army and the British government might think this attack on four police officers represented a serious breach of the Republican cease-fire. It might mean a redeployment of the army on the streets and a rearrest of remand prisoners. That in turn might lead to a spiral of retaliatory violence. The Loyalists would probably respond with their own assault on a Catholic bar or something, a retaliation for that would be forthcoming, and who the hell knows, it might mean the start of a summer of slaughter.

So, as a good deed for my fellowmen I couldn't kill this character. I had to let him live and tell the cops that no, he wasn't aiming an RPG at them, but in fact was after a man called Michael Forsythe.

"One last time, you have no idea why me?" I asked.

"I told you, I don't know."

"They didn't give you a fucking reason?"

"We didn't have the time for that. They said that this was a time-imperative op and we had to get cracking. They knew you were going to the boat, but didn't know where you'd go after. Had to hit you there."

"Ok. I suppose I'll have to talk to your boss. Where's he?"

"I'm not going to tell you that."

"No?"

"No."

I stood, reloaded the .38, put my Stanley boot on his left hand, took very careful aim, and shot his thumb off.

He screamed, rolled on the ground, and tried to crawl away from me. I kicked him in the stomach, knocking the wind out of him. I picked up the bloody thumb and knelt beside him.

"Now listen here, mate. Give you a choice. I'll put this here thumb in your pocket and maybe the surgeons at the Royal can sew it back on. Maybe not, but at least you'll have a chance. Otherwise I'm going to shoot your other thumb off and I'll take both with me. How does that sound?"

"You fucker, you fucking fucker," he managed between gasps of pain.

"Hey, maybe I'll shoot your balls off too, what do you think?" I said breezily.

"What do you want?"

"Well, let's take it slow. Sure O'Neill ordered the hit?"

"Yes."

"And where would I find him right now?"

"Right now, he'll be in the Linen Hall Library," he said.

"You're kidding me?"

"Linen Hall, I swear it's true. He goes there from two to five every single weekday like clockwork. Upstairs in the reading room. He's writing a book. I think it's his reflections or something."

"Better not be yanking me, Jimmy."

"I'm not, I swear to God," Jimmy said.

It was an unlikely place to find a commander of the Belfast Brigade of the IRA, but it was an unlikely place to make up out of the blue. I believed him.

I threw the thumb down beside him and as a further public service—to prevent him running away before the cops showed up—I clobbered him on the head.

I ran between the buildings until I came to the main road.

I wasn't entirely sure of my bearings, but then I saw the gleaming dome of the city hall. The Linen Hall Library wasn't too far from that, I seemed to remember.

"Onward and upward," I said and jogged toward the center of town.

I didn't know what I'd done to annoy Body O'Neill, to make him send assassins to Dublin to get me, to make him risk the cease-fire, but I was going to find out. I had a job to do and I didn't have time for subplots.

8: SCYLLA AND CHARYBDIS (BELFAST—JUNE 16, 6:00 P.M.)

He had finally gotten my attention. Having failed to kill me three times in half a day, each time a little more spectacularly, I knew I had to sort him out before I did anything else. Body O'Neill, whom I'd never even heard of before. Belfast Commander of the IRA.

Probably Darkey White's long-lost brother. Or Bridget Callaghan's tragic lover. Or a kid I used to bully in primary school. It would be something stupid. And if I had to murder the son of a bitch so he'd leave me alone, then so be it.

I wasn't exactly sure where the Linen Hall Library was, but everybody else in Belfast was, so I was there pretty sharpish.

An attractive, dark, squarish building near the city hall with a bunch of people outside standing around a stall that was selling books, bootleg videos, and "comedic" singing fish.

"Get your copy of *Star Wars: Episode III*, the final film in the series, release date May of next year," a hawker called out.

"Is this the entrance to the Linen Hall Library?" I asked him pointing at a pokey wee door.

"Aye, up the stairs. You want to see the new *Star Wars*? It's got wookies in it."

I ignored him and entered the building. An old concierge sitting at a desk. Behind him a glass door that led up the stairs to the library.

"Evening," I said, walked past the desk, and tried the handle on the glass door.

"See your card," the concierge said.

"I don't have a card."

"No card, no admittance."

He was one of those sons of bitches who had spent their entire lives thwarting the interests of people like me. Sleekit wee bureaucrat. It had made him shriveled, small and boney. He looked half dead under a peaked security guard's hat.

"Listen, I need in to the library," I said.

"Well, you can't get in without a card. You'll have to get a card."

"I don't want a card, I just want to see somebody up in the reading room. I don't need to join or anything."

"I cannot let you in without a card," he insisted.

"This is ridiculous, I just need to see somebody in the bloody reading room."

"Well, you'll have to go through me," he said, eerily echoing the extremely violent thoughts that I was having that very moment. Let's see, shoot the bastard, break through the door, run upstairs . . .

But that was a crazy idea. This was the center of Belfast, the cops would be here in two minutes. And besides, a gunshot down here would send everyone upstairs into a panic. Give O'Neill a chance to run for cover.

"Can I send a message up to someone in the reading room? It's quite urgent."

The concierge thought about it for a moment.

"Shall I send Miss Plum down to see ya?" he asked.

"Miss Plum from the library?"

"Yes."

"Aye, and get Colonel Mustard with the lead pipe as well," I said. "What?"

"Please get her, it's quite urgent, it's a matter of life and death," I said solemnly.

He raised an eyebrow and picked up the phone.

"Miss Plum, yes, it's Cochrane. I've got a young man here who wants to get in to the library. He says it's very urgent. Could you see your way to coming down here with a temporary card at all?"

Apparently Miss Plum said yes.

"She's coming right down," Cochrane told me.

I tapped my foot on the floor. I was bristling with anger and impatience. I had to deal with O'Neill right now while my blood was up. I had to know why he had been trying to kill me ever since I had arrived in this fucking country, and I had to put a bloody stop to it. Three attacks in one day: that was miles better than even Bridget's record. And holy mother of God, now they'd even taken to sinking ships in order to nail me. What would be next? Aerial bombing? Anthrax?

Aye, well, we'd see O'Neill about that.

But there was another reason for seeing him too.

Something that had been nagging me since I'd been in the Rat's Nest, and had become apparent on the *Ginger Bap*.

Something Seamus Deasey had said. Outside the pub, when he had told me Barry's name and the fact he lived on a boat on the Lagan, Seamus had slipped in a boast that having Barry's name and address wouldn't do me any good. At the time I hadn't even considered it, but now it seemed that Seamus had known that Barry was already dead. Seamus knew that Barry had been murdered.

How?

Unless he was the all comers' lying champion of Sicily five years in a row, I didn't think he was stroking me. When I'd looked in Seamus's eyes, he seemed to have no knowledge whatsoever of the kidnap. I think the word *kidnap* even surprised him: he thought wee Siobhan was still missing. And he was genuinely shocked when I'd suggested that one of his boys might be involved.

I could be wrong, though. He could be in it up to his eyeballs and I might have missed the one chance to break the case wide open. Would have been easy: kidnap Seamus, take him to a wee hidey-hole, and get cracking with my experimental interrogation techniques. But nah, even then I don't think he would have fessed up to knowing anything about Siobhan Callaghan.

So where did that leave things?

It meant Seamus didn't know why Barry had been killed, but he knew that he was dead. And thinking back, I'm no crime-scene expert but I don't think Barry's corpse had been disturbed. Donald hadn't seen anyone go on board the *Ginger Bap* and that lock looked untouched since the murderers had jury-rigged it.

Since no one had messed with the scene, the only way Seamus could have known about Barry's murder was if something had leaked out about it, or he had heard some word on the street, or perhaps the murderer had actually asked for Seamus's permission to kill his boy. If he'd been a Belfast assassin, he probably would have had to do that. You don't go around whacking members of other people's crews, be they capo, soldier, or lowly drug dealer, without getting the ok from on high. 'Course, if the hit men were from abroad, London or Dublin, say, then it wouldn't matter, but a Belfast-based assassin would have had to get a permission slip. Oh, you'd maybe explain that Barry had raped your sister or insulted your granny or some such shite like that. You'd give Seamus a couple of grand blood money and he'd be happy enough.

It was pure speculation. But the more I thought about it, the more I was reasonably certain that Seamus had not only known that Barry was dead but that he had a fair idea who'd been involved in it. Following my little stunt in the Rat's Nest, I wouldn't be able to get within a million miles of Seamus, but Body O'Neill was one floor above me. One minute up the stairs. For if Body O'Neill was the commander of the IRA in Belfast, it meant he was Seamus Deasey's superior. O'Neill could order Seamus to tell me what he knew about young Barry. All it would take would be a sufficiently persuasive argument to convince O'Neill of the justice of my cause.

Maybe a Belfast six-pack would do the trick.

But certainly he could solve a lot of the questions that were troubling me. And I was damn well going to get the information I bloody needed about the hits on me and everything else I wanted to know.

I looked at the concierge.

"She's taking her time, isn't she?"

He nodded awkwardly.

"Know much about the library?" he asked.

"Not really," I said with the sinking feeling that he was going to tell me.

"When the Luftwaffe bombed Belfast in '42, the military target was the docks and the shipyard but Göring instructed several Heinkel 111s to hit cultural and civic targets, and among those were the city hall and the Linen Hall Library."

"Is that a fact?"

"Thousands died but the incident doesn't even merit a mention in most histories of World War—"

"Shocking."

"And did you further know—"

I had to interrupt.

"Look, I'm sorry to be rude, but you wouldn't mind paging Miss Plum again, would you?"

He paged her.

"Miss Plum, that gentleman is in quite a rush to get in," he said into the speakerphone.

"It's not André with the lobsters, is it?" Miss Plum's voice replied.

The concierge looked at me.

"You're not André with the lobsters, are you?"

My knuckles whitened.

"Do you see any lobsters?"

"It's not André, Miss Plum," the concierge said.

"But it is very urgent," I said into the intercom.

"I'll be right down," she said.

"Great."

Eventually, after I'd endured more tedious tales of the library's fascinating history, Miss Plum's legs appeared at the top of the stairs.

She opened the glass door and came out to meet me.

A chubby, red-faced Kate Winslet type, brown eyes, tight skirt, pert, snarky mouth.

"Hello," she said.

"Hi, look, I have an urgent message for a Mr. O'Neill upstairs."

"Oh?"

"Yes, do you know Mr. O'Neill? Is he here today?"

"He's here," she said.

"Well, I wonder if you might let me up to see him."

"I'm afraid that's not possible. You'll have to join the library to get in, at the very least you'll have to get a temporary card. Oh, don't get so worried. You just have to fill out a few forms, provide proof of residence," she said, looking with displeasure at the burnt fiberglass that had stuck to my leather jacket.

"Please, I'm in a big rush, I don't have time for forms, I really just need to see him," I said. I didn't have time for bloody paperwork, and it was years since I could produce any proof of Belfast residence.

"I'm sorry, it's the policy, this is a very select institution," Miss Plum said with a winning smile.

She was a charming girl and in general I avoid killing women, but I was right on the goddamn edge here.

"Ok, look, Miss Plum, what's your first name?"

"Jane," she said with a tiny sniff of suspicion.

"Look, Jane, first let me say I completely understand the policy. Very sensible, keep out the riffraff. Second of all, let me compliment you on your style, appearance, and professionalism. Has anyone ever told you that you resemble a thin Kate Winslet? You have an extraordinary skin tone. If you ever want a job with the Olay people, look me up, my cousin's the vice president. But this is an emergency. Mr. O'Neill's mother is dying. He's turned off his cell phone and I just need to see him, to let him know, so he can rush to her side for the final moments. The priest has already read the last rites, we all believe she'll pass within the hour."

"His mother?" Jane said, shocked.

"Yes, his poor wee mother," I said, staring off into the middle distance.

"Bloody hell, she must be over a hundred," the concierge said.

"O'Neill's an elderly gentleman then, is he?" I thought but somehow also said aloud.

"Oh aye, he's well into his seventies," Jane said.

"Well, I'm just the messenger," I said, a bit thrown.

"His poor old ma, she's probably in the *Guinness Book of Records* or something," the concierge mused.

"Could be," I began hesitantly. "But the information I have is that she's on her last legs. Could I just go up and let him know? It really is at a matter of life and death, surely you can make an exception for that?"

I smiled at her and placed my hands in a pleading gesture.

"Well, it's not really the done thing. . . ."

Thank Christ, I thought, and followed her up the stairs.

I was in such a hurry now that I didn't even admire her bum waggling from side to side as it rose up the marble steps.

The reading room was a charming little affair, with old book tables, neat shelves, and a tidy Georgian appearance. Various oddball types reading magazines, newspapers, and books. The more stereotypical iron-faced librarians, with horn-rimmed glasses and a capacity for unspeakable deeds, patrolled the reference area, enforcing the strict rules on silence, shelving, and pencils only.

"That's him sitting at the alcove behind the window seat," Jane said.

"I don't see him."

"That's because he's in the corner, in the alcove."

"Ok, yeah, that's the top of his bald head, is it?"

"Uh-huh."

"Thanks very much," I said.

"Now please, try hard not to cause a disturbance," she said.

"Oh, don't worry, love, disturbances are not my thing at all."

I thanked her and walked to the corner alcove. The most secure spot in the whole place. Walls on three sides, near the emergency exit, but his one mistake—he had shifted his chair around so that he could get more light on his book from the alcove window. Silly old fool. Now his back was to the entrance. Anybody could just walk over.

I watched him for five minutes to check for goons. Really should have been a couple of hours, but time was of the essence. No one that I saw. No one that wasn't born before World War I, anyway.

I stood next to him.

A bald, wizened seventy-year-old, with a bit of a Parkinson shake, round reading glasses, and a wispy beard. Depressingly, this scholarly looking gent, who apparently was one of the most feared paramilitary commanders in Belfast, was also dressed in leisure wear: a white UCLA sweatshirt and black jeans. I checked that no one was paying attention and removed the .38.

"Body O'Neill?"

He looked up.

I pointed the revolver at him, real close so that he could see it through those thick lenses.

"Yes?"

"I want to ask you some questions."

"Who are you?"

"Michael Forsythe," I said.

Mild surprise in his watery yellow eyes.

"Ahh, I see, Michael Forsythe. For some reason I thought you might be dead by now," he said.

"You know, funnily enough, that's what I want to talk to you about," I said, winking at him.

He smiled, stroked his limpid cheeks, looked around the room.

"Sit," he suggested.

"Why not?"

I sat beside him.

"You don't mind if I just check you for a gun?" I said.

"I would rather you didn't touch me. I assure you, I am unarmed," he said.

"Well, just to be on the safe side," I said and patted him down. He did not have a gun, which was a bit odd, but there was a little lump under the *L* in UCLA.

"What's that? A pacemaker?" I asked.

"I asked you not to touch me," he said, embarrassed.

"Yes, but I have the gun," I explained.

He frowned, looked around the room.

"You know why I like this place?" O'Neill said.

"What place, the city?"

"No, the library," he said.

"No, why?"

"It's eclectic. Postmen, dockers, students, everyone. You can bump into Seamus Heaney, and occasionally you'll see Gerry Adams in here researching his so-called memoirs."

"Now listen to me, O'Neill. I'm sure you're just fabulous at playing for time, but I have a whole series of questions and my patience is already stretched very thin."

"You have questions for me?"

"Yes, I bloody do. First, why have you been trying to kill me since Dublin?"

O'Neill regarded me with some distaste, not fear, but rather a condescending scowl that verged on utter contempt. I wasn't going to let the old bat intimidate me. I *was* holding the gun, after all. I leaned back in the chair and rested the revolver on the book he'd been reading. I closed it with the barrel, aggressively snapping it shut.

"Better start talking, O'Neill," I said with menace.

"The interview form is not one I enjoy, Mr. Forsythe. Question-and-answer is such a barbaric manner of discourse. If you have any questions, you should probably take them up with Mikhail."

"And who the fuck is Mikhail?"

"I'm Mikhail," Mikhail said, thumping my hand with a knuckle duster and removing the revolver from my grip in a fast, continuous motion. I winced and turned. Mikhail was a six-foot-six Neanderthal. Shaven head, narrow Mongolian eyes. Clearly the bloody bodyguard, fresh in from slaughtering insurgents in Chechnya.

My hand was killing me. Mikhail shoved a snub-nosed silenced .22 automatic into my ribs. He passed his boss my .38.

"We don't want a scene, Mr. Forsythe, but Mikhail will kill you stone dead if you say another harsh word," O'Neill said quietly.

"Kill me in front of all these witnesses?" I asked.

"What witnesses? No one will hear a thing and we'll shove you under the alcove desk and walk straight out of here. No one will find you until closing time and by then I'll have an alibi and the case will be insoluble," O'Neill said.

"Miss Plum knows I wanted to talk to you."

"Look around, no one can even see us here, and I assure you, Mikhail is very nervous about going to prison. He had a bad experience in a Communist gulag. If you look even a wee bit like you're going to shout or cause trouble, he'll shoot without a second thought," O'Neill said.

I nodded.

"Ok, or what?" I asked.

O'Neill looked baffled for a second. He hadn't thought about the "or."

"Or you come with us outside," O'Neill said.

"I'll think about it," I said.

"In case you decide you'd like to join us, I'll just make a phone call," O'Neill said sarcastically.

He popped open his cell.

"You won't bloody believe it, Tim. Meet me outside the Linen Hall right now with the van and a couple of heavy lifting boys," he said.

I nodded at Mikhail.

"How did you get a library card, you don't seem the literary type?" I asked.

Mikhail ignored me. O'Neill hung up, smiled.

"I'm curious, how did you find me here, Mr. Forsythe?" O'Neill said.

"I'd love to tell you, but question-and-answer is just such an uncivilized form of discourse. Spot me a couple of Manhattans and we'll have a right old chin wag about anything you like."

"Oh, I don't think we'll be doing much talking, Mr. Forsythe. Very little of what you could say would interest me," O'Neill said.

"I think you'll find you're mistaken, I'm quite the amiable companion. For instance, I'll bet you didn't know that today is Bloomsday. Down in Dublin they are having a real shindig. And this might interest Mikhail: on this date in history Yuri Gagarin—"

I'd been trying to say all this in an increasingly loud voice, not so loud that Mikhail would pop a cap in my stomach, but loud enough to bring Miss Plum over. Regardless, O'Neill stopped me with a wave of his hand since his cell phone was vibrating.

"Hello. . . . It is. . . . Excellent. . . . We'll be down in two minutes," he said.

He turned to face me with the grisly smile of an executioner.

"Stand, please, Mr. Forsythe."

I stood.

"Mikhail, I think Mr. Forsythe and you and I will take a walk outside. We'll go down the fire escape. I'll want you to walk ahead of us very slowly, Mr. Forsythe, and if you stumble or fall, or cry out or do anything I don't like, Mikhail will shoot you in the brain."

I hesitated and stared at him.

"But I have no real incentive to go, do I? You're going to kill me once I get outside and into that van," I protested.

"We'll kill you right now. The .22 won't make a sound. At least if we postpone it, you'll have more of a chance. Maybe once we get in the van, you'll talk me out of it, who knows?"

"I might convince you not to top me?" I said.

"I'll be honest with you, Mr. Forsythe, it's unlikely, but stranger things have happened."

I had no choice but to do what he said. I began walking toward the fire escape.

O'Neill beside me, holding my gun, Mikhail behind us.

"Maybe you should go back and put your book away. That Miss Plum is terribly overworked," I said to O'Neill. He was tiring of my glibness now. His lips narrowed into a grim slit.

We reached the stairwell.

An echoing concrete space, devoid of people.

"We could kill him right here," Mikhail said in some kind of Yugoslavian accent. I knew this because my old landlord in New York City had been a Serbian.

"Let's not bring the library into it all," O'Neill said with distaste.

"Dobar dan," I attempted, trying to get Mikhail on my good side, but the bastard appeared completely unmoved.

Mikhail did a thorough search of my body, gave O'Neill my bag of .38 shells and all the money I had left in my pocket.

We walked carefully down the concrete steps and reached the fire exit door. O'Neill turned to Mikhail.

"You keep the gun on him, I'll go out and see if there's any peelers. Shoot him if he so much as blinks."

O'Neill slipped out into the street. When he had gone, I turned to the big guy.

"Don't take him literally on the blinking thing," I said.

Mikhail nodded sullenly.

"Dobar dan again, Mikhail. Misha, my old mate. This could be your lucky day. I work for Bridget Callaghan and she's the head of the Irish mob in the United States. We'll pay you ten times what you're getting in this small town, ten times and a green card, what do you say?"

Mikhail laughed, said nothing. Before I could think of anything else, O'Neill came back.

"It's all clear, Tim has the van," he said.

He looked at me.

"One move, one sound, Forsythe, and we'll fucking kill you in the street, understood?"

I nodded.

He opened the fire exit door.

I stepped outside.

A big red Ford van double-parked twenty feet away along the pavement. A couple of meatpackers waiting beside the rear doors.

I walked slowly onto the sidewalk. The streets were comparatively empty. It was nearly six o'clock and Belfast has a short rush hour. Everyone who needs to get home is usually on a train or a bus by 5:30. Thursday was late shopping night, but today was not, alas, a Thursday. Only two witnesses on the whole street. A religious preacher with a megaphone and the bootleg video salesman.

"Faster," O'Neill instructed.

The preacher spotted us and asked Mikhail and myself if we knew that our lives were hanging by a thread. Mikhail prodded me with the gun before I could give my ironic answer.

We stopped at the van. One of the meatpackers looked at me.

"That runt's Michael Forsythe?" he said skeptically.

"That's him," O'Neill said. "Mikhail, help him inside."

I didn't want to get into the van. The van meant death. I made a last desperate plea to O'Neill.

"Look, please, whatever I've done, I don't think this will solve anything. I'm not a bad lad, I don't care what you've heard. Really, we should talk this over," I said.

"Just get in the van," O'Neill demanded.

No way. If I got in that van, I was toast. This would be my last opportunity to make a run for it, even if Mikhail did bloody shoot me.

I dropped to the ground, breaking Mikhail's hold on my shoulder. I scrambled to my feet.

"Help, they're gonna murder me," I screamed at the top of my voice, tried to push past Mikhail and the other goons.

Someone thumped me in the head, I ate tarmac. Mikhail and one of the other boys picked me up bodily and threw me inside the van. I screamed all the louder, attracting the attention of the only person now left on the street.

"What the hell is going on there?" the video guy shouted.

"Get the police, I'm being kidnapped—" I managed before someone belted me in the mouth, the boys jumped in, and the van doors closed. O'Neill and Mikhail got in the front while three goons grinned at me in the back. We sped off into the traffic, Mikhail driving fast for some safe location.

A pretty large van that you could almost stand up in, about ten feet long. It was basically a shiny box with hooks in the ceiling that I didn't like the look of one little bit. It was either a dry-cleaning delivery vehicle or a portable torture chamber. They weren't meat hooks because the van wasn't refrigerated.

The three boys were crouched at one end. I was up near the cab. No chance against the boys, but maybe if I could smash the glass through to the driver's compartment I could cause an accident.

I thumped the glass with my elbow, it bounced off harmlessly, the van turned a corner, the three boys jumped me at once. I tried to clobber one, but these were big shits who knew exactly what they were doing. We didn't even fight, they just grappled me to the floor and pinned me down.

One sat on my legs and the other two held down each arm.

O'Neill slid back the glass partition.

"Do you have him, Tim?" he asked.

"Aye, we got him."

"Good."

"What do you want us to do with him, Mr. O'Neill?" one of the goons asked. This eejit seemed to be the leader. Tim, tall, well built, viciously scarred, wearing a Man. United goalkeeper's shirt and a Yankees cap.

"Well, first thing. We just did a cursory pat down, make sure he's got nothing on him," O'Neill said.

They violently searched me.

"Hey, he's got no left foot, see that?" Tim said.

They stared at the prosthesis.

"You would never have known, I seen him walk just like a regular person," Tim said.

"Get off me, I'll fucking kill you all," I yelled, but Tim bitch-slapped me across the face and shoved a handkerchief in my mouth to shut me up. Now that I was restrained and quiet, O'Neill could give full vent to his fury.

"What in the name of God is going on, Tim? I thought people were taking care of him and, lo and behold, he comes up to my private sanctuary. You know he pointed a gun at me while I was working on my book?"

"Sorry, Mr. O'Neill," Tim said.

"He came into my holy of holies and shoved a .38 in my face. You can imagine how surprised I was. I thought he was bloody dead already."

"Really sorry, Mr. O'Neill."

"I thought Sammy was going to take care of him at that boat? Eh? Was that not the plan? And it turns out Sammy did not take care of him at the boat?" O'Neill asked.

"Sammy's dead, Mr. O'Neill, the whole thing was a disaster. Jimmy fired the RPG at a peeler foot patrol. There were injuries. I don't know what went down. But the cops killed Sammy," Tim said.

"Hey, where to?" Mikhail asked from the front.

"Just drive around for the moment, eventually we'll have to take him out to the country," O'Neill said.

Mikhail nodded.

"Tell me what happened," O'Neill demanded.

"It's not that clear yet but apparently Jimmy fired the RPG at him on the boat at the same time a foot patrol was coming. I suppose Jimmy thought he could get him and get away before the peelers got involved," Tim explained.

"Jesus Christ. And you're telling me there were casualties?" O'Neill asked. "Did anybody die?"

"I don't know yet," Tim responded.

"Holy Mary. Where's Jimmy now?"

"He's in custody."

"Oh for Godsake, that's just terrific," O'Neill said.

We drove in silence for a moment.

"What do we do about Forsythe?" Tim asked.

"Next time Seamus Deasey asks me to help him out, somebody remind me that wee shite is more trouble than he's worth. Have to see about replacing him," O'Neill said almost to himself.

"Aye, but what do we do about Forsythe?" the goon persisted.

"Oh, I suppose we have to top him now, it's the very least we can do after this bollocks," O'Neill said.

"Aye, he's a rat anyway," Tim said.

"Aye, he is too, he is too," O'Neill said reflectively.

"Take us out of town, the usual spot," he told Mikhail, and he leaned back to us.

"Aye, lads, better get this over with."

I writhed, but it was useless. Tim was kneeling on my left arm. And the others had me locked to the floor. The only way I was getting out of this was to talk my way out. I cleared my head fast. I stopped struggling, bit the handkerchief, partially swallowed it, gagged, and managed to puke it out of my mouth.

"O'Neill, listen to me. This will start a mob war with America. I'm working for Bridget Callaghan now, I'm trying to find her wee girl. You don't want her pissed off at you, do you?" I screamed.

"You say you're working for Bridget Callaghan?" O'Neill asked, surprised.

"Yeah, ask Seamus, I'm working for her. I'm looking for her daughter. Ask Seamus if you don't believe me. That's what this is all about."

"Seamus wants you dead. Bridget Callaghan wants you dead. We'll be doing everyone a favor," O'Neill said.

"No fucking way, you haven't got the latest news. Bridget does not want me dead. I'm working for her now. If you kill me, Bridget will make sure you all pay a very heavy price."

O'Neill shrugged in the front seat, took off his bifocals, cleaned them.

"Ach, they'll never find you, will they, Tim?"

"No, sir," Tim said, placing the handkerchief back in my mouth and attempting to squeeze my jaw shut with his big hands.

"How will we do it, Mr. O'Neill, cut his fucking throat?"

"No, no, no, I don't want blood all over the van, and you can put your guns away. I just bought this wee number and I got to move the grandkids' play box on Saturday. I do not want blood or holes in the bodywork."

"So what do we do?" Tim asked.

"Throw one of them plastic bags over his head. Suffocate him. Anybody ever seen someone die like that? It's very instructive. Completely bloodless. Very efficient way to do someone if you do it right."

"Sounds good to me," Tim said.

"There's some rubber bands back there, you can use those to keep it tight, ok?" O'Neill said.

Tim reached behind him and the other two lads gave him one of the bags. With his hands off my mouth, I could just about speak.

"Now wait just a goddamn minute, I haven't done a thing to any of you people, this is a huge mistake," I said.

O'Neill turned around to face me.

"Make your peace, Forsythe, it'll be easier on yourself. Just get composed, this doesn't have to be ugly for anyone. We all have to go sometime and it's the manner of our death that tells us whether we have dignity or not."

"Nice speech, but you're not killing me," I said, and struggled as hard as I could against the three men. But they were over seven hundred pounds of deadweight. I had no chance.

"You're making a huge mistake. I'm the only one that can bring that girl back alive. Bridget will have you all killed. She'll have every one of you executed, you don't know the depths to which she—"

They slipped a clear plastic bag over my head and fastened it around my neck with a thick rubber band. Almost immediately I found that I was having difficulty breathing.

I tried to bite the bag, but it was thick, heavy-duty material. I tried to claw Tim with my fingernails, but he simply adjusted his weight so that he was sitting on my wrist rather than my hand.

Within seconds all the good air in the bag was gone.

"Help," I called out. "Help me, please."

The three men looking at me through the clear plastic. The inside of the bag filling with condensed water vapor from my lungs. My temples throbbing. My eyes stinging.

Not this way, not now. No. Please. I have so much to do.

I bit at the bag, thrashed my legs and arms. Screamed. I lifted my head off the van floor and banged it, trying to create any kind of rip in the plastic. Tim simply forced my head down with his fist.

Tim's hand and the wet plastic on my forehead—the slimy touch of death.

The bag full of CO_2 now. The oxygen had been burned away. I panic-breathed, dragged the poison down into my lungs. My throat burned and I breathed even deeper. In a few seconds the lack of oxy-gen in my brain would force me into a blackout and that would be the—

All three men clattered down on top of me.

A pocket at the bottom of the bag.

I sucked air.

A siren.

Something was happening. The car violently skewed to the left and then to the right, accelerated.

I managed to free a hand. There was a huge crash and I was smashed against the roof of the van, just missing one of those ugly hooks. Suspended for a moment in free fall, I ripped the bag off my face as the van turned over on its side and tumbled onto its roof be-fore the windshield smashed, the ceiling buckled, and the air bags in-flated in the front seat.

We were still moving upside down, me and the three goons tangled up together. I elbowed the nearest one in the eye, sticking my elbow deep in the socket. I grabbed his fat head in my two hands and banged it into the side of the van. I reached inside his coat and pulled out an Uzi machine pistol.

The van continued skidding on its roof for a second before smash-ing into a wall. Tim thumped into one of the meat hooks, his flesh neatly skewered through the neck, the other two goons tumbled into the rear doors.

I dropped the gun, regrabbed it, braced myself.

The van stopped spinning and came to a dead halt.

I got into a half crouch, took the safety off the Uzi, made sure the magazine was slammed in properly, and machine-gunned all three of them, riddling them with bullets, for a blast of about three seconds. Two were unconscious, but the third put his hands up defensively. I shot through his palms and pumped a dozen rounds into his neck and head.

I Uzied the rear doors, kicked them open, and jumped outside.

We were still in Belfast, on a blasted piece of waste ground, which was what was left of the projects near the old markets district. The tenements had been demolished and were being replaced with neat semidetached houses. The van was upside down and the cab had a police Land Rover wedged into the side of it, the Land Rover lying on its side with the wheels spinning. Mikhail's mangled body cut in two, his legs in the van and his torso on the Land Rover's windshield.

I didn't have much time. The cops would be out of there just as soon as they recovered and got those big armor-plated rear doors open.

I ran to the front of the van, saw that O'Neill was bleeding from a scalp wound but very much alive. I pointed the Uzi at him.

"You're coming with me, you old bastard," I said.

I dragged him out of the van, ran, and practically carried him away from the scene before the peelers got out and shot or lifted the both of us.

The rain fell and muddied grass, flooded drains, and made petrol float and turn to filthy rainbows, manufacturing a slimy membrane on rooftops, streets, and lanes.

I let it drip onto my tongue.

Where were we?

Safe.

An alley behind the Peace Line between two rows of new houses. The Peace Line, a twenty-foot-high wall that separated the Protestant housing development from the Catholic one.

No one around here, but they were close and they were coming.

Cops starting to mill about the crime scene. A helicopter flying above us. I had about five minutes to question the old man. We were three hundred yards away on the other side of a playground from where the police Land Rover had rammed the van. Already there were two other cop Land Rovers there with a forensic team.

We'd gotten away so fast the peelers hadn't seen us. But it was standard cop procedure to fan out from the scene of a violent incident. Soon there would be dozens of constables walking three-sixty in every direction, looking for witnesses. We'd have to move on if we didn't want to get arrested. Like I say, five, ten minutes tops.

But that was ok.

All I needed was a quick debrief with O'Neill and then I'd pop the old git and make a run for it.

And if I survived this day, I'd make sure I bought a bloody copy of *Star Wars III* from that bootleg video man. His phone call to the peelers had undoubtedly saved my life. I'd thank the coppers, too, if I hadn't made it a rule never to thank the peels for anything.

O'Neill was slumped against a wall. Breathing hard, dabbing at his scalp. Let him bleed, let him fucking hemorrhage. But be damn quick about it. The helicopter might spot us and sooner or later the police would realize that someone had run. I needn't worry about eyewitnesses, at least, there'd been no one about. (Even if there had, nobody would have seen a thing.)

O'Neill coughed and spat blood.

Didn't look like an internal wound, just a gash in the mouth.

I was still holding the Uzi but I felt uncomfortable with that bulky weapon, so I searched O'Neill, removed my .38, the bag of shells, the money he'd taken from me, and all his dough too. I wiped the Uzi clean of prints and threw it over the Peace Line.

"Open your eyes," I said.

O'Neill looked at me.

"If you're going to kill me, just fucking kill me," he said.

"Patience, Body, patience; we don't have a lot of time, those pigs are going to be over in a minute and we want to be gone."

"You're not going to top me?"

"I haven't decided. O'Neill, listen, I want you to answer some questions for me, I don't want you to piss me about," I said.

O'Neill sat up.

"There's some pills in my trouser pocket, can I get them? For my angina."

"Get your pills, but hurry up."

O'Neill reached into his pocket, pulled out a bottle of morphine pills, and chucked a couple into his mouth.

"I'll take a few of them too," I said, and pocketed a couple. I was in a hell of a lot of pain myself. O'Neill breathed deep and seemed a little better now.

"Ok, what do you want to know?"

"I want to know why you've been trying to kill me since I landed in Dublin," I said.

He looked puzzled.

"I haven't been trying to kill you since you landed in Dublin."

"You bloody have. Your wee pal Jimmy told me you authorized the RPG attack on me. You said so yourself in the van."

"I did. But I didn't try to get you in Dublin," O'Neill said.

"Why did you try to kill me at the boat?"

"You fucked with one of my boys. Seamus Deasey. You embarrassed him in front of his men, you hit him, you came into his place of business and you shot Eliot Mulroony, who was his right-hand man. I couldn't let you get away with that. Seamus was furious. He told me where you were going to be and I told him I'd take care of it."

"You're lying to me. You sent that guy to the airport and the other guy in the brothel. You tried to get me twice in Dublin."

"No, I didn't."

"You did. I talked to Moran and he told me that it wasn't him. I looked him right in the eye and he said it wasn't him."

"Listen, Michael, can I call you Michael? The first time I heard you were in the bloody country was this afternoon when that eejit Deasey calls me gurning that you've humiliated him and he wants you dead."

I sat on my hunkers in an uncomfortable squat.

"You're saying you haven't been trying to kill me since this morning?" I said.

He shook his head.

"Believe me, Michael, I just did what I had to do to keep my boys in line. It was nothing personal, it was nothing to do with you being a rat, er, I mean . . ."

"It's all right. . . . So it wasn't you."

"It wasn't me."

"So who was it?"

"Maybe you have old Belfast enemies."

"I don't. I was small-time. Nobody that would want to kill me that bad."

"Maybe somebody who knew that there was a bounty on your head."

I sat on the pavement beside O'Neill. The cops were starting that line thing they do, where they pace very close to one another, looking for evidence. Be over here sharpish.

"You're telling me that it wasn't you?" I muttered to myself. It was a rhetorical question, but O'Neill wanted to reassure me.

"It wasn't me, Michael. I authorized just the one attack on you. That's all. I don't know about these others you're talking about. Just the one attack."

"The RPG hit at the boat," I said.

"Aye, the apparently fucked-up RPG attack on the boat."

I looked into his tired eyes. I believed him; there was no reason for him to lie. It was just that one op. Which unfortunately reopened the question, what the hell was going on? Two attacks in Dublin, not by Bridget, not by the IRA. Someone as yet unknown. I put the .38 back in my pocket. I offered him my bloody palm.

"Listen, Body, I want to talk truce."

He shook my hand.

"Talk away."

"Ok. I messed with your boy Seamus and you're pissed off about that. But I have other things on my plate. Bridget Callaghan's right-hand man, David Moran, wants to see me dead. He's vowed to kill me when they get Siobhan back at midnight. If they don't get her back, he's going to kill me anyway. Now, as I see it, it would be bloody redundant of you to waste your time trying to kill me. You've more than paid me off for Seamus, ok?"

He nodded.

"So what do you want?" he asked.

"I want you to leave me alone. You don't want me around. Ok. Give me twenty-four hours to leave Ulster. One way or another, I'll either be out of here or I'll be dead. Keep off the goddamn hounds until then."

He straightened himself, thought about it.

"Michael, if you're sparing me right now, and it sounds like you are, you're a bigger man than I thought. I wouldn't have hesitated to kill you; if the peelers hadn't rammed the van, you'd be dead. It's rare to see that these days. I know what they say about you, you're a rascal and all that. But I give you my word that no one from the IRA or any other group that I have influence over will bother you in the time you're in Belfast."

"Including Seamus?" I asked.

"Including Seamus," he confirmed.

"Do you have the clout to do it?"

He seemed offended.

"I do."

"You'll keep Seamus Deasey off my back?"

He nodded.

"And there's something else. I need Seamus to do me a favor," I said with a little smile.

"From Seamus? Of all people in the world, you need a favor from Seamus? That's not happening, mate," O'Neill said doubtfully.

"Bridget Callaghan hired me to find her daughter. The person who lifted her was on that boat, the *Ginger Bap*. Kid called Barry. He'd been murdered, execution style. Seamus knew he was already dead. Don't ask me how he knew, because I'm damned if I know."

"Seamus is mixed up in the disappearance of Bridget Callaghan's daughter?" O'Neill asked. The old man's face looked even more ashen. His lip was trembling. He was clearly upset.

"I don't know about that. But he knows something about Barry's death. Maybe the gunman needed Seamus's permission to kill one of his dealers."

O'Neill scoffed. "Seamus couldn't give permission to get a dog's hair cut. I'm in charge round here and nobody asked me about it."

"Well, he heard something. I need to know about it. Time's running out. When Seamus told me where Barry lived, he told me specifically that the information wouldn't do me any good. He knew Barry was topped. The cops hadn't found him and the neighbors didn't know."

O'Neill looked thoughtful.

"You really think the person who killed this Barry is involved in Siobhan Callaghan's kidnapping?"

"He has to be."

"And Seamus knows who did it?"

"I went to the boat before it sank, nothing had been touched. The lock was all done up with wire. The last person there was the killer."

"Maybe somebody blabbed," he said, coming to the conclusion that had also occurred to me.

"Belfast's a pretty closemouthed town," I added with a touch of skepticism.

"Aye, but it's not like in your day, Michael. We can't go around murdering witnesses anymore, not with the cease-fires."

"Will you help me?" I asked.

"Michael, we're both intelligent men. You and I know that it's in our own best interests that Bridget Callaghan gets her daughter back in one piece. If finding who killed that boy can bring you closer to Siobhan, I'm sure Miss Callaghan will look more favorably upon us rather than her other potential business partners."

"I'm sure she would."

He nodded.

"Give me a minute," he said. He pulled a cell phone out of his inside pocket and dialed the number. He turned the volume loud so I could hear the conversation too.

"Seamus, it's me," O'Neill said.

"Are you ok? Been hearing lots of things," Seamus said with a tiny trace of disappointment in his voice that both O'Neill and I picked up on.

"Seamus, you listen to me and you listen good. I have heard that you have been fucking playing me. I have heard that you have been trying to make a fucking monkey out of me," O'Neill began.

"What are you talking about?" Seamus complained.

"You better start packing your bags, Seamus, because I'm putting a contract out on you right now. You only wanted Michael Forsythe killed because he was close to finding out that you were involved in Siobhan Callaghan's disappearance. That whole fucking operation at the boat was to cover your white Irish arse."

"It's a lie. I had nothing to do with that wee girl's disappearance," Seamus protested.

"Did you not? Well, I have information to the contrary. You wanted that boat sunk, you wanted Forsythe dead because one of your dealers lifted her. You wanted Forsythe out of the picture because he knew the fucking truth."

Body's eyes twinkled with merriment. He was enjoying this.

"That's bullshit, I didn't know the boat was going to sink. I swear to God, Mr. O'Neill, I knew nothing about any kidnapping," Seamus said in a panic.

"How did you know Barry was already dead on the boat? How did you know he was fucking dead?"

"Gusty McKeown did it. Him and some fella from out of town. Gusty got the guns from me. Wanted a whole lot of guns. I had to ask him what it was about and he told me they had to top some wee fuck for reasons that he wasn't allowed to divulge. So I said what wee fuck is that and he tells me and I say that's my wee fuck and I ask for extra as compensation, you know. But I says ok cos they wanted Russian machine guns and Glock pistols and the whole works and were paying top dollar. With the guns and the compensation, it was fifteen large. I swear to God I was going to give you your cut, but I just hadn't got round to it."

O'Neill put his hand over the receiver and looked at me.

"Is that what you need?"

"Where would I find Gusty?" I said.

O'Neill spoke into the phone again.

"Where would I find Gusty?" he asked Seamus.

"Shit, I have no idea, Mr. O'Neill, he lives in the . . . oh, wait a minute, I think Andy knows something. Hold on. . . . Mr. O'Neill, Andy says he'll be at the fights at the Dove Tavern on Brazil Street."

I nodded at O'Neill. That's what I wanted.

"Talk to you later, Seamus," O'Neill said and hung up his phone.

He looked grim. He had discovered a lot about Seamus. The poor wee blabbermouth would be lucky if he saw out the night.

"You going over to the Dove?" he asked me.

"Aye."

"You'll need a password to get into the fights. It's always a historical figure. This week I think it's Henry Joy McCracken."

"I just say 'Henry Joy McCracken'?"

"Aye, that's it."

O'Neill put out his hand. I shook it and helped him to his feet.

"I like you, Michael, I'm glad things worked out the way they did," he said. "You are not lacking in honor."

"Thanks," I said. "I better get cracking. You, too, if you don't want those peelers down your neck."

"Good luck. And remember, Forsythe, this is my town. I hope you don't keep leaving a trail of bloody destruction in your wake."

"Well," I said, reflecting upon his words, "the night is young."

9: HADES
(BELFAST—JUNE 16, 7:45 P.M.)

The day has shed its skeleton and the dark is finding corners all over the city. It has taken until this time for the sun to finally dip behind the surrounding hills. A night of smothering blackness and a yellow moon. Stars beginning to show between the clouds.

Dusk is when Belfast really clicks. Fights. Murders. Burglary. A thousand calls about someone we're doing over. Someone we're lifting. Sober men rubbing their hands and performing with clear consciences wee jobs and the breaking of bones.

Not that it bothers me. I'm impervious. My story is that of the escape artist, the killer. It's taken me a while but now I have momentum.

Children in front of me throwing footballs at one another across the street. Not much younger than Bridget's child. That poor lost girl.

"My turn, mine."

"Is not."

"Is too."

I give the ball to the nearest kid, a redhead whose face is one big freckle.

"It's her turn," I insist.

The girls look up from their game and their dirty summer clothes. Glad that an adult has restored order.

"And can somebody please tell me where Brazil Street is?"

"Down there on the left. Are you looking for the Dove?" Red says.

"Aye."

"It's right in the middle of the street, the steps that go down," her friend explains.

I thank the kids and reach the corner. I'm ready. I see a board above a small entryway with an arrow pointing to the basement. A neon sign that says "The Dove."

I cross the street, walk down the steps, and knock the door. A big metal job that can sustain a petrol bomb attack or a police battering ram.

A man opens it a crack. A sleekit character with a reconstructed nose, no hair, paramilitary tattoos. Bouncer type.

"What do you want?"

"Here for the fight," I say.

"What fight?"

"Henry Joy McCracken."

"Why didn't you say so, come on in."

I hear a heavy chain being unhooked and the door swings open.

"Two-pound cover," the bouncer says.

"Ok," I say, and give him a two-pound coin.

"Down the bottom," he says, and goes back to reading *The Bridges of Madison County*.

Murk. A stink. A creaky set of wooden stairs.

"Down these steps?" I ask.

"Aye, watch you don't break your neck," he says without looking up.

Carefully I walk down the steep staircase.

A lot of noise coming from behind a metal door. I push on it, go in.

A wall of cigarette smoke. Screaming, shouting, yelping. The aroma of defecation, blood, spilled beer, and sweat. A gloomy room with an arc light swaying from a concrete beam. From the noise, the fight must have already begun. A ring of about thirty men. I walk closer. A barrier of sandbags, sawdust on the floor, and two pit bull terriers tearing the hell out of each other. A brown one and a black one. Both dogs are caked with gore, the brown one's ear has been ripped off, the other's eyes are filled with blood. They're tired and snapping at each other with desperate weary lunges. But it's clear that no one is going to stop it. This is a fight to the death. I watch for a moment and then head farther into the crowd. Don't want to stand out. Maybe all these men know one another.

A bookie comes over to me. Skinny character in a suit, tie, and chestnut wig. You can tell he's a bookie even without the chits he's carrying, because he has that wiry bookie energy and a hungry look.

"Wager?" he asks.

"It's all over by the looks of it," I say.

He gazes back at the fight.

"Give you two to one on Danielle," he says.

"Which one is Danielle?"

"The bay," he says.

There's no point on getting on the wrong side of him, and bookies love marks more than anything in the world. I give him a tenner and he gives me a paper chit.

"Listen, it's my first time here. Supposed to meet a mate of mine, Gusty McKeown, you know Gusty? Bit of a joker. Whereabouts is he?"

"Gusty's right over there," he says, pointing to a tall, spiderlike man with a black bowl haircut and hollow eyes.

Just then the black dog falls on the brown one, sinks its teeth into its throat, and begins biting through its windpipe. It's something I've seen lions attempt on TV but never witnessed a dog do. It's awful. The brown dog's howls are silenced and it slowly suffocates.

"You can't win them all, sorry," the bookie says.

"Should have offered me ten to one," I tell him, to keep him sweet.

He smiles.

I edge around the ring of perspiring, heaving low-lifes and find Gusty yelling as the brown dog expires in a blood-curdling spasm. When the cheering dies, a man comes in with a snow shovel and scoops up the dead dog. Another man muzzles the winner and leads it off. A third man throws more sawdust on the floor. The crowd is buzzing with cathartic release and expectation about the next bout on the card. Mixed crowd of Prod and Catholic paramilitaries together— you can tell because of the tattoos. Maybe underground dog fighting is one of those cross-community schemes everyone is always trying to encourage.

The bookie, who seems also to be master of ceremonies, walks into the center of the ring and begins a spiel about the next two unfortunates.

"Gentlemen, I hope you enjoyed our pedigree tussle. Quite a performance. Now it's a mongrel battle. Sparky is a wee fighter from Doagh, this is his first time in a formal competition, but let me tell you, I have seen this dog go on mutts twice his size. . . ."

"Gusty . . . Gusty," I whisper in the big lad's ear.

He turns and looks at me.

"Who the fuck are—"

I get real close, lift his T-shirt, and put the snub of the .38 against his belly fat. I grin at him for show and pat him on the back like we're old mates. But I'm angry now. Those kids outside, all this, what's happening to Siobhan, it's finally getting to me.

"Gusty, listen to me, me old china plate, this is a fucking .38-caliber revolver and I'm going to blow your guts apart if you don't tell me what happened to Siobhan Callaghan," I say quietly.

"I don't know what the fuck you're talking about."

I push the revolver tight into his stomach so hard that it's bound to be hurting.

"Gusty, I'm serious here," I say.

The arc light swaying on the crossbeam swings above our heads and the bookie ringmaster catches my eye. The bottom halves of our bodies are blocked from him by the people in front, so he can't see the gun, but Gusty has turned several degrees paler and it doesn't look so good.

"Another wager, stranger?" he shouts over. A few men turn to give me the once-over. Have to reply fast.

"Aye, twenty quid on that thing on your head against any dogs you got back there," I shout back and keep the revolver tight on Gusty's belly button so he won't try anything heroic. The crowd hoots with laughter and the bookie gives me a black look and goes back to his spiel.

I pull Gusty's hand behind his back and twist it hard. Gusty winces. The bookie gives me another suspicious glance. That son of a bitch doesn't like the look of me one bit, but he's immediately caught up in a dozen wagers; while he writes them down, two unfortunate terrier mixes are led out on ropes.

"Who took Siobhan, Gusty? Where is she?"

"I don't know."

"I'll kill you right now, Gusty. I don't give a shit what happens to you or me; tell me where Siobhan is and you'll live, don't tell me and I swear to God I'll fucking plug you in two seconds," I say, looking him square in his dilating pupils—attempting in that look to convey what a badass motherfucker I am, how little Gusty's life means to me, and how easy it would be to let him die.

Gusty gets some of it but not enough. He's still more afeared of them than he is of me.

"Gusty, I know you murdered Barry on the *Ginger Bap*. I know you're working for the kidnappers. Tell me where she is," I say.

The dogs begin ripping each other to shreds.

The room. The sweat. The stink. The bookie yelling. Me pushing. Gusty trembling.

And then just like that, a tidal wave of exhaustion ripples through me. It's hard to keep this up. Hard to go at it hour after hour, day after day. Tired of all of it. This sordid wee place. People like Gusty. This whole town, in fact. Belfast with its surface changes. But these generations of old blue-white fat men have to die first for real change. Gusty'd be a good start.

"Ok, mate, you're done, I've had it," I say and make the mental decision to kill him just to see what happens. I squeeze the trigger.

Luckily, in a piece of telepathy or empathy, he sees exactly what I'm thinking and starts begging for his life.

"Please don't. I don't know where you get your fucking information, but really I don't know a thing about that wee missing girl," he says rapidly.

Make the present terror more incipient with a countdown, I tell myself.

"Ok, Gusty, it's an old saw, but I'll give you five seconds and then I'm going to shoot you in the kidney. One—"

Gusty's no Braveheart. No one who goes to a dogfight is a bloody Braveheart.

"Ok, ok, fucking Jesus. Don't shoot me, I'll tell you everything. Don't shoot me for fucksake, my wife just had a bairn."

"I don't give a damn if she gave birth to the bloody Messiah, now talk."

"Ok, ok, ok, I'll tell you everything I know, which isn't fucking much," he says.

To show that there's a bit of quid pro quo in the transaction, I remove the gun from his gut but I keep my hand as close to his belly as if it were J.Lo's arse.

Time must have passed because two more dogs begin ripping each other to shreds and it occurs to me that we seem a wee bit suspicious standing here stock-still, whispering.

"Go on, my son," I yell when one of the dogs bites the other on the bridge of the skull.

"Cheer the dog," I tell Gusty.

"Kill the fucker," he yells.

"Ok now, Gusty, you better talk; I'm like Doctor Kevorkian, no fucking patients left," I say.

"Ok, yeah, I helped top the kids. It was ugly. I didn't do the actual killing. A boy from County Down did it. Bangor, I think. I didn't know him. He was working for an outfit from out of town. I swear I didn't kill them boys."

"I don't give a shit; what was your partner's name and who was he working for?"

"All I have is the name, that's all I know, I wasn't involved. I swear it."

"Give it."

"Slider McFerrin."

"Address?"

Sweat on his forehead. His eyes darting from side to side.

"I don't know. He's from Bangor. I didn't know he was a player. I had no idea it was to do with Bridget Callaghan's daughter."

"There was no girl on the *Ginger Bap*?"

"Fuck no, I would have told Seamus if I'd thought there was more to it than a wee hit."

A fake smile of reassurance over his pallid face.

"What exactly did Slider say to you?" I ask him.

"First of all, Slider heard about me as a man who could get him guns. He needed guns. He said he was working for a serious hardmen outfit from over the water and he was coming into a big score on June sixteenth and I'd get a cut of it if I could get him all the weapons he needed."

"And?"

"I said no problem, for the right dough I could get him anything."

"Where did the kids come in?"

"Well, after I said I could get him the guns, he wanted to know if I'd be willing to help take care of one of his boss's enemies. Kid called Barry, who was a drug dealer working for Seamus Deasey."

"What did you say?"

"I told him it would be tough, you'd have to sweeten Seamus; and Slider says, there's ten gees to kill Barry, ten gees for the guns, ten gees to sweeten Seamus, and ten gees for me to keep my mouth shut."

"You couldn't say no to that, could you?"

"No."

"What next?"

He gulps, tilts his head to the side, takes a breath.

"I got the guns from Seamus; they wanted Pechenegs, big Russian jobs, handguns, silencers, the works. I paid Seamus off, had to tell him about Barry, but he knew to keep mum; it was a big score for him and he didn't want to pass the cut on to Body O'Neill."

"And then you killed Barry and his mate?"

"No, no, I didn't touch them. I just showed Slider where the boat was and helped him out. He shot the Scottish lad, but he had to question Barry first to make sure he hadn't blabbed."

Another fake grin.

"Then what?" I ask.

"That was yesterday. He gave me half my score. The rest tomorrow by FedEx when he gets the big money. Haven't seen him since then."

"And you knew nothing about the kidnapping?"

"Not a thing. Slider's a hard case and says if I ask any questions or breathe a word, no kneecapping, no Belfast six-pack, but instead a bullet in the neck from those over-the-water types."

"Better not be lying, Gusty," I say.

"It's fucking gold, so it is. I swear it."

I nod.

I know with a dead certainty that Gusty is lying through his teeth. He didn't stand idly by while Slider topped those two lads on the boat. It's more likely that Slider is the middleman and Gusty iced them. He certainly helped. Whether he's deeper in the kidnapping than this I don't know, but somehow I doubt it. Probably hired him for this one job. Doesn't seem like a criminal mastermind. The real person I need to speak to is Slider McFerrin.

"Slider told you nothing about these over-the-water players?"

"Nothing. He was keeking it, no way he was saying."

"I swear to God, Gusty, if you're keeping anything back, you're fucked. Slider and Barry are mixed up in the disappearance of Bridget Callaghan's daughter. Bridget'll fucking kill you and Seamus'll fucking kill you and O'Neill will kill you."

"I don't know anything about any kidnapping. This was just a wee job. Guns and a hit. That's all," Gusty says.

"Whereabouts in Bangor is this Slider fella?"

"I don't know. He let it slip he was from Bangor, but he wasn't saying. I don't know any of the hoods from Bangor, but you could ask around."

I grimace and take a step away.

"You keep your trap shut until the girl's back with her ma. Understood?"

"I understand."

He nods at me and I begin making my way through the throng. What next? Up the stairs, out into Belfast, somehow get to Bangor. A town about fifteen clicks away in northern County Down. Make sure I call the cops about that murdering bastard Gusty, although that can wait until after midnight too.

Never turn your back.

It's an old lesson and a good 'un.

"He's a fucking peeler," Gusty suddenly screams at the top of his voice. "He's a fucking undercover. Get him."

Like in a club when a drunk falls into the DJ's turntable, the noise in the room immediately ceases. Even the dogs stop killing each other for a second.

I run for the stairs.

I don't make it.

Two men immediately on top of me hammering punches into the side of my head. I thump one off. The other tries to butt me in the nose, misses, and smashes me in the forehead. I stick a fingernail in his right eye and kick him away. But it's too late now and the rest of the room is running over. A couple of punches and then an aluminum bat smacks into my ribs. You know you're in trouble when someone produces a baseball bat. Baseball isn't played in Ireland. Men who carry baseball bats for a living are professional skull smashers. Another bat crashes into my legs. I go down yelling. A kick lands on the side of my head. More kicks in my ribs. I see the glint of a knife. Baseball bats and knives. Well, that's it then. They're not messing about, they're going to kill me. An undercover cop, fair game in their eyes.

The bat comes down heavily a couple of inches from my head, breaking someone's foot instead. A kick just misses getting me in the balls. But someone succeeds in stamping on my chest, knocking the wind out of me.

And finally I manage to pull out the revolver.

I shoot someone in the leg and someone else in the gut. Both men fall to the floor with heavy thuds, too shocked even to yell.

The kicking stops, the men freeze for a moment. I fire into the ceiling. The attackers take a step back.

I am badly hurt and I realize immediately I've a window of only a few seconds before I'll pass out. Blood is pouring into my mouth, my head's pounding. I get to my feet. Almost fall, steady myself.

"I'm not a fucking cop," I say and swing the pistol around wildly, pointing it at various individuals. They're scared now, ready to believe me. "Gusty owes me ten grand, I'm his collector."

They turn to look at our old pal.

Need to further concentrate their minds. I shoot him in the crotch. He falls to the ground, screaming.

"Next person to fucking look in my direction is off to the fiery pit," I tell them.

I shamble-run to the stairs. The doorman blocking my path. I shoot him in the left thigh, push past him, and scramble up the steps. The mob boiling behind me, debating whether to follow me or not. Am I a cop? Am I not? A confusion in the stories and the fact that I still have a gun. I have one round left. One for any one of them.

I open the metal door and run into the street. Down one alley, then another, losing myself.

Losing myself.

The blood pouring out.

My head throbbing.

Pain mounting.

Those flashing lights again.

Take a look back, no pursuit.

Another alley. I slip, fall into a pile of garbage cans.

Aye, that's me. In the goddamn rubbish. At home here.

In Belfast.

In Dublin.

And back.

I fall way back.

Across countries. Oceans. Years.

Lima.

Los Angeles.

Farther.

All the way to a cold January in the Bronx, where my mind wants to take me for reasons that I don't get now but I'll understand by midnight.

❋   ❋   ❋

Tsssfffff . . . We came running down the lane, between the railway tracks and the security fence. A red number 2 train approaching and Andy afraid that we were going to be sucked over onto the line the way Goldfinger got sucked out of the plane in the Bond flick.

"There's no way," I tried telling him. "It's all to do with pressure."

"Aye, you say that, and when I'm mashed up against the carriages you can tell my ma."

The train was accelerating and we still had about fifty yards until we got to the steps at the platform.

"We're not going to make it," Andy said. Fergal was leading us, but he was so looped on paint thinner he thought he was back in the OC, hare coursing or something, screaming and hooting and generally spooking Andy and me.

"Will you shut it, you big glipe," I told him, but he was uncontrollable.

The train was bearing down and those buggers in the MTA never stop.

"We're gonna die now," Andy said behind me.

"We're not going to die," I assured him.

But the gap between the line and the security fence was only about a yard wide and for the first time I began to think that Andy might be right. Maybe the bloody thing was going to hit us. It was coming at a fair oul clip, that was for sure.

"If we cut over to the other side of the tracks, there's more room," Andy suggested.

"Go and you'll trip and fall and get bloody electrocuted and then beheaded and I'll have to explain that to your ma," I said.

"Well, big Fergal's going to get it first, the way he's carrying on."

"And he deserves it, his idea."

I looked up the track to see where Fergal was, but everything was absorbed into the train's headlights. It couldn't be more than ten feet in front of us. Jesus, Mary, and Joseph.

It sounded its horn and I found myself screaming.

"Oh my God," Andy yelled out and then the thing was on top of us.

"It's sucking me in," I heard myself shrieking. "Sucking me in, so it is."

Couple of people staring at us from their seats, lights, clattering wheels, sparks. In a few seconds the train was past. Fergal was giving it the fingers from the side of the track. I was hyperventilating. Deep breaths, I told myself, deep breaths.

Andy put his hand on my back. I shook my head.

"That boy is going to get us killed," I said, pointing at Fergal.

"More than likely," Andy agreed.

We headed up the line, caught Fergal, grabbed him by the jacket, and trailed the useless ganch after us. We exited the subway station and found the steps down the hill. Sure, it saved us about fifteen blocks by going over the fence and along the tracks, but it had taken years off our lives.

A minute later we walked into the brightly lit bar, more or less in one piece. Fergal looked at his clunky digital watch and told us that it was exactly nine o'clock.

"My shortcut paid off. We'll be able to get a seat now," he said, sliding his way among the patrons. Andy gave me a disgusted glance and I validated it with an eyebrow raise.

We walked to the bar, but before we got five paces a bouncer tapped me on the shoulder.

"How old are you boys?" the bouncer asked in a monotone.

"How can you ask me that question?" Andy said. I groaned. Just answer, you bloody big stupid eejit. "Can't you see that I'm twenty-five?" Andy continued. The bouncer looked at him with skepticism as Andy rummaged for the fakest of fake IDs. Fergal waved his hand in front of the bouncer's face.

"These are my mates," he said.

Fergal was five or six years older than Andy and myself, but even so, that wouldn't matter to the bouncer. I sighed. All this way into the heart of the Bronx and then risking death on a shortcut along the elevated subway tracks. All for some mythical bar that would probably be shite. Moot, anyway, because it looked like we were going to get chucked out after just two seconds inside the establishment.

"I'm twenty-five," Andy insisted and showed the ID.

The bouncer looked at Fergal for a second.

"Wait a minute. Do you work for Sunshine and Darkey White?" the bouncer asked.

Fergal's eyes narrowed. He drew himself up to his full height.

"Aye, I do," Fergal said.

"And these are your mates?" the bouncer asked him.

"Aye, they're tagging along. Andy here has been with us about six months, and for young Michael, this is his very first week in America."

The bouncer looked upset and then afraid.

"Sorry, I had no idea, I had no idea," he said apologetically.

"It's ok," Fergal said.

He backed away.

"Sorry for grabbing you on the shoulder, pal. I didn't know you were working for Darkey White," he said to me.

"Forget it," I muttered. "It's nothing." Although it wasn't nothing, and Fergal suddenly gained stature before my eyes.

We walked upstairs to the top bar, our ultimate destination.

Of course, we could have gone drinking anywhere in Riverdale or Manhattan but what was special about this place, allegedly, was that it was full of underage Fordham girls, who, Fergal claimed, were gagging for it all the bloody time. Beer, underage girls, Fergal on paint thinner. Quite the mix.

"My prediction," I told Andy, "is that it's going to end in tears."

"Lucky if it's only tears."

We opened the door of the top bar and went in. But for once, Shangri-la wasn't over the next mountain. It was right bloody here, if your particular utopia was heavily made-up seventeen-year-old Catholic girls, in slut skirts, heels, jewels, and perfume from their ma's closet.

There were mirrors everywhere and bright interrogation-style lights. MTV was playing on two TV screens, the music so loud that everyone except the bar staff had to shout. The girls had attracted a rough crowd of ne'er-do-wells from Long Island—surly suburban kids, looking for action of any description: girls or fights, either would be acceptable.

Fergal sussed a vacant table near the corner right under one of the TVs. He led the way, his big arms swinging wildly at his sides, terrifying me into thinking that he was about to knock over someone's pint. He could handle himself, but it was inevitable that Andy and me would be drawn in to any fracas. A couple of silent prayers and mantras kept him safe all the way to the corner. We sat down and took off our jackets.

"My shout," I said, and asked the boys what they were having. Everyone was on lagers, so that was easy to remember. The barman caught my eye as soon as I pulled out a hundred-dollar bill. Part of the advance Sunshine had sent me to bring me over from Belfast to New York.

I ordered three pints. I paid with the bill, got the change, and put the three pints into a triangle. I weaved my way back through the tables, avoiding obvious booby traps in the shape of extended legs or handbags or the belts of folded-up coats.

"Cheers," Fergal said, grabbing his pint right out of my hand and drinking half of it in one gulp and then belching. It was tough to be seen with Fergal. He played quite the rube. Eccentric one too. He was dressed in a tweed jacket and trousers and tatty woolen waistcoat. He had a red beard that looked like a case of scrum pox gone awry. Andy claimed that Fergal was a sophisticated thief back in the OC, but it was hard to credit.

I sat down, looked at Andy, and we both took a sip of beer.

"So what's the *craic*?" Andy asked me. "How's America treating you so far?"

"It's ok."

"How's your place?" he asked.

"Fucking shithole."

"Be it ever so humble . . ."

"Ok, boys, listen," Fergal said, looking serious and conspiratorial. With the getup he was in, the conspiracy could have involved a plot against Queen Victoria, but more likely it was about the girls.

"Listen. I've been checking out the table under the clock. Don't all look round at once, but tell me how old you think the brunette under the *R* in Rangers is?"

Fergal was checking out a brazen wee hussy with a six-inch-high beehive hairdo, hello-sailor lipstick, and pancake to cover the acne. She was with her older sister, who, after a great deal of pestering, was obviously taking her out on a Saturday-night thrill. Neither sister was going home with anyone tonight.

"Sixteen," Andy offered.

Fergal looked at me.

"Not sixteen, no way," I said. "I know for a fact how old she is."

"Seventeen?" Fergal suggested.

I shook my head again, taking a big sip of my pint to keep up the suspense.

"That girl is fourteen years old," I said at last.

Both of them were suitably impressed, taking unsubtle double takes.

"No way," Andy said.

"Believe it, kiddo. I'll go ask her, if you don't believe me."

They didn't believe me. I asked her. She said she was twenty-one and I told her I heard there was going to be a police raid to check IDs. The whole table cleared out five minutes later and once the rumor was out, four other tables after that.

Andy's round. He went to the bar, but despite being a giant he had some trouble getting served. Fergal, fully recovered now from his paint-thinner experience, was in a reflective mood.

"Yon Andy boy is encumbered not just by imposing stature but also by his astounding lack of bar presence," Fergal said.

"Explain."

"Certainly. He's not ugly, not handsome. And to have presence at the bar you need to have either a very handsome noticeable face or a very ugly noticeable face. Andy is right in the middle," Fergal said.

"Whereas you, Fergal, are a big lanky bugger with a horrible beard, the dress sense of a street person, and a nose that's bigger than some of the smaller hills in the Netherlands," I said, just to see how far I could push Fergal boy. But he wasn't fazed.

"All very true, and explains why I never have to wait more than thirty seconds at the bar. You get served very quickly because, I conjecture, the barman is thinking that anyone with your evil eyes is liable to do just about anything if he doesn't get his pint pretty sharpish."

"I take evil eyes as a compliment," I said.

"As you should."

Andy came back and asked what we were talking about.

"Just oul shite," I told him truthfully, and got stuck into beer number three.

Fergal finished his pint and looked around the bar.

"Boys. Sorry I brought you. This place is a bust, let's get over into the city," he said with ennui. We all agreed, drank the rest of our bevvies, and grabbed our coats from the backs of the chairs. We had all just stood up when the bar door opened and Scotchy Finn came in.

Scotchy Finn. Finally.

"There he is," Andy said. "That's Scotchy, he bloody said he was coming, but you never know with him."

"That's Scotchy?" I asked, staring at a dangerously thin, pale-skinned, orange-haired, bucktoothed, sleekit wee freak.

"That's him," Andy insisted.

I hadn't encountered Scotchy yet, but his reputation had preceded him. He was supposed to have met me at the airport, but he hadn't. He was supposed to have gotten me an apartment in Riverdale, but he'd found me one in Harlem instead. He was supposed to have taken me around the city, but he'd left all that to Andy. To cap it all, the story was that if Sunshine liked me, Scotchy was going to get his own crew, with the three of us under him. Our new boss.

Scotchy saw us and beamed from ear to ear.

"Boys, you weren't heading out, were you? Rounds on me,"

Scotchy said, and threw his jacket into the corner. We all sat down again. Scotchy went to the bar and came back almost immediately with four pints and whiskey chasers.

"Death to death," Scotchy said, and knocked back his whiskey.

We all followed suit.

"You're the newie, right?" he asked me.

"That's right," I said.

"Heard you were in the fucking British army," he asked aggressively.

"Aye, right again."

"Well, ya bloody collaborator, I spent my time blowing up the British army, trapping them, killing 'em, sniping them, down in South Armagh," Scotchy said with a touch of hammy malevolence.

"Aye, I thought I could detect a culchie inbred-hillbilly accent. South Armagh. Surprised you had the time to fight the Brits when you were fucking your sister and the various domestic farm animals that were handy, not that you could probably tell the difference between your sister and the farm animals," I said, and took a drink of my pint.

I wasn't sure how he would react to that and I was nervous for about half a second before Scotchy opened his fangy chops, grinned, and broke into a laugh.

"I think I'm going to like you, Michael," he said.

"Well, I'd love to say the same, but I'm not too sure, Scotchy," I told him.

"Forsythe, is it? Like Bruce Forsyth, that fucking shite comedian?"

"Aye, like Bruce Forsyth the shite comedian," I said.

"Ok, from now you're fucking going to be Bruce," Scotchy said.

"I don't think so, mate," I replied.

Scotchy ignored me and turned his attention to Andy and Fergal.

"Well, boys, how have you been while I've been dodging bullets and making us all rich in Washington Heights?"

"Good," I said, still speaking for the group, my first attempt to assert my dominance over them and, hopefully, one day over Scotchy, too.

Scotchy ignored me again, then went on to tell us what particular mischief he'd been up to all night with Big Bob and Mikey Price and the rest of the crew. Extortion, muscle, threats—fun stuff. After a couple of bloody anecdotes, Scotchy looked at me and grabbed me by the arm.

"Come on, new boy, get those down your neck and it's back to my place. Having a party for ya. Just decided. Get youse fixed up yet, even Andy over there, the big scunner."

We wolfed our pints, barely able to keep up with Scotchy as he got in another and ordered a keg of beer to carry out. Scotchy tried to pull the remaining jailbait, but no one would go with him. He went to the bog while Fergal and I lugged the keg to Scotchy's Oldsmobile.

"Are you sure you should be driving, Scotchy?" Andy asked him as we got in the back. Scotchy swiped at the top of his head.

"Ok, ok, I was only asking," Andy muttered.

Scotchy put the car in gear and spun the wheels out of the car park. Scotchy was a terrible driver—even when fully sober he fiddled continually with the washer fluid, the mirror, and the radio; and now he was half tore.

Twice he almost got us into accidents, one of them with a police car.

He flipped the stations and when Karen Carpenter's warble came on, Andy asked him to leave it.

"I like that song," Andy said, in vino veritas.

"I like it too," Scotchy concurred.

I rolled my eyes at Fergal, but he also appeared to like the Carpenters, making me think that I alone in the vehicle hadn't been body-snatched.

We arrived at Scotchy's pad in Riverdale at 10:30. Nice place, with a balcony and a view across the Hudson. Scotchy had done minimal decorating. A few posters of Who and Jam concerts he'd attended. A sloppy paint job in the kitchen. A proud display of beer bottles from all over the world on his long mantelpiece.

Scotchy showed us to the liquor cabinet and started making phone calls. By twelve, there must have been forty people there, but only about a quarter of them girls. At least the booze was good. Scotchy had boosted a huge case of single malts from the distributor. Twelve-year-old Bowmore, seventeen-year-old Talisker, and an Islay laid down in the year of my birth.

Just after midnight, Sunshine showed up. A saturnine, balding

Steve Buscemi type who was Darkey White's number two. I'd met him once before, when he'd interviewed me about working for Darkey. Even more than Scotchy's, it was Sunshine's call whether I got the job or not, so I made a point of talking to him about movies old and new. Sunshine liked me and introduced me to Big Bob Moran and his brother David. Bob was already drunk and complaining about the Dominicans who were invading his neighborhood in Inwood. He was going to move back out to Long Island, he said. David Moran was a more complicated character, who worked directly for Mr. Duffy, the reputed head of the entire Irish mob in New York City. David and Sunshine had a lot in common: they'd both gone to NYU, were both thinkers. Both white-collar types, unlike me and Scotchy on the bloody coal face.

"Sunshine says you'll be joining him very shortly," David Moran said.

"He hasn't told me yet, at least not formally."

"Sunshine has heard great things about you; you ran a couple of rackets when you were a teenager in Belfast and you were even in the army for a while. Remember, we're all one big family here," he said. He patted me on the cheek.

Scotchy noticed Bob, David, and Sunshine for the first time and came running over. He shook hands and dragged them outside to see his new car.

Andy found me and took me to one side.

"Listen, Michael, let me tell you who's just arrived," he said in hushed tones.

"Is it the pope? Madonna?" I said breathlessly.

"Bridget Callaghan," he said.

"Who's that?"

"Pat's wee girl, the youngest. She's just back from university. She's dropped out, so don't say anything about that, it would upset her, ok?"

I nodded. But there was something else. I could read Andy like a book.

"What?"

"What do you mean what?"

"Tell me."

Andy sighed.

"Darkey's very fond of her, she's very beautiful. Darkey treats her like a daughter. He told me specifically he wants me to look after her now she's back in New York, so she doesn't get in any trouble. Now, Michael, that means you, too, I don't want you trying to go off with her, ok?"

"Ok."

"Promise me," Andy said.

"Jesus, I promise," I said.

"Ok, let's go meet them, she's got a couple of wee friends with her, I think."

"And can I ask them out?"

"'Course."

We met Bridget.

She had dyed blond hair and freckles. It might be that she was beautiful, but I couldn't get a good look at her under the party lights. She offered her hand. I shook it.

"Michael Forsythe," I said.

"Andy told me you were here. I'm Bridget. He says you'll be working for him," Bridget said in a bubbly New York accent.

"Yeah, right, I'll be working for Andy," I said sarcastically.

"Listen, it's nice to meet you, but I'm not stopping, the last place on earth I'd want to be on a Saturday night is a party at Scotchy's house."

"I can see why," I said.

There was a long awkward pause during which I identified her perfume as something refined from citrus zest.

"Well, it was nice meeting you," she said and turned to find her friends. I watched her bum sashay through the party. She gave Andy a friendly kiss on the cheek. Much to my surprise, I found that I was jealous. I quickly barged through the crowd and stood beside her.

"You don't have to go yet," I said to her.

"I do, I have to find my friends," she muttered.

"Yeah, Michael won't keep you," Andy said.

"Well, Andy won't keep you, he has to get back to listening to the Carpenters," I attempted weakly.

"Being a wetback, Michael has to go home early and hide from the INS," Andy said, giving me the skunk eye.

"At least I don't have zero bar presence," I said.

"At least I don't smoke," Andy replied.

"At least I'm old enough to smoke."

"I'm the same age as you," Andy said.

"Why don't you two boys just kiss and make up," Bridget mocked.

Andy and I were put in our place, and we both laughed. Bridget was quick as well as cute, and I was now officially captivated. I tapped Andy on the back five times, which meant that all I wanted was five minutes alone with her. He gave me a suspicious look but went off to refill his drink.

"You're a student," I asked her when we were alone

"I *was* a student. I left after two semesters."

"Where were you at?"

"University of Oregon."

"Beautiful place, I hear."

"Yes," she said.

"Doing?"

"Celtic studies."

"Interesting stuff?"

"Yes."

"You enjoyed all those trees?"

"Uh-huh."

Her one word answers were a clue things weren't going well. I stopped the patter and looked at her.

"Ok, Bridget, so you're beautiful, you're smart, and you're pissed off because you can't believe you're at this party with a bunch of drunken hoods, and that might have appealed to you once but for the last half a year you've seen the wider, more cosmopolitan world, and now it's a bit too *Return of the Native* and you're thinking how long do I have to talk to this imbecile before I can get my friends to go the fuck home. Perceptive, huh?"

She smiled.

"Perceptive," she agreed.

"If it's not a sore topic, why did you drop out?"

"Well, you were wrong about one thing, I'm not smart. I do hate it here, but I'm not clever enough to get away from here. I don't suppose I'll ever get away from here. From all this. Not now. I didn't drop out, I flunked out," she said.

"You don't seem like a dummy to me," I told her.

"Thank you, Michael," she said and smiled so sweetly it nearly broke my heart, and things could have gone swimmingly after that had not Scotchy and Andy got into an argument about something and began screaming at each other. Scotchy and Andy? It seemed unlikely, but there it was. Sunshine and Big Bob were holding back Andy; Mikey Price and David Moran were holding on to Scotchy.

I found Fergal.

"What's going on?" I asked him.

"Andy's had a bit too much to drink, he says Scotchy's been robbing him blind," Fergal explained. "Scotchy says he's going to kick his fuck in."

"Jesus."

"Sunshine won't let them come to blows, but the problem is Andy's right, Scotchy probably *has* been robbing him blind," Fergal continued.

"That Scotchy seems like a nasty wee shite," I said.

"Oh, you don't know the half of it."

"I'm going to shoot him in the kneecaps," Scotchy was yelling.

"Aye, resort to fucking firearms, cowardly fucking shite," Andy said.

"That's enough, for God's sake, you stupid fucks," Sunshine said, very atypically losing his cool. Andy and Scotchy stared at him, chastened.

Sunshine whispered something to Scotchy. He shook his head and stormed off.

The party continued for about five minutes, but suddenly the music stopped and everyone turned around to look at Scotchy, who was standing on top of his massive stereo speakers.

"Everybody shut up," Scotchy yelled.

In a second the whole place was as quiet as a funeral parlor.

"Wee Andy and I have had a disagreement about something and he called me a coward. Now, I've thought about it and I cannot let it lie. If there's one thing I can't stand for, it's being publicly called a yellow bastard. I'll take anything else but not fucking that."

"Get down from there, Scotchy," Sunshine said from somewhere.

"No, Sunshine, not this time; I fucking respect you, but you have to respect me. We are going to play a wee game to see who exactly is the toughest, baddest black hat in town."

Everyone cheered, thinking that this was some powerful new joke of Scotchy's.

Scotchy quieted them down with a wave of his hand and then whispered to Big Bob, who was standing next to him. Big Bob nodded and ran into the bedroom at the rear of the flat. When he came back he was holding something. I pushed my way to the front and saw that it was a gun. Six-shot revolver. Scotchy took it from Big Bob and held it up in the air. Everyone gasped. A few backed away.

Andy was looking at Scotchy, swallowing hard. His face white as a funeral notice. Holding on to a chair back like it was the stern rail on the *Titanic*. He was trying hard to stop himself from shaking, stop himself from going down.

"Ok, everyone knows the rules, so I won't bother to explain. I'm taking out five bullets, as you can see. That leaves one left. Look."

"Wait a minute, Scotchy," Sunshine said from the back, but even he couldn't stop this now. The crowd shushed him and wouldn't let him through.

Scotchy took out five rounds and put them in his pocket.

"Fucking wise the bap, Scotchy," I said, since no one else was going to.

"Bruce, new boy, you shut the fuck up and learn your fucking place," Scotchy said with menace. I wanted to reply, but when I opened my mouth, it was dry. I saw Fergal and caught his eye. He seemed as frightened as I was.

Scotchy climbed down off the speaker and cleared a circle around himself.

"Me first," he said.

He took the revolver and spun the chamber. He pointed at his head. He closed his eyes and pulled the trigger. The barrel revolved, the hammer went back and came down on an empty chamber. No bullet.

The place erupted. One of the girls fainted, a biker threw up, and everyone else cheered hysterically. Andy looked as if he was about to pass out.

"See, everybody. No chicken, me," Scotchy said. He called for silence and passed the gun first to Bob and then to Andy. Andy took it as if it were a dead animal. I tried to find Sunshine in the crowd to see if he would stop what was happening, but he was lost in the sea of faces. Everything was blurring up and dissolving.

Andy took the revolver and put it to his right temple. The muzzle caressing his blond hair. Andy seemed so young, like a farm boy from Galway or Iowa or somewhere.

"Don't," I said, but no words came out.

Andy closed his eyes and pulled the trigger.

There was silence. The hammer came down. Then everyone was cheering again. Scotchy lifted Andy up into the air and proclaimed him the winner. He took the revolver and showed us that it had been empty the whole time. Scotchy carried Andy around the flat twice and set him down on the sofa. Strangers were coming over and patting him on the back. Scotchy was laughing hysterically with Big Bob, who'd been in on the whole thing. I found Bridget practically sobbing in a corner.

"You left me," she said.

"I didn't. I wanted to see what was happening to my friend, I—" I tried to explain.

She looked at me in disgust.

"A man pulled a gun out and you left me. You are just like all the rest. It's all a fucking boys' club, isn't it?" she said.

I didn't know how to respond. She shook her head and wiped away a tear.

"I'm leaving," she said.

"Can I, um, escort you home or anything?" I asked.

"No."

"I suppose I'll see you around," I said.

"If you're working for Darkey, yes, then I probably will see you around," she said coolly. She found her remaining friends and stormed out.

Fergal found me sitting on the balcony looking out at the black Hudson and the George Washington Bridge. I was beginning to have serious misgivings about coming here to America. About working with Scotchy. About doing what they wanted me to do for them.

"Get you a beer, it'll cheer you up," Fergal said, reading my thoughts.

"Nah, no beer, just need a bit of peace and quiet," I said.

I shook my head. That thing with Bridget had seriously depressed me. And it was too late to go back to Ireland. I owed Darkey five hundred bucks and the money for the flight. I'd have to work that off at least. Fergal saw that I was troubled.

"We'll go get Andy and go home," he said.

We found him sitting in a corner, trying not to cry.

"You're tonight's big winner," I told him.

He nodded.

"Let's go home," I said. All three of us went outside. Andy was still shaking, and I had to steady him with my arm.

"You think you can walk?" I asked.

"I'm fine," Fergal answered.

"I wasn't talking to you, ya big ganch," I said.

"I'll be ok in a minute," Andy said.

We walked east in silence in the direction of the IRT stop. It was a cold, cold night and the hazy stars were out.

"Bob told me that Scotchy had a live round in it when it was his turn, but he made him take it out for Andy," Fergal muttered at last.

"He's still fucking crazy," I said.

The IRT stop was deserted, but in New York, I learned, the trains run all night. It appeared at two-thirty. We got in. For Fergal and Andy it would be just a few stops, me all the way down to 125th Street.

"Well, you finally met Scotchy, our new crew chief." Andy said sardonically.

"I finally did," I agreed.

"He's not as bad as all that," Fergal said. "You'll see, a year from now, we'll have the finest crew in the city and we'll all be the best of mates."

A year from then, Fergal, Scotchy, and Andy were dead in Mexico. I had lost a foot and I had killed Bridget's fiancé, Darkey White.

The subway car rattled. The lights flickered. Andy got off. Fergal got off. I lit a cigarette.

"The best of mates," I said drowsily, let the fag slip between my fingers, and dozed long past my stop and all the way down to Ninety-sixth Street.

❖ ❖ ❖

A helicopter gunship flying overhead. Baghdad? Nah, it's raining. The other B. Belfast.

Stars.

Stars that are still there when I close my eyes.

Sheesh.

Why, of all memories, this one?

Why, indeed. I get to my feet. I'm in an alley. My face covered with blood.

My cell phone ringing.

"Hello?"

"Michael, where are you?" Bridget asks.

"Town."

"Have you found anything?"

"Aye, a name, it might be good."

"Look, I want you to forget it. We've been instructed to go to Arthur Street police station. They're calling with specifics and I'm having the money delivered. We're getting the call in a few minutes. I'm cooperating fully. It's too late now. We're doing the exchange at midnight. I don't want you to fuck it all up."

"Bridget, wait a minute, this is a good lead, I—"

"Michael, I told you to forget it, Siobhan's life is at stake here. The most important thing is Siobhan. I want you to back off. I'll send you something for your time. Ok, hold on. . . . Ok, I have to turn the phone off now, Michael, I don't expect to see you again."

The dial tone.

Silence.

What had happened to that little freckled frightened girl?

Darkey had schooled her.

I had schooled her.

She had schooled herself.

No one messed with her now.

But even so. Back off? Like hell.

She doesn't see the big picture. This isn't going to end with an exchange of girl for cash. This is going to be bloody. These people are ruthless.

And what's more, I nearly have the bastards.

I look at my watch. It's not even nine o'clock. Plenty of time left.

I head out of the alley, toward lights. I find a bar. Stagger to the bathroom. Take off my jacket, Zeppelin T-shirt. Examine myself carefully in the mirror. Bruises all over my rib cage, scrapes, cuts. No sign of internal bleeding, though. Nothing protruding through the skin. I touch individual ribs.

A couple might be cracked. Not that you can do anything about a cracked rib. I fill the sink with hot water and wash the blood off my face. Rinse my chest and clean the wounds with a paper towel. Couple of nasty cuts on my forehead. I stick my head in the sink and try to get the clotted blood out of my hair. I click the hand dryer and blow hot air on my face and arms. Read the graffiti while I'm drying. "Death to Prods." "Death to Fenians." "Fuck the Pope." "Fuck the Queen." And, a new one on me: "Asylum Seekers, Go Home."

Fix the duct-tape bandage, adjust my prosthesis, T-shirt on, jacket on. Check the revolver. Reload. Exit.

"Arthur Street police station?" I ask the keep.

"Who wants to know?" he says.

No more time for this shit. I pull the revolver out of my trousers and point it at his face.

"Arthur Street police station?"

"Go out of here, straight on, till ye hit Powers Street, make a left at the Boots, then another left, ya can't miss it."

"Thank you," I say, put the revolver away, and leave his bar, vanishing out into the creeping, cold Belfast night with all the other gun-toting villains.

10: THE LOTUS EATERS
(BANGOR—JUNE 16, 9:15 P.M.)

The police barracks was a fortress. Twenty-foot-high redbrick walls reinforced with concrete layers and steel piles. On top another fifteen feet of fencing angled outward so that grenades and handheld bombs would slide off. The gate was shipyard steel, running on rollers that could open quickly to let a vehicle in or out. A guard tower watching the entrance was surrounded by sandbags and in front of the barracks and all the way around the wall there were TV cameras and mirrors. The road leading to the station was shut on three sides and the fourth had speed bumps every fifteen feet. Even with all that, in the old days, the police station got attacked about once a week. Sometimes with mortars fired over from the nearby housing estate, sometimes by kids with coffee-jar bombs thrown in a night attack, and occasionally, a sophisticated terrorist would fire off a Libyan-assembled Russian rocket. There would always be collateral damage and for every cop there'd be one or two civilians hurt too.

But that was then. A lot had changed in Belfast since and the cops had gotten fat, lazy, and inattentive, no longer dressing in full riot gear or carrying submachine guns. But still, you'd think after today's incident the peelers would be on high alert. For all they knew, the failed RPG attack on their colleagues could be the herald of a big breakdown in the six-year-long IRA cease-fire. Dozens of attacks might be on the way this very night. A major IRA assault with bombs, guns, rockets—it could be the start of the Northern Irish civil war. So either they'd gotten information from O'Neill and the IRA brass that the RPG attack was nothing to do with them or they were even more bloody complacent than I thought. Probably the latter. The peelers inside the gatehouse didn't even notice when I knocked at the bulletproof window. They were drinking tea, laughing, and watching a football game on a portable television.

"Hey," I said, and knocked even louder to attract their attention.

"What is it?" an irritated copper yelled through the glass.

"I'm with Bridget Callaghan," I said. "She's supposed to be here?"

"You're late. They're all here already," the policeman said.

"Ok, where am I supposed to go?" I asked.

Man. United scored a goal on the telly. One peeler cheered while another one groaned, reached into his pocket, and gave him a fiver.

"Bridget Callaghan?" I tried again.

"Oh, aye. Across the yard, present yourself at registration," a copper said. I hesitated at the gate and went in. They didn't even want to search me. So here I was, walking into a police station in Belfast with a handgun in my pocket.

I skipped around the puddles in the courtyard, entered the main barracks. A sergeant with a walrus mustache was flipping through the *Sun* and talking to a young constable. Both purposely ignored me as I walked up to the desk.

"You see, that's why so many Americans are dying in Iraq. If a Humvee gets hit by an RPG, it just sits there and blows up. A Land Rover or any other high-sided vehicle will roll over and the impact will be much, much less. The low center of gravity actually works against the bloody Humvee," the sergeant was explaining.

"Is that so?" the constable said, concealing a yawn.

"Aye, it is, that's why our boys survived today's incident," the sergeant said.

"They weren't even in a Land Rover, they were on foot patrol," the constable said, rolling his eyes, as if he'd heard this and similar crazy arguments too many times before.

"Excuse me," I said.

"What do you want?" the sergeant asked, glancing over the topless woman on page three.

"I'm looking for Bridget Callaghan," I said.

"Did you kidnap her wean and now you're turning yourself in?" he asked deadpan.

"Aye," I said. "That's exactly it."

"What do you want?" he asked.

"I work for her, I've got some information."

"Interview room three, she's with the chief super. Chief super, indeed. We're pulling out all the stops for her even though we had four officers attacked today," he said with obvious distaste.

"Thanks," I said and walked down the corridor.

"Aye, you go to your fucking hoodlum bitch boss," the sergeant muttered under his breath.

I stopped, turned, went back to the desk.

"What did you say?" I asked.

"I said your boss, Bridget Callaghan, is a fucking American hoodlum bitch, who we should be fucking deporting, not helping," the sergeant said.

"Take it easy, Will," the constable said.

"Take it easy? Take it easy? Four good coppers nearly topped today and some snatch from America has us running through hoops because she's lost her fucking slut of a daughter. I mean, Jesus Christ, talk about priorities."

I stared at the sergeant. Even if the other peelers around here weren't upset about the RPG attack, he was old enough to remember when such things were a daily occurrence. It was really sticking in his craw. Still, that was no bloody excuse.

"Listen, mate, you might not like Bridget Callaghan, she's not exactly my best friend either, but you better take back what you said about her kid."

"Or you'll what?"

"Or I'll tell her what you said," I said, grinning, to show I meant it. The sergeant thought about it for a moment. He didn't want to lose face in front of the constable, but even so, Bridget had a reputation. He hesitated for a second or two and then looked down.

"No offense meant," he said quietly.

"None taken," I replied, and hurried down the long beige hall.

A door was open to one of the interview rooms. I knocked and peered inside. Two peelers watching a porn movie, writing things down on clipboards, a stack of fifty more tapes on the floor. On TV a heavyset German woman beating a naked German man. *"Ach, ach, mein Schwanz,"* the man protesting.

"Bridget Callaghan?" I asked.

"Next door on the other side of the corridor," one of the peelers said.

I crossed the hall and knocked on the door.

"Enter," a voice said.

I went in. A bunkerlike room with no windows and big Ordnance Survey maps of Belfast plastered over the flaky white concrete walls. An oak table with coffee cups, ashtrays, and several phones. Three uniformed female cops, two uniformed male cops, half a dozen plainclothes detectives, Moran, Bridget, the two goons from the elevator, the goon from the Crown wearing a bandage, a female assistant, a priest, and the chief superintendent, who was a forty-year-old high flier with a leather jacket, purple silk shirt, purple tie, and a blond ponytail. I could tell before he said anything to me that he was a wanker. He was explaining something to Bridget. No one saw me come in. I let him finish the sentence before I walked over to her.

Bridget looked up.

"Michael."

"How you doing?" I asked.

She smiled a little, thought about the question, closed her eyes, and then her body slumped forward slightly. She almost fell off her seat. Moran, the chief super, and I all made an attempt to steady her, but Moran nodded to one of the goons, who got between me and her. He placed his hand discreetly on my elbow and kept me from touching her. Moran and the chief super grabbed Bridget, helped her regain her composure. Moran looked at me furiously. I wasn't to touch her. Not now, not ever. I nodded to show that I understood him. There was no point making a scene.

"Michael, what happened to your face?" Bridget asked, her eyes widening with what in the old days one might have thought was concern. It threw me for a moment. Bridget brushed the red hair from her forehead and waited for an answer.

"I fell down a set of stairs, I'm fine." I said.

"Who are you?" the chief super asked, looking at my damaged leather jacket and Led Zeppelin T-shirt.

"I'm just a friend."

"Yeah, well, you and all your other mates better keep out of it. They're calling in ten minutes," he said.

"How do you know when they're calling?" I asked Bridget.

"They phoned the hotel and told me to get on over to the police station. They're going to want street closures and full cooperation from the police. They want the police to assure them they're going to back off. But it's ok, Michael, they just want the money, they don't want any trouble, they're going to let Siobhan go as long as we cooperate," Bridget said, her eyes brightening with hope.

I nodded. The kidnappers weren't so dumb. They appreciated that if the police were running things there was less chance of a cock-up. Bridget's men might fly off the handle or do something unpredictable, but the cops would not. All in all, sensible policy. But then what? How do you do it? How do you keep the peelers from following Bridget? How do you ensure that you get the cash and get away with it?

"Ms. Callaghan," the chief super said. "If I could get your attention, please . . ."

Bridget gave me a dismissive wave and began talking to him again. She was wearing jeans and a black sweater. She was beautiful. As devastating as ever, despite the circumstances. She couldn't help looking sexy. I couldn't help thinking that she looked sexy. Those eyes, those cheekbones.

Bridget would be a flame at seventy.

Moran approached me, took me to one side.

"What have you got, Forsythe?" he asked in a low tone. My ribs were killing me. I ignored Moran, grabbed a cold cup of coffee, swallowed one of the morphine pills I'd taken from O'Neill.

"What have you got, Forsythe?" Moran asked again.

I looked at him closely. What was his game? Could he be trusted? How many angles was he playing at once?

"I've got a name," I said. "A man called Slider."

"What about him?"

"He might be part of the gang that lifted Siobhan. But if not, he might be involved somehow. I'm really not too sure," I said, deciding to be honest with him.

"Is that it?"

"That's it."

"It's a bit fucking vague, isn't it?"

"Well, it's not much of a lead, but—"

"Do you see what time it is?" he interrupted.

I looked at my watch. It was almost nine o'clock.

"Nearly nine," I said.

His eyes narrowed. He'd given me the chance to do something, to pull myself out of the trough. A narrow shot at redemption and I hadn't come through.

"It's too late. It's over. Can't afford any interference. Everybody's rolling now," he said.

"What do you want me to do with the name?"

"You've got the name of somebody who somehow might be involved. Terrific. Tell the cops after the exchange. After the exchange. We can't have them or you messing things up, as per fucking usual."

"I never messed anything up in my life," I said.

"You haven't fucking messed up? You killed my brother and Sunshine and Darkey White and ratted out the rest of the fucking crew," he said with fury.

"Yeah, that wasn't a fuck-up, mate, that was deliberate," I said.

His fists clenched, his face reddened, and he gave me a look of cold, calm hate.

He was about to say something else but just then the phone rang. Everyone in the room stopped what they were doing and looked at it ominously. Bridget picked it up, the chief super nodded to a peeler next to a bank of electronic equipment, signaling him to begin recording the conversation and put it on the speaker. He put his finger to his lips and nodded at Bridget.

"Hello?" she said.

It was the switchboard.

"I have a call for Bridget Callaghan," the switchboard operator said.

The chief super leaned into the speakerphone.

"Put them through to interview room three, keep the line open, and start the traceback," he said.

Static, a long pause, and then a voice:

"Hello?"

"Hello," Bridget said.

"Bridget Callaghan?" the voice asked. A foreign accent, and there was something about it that immediately tweaked me. It sounded European, Spanish maybe. Very old. A man in his late eighties or nineties.

The interview-room door suddenly opened and another young peeler came in; he gave the chief super the thumbs-up. The trace was on.

"I'm Bridget, I want to speak to Siobhan," Bridget said, the way she'd been coached.

There was a silence on the line and a voice began to speak. This time, a different person. A young man, definitely from Belfast. North Belfast, if I had to guess.

"Your daughter is still alive, I can assure you of that. Now, about tonight—"

"I want to speak to her," Bridget insisted.

"You'll do as you're fucking told," the voice said.

"I won't do anything until I speak to Siobhan," Bridget said.

Another pause. Longer.

"Siobhan, say something," the second voice finally demanded.

A brief silence and then a tiny "Mommy? Mommy?"

"Oh, Siobhan, honey, are you ok?" Bridget said, bursting into tears, barely able to control herself.

"I'm ok, Mommy, I'm ok, Mommy, I'm ok—"

"What have they done to you, have they been feeding you? Are you ok?"

"Um, I'm ok. . . . I feel funny."

"Oh, Siobhan, darling, it's going to be ok, I'm going to see you in a couple of hours, be brave, honey, I love you so much," Bridget said soothingly.

"Love you, Mommy," the girl said dreamily.

Silence. Bridget choked down sobs and the second kidnapper came on again.

"Did you get the money?"

"I got the money," Bridget said.

"Good. Ok, you know she's alive, and you'll get her back and everything is going to go very smooth if you fucking cooperate. Ok. I have a list of things to tell you. Tell the fucking peelers to write this down. The first thing is this. All helicopters in Belfast need to be grounded at eleven o'clock. If there's one helicopter flying in the sky after eleven, the deal is off and the girl dies. Second, there's a phone box at the Albert Clock. We'll be calling at twenty to twelve. You have to come there alone with the ten million. If we see one peeler, or one of your fucking boys, the deal is off and the girl dies. Third, we are going to be bouncing you all over the city, so you better come in a car, and you better fucking know how to drive, because if we see anyone else in the car, the deal is off and the girl dies. Fourth, do not let anyone try to follow you, if we see anyone following you, the deal is off and the girl dies. Fifth, when you meet with the middleman, he is going to search you. If you don't have the money or you're wired up in any way, the deal is off, he walks away, and the girl dies. No GPS, no bugs, no transponders, no mobile phones. Have you understood these arrangements?"

"The pay phone at the Alfred Clock," Bridget said.

"The pay phone at the *Albert* Clock. Twenty to midnight. There you'll get your initial instructions. Bring a car and bring the fucking money and come alone. If you're a fucking eejit, you're going to lose your daughter; if you play it cool, everybody's going to be happy."

The line went dead.

The constable who had given the thumbs-up came back into the interview room.

"Well?" the chief super asked.

"Oh, we traced it, no problem, sir, but the bad news is that it's from a batch of phones stolen from a shop in Larne. The cards were all canceled, but they've obviously reactivated them somehow," the constable said.

"So you couldn't find out anything?" the chief super asked.

"Well, they're almost certainly calling from Belfast. It was a strong local signal. Tech boys say a radius of about five miles. That's about all we can tell," the constable said.

The chief super groaned.

While the two cops talked and the other peelers pretended to be busy, Bridget was quietly sitting there sobbing. Gone was the general, the bitch boss, all that was left was the frightened mom. I pushed past Moran and the goons and sat next to her. Gently I put my arm around her.

"Bridget, are you ok?" I asked.

She nodded, didn't push my arm away, continued crying.

"Siobhan is still alive, it's wonderful. I knew she would be, anyone with your genes is a survivor. She's alive and she sounds good. And you'll be seeing her really soon," I whispered.

Bridget smiled.

"Oh, Michael, I hope you're right," she said.

The chief super began barking orders to the peelers, who were standing around gawking.

"Oliver, you see about the helicopters, get on to the army and the airports. Pat, get a team of detectives over to the Albert Clock; Erin, you see about a car for Ms. Callaghan, get a bug in it, get a camera in it if you can; Lara, you make sure Ms. Callaghan gets rigged up. Sam, he said no helicopters, but see if we can get a microlight up there with a camera. Ari and Sophie, find out the locations of all the phone boxes within a mile radius of the Albert Clock; we'll stake out every bloody one of them if we can."

Bridget stood.

"He said no cops," Bridget said. "He said if he saw one cop, he'd kill Siobhan."

"Don't worry, miss, these will be plainclothes detectives; he won't even notice us, it'll be very discreet, I assure you," the chief super said.

Bridget was angry now.

"No fucking cops. Ok? This is my show. I'm cooperating with those sons of bitches. Cancel your fucking microlight and call back those detectives," she said vehemently.

The chief super shook his head, but her eyes turned him.

"Ok, if that's what you want," he said reluctantly.

"It's what I insist upon," Bridget said.

"At least let us put a bug in the car and on your person—"

"You can bug the car but not me, he was perfectly clear about that.

I don't want you Paddy fucks ruining this for me. You haven't been able to find my daughter, you haven't been able to do anything. So now it's over, just keep out of it and let this go ahead. Once I get Siobhan, you can do what you like finding these bastards."

The chief super was about to add something but bit his tongue instead.

"If that's what you need, fine," he said finally.

Bridget dabbed her eyes, took a sip of water.

"It is," Bridget said. "Now, if you'll excuse me I have to go to the ladies' room."

She got up. A female constable helped her out.

Moran stood behind me and hauled me to my feet. I would have smacked the fucker but for the presence of the Old Bill. I pushed his hand away from me.

"Keep your fucking paws off me. Touch me again and you're a dead man, peelers or no peelers," I snarled.

"Yeah, well, you heard the lady. You better pull the cord and get out of here, Forsythe, your services are no longer required," he said.

"I have things to do anyway. Don't be such an asshole."

We stared at each other and one of the younger detectives came over.

"Is there a problem here?"

"No problem, run along, sonny, the adults are talking," Moran said.

The cop couldn't think of a reply and walked shamefaced back to his colleagues.

"Ok, Moran. Fine, you're a big man. Great. It's not midnight yet. You can tell me this—Bridget's pretty emotional—was that definitely her? Definitely Siobhan?" I asked him.

"It was her," Moran said.

"And that first voice, have you ever heard it before?"

"Nope."

"It was foreign, wasn't it? There was something about it," I said.

"I told you, I haven't heard it before. You're trying my patience, Forsythe. Well, you won't be trying it for too long. As soon as we get Siobhan back—"

"Aye, I know. Well, like I say, join the queue, I'm not exactly Mister Popular round these parts."

"Price you pay for being a rat murderer," Moran said.

Bridget came back into the interview room. She couldn't stand now. Moran helped her into a chair. She blew her nose. She'd been crying on and off for hours. For days, really, but once again I was struck by her. She was haggard and she was older but she looked extraordinary. Age had only deepened her loveliness. It had removed the rawness of youth and replaced it with an elegance, a charm, a breathless quality. No longer a bubbling champagne. Now a cognac of the first reserve. Smoldering, earthy, vulnerable, pure.

And in a way, looking at her was like looking in a mirror. We had both done terrible things. We had both changed so much.

And I saw something else.

I knew I loved Bridget now. I'd always loved her, from that very first moment, and all through the years and even now when she was trying to kill me. I couldn't help it. No one could. I could even forgive Darkey White for what he did to us, to me and Scotchy and all the rest. Our lives were worth it, for a chance of happiness with this woman.

A constable came in with a large briefcase full of money. It brought me back to my senses. Ten million in sterling and international bearer bonds. How much was that in dollars? Was Bridget worth that much? Of course she was. That and much more. She'd have paid fifty million to get Siobhan back. Kidnappers couldn't be that savvy, then, or they would have known that. Or maybe they did know it, but wanted a sum she could raise quickly. Or perhaps there was more to all this than just the cash.

"Let's get you a cup of tea and get you prepped," the chief super said to Bridget.

"Ok," she replied meekly, tired now, close to the edge.

She was led away by the chief super and one of the female constables. She didn't get a chance to say goodbye to me. I stood awkwardly for a moment, wondering what to do next. Moran made his presence felt at my arm.

"Make yourself scarce, Forsythe. We'll count to a thousand and then we're coming," he said. No smile on his face, just those brutal, vengeful eyes.

"Ok," I said, stole his cigarettes and lighter from the table, and walked out of the interview room.

In the corridor I found the constable who'd been doing the trace. He looked keen and amenable; he might do.

"Listen, mate, I'm a private detective working for Bridget, can you do me a wee solid? I need the address of a Slider McFerrin in Bangor, he might be involved in all of this. I don't know, but I think he might be the one that stole those phones of yours."

"Do you now? Slider what?"

"McFerrin, he lives in Bangor."

"Ok," he said, but he didn't rush off to go check it out.

"Come on, mate, quid pro quo, I gave you the name, tell me his address and I'll check it out. It might be a dead end, but I promise I'll give you everything I get," I said.

"You'll give who?"

"I'll give you personally."

"Fair enough. I'll see what I can do, hold on there."

I took a seat in the corridor and closed the door on the two peelers watching the German porn flick.

The keen copper came back.

"Slider McFerrin?" he asked.

"Aye."

"James McFerrin, lives with his ma at 6 Kilroot View Road, Bangor. You think he's mixed up in this?"

"He might be."

"Well, he's a player all right."

"What can you tell me?

"I can't tell you anything. Watch your step, though. Bad family. He's one of six boys. Eldest was killed by his own side, the ma runs bootleg whiskey, and he's done time in the Maze for murder, assault, and grievous bodily harm. He was released under the Good Friday Agreement. Nothing about theft, phones or otherwise, but he's a bad 'un."

"Cheers, mate."

I walked out into the station car park. It was raining again now. The drains had been blocked up and narrowed to tiny slits so that a terrorist couldn't crawl into the sewers and blow the police station up from underneath. The car park was flooding and a peeler with a foot pump was trying to get the water out of the bigger potholes. It was a sorry sight.

"You couldn't give us a hand there?" the peeler asked, mistaking me for a plainclothes detective.

"Fuck, no," I told him.

I left the cop shop, walked a few blocks, found a taxi stand outside the Ulster Hall. They were just letting out a revival preacher, a Dr. McCoy from the Bob Jones ministry in America. Revival meetings were popular in Belfast. From the airbrushing on his poster, Dr. McCoy seemed a wee bit more suspicious than most, and sure enough, the patrons had been so thoroughly fleeced that no one even had any dough left for a taxi. I skipped to the front of the line.

The driver of the black cab was glad to see me.

"Hanging about here for bloody ten minutes," he complained. "I suppose the rest of your mates are waiting to get beamed up."

I got the joke, told him the address in Bangor.

"I see you're wearing a Zeppelin T-shirt. Did you know that the Ulster Hall was the very place where Zep played 'Stairway to Heaven' for the first time?"

I said I didn't know, but there was an extra fifty quid in it if he shut up and another fifty if he drove to Bangor like the hounds of hell were after him.

✾　✾　✾

A wind from the Arctic taking the black smoke from Kilroot Power Station and blowing it down over the bad facsimiles of houses in the dour northern part of Bangor. The shore and the oily sea slinking back into themselves and the smell of burning permeating everything. Ash on clotheslines and whitewashed walls and on almost all the windward-facing surfaces, as if the golden head of the enormous belching chimney top was in some sinister coitus with the dank and cheerless settlement.

Kids out playing football, older folks sitting in deck chairs, chatting. It was a break in the rain, and in Northern Ireland you used those breaks when you could get them.

The people were Protestants. I knew this not because they were physically unlike or dressed differently from Catholics—indeed, anyone who says that he can tell a Catholic Irishman from a Protestant Irishman by looking at him is a liar, since a third of all marriages in Ulster are across the sectarian divide. Nah, I knew it because the curbstones had been painted red, white, and blue, there were murals of King Billy at the ends of the street, there was a painted memorial for the battle of the Somme on the side of a house, and the flags flying in this neighborhood were the Scottish saltaire, Old Glory, the Union Jack, the Ulster flag, and the Israeli Star of David. If there were Catholics on this street, they kept bloody quiet about it.

I knocked on the door of number six.

A kid answered. About ten, freckles, brown hair, patched sweater, cheeky looking.

"What do you want?" he asked.

"I'm looking for Slider."

"He's away," the kid said.

"Where is he?"

"Don't know."

"Who does know?"

"Ma."

"Is she home?"

"She'll be back in five minutes. Down the shops. Do you want to wait inside?"

"Well, are you sure that would be ok?"

"Aye. It's fine."

I followed the kid inside the council house.

A broken light and a narrow hall filled with a death-trap assortment of toys: skateboards, roller skates, cricket balls. The kid opened a door to the left and I followed him into the living room. Boards on the floor, bare walls, and some kind of grotesque papier-mâché statue in the middle of the room. Another kid, a little younger than the first, adding more wet paper to the statue.

"What in the name of God is that?" I asked.

"It's the fucking pope, what do you think?" the first kid said.

I looked again. The Holy Father's head was lying on some old plywood and empty vodka boxes. It was still crude, with black-marker facial hair and possessing only a hastily drawn lopsided grin, instead of the full black-toothed variety that would frighten even the youngest children. Just over six feet high and draped in a white sheet, it looked more like a Klansman than the leader of the Catholic Church.

"Do you not think it's any good?" the younger kid asked.

"What are your names?" I asked the first.

"I'm Steven, he's Monkey," the first kid said.

"You're telling me that that's supposed to be the pope?" I asked Steven, looking at my watch.

"Aye, it is."

"What's it for?"

"Are you not from around here?" Steven asked.

And then I remembered. Of course. The Twelfth of July was coming up. The anniversary of the Battle of the Boyne, when Protestant King William defeated Catholic King James, a victory celebrated every year by burning the pope in effigy.

The kid looked at me for an answer.

"No, I'm not from around here."

I lit a cigarette and sat down on a ripped leather sofa. The kids demanded a share and so I lit a couple more.

"Well, what you think of the pope?" Steven asked, smoking expertly.

What I thought was that that was the whole problem with Protestant ideology in Northern Ireland. They had gotten it all wrong—the way to really preserve a culture was to celebrate and nurture the memory of a glorious defeat, not a famous victory. That's why Gallipoli, Gettysburg, the Field of Blackbirds, the Alamo became the foundation myths for the Kiwis, the American South, Serbs, and Texas. Every year the Shi'a celebrate a massacre and, of course, Christianity is founded upon an execution.

"The pope doesn't have a beard," I said.

"See," Steven told Monkey, shaking his head dramatically and dropping the ash from his cigarette onto the bare floor.

"What exactly are you saying, wee lad?" Monkey said.

"I told ya," Steven said with satisfaction.

Monkey's face went through a spasm.

"You told me he had a beard like Jesus in *The Passion*."

"I did not," Steven replied indignantly.

"Did so," Monkey said, clenching his fists.

"Not."

They had both forgotten I was there. They were about to come to blows and even if they didn't, they were giving me a bloody headache.

"Ok, lads, give it a rest. Steven, here's a fiver, away you go and find your ma for me," I said.

The kid took the note and sprinted out into the street. The other wean looked at me suspiciously, puffed on his cigarette, and went back to his work.

"Are you from America?" he asked after a while.

"Aye, now I am," I said.

"What's it like out there?" he asked wistfully.

"Exactly like the movies," I said.

The kid nodded. Just as he had suspected.

"I saw that Beyoncé Knowles the other day at the supermarket. Boy, is she a hottie," I said.

"You saw Beyoncé at the supermarket? What was she buying?" the kid asked.

"She was with Madonna and J.Lo; there was a special on Rice Krispies, they all had their trolleys loaded up."

"Beyoncé was getting Rice Krispies?" he asked, impressed.

"Uh-huh."

But before I could build an entire cathedral of lies, the living room door opened and a breathless Steven brought in a plump fifty-year-old woman wearing a Yankees cap, a bright yellow dress with green hoops, and sand-covered Wellington boots. She had the circumspect dark eyes of a sleekit old cow, so I knew I'd have to go careful. Monkey had stubbed his fag in the ashtray, but the woman immediately began sniffing the air. She grabbed Monkey by the ear.

"Aow," he said.

"Have you been smoking, young man?" she asked him.

"Nope."

"Don't lie to me," she said, twisting the ear a little more off the vertical.

"I haven't, honest."

"You better not. Stunts your growth and you're not shooting up as it is, so you're not."

That was a low blow and both boys knew it. They winced. I stood.

"Mrs. McFerrin, I was smoking, the boys weren't smoking, it was me."

She looked at the three cigarette ends in the ashtray and eyed me suspiciously.

"What are you doing here?"

"Well, I wanted to talk to you about some business. . . ." I began.

"Business, is it? Well, sit down, I'll go to the kitchen and make some tea."

"I don't have time for tea. I'm in a rush to make a flight," I said.

Her eyes narrowed. Her face scrunched up impressively. She looked for a moment like an accordion that had fallen from the cargo hold of a 747.

"No tea, no business," she said coldly.

I had clearly insulted her by declining her hospitality, and that in Ireland was a huge mistake.

"I would love a cup of tea, if you don't mind," I said. She went into the kitchen and I heard the kettle boiling. I looked at my watch. I really had no time for this shit, but I couldn't beat the information out of her, not in front of her weans. The two kids went back to their pope.

"Maybe he needs a belt or something," Monkey said as he looked at the effigy anew.

"You ever see the pope wear a belt?"

"What about those ropy belts that monks wear around their cassocks?"

"Around their what?" Steven asked, and both boys cracked themselves up laughing. I didn't see the funny side of anything right now.

"Mrs. McFerrin, I have to get going," I shouted into the kitchen, straining to keep calm.

She came back in with a teapot and a selection of chocolate biscuits. She poured some tea and I took a biscuit.

"Well," she said finally in a whisper. "How much poteen do you want?"

"I don't understand," I said.

"You're here to buy poteen, aren't you?"

"No, no, I'm not, I'm looking for Slider, my business is with him."

"Slider? I wouldn't have a clue where he is. I haven't seen him for two days," she said.

My heart sank.

"It's really important. Slider and I go way back, but you see the thing is, Mrs. McFerrin . . . um, I'll tell you what it is, I was just at the Ulster Hall there, Dr. McCoy from the States was in town doing a revival, and the thing is, I've been born again, but now I'm going back to Beverly Hills. I work over there. And I want to clear all my debts now that I've seen the light. You see, I owe Slider a thousand pounds, and I want to pay him before I go."

It was a crazy story, but this was a crazy house.

Greed lit up the fat lady's face.

"Well, son, that's a wonderful thing, you finding the Lord Jesus and everything. But I just don't know where he is or where he's been," she said.

"Doesn't he live here?"

"Not the last wee while; oh, but you know who might know, wee Dinger," she said.

"Who's Dinger?"

"He's my youngest; he's a wee bit, a wee bit, you know, special, that way . . . but Slider looks out for him. Takes him on trips and stuff. He's been taking him somewhere all this week, just for the run in the car. So Dinger might know."

"Where's Dinger now?" I asked.

"Where he always is. On the beach," Steven said.

"Whereabouts?"

"He'll be the only one out there."

"Well, it's been great talking to you, thank you very much, Mrs.—"

"Houl on a minute, big fella, I get a finder's fee, don't I? I told you where Slider is, or at least someone who knows where he is, so that's five percent. That's fifty quid," she demanded. I didn't want her to kick up a fuss. I give her five tens. She smiled and put it in her pocket. I hope it chokes ya, I said to myself, and went outside to look for the youngest member of the clan.

❊   ❊   ❊

The moon unhooking itself from the sea. The first stars. It was the gloaming now. The lingering summer twilight that in Northern Ireland and Scotland can last until nearly midnight at this time of year.

The tide was out and the sand was wet and freezing. Seaweed on the dunes. A few beached starfish and transparent jellyfish. You could see most of Belfast Lough spread in a big U-shaped curve, and from here in Bangor it was only about twenty miles across the water to Scotland. Tonight with the setting sun illuminating the hills in Galloway it seemed much closer.

Dinger was alone on the beach, gathering shells. I walked over from the seawall.

"Good shells?" I asked.

He dropped the collection with contempt and stomped away from me. He was in bare feet and jeans and a sweater too big for him. He had black hair and big eyes. He was about nine. He didn't look "special" or any more special than his brothers or his hatchet-faced ma. When he was far enough away from me, he began singing. He drew something in the sand with a piece of driftwood. He looked behind him to see if I had gone yet, and then he picked up a length of seaweed and popped some of the float pods on the strands. They went snap and briny water came out of them, trundling down his fingers onto his sweater. Some of the weeds were covered with diesel and were slimy and difficult for him to pull up.

"Can I help you with that?" I asked.

"You'll have to clean your shoes before you go in the house," he began, and then ran from me again.

Jesus, this was going to be more difficult than I thought. I had trouble catching him with all my injuries and my fake foot.

Dinger stopped abruptly and sat down next to a dead seagull, its wings covered in what looked like a thick glue and its head completely black. Tankers occasionally came down this way on their journey to Belfast, so it was possible there had been a small slick or an illegal dumping.

"It's dead," Dinger said to me.

"Yeah, I see that, it's very sad. You're Dinger, aren't you?" I asked.

"Everything dies," Dinger said. He regarded the seagull for a moment. He picked it up by the wing and offered it to me.

"No, thanks. Listen, Dinger, I want to talk to you about your brother Slider," I said.

"What's that?" Dinger asked, pointing to a rock covered in the brown edible seaweed called dulse. Dinger crawled over to the rock, lifted up the dulse, pointed at it.

"You know what that is?" Dinger asked again.

"Of course, it's dulse," I said.

Dinger broke off a dry piece and offered it to me. I took it from him.

"Eat it," he said.

I put it in my mouth. It was salty and revolting. I swallowed and struggled to keep it down.

"Thank you," I said.

"What it taste like?" Dinger asked.

"You never tasted dulse?"

"No," he said, his mouth opening and closing like a suffocating fish.

"What it taste like?" he asked again.

It tasted like something that had been shaved off the bottom of a trawlerman's seaboot and then matured by nailing it to the floor of a particularly nasty whorehouse for a couple of decades.

"It tastes ok," I said. "You wanna try?"

Dinger shook his head. He wasn't a complete fool. It started to rain. He pulled out a Glasgow Rangers hat and put it on. It was wool, so it didn't do much against the rain but it kept the wind out of his ears.

"Dinger, I want to talk to you," I tried again.

"Do you want to go on an adventure?" Dinger asked me.

"Dinger, I'd love to, some other time, but listen, I wonder if you could do me a favor? I'm looking for your brother Slider and your ma said that you knew where he's been going all week. He's been giving you a ride in his car, hasn't he?"

"You talk to my ma?"

"Aye."

"Huh. We go on an adventure."

It was really getting late now and I wondered if I was wasting my time with this wean.

"If I go on an adventure with you, will you tell me where your brother is?" I asked him.

"Yes, I tell if you do dare," Dinger said conspiratorially.

"I already ate the seaweed, isn't that enough?"

"You do dare," Dinger insisted angrily.

"Ok, ok, what's the dare?"

"I dare you to walk along the pipe," he said, pointing to a sewage outflow pipe that led from the shore to the lough. It didn't look like a particularly dangerous task, even though it was covered with seaweed and barnacles. The tide was still out and the water was only a few feet deep.

"Ok. If I walk along that pipe for a minute, you'll tell me where Slider is? Agreed?"

Dinger nodded.

"Shake on it," I insisted.

Hesitantly and with a great deal of consideration, he put out his left hand. His fingers were crossed and I knew that he was trying to stroke me.

"Ok, Dinger, your right hand and no crossies," I said.

Dinger frowned and put out his right hand instead.

I climbed on top of the sewage pipe and walked along it for a few paces. It had the worst smell in the world and a few sad-looking gulls flying about picking up complete turds from the water. The stench was too fucking much. I jumped off and walked back to Dinger, who was now petting a stray dog.

"Dogs hear things in ultraviolet. They hear everything high pitched, like Batman. No, it's not called ultraviolet, it's something else. Ultrasomething but not ultraviolet," he said.

I grabbed Dinger by the arm and held him tight. I bent down so that I was eye level with him.

"Now, Dinger, listen to me. I kept my part of the bargain, I walked along the pipe. You have to keep your end. Where's your brother?"

"I don't want to tell you," Dinger said, tears coming into his eyes.

"Why not?"

"If I tell you, you'll go away and I will have nobody to play with. Monkey and Stevey don't play with me."

"I'll come back and I'll bring Slider with me. You like Slider. Slider takes you places, doesn't he? Slider takes you on adventures."

Dinger's face brightened.

"Slider takes me on adventures. He says secret missions like on TV."

"Slider took you on a secret mission?" I asked, letting go of his arm and sitting next to him on the sand.

Dinger shook his head.

"Secret," he insisted.

"Oh, you can tell me, I'm Slider's best and oldest friend and I want to find him. We'll all go on an adventure together, would you like that?" I said.

Dinger grinned.

"And we can go in Slider's car?" Dinger asked.

"Of course we can go in Slider's car, and we can get ice cream afterwards. You and me and Slider."

"Yeah, and we don't ask Stevey or Monkey."

"No, we wouldn't ask them. Just the three of us, you and me and Slider. Now, where is Slider?" I asked softly.

"He's with the car."

"Where did he go in the car? On a secret mission?"

Dinger nodded solemnly.

"Where in the car?" I asked.

"To the secret place. To the lodge, the old lodge with the arch," Dinger said in a whisper.

"Where's the old lodge, Dinger?"

"I don't know."

"You don't know," I persisted.

"No."

"Oh, that's a shame, we won't be able to get Slider and go on an adventure," I said.

"We go adventure," Dinger said, bursting into tears.

"Dinger, you think for a minute, where is the secret lodge?"

Dinger stopped crying immediately, closed his eyes, and held his breath.

"Orange Lodge," Dinger said.

"Yeah, it's an Orange Lodge, where is it?"

His brow furrowed and he touched his forehead onto the sand.

I knew hardly anything about the Orange Order, just the basics: it was a working-class Protestant secret society founded in the eighteenth century. It honored the memory of William of Orange, who had become king of Britain and Ireland after he defeated James the Second, the last of the ill-starred Stuart kings.

Dinger stood up.

"Go home, Lucky, go home," he said to the dog, who looked at him for a second and then ran across the sand. When the dog was definitely out of earshot, Dinger beckoned me close with his finger.

"I know where," he whispered triumphantly.

"Where? Where's the lodge?"

"Near that big monument," Dinger said.

"What big monument?"

"The big monument across the water."

"In Scotland?" I asked, stifling a panic.

"No, no, no, just over there," he said, pointing out across the lough.

A monument over there.

I tried to see what he was pointing at, but it was so dark that you couldn't see anything across the lough except the lights of Belfast, Rathcoole, and Carrickfergus.

And then it came to me.

"Jesus, you don't mean the Knockagh Monument, do you, Dinger?"

The Knockagh Monument was a huge war memorial that had been placed on Knockagh Mountain near Belfast. I didn't know much about it, except that it was a massive granite stone, which I think was carved with the names of the Irish dead from the two world wars. It was certainly enormous, and from up on top of the mountain you could see fifty miles in every direction. It was a make-out place for teenagers. A single road to the monument surrounded by forest and farms. An isolated, out-of-the-way spot. I didn't recall any old abandoned Orange Lodges around there, but I didn't know the area that well.

Dinger nodded excitedly.

"Dinger, let me get this straight. Slider took you to an Orange Lodge near the Knockagh Monument?"

"Bird kite, an eagle kite," he said.

"You flew a kite at the Knockagh?"

"Aye. Knockagh, Knockagh, Knockagh. Slider said wait in car and we go see all of the world and fly the kite. Eagle kite."

"He told you to wait in the car outside an old abandoned Orange Lodge near the Knockagh, right? And there was an arch outside the lodge?"

"Secret mission. Wait in the car at the lodge. Doink, doink, doink."

"Did he ever mention a girl, a little girl?" I asked.

"We fly the kite, very windy."

"Ok, forget the girl. Can you tell me anything more about the lodge?"

"We fly kite," Dinger insisted.

"You went from the lodge to the Knockagh Monument and flew the kite?" I asked.

"Yes," Dinger said, exasperated with all the questions. He started walking away from me. But I had enough.

"Thanks, Dinger," I said and ran across the beach.

I digested the information. The kid might have made up the whole story and he was a bit of a looper, but Slider had been taking his kid brother somewhere this week. It could be that they were holding Siobhan in an abandoned Orange Lodge with an arched gateway not too far from the Knockagh Monument.

Slider tells Dinger to wait in the car while he delivers food or whatever to the rest of the kidnappers, and then immediately afterward he takes Dinger to the Knockagh, where they fly their kite.

Well, no good deed would go unpunished. Slider was only looking out for his retarded kid brother, but holy mother of God, I'd fucking kill him to get the girl.

And I really felt that I was close to her. This was a good lead. Slider was part of the gang. And if I were a betting man, I'd give you evens that Slider's wee brother had just told me where they were holding the girl.

I might have to top you, Slider, but it's your mistake, you're not supposed to tell anybody. Nobody. Not your ma, not your da, not your bro. You certainly don't bring him with you and tell him to wait in the car. Your mistake. . . .

I ran off the beach and into the center of town. I saw a taxi. Flagged it down.

"I'm on a call, you can't get in," the driver said.

I opened the door and got in the passenger's side. I gave him most of the money I had left in my wallet. Several hundred dollars and euros. I took the gun out of my pocket and held it in my hand. I didn't point it at him. Carrot and stick.

"Listen, mate, I need your fucking cab. You're going to tell the peelers that I hijacked ya, but you're going to wait till after midnight. Ok? Do we have a deal?"

"You need my cab for a couple of hours and you want to pay me five hundred euros? Fucksake, mate, you didn't need the gun."

"So we have an agreement?" I asked.

"I won't call the cops at all. But you've got to tell me, where are you gonna leave the car?"

"I don't know. I have to go. Take the money, and if you're calling the peelers, you better fucking wait till midnight. Ok? I won't need it after that," I said.

"No problem, squire, no skin off mine. Ratty old beast, just make sure you keep the clutch way down when you're changing gears."

The driver and I swapped positions.

I drove out of town.

The Knockagh was, of course, all the way on the other side of Belfast Lough. You had to go through the city to get there. I checked my watch. It was almost ten now. But that was time enough. More than time enough. No need to be reckless. I slowed from ninety to seventy-five.

"Hold on, Siobhan, hold on, ya wee skitter," I said to myself. Words affectionate and reassuring. Affection for *her* and her wean. Darkey's kid, yes, but half the genes belonged to her. And for Bridget's girl I would move the Earth. I'd done a lot already. I'd do more.

And you behind the mask.

It's already been decided.

Long before you or I was ever born.

Sit tight. In your bolt-hole a world away, a drive away, from here.

Do you feel that breeze on the back of your neck?

That's me.

Aye.

Sleep soft, assassins. Embrace your loved ones. Kiss your wives. Drink your fill of the cool night air.

Your days on this world have been reduced by the thousand and the ten thousand.

For I am coming.

I am coming.

11: THE WRATH OF ODYSSEUS
(THE KNOCKAGH—JUNE 16, 10:15 P.M.)

Silver light along the motorway. A darkening horizon. A gray road. The moon a yellow sickle above the sea.

Salt haze. Deserted shore.

Vehicles leaving the city. And farther, behind those hills, a gang of hoods and a sobbing, terrified kidnapped girl.

Something up there. Shapes just outside my field of vision. The songbirds are down. The seabirds, too. And, as per instructions, the helicopters are landing—abandoning the night to the insects and the doves navigating the magnetic field.

Something that's bigger than dragonflies, pigeons.

A look of recognition.

Ahhh, I know what they are.

Imaginary things—specters, furies, impatient gods hovering above the car. Watching me, hurrying me.

"Faster, faster."

They know it's barely started. Pain behind. Pain ahead. They feed on it. It nourishes them. Go ahead, dip your talons, have a taste.

"We'll assist you, death bringer."

The taxi driver left a thermos. I open it and drink some lukewarm tea. Another morphine pill. No more of those. In the army they'd ink an *M* on your forehead by this stage. Ignore the creatures, smell the night, the lough. Relax.

My palms on the steering wheel. My fingers loose. My fingers.

Look at them. Aye. Those hands were not made for reaping wheat or serving food or welding steel.

Death bringer is right.

I don't know what I'll do when I have to stop, but for now I'll let them do what they do best. A trigger squeeze. A knife flash.

Yes . . .

Fifteen minutes along the motorway and I was approaching Belfast again. This morning I'd been excited about coming home. But not now. I'd been inoculated against nostalgia. An RPG attack and a good kicking will do that for you.

I wound down the window.

Rain and briny water and cold air.

But no magic. Belfast, a place like any other. A few landmarks. A few memories. The aircraft factory. The airport. A big poster advertising the book *Evolution: The Fossils Say No!* On my right the massive cranes of Harland and Wolff shipyard, where they built the ill-fated *Titanic* and her equally doomed sister ships, *Britannic* and *Olympic*. My father had worked in the shipyard. His father too, before going off to sea. Where was my da now? Did he still live here? My beloved nan was dead and she was the woman who had really raised me. No, my ma and da weren't relevant anymore. I didn't care. The psychic weight of the city wasn't pulling me in. I was just passing through. My home wasn't Peru, wasn't America, but it certainly wasn't here.

Still, Bridget had been correct to call me. Correct in her assumptions. Even after all this time it was as much my city as anyone's and she was right to think that I was the man who could find her kid. Her goons couldn't have gotten this close. Never. Throwing money is the Yank cure for everything. But in a society like Ulster or Afghanistan, money won't do it. Not the peelers, either. In Belfast if you've a real problem, you don't call the cops.

Aye, even now, I knew how the city ticked. I could feel my way through the streets. It wasn't geography, it was just the way things worked. Same as New York, and Lima, too, come to that. Probably everywhere in the world. The same five hundred people at the top, the same five hundred people at the bottom. And everyone else in between. Little people. Extras. I could feel it out. I had felt it out. The trail was good. It was simple. There were three acts. She had given me a job to do and I was doing it. And the third act would work out too. Oh yeah. Deus ex machina. Me as both God and the instrument of destruction.

Over the motorway and through the city.

New roads that I didn't know how to negotiate.

New buildings.

But eventually the signs took me out onto the M5, which led northeast along Belfast Lough. Traffic roaring by at eighty miles an hour.

The motorway had been built on reclaimed land. Four or five artificial lagoons created to prevent the road from being eroded by the lough water. Had this been here when I'd been here? I couldn't remember. The lagoons were full of herons and oystercatchers stretching, squawking, settling down for the night.

Birds. Water. Clouds. Me.

The big sopping city retreating behind. Belfast receding in the mirrors for what could be the last time in my life.

I could just keep driving north to the ferry port at Larne.

I could. But I won't. Bridget, Moran, the cops, everybody wanted me to stay out of it now. Time pressing and the kidnappers couldn't have been more explicit. But Moran was wrong. I had never fucked up anything I'd tried. Clumsy sometimes and I'd taken hits, but I'd always seen things through. Maybe that's why she'd asked for me. She understood that. Her speaking voice might be saying "I want everyone to pull back, to keep out of it, we should all do what the kidnappers say," but the secret message to me was "Michael, I love you, I trust you, you can do this. Do it for me, Michael. Find my girl. Find her. . . ."

I let this thought sit with me for a moment, and then I laughed at my reflection in the windshield.

"Always the fantasist," I said.

Still, I'd had it up to here with words and memories. I was full. There wasn't any room for insults or accusations. From Moran or Bridget or anyone.

Slán agat, mudflat city.

Slán abhaile. I won't be returning. I know that.

But I wasn't so proud that I wouldn't look back in the rearview mirror.

And I was eager to know how things were playing out. What were they doing there? Had Bridget convinced the cops to stand down? Of course she had. That imperious red hair and that cold smile and bending body. She could be the offspring of Elizabeth and Essex. She could be Queen Boudica. She could be . . . Fuck it, she could be the most powerful female mobster in the United States.

Aye, she'd tell them to get lost and it would just be her at that phone box near the Albert Clock. I could see the scene. The rain's stopped. The streets are slick. She'll pull up in a rented Daimler. She'll get out. She'll be wearing a raincoat and carrying the briefcase full of cash. Her face haunted, worried, cautious, pale. You ever see *Odd Man Out* or *The Third Man*?—it'll be like that. It'll be in black and white.

That clock, the touchstone for someone. Not a Belfast native. Unlikely anyone from the city would pick an exposed location like that, even for a preliminary phone call. But I'd bet a little money that that old man on the phone, that first voice we'd heard, had thought of that famous landmark as a good place to have Bridget wait. An old man, who maybe was from here originally but had spent many decades abroad.

Speculation.

In any case, now when I looked in the mirror, the city was almost completely gone. Only the choppers landing and the lights distorting on the black lough water. Even the traffic diminishing. Everything easing down on this, another wet Wednesday night in June.

Good.

＊　＊　＊

A green Toyota taxi weaving up into the hills. Farms dotted around the fields. Stone-made. Whitewashed. Buttressed against the elements. Slurry pits and green plastic over the hay crop. The road narrow. The low gears having difficulty on the higher inclines. The driver's side: bog and black bags tangled on the wire, lights weaving down to the Irish Sea and eventually dissipating into the hazy outline of the island of Great Britain. It's pretty, sickeningly so in the present circumstances. For I'm close now.

Toy boats on the lough. The outlands of the islands and the hills that make up southern Scotland. A green backdrop, a Celtic sky, and the indigo water setting everything in place like a quilt or jigsaw map of this portion of the world.

Big sky, big land, big sea, and then, suddenly, it's all just too much. Overwhelming. Those lights in front of my eyes, my head pounding, my cracked ribs throbbing, a dazzling feeling of vertigo. I dry heave. I put my foot on the clutch, slide the gear stick into neutral, slam back the handbrake, open the door, and climb out of the car.

I stumble to the grassy verge, sit, and try to get a breath. Hyperventilating. I lie backward on the grass, my arm falling in a sheugh. Not that it matters. I suck in the damp Irish air, rip my jacket off.

Get back in the car, get back in the car, the voice commands.

But still gasping, I lie on my chest and spread my arms. The overpowering smell of slurry, silage, and sheep shit.

I begin to breathe easier.

Where am I?

The hill country leading up to the Antrim Plateau. On the way to Knockagh Mountain. Aye, that's right. A slight drizzle and the sky its usual low-key gray-green shading into black. The stars when they all come out will be different from those I've become accustomed to in the last few months.

Gusts of wind wheedling their way down from the peaks. A williwaw. I stand and walk a little along the road, away from the car. My breathing almost under control.

Are you ok now? What happened there? Were you losing it? You can lose it at 12:01, but not now. After it's done, but not yet. Get a grip, you son of a bitch. It's not just your life at stake. Another human being might be depending on you. A girl. A mother.

"Just another minute," I say, sitting again, reaching for the pack of cigarettes in my jacket pocket. Flies buzzing at the puddles in the ditch. Clegs and midges. And that smell. That dungy brew of cows and damp. I'm underdressed and cold. But the fag will help. Marlboro Lights, weak-kneed, but I hardly ever smoked now anyway. I light a ciggy and hold it between my thumb and my fingers, the way I used to before I quit, feeling the anticipatory heat of it in my nostrils in contrast to the crisp cold air on my fingertips. I drink in the smoke, cough, close my eyes. Oh yeah, that's what it was like. I remember. The tobacco warming my lungs, toasting them with its flavor. Burnt and sharp like ocher. Aye. Is that the ticket to keep away the cold.

I take another hard draw and walk back to the car.

I'm ready.

That won't happen again

No . . .

I drove deeper into the Belfast hills and eventually found a sign pointing to a narrow single-lane track that might be the Knockagh Road. An old lady with a Scotty dog.

I leaned out the window.

"Excuse me, does this go up to the Knockagh?"

The dog was taking a dump and the old lady was trying to pick up the droppings with a cellophane bag over her hand. She couldn't bend down too well because of osteoporosis and the dog wasn't too happy about her interfering with its rear end before it was done with the business. A man in less of a hurry would have been amused.

"Does this go up to the Knockagh, this road?" I asked again.

"Where are you trying to go?"

"There's an Orange Lodge near the Knockagh, I need to be there for a meeting."

"There's no Orange Lodge up there, I can tell you that," she said.

"Well, is this the right road, at least?"

"Aye, this'll take you there," the old lady said, and breathtakingly slowly got out of my way. I resisted the temptation to run her over. She gave a friendly wave, and I sped up toward the mountain.

After a few turns, I saw that it was indeed the right road. Blocks of managed forest began appearing next to the farms. Dense, fast-growing pine trees, where you could probably hide out for months without anyone ever finding you. I hoped the mysterious lodge wasn't buried deep within one of those.

I drove higher still until I was right at the top of the plateau. The big granite war memorial was hard to miss standing up about a hundred feet from the mountaintop. I got the car as close as I could, parked it, and ran to the monument. The view was of the whole of Belfast Lough and the surrounding countryside. From up here in the western hills you could see a lingering, fragmented sunset, but in the east, down to water the sky was black and already most of the settlements around the lough had turned their streetlights on.

I climbed on top of a wall, scanned the surrounding fields. No ruined buildings, no parked cars, no secret hiding places, no arches, no fucking lodge. Nothing.

I'd cocked it up.

Moran was right after all.

I should have taken the kid with me. Dinger. Should have made some fucking excuse and grabbed the wean. Oh Christ. He could have shown me exactly where his brother had taken him.

Shit on a stick.

"You eejit. You brainless twat."

I railed at myself for thirty seconds, got a handle on it.

Ok, calm it, cool it, what if I went and got him now? Aye. Get him. Get the wee shite. His ma would fucking sell him to me for a hundred quid.

I looked at my watch. Nearly ten. There was no way I would ever make it to Bangor and back before midnight.

"Damn it."

And now, just for good measure, a haar fog was descending over the plateau, coating everything in wetness and a damp cloak of invisibility. Not that there was anything to see: scrub grass, heather, and bog.

A complete dead end. In the dying light, I desperately tried to find a building, but there was nothing that even remotely resembled an Orange Lodge. There were some ruins, but not Orange Lodges; these were little crofts that had lain bare and deserted since the time of the Great Hunger: all that remained were four gray walls. The whitewash long gone, the thatched roofs caved in. They weren't for human habitation and farmers used them now as sheep pens.

"Jesus, Mary, and Joseph. To get so bloody close," I cursed and sat down. Took out the pack of cigarettes. Changed my mind, threw it away.

Ok, what now? No point lingering around here. Back to the car. Somebody must know about an old Orange Lodge nearby. Yeah, ask around. There might have been a few funny comings and goings the last few days.

I ran to the Toyota and drove back to the main road.

But it was just a country track and there were no signs of life. No houses, no cars, no tractors; now and again an insomniac cow wandering along munching at the verge.

The fog grew thicker, the night descended.

Taking no chances on an accident, I slowed to five miles an hour.

Not a single bloody farm.

I crossed a stone bridge over a stream and turned into a bleak wetland that no longer had fields or fences or any trace of a life at all. I drove up and down looking for anybody, anything. Getting farther and farther away.

Hit the brakes.

Holy shit, this was all wrong. I was just driving aimlessly. Had to get a plan. Had to get help. I rummaged for my cell phone and dialed the operator. I couldn't get a signal, but when I climbed out of the car and onto the roof, mercifully, I got through.

"Hello," she said.

"Hi, I'm driving and I'm lost. I need the number of the car help people," I said rapidly.

"You're driving and you're lost? Do you want the AA?" the operator asked.

"Bloody hell, is that your solution to everything in this country? Alcoholics Anonymous? I said I was lost, I'm not bloody wasted."

"The Automobile Association," the operator said with a hint of world weariness.

"Oh, yeah, AA, aye sure, terrific, fire it on over, love," I said.

She gave me the number. I dialed them up and explained my predicament.

"Look, I don't know if you can help me, but I'm completely lost; I'm up somewhere in the hills near Belfast. Two minutes ago I was at the Knockagh Mountain; I'm looking for a pub or a hotel or a police station or anyone who can give me directions. Is there anything you can do to help? You must have a big map of Ireland with a list of pubs and gas stations and stuff. Is there anywhere like that around here?"

The man had a soothing County Kerry accent.

"Well, can you tell me what road you're on, while I call up the map on the screen here."

"I don't know what the road is, it's a very narrow road, single lane."

"Is it a B road?" he asked.

"That's very possible," I said.

"Ok, I think I see roughly where you are. You say you were at the Knockagh viewpoint a few minutes ago?"

"That's right."

"Well then, you must be on the B90."

"Ok. So what do I do? I need a gas station or a bar or something. Anything."

"Well, if it really is the B90, you should go north and turn left at the very first junction you see. About a quarter of a mile down that road, there's a place here on our map that we've given a star to," the man said.

"Yeah, mate, unfortunately I can't tell north from south, it's dark and there's a fog," I explained.

"Just keep going the one direction. If you don't come to the junction within, say, ten minutes, turn round and go the other direction. It's called the Four Kingdom View Pub and Restaurant."

I thanked the man, got his name in case I had to call again, and hung up. I climbed down off the roof, got in the car.

I put the fog lights on and followed the road as it grew narrower, the car weaving between and almost touching bramble bushes. I was about to give it up as a bad job, do a U-y and try the other bloody direction, when I saw the junction. I turned left and almost immediately came to a large posthouse-style mansion. White walls, a thatched roof, hanging baskets of flowers under the eaves, and tiny stained-glass windows on the ground floor. A small hand-painted sign said "Four Kingdom View Pub and Restaurant." Thank God. I pulled into the driveway and parked the car.

The path around the side of the restaurant ended on a rocky outcrop that overlooked a garden of neat hawthorn hedges and a pile of garbage.

"Charming," I said, and went inside.

A low-ceilinged, timber-framed room. A tiny kitchen giving off a smell of old socks and rat poison.

Through the tobacco haze I could see that I was in yet another sinister little pub, with unhelpful-looking locals eyeing me from the shadows. Barely half a dozen people in the place. All of them farmers wearing tweed jackets and flat caps. No one sitting next to anyone else. Everyone left to their own morose thoughts and reflections. It was your typical suspicious, superstitious, closemouthed, dour Irish country pub. The sort of pub you never see in the tourist ads for Ireland but which are just as common as the singing-and-dancing happy pubs celebrated on the screen.

The only way the Automobile Association could have given this place a star was if the proprietors had threatened the reviewer with a ritual murder.

It certainly wasn't the sort of place to come blazing in, asking questions about a ruined Orange Lodge. Asking any questions, come to that. They wouldn't kill me like they would have earlier in the Rat's Nest, but they wouldn't rush to give me the Heimlich maneuver, either.

"What'll ye be having, sir?" a barman asked in a not unfriendly manner. He was a tall, ungainly man in a filthy smock who moved so incredibly slowly that he was either in a partial body cast or he was drunk out of his mind and trying not to show it.

The locals were all nursing hot whiskies. That would be one way to ingratiate myself.

"Oh, I'm driving. Just a lemonade. But I'll give everyone in the bar the same again. Have one yourself."

"Very good of you, sir."

"My pleasure," I said. The barman stared at me.

"And for you, sir, what kind of lemonade?" he asked.

"There's different kinds of lemonade?"

"Aye, there's white or there's brown."

"What's the difference?" I asked with mounting irritation.

"One's white, the other one's brown."

"I'll take white, then."

"Fine."

He brought me a glass of white lemonade. I put a fifty-pound note on the counter. He took it greedily.

"Drinks are on this gentleman," he announced when he had thoroughly examined the bill.

A few of the old codgers nodded, but the rest kept their own counsel, disdaining to even look in my direction. They certainly didn't seem a cooperative bunch despite my largesse. I'd have to try the bar-man. You couldn't just ask him outright, though. I'd work my way around. At the very least, I'd try and do this without making a scene, but if things went on for more than five minutes without progress, I was willing to shoot every one of these old bastards until they told me what they knew.

"What are the Four Kingdoms?" I asked the barkeep.

"What are you talking about?"

"You're called the Four Kingdom Restaurant," I said quickly.

"Oh, that. Supposedly that's the view from the top of the Knock-agh. Kingdom of Ireland, Scotland, the Isle of Man, and, of course, the Kingdom of Heaven."

"That's fascinating. Fascinating stuff. I bet you know a lot of local geography and stuff like that," I said.

"Not really," he replied.

"Well, uh, listen, uh, I was wondering, I was looking for this old lodge that was supposed to be around here, did you ever hear of any-thing like that?"

"No."

"No old Orange Lodge, around here, nothing like that?"

"No."

"No ruins of any kind?"

"No."

"Are you sure?"

"Perfectly sure."

A man came out of the toilet and sat back down at the bar. He grabbed a pint of Guinness as if it were a life belt, nodded to me. He was a younger man, thirties, wearing a tweed suit but with a yellow silk waistcoat. His slightly wild blond hair was unadorned by a flat cap. It was a stroke of luck; this level of unconformity might also stretch to the possibility of being open for questions.

"How do?" I asked.

"Not too bad," he said.

"Well, a bad pixie must be following me around because I am com-pletely banjaxed," I said, coming straight to the point.

"What's the problem?" he asked.

I summoned over the barkeep.

"Another pint of Guinness for my friend here," I said, and offered him my hand. He shook it.

"Brian O'Nolan," I said.

"Nice to meet you, Brian, my name's Phil, thanks for the pint," he said.

"My pleasure, Phil."

Phil looked at me, eager to hear the nature of my difficulties.

"Ach, I'm in a wee spot, Phil," I said, trying not to appear too anxious.

"What do you need?" Phil asked, finishing his own pint and starting on mine.

"Well, I'm a bit disappointed, to tell you the truth."

"What's the matter?"

"Uh, it's not important," I said with a sigh.

But the man's interest was piqued. I had him on the hook now.

"No, tell me," he said.

I laughed.

"It's probably a stupid thing. But me dad, we live in America now, he moved us out there in the seventies when I was just a wee boy. And, well, he used to be in the Orange Order. You'll think it's stupid."

"No, go on."

"Well, he used to go to an Orange Lodge round here, and I was coming over to Belfast for business and so he asked me if I could find his old lodge and take a picture of it for him. Well, wouldn't you know it, business took me a little longer than I thought it would in Belfast and now it's dark out and I've been driving around for a couple of hours and I haven't been able to find it and, ach, I'm just a bit upset for me da."

The man nodded solemnly. I had hit all the right buttons. The Orange Order, family, tradition, a son's duty, if only I could have worked a dog in there it would have been a home run. Phil looked upset for me and gulped down his pint. I put a fiver on the counter and nodded at the barman. He started pouring another.

Phil cleared his throat.

"Well, Brian, you shouldn't be giving up yet. I don't know too much about that sort of thing; I'm not really from around here, but Sam Beggs over there, he knows this area like the back of his hand."

"That guy in the corner?" I asked, looking at a haggard, blue-nosed yokel chain-smoking his way through a packet of loose tobacco.

"Yeah, that's our Sam."

"Thanks very much, I'll go ask him," I said.

Phil shook his head.

"You better not, he's not exactly a big fan of strangers; you know how it is with some of those culchie types, wee bit sleekit, you know. I'll just go over and ask him for ya," Phil said.

"I would be much obliged."

"Sure, 'tis no problem at all. What's the details?"

"All my dad said was that he used to go to an Orange Lodge within a stone's throw of the Knockagh; he said it might be a ruin now, could be an arch over the gate or something," I explained.

Phil walked to the character in the corner of the room while I sipped my lemonade and tried desperately not to look at my watch. Five agonizing minutes went by as the two men chatted.

Phil came back with a smile on his face.

"See, never say die, he knows the very place. The arch you're talking about must be what's left of the old narrow-gauge viaduct, the lodge is the next field over. About two miles up the road from here, a wee lane you turn off and go down. The lane has a big sign on it that says "Trespassers Prosecuted, No Shooting." You can't see the old lodge from the road, you have to go down the lane a good bit. He says that he thinks it is a ruin, mind, but if you've a flash on your camera it might come out."

I thanked Phil profusely, ran out to the car.

I reversed the taxi out of the pub car park, sped along the Knockagh Road, hammering down the foggy track at ninety miles an hour. A Jeep passed me doing fifty in the other direction and it distracted me enough so that I almost drove straight past the lane.

Almost.

I slammed on the bloody brakes, skidded, nearly rolled, recovered, stopped, reversed, read the "Trespassers Prosecuted, No Shooting" sign, pulled in, parked the car, and grabbed the gun.

✵ ✵ ✵

A smell of burned gorse over by the tarn. That or a bonfire. Or perhaps someone lighting turf in an old Orange Lodge in an attempt to keep warm. The path led down to a field. But there was a haze in the glacial mouth of the valley—a gluey sea mist snaking its way up from the ocean at the head of a cold front and storm from the north. That, coupled with the fog on the mountain and the coming night, had closed the visibility to almost zero.

I felt my way forward gingerly and arrived at a second barbed-wire fence and a gate with another sign, which said "Keep Out. Trespassers Strictly Prosecuted." This sign was new and there were tire tracks in the mud.

A big vehicle and a couple of smaller cars. I bent down to examine them. Definitely fresh, in the last day or so, I would have guessed.

The path seemed to diverge now, left along the contour of the hill, but straight on took you farther down the slope. A bite of wind came from the high bog, a cold blade moving over the shadowy hills. While I zipped my jacket, the gust opened a gap in the mist. Fences hugging the hills, separating one desolate little sheep field from another. But what was that at the bottom of the slope? A house, a ruined lodge? Definitely worth investigating. I'd have to get closer. My hands tensed on the cold fence.

I opened the gate and walked onto a metal cattle grid, got one pace, immediately skidded, slipped, and fell. One of my Stanley work boots came off and my plastic foot got caught between the gaps in the metal rollers.

"Bloody hell."

A cattle grid is a series of metal tubes usually placed over a trench in front of a gate. People can walk on the rollers and cars can drive over them, but cows cannot cross them. The cows don't even have to fall one time to get it, instinct keeps them away. It's a handy device that allows you to keep your gate open without worrying about your cows, pigs, or horses bolting.

A clever contraption, and it's the rare fucking eejit that gets his foot caught in a cattle grid. But he was here tonight. I tugged at it, but my artificial foot was completely wedged. I unhooked the straps and pulled as hard as I bloody could. It didn't move an inch.

I removed the sock and heaved on the bastard, but there was still no way it was coming up. A better option would be to push it through the rollers. I could get the whole weight of my body behind it, but the problem there was that I couldn't see how deep the pit went under the rollers. I didn't want to lose my foot in a bottomless hole, not when I might need to run on it in a second. And anytime now the car with the kidnappers and Siobhan inside was about to drive up from the house.

That would be a nice fucked-up and ignominious way to end my existence on planet Earth. Hunting for my foot in a cattle grid while they drive past, stop the car, look at me in amazement, and then shoot me to blazes.

"Come on," I said as I tried pulling it again, but it was pointless. I would have to push it through. The pit couldn't be that deep. They didn't want cows to break their legs. They just wanted to spook them a bit.

Have to check it out. I lay down on the metal rollers and felt underneath. I stretched my arm to full extension and touched years' worth of sheep, cow, horse, pig, and dog shit, as well as leaves, garbage, and other assorted filth. Disgusting, but not deep.

I leaned with my full body weight on my foot. I pushed, and it sank through the rollers and landed in the shit.

"Ah, Jesus," I said aloud.

I reached for the foot, found it, grabbed it between my fingers, and maneuvered it to the big gap in the rollers at the edge of the pit. I pulled it out, cleaned it as best I could, and strapped it back on. I spent another two minutes rummaging in the murk to find my boot. I saw that the cause of this minicatastrophe had been when the lace had broken and the boot had skittered off. The lace was neatly bisected, so I could tie up only the top four holes.

I stood. The boot didn't feel remotely comfortable on the stump, but it would have to do.

The wind had killed the fog completely now and I found that I was looking at a one-room building. Very old, but far from being a ruin. It had a corrugated iron roof, a working chimney, and glass windows. It was a very old Orange Lodge, perhaps one of the original ones, and the fact that the kidnappers were using it made two things clear. First, whoever had kidnapped Siobhan certainly wasn't a member of the Orange Order or the Protestant paramilitaries. They would never countenance the possibility of being traced back to an Orange Lodge. It wouldn't look good within the community to use a semisacred place, even a partially ruined one, for a high-profile organized crime. This in itself was also puzzling because it didn't seem likely that Catholic paramilitaries would use such a place either. They'd pick somewhere they were comfortable in, safe, a territory they knew well. An old Orange Lodge deep within a Protestant farming area? No chance. Bridget had been told the same thing from both sides and Body O'Neill hadn't known a thing about the kidnap.

But if it wasn't the Protestant paramilitaries and it wasn't the Catholic paramilitaries, who in the name of God had grabbed the wee girl? Try to be an independent hoodlum in Ulster without being allied to one of the two sides and you'd very quickly end up as fish food. Was it a foreign organization? If so, they'd recruited local talent; but the masterminds could easily be from abroad—like that old guy on the phone. A risky game, but why not?

Well, we'd soon fucking see.

I crept my way closer. The lodge fifty feet away. Two cars outside. A beat-up Ford Sierra and a new Camry. Two cars—so what was that, maybe eight or ten guys?

If time wasn't such a big factor, I would have stalked the place for at the very least twenty-four hours. In the gorse and heather there were dozens of places to hide. A pair of binocs and a notebook and I could have sussed the whole operation.

But I had no time for that shite.

Close enough to be seen, so I got down on my belly. The smell of slurry was strong and the ground was damp from a rainstorm earlier in the day. I slithered through the tuft grass until I came to a small stone wall that surrounded the building.

I looked at my watch. Ten-fifteen. They wouldn't be on the move just yet. They'd be nervous; but they wouldn't be shitting bricks. Keeping up one another's bravado. I looked over the wall. Just a few paces to the lodge. If she was still alive the girl would be there with them, so I couldn't just storm in, killing everything that moved.

There was only one way. In with the gun. Give them a chance to put their hands up, and if they tried anything, shoot the fuckers. But protect the wee lass at all costs.

I slithered over the wall.

I could hear voices now. At least two, possibly three men. I crawled my way around the lodge so that I was facing the only door.

The voices were quite distinct. All of them Northern Irish, all from the Belfast area.

"See this in the *Tele*, attacking the peelers again, so they are."

"Fucking peelers deserve it."

"Aye, you're right, they've had it far too easy."

"What's that about a wedding, it's not Charles and Camilla, is it?"

"Nah, it's about Paul McCartney, getting married to yon awful woman."

"I had one of her pies once, it was lovely."

"She doesn't make pies, you're thinking of Linda. Hey, I'm going for a jimmy."

More like three or four different men speaking. Maybe another two or three keeping their own counsel. Could be seven targets in there. I'd have to reload the bloody gun. Tricky, but you could do it if you'd practiced. And I'd have surprise. I grabbed three shells and held them in my left hand. I checked the .38. It looked clean. I eased the hammer back.

Here goes, I thought, just as the door opened. I ducked into the shadow beside the wall. A heavyset man in a checked shirt and body warmer came out carrying an old-fashioned shotgun. He didn't see me. Even though the fog was gone, it was close to full dark now. He walked to the wall, set down his shotgun, opened his fly, and pissed.

Quietly I got to my feet, eased in behind him, put the gun to his neck.

"This is the police, don't move a fucking muscle or I'll top you, do you understand?" I said in a whisper.

He flinched and urinated on himself.

"I understand," he said in a croak.

"Keep your cock out and put your hands on your head. If you make one sound I'll shoot your dick off. Get me?"

"Aye," he said, frightened out of his mind.

He put his hands up and I patted him down. He had a penknife in his back pocket, a wallet with some low-denomination bills, and the driving licenses of three different people.

I dropped the wallet in the mud. I knew I had to work fast.

"Ok, get down on your knees. Keep those hands on your head," I said.

He knelt down. He was physically shaking. Terrified I was going to kill him.

"Ok, what's the story, pal? Tell me everything in a fast whisper," I said.

"What about?"

"The girl."

"I didn't touch the girl, I promise, I didn't touch her, the—"

He was starting to raise his voice.

"You better learn how to fucking whisper pal or you're a dead man," I said.

"Sorry," he whispered.

"You were talking about the girl," I said.

"I didn't touch her. The boss said no one was to touch her. He gave her the drugs, and we weren't supposed to go near her, it was Slider, it wasn't me, I didn't lay a finger on her."

"What did Slider do?" I asked coldly.

"He felt her tits, that's all, I tried to stop him. He said he wanted to see if they were coming along. He made me do it. I didn't even want to. I mean, the boss told us not to. He said we weren't to do a thing while he was away. I only did it once. Not like Slider. She was out the whole time, mind. Well out."

"Is she ok?"

"Where's the other cops?" he asked.

"Never mind that. How is the girl? Is she ok?"

"She's alive, she's fine, doped up but fine. I promise."

"Ok. How many people in there with you?" I asked.

"Three people."

"Only three, don't you bullshit me, I saw two cars out front," I said.

"The others have left," he said.

"Left where?"

"Left with her."

"Fuck," I said, biting down an urge to yell the word. "Ok, ok, when did they go?"

"Twenty five minutes ago," he said.

"Twenty-five minutes ago. Jesus. Not in a goddamn Jeep?" I asked.

"Yes," he said.

I cursed inwardly.

"Where did they go?"

"I don't know."

"I said where did they fucking go?" I demanded, pushing the revolver between folds of fat in his neck.

"I don't know, Slider knows, he talked to the boss, he suggested the handover place, I don't know where it's going to be, I'm not supposed to know. I promise, I don't fucking know."

"Slider's still in there?"

"Yes."

"And the boss?"

"He left with the others and the girl."

"You have no idea where they went? You better not be lying."

"I don't, I really don't know," he said.

"How's your shotgun? Do you keep it clean?"

"It's clean, but I only have the left barrel loaded."

"Ok."

I didn't have time to tie him up. If I knocked him out he could come to at any time. Really, there was only one course of action. And he had fondled her breasts while she was unconscious. That was enough for me. I unfolded the penknife. I put the gun in my jacket pocket. I quickly threw my hand over his mouth and locked his head between my shoulder and arm. I shoved the blade into his throat, missing the carotid artery by an inch. It was ok, I dragged the blade through his flesh, found the artery, lifted it out, and cut through it. Blood spraying everywhere.

That would kill him in two minutes, but I didn't have two minutes. I took the penknife and stabbed him in the voice box. Couldn't risk a scream while he bled to death. I kicked him to the ground and let him gurgle there. I was drenched in arterial blood but time was pressing. I picked up the shotgun in my left hand, held the revolver in my right. I walked to the building and slowly began turning the door handle. No profit in kicking it in. That would just alert them. This way they'd think it was their mate coming back from his piss—give me a second to analyze the situation.

I inched opened the door, raised the shotgun.

A single room, twenty feet by fifteen feet. A fire burning in a grate. A camp bed. Recliner chairs and deck furniture. A table with a gas stove and an oil lamp. Three men. One sitting in the old leather re-cliner reading tonight's *Belfast Telegraph*. The second cooking a plate of sausages over the gas stove. The third lying on the bed looking at a chess problem.

"Which one of you is Slider?" I asked.

None of the men answered, but the one looking at the chess set nearly leaped out of his fucking skin. I shot the one cooking the sausages with the twelve-gauge, the impact blowing his shoulder and the side of his head clean off. I dropped the weapon and with the .38 shot his mate reading the paper, the bullet sailing through the color picture of the half-sunk *Ginger Bap* on the front page and catching him in the stomach. I shot him twice more in the chest. Slider, mean-while, had produced a gun of his own, a semiautomatic, which he was trying to load with a clip. He got the clip nine-tenths in and attempted to pull the trigger, but the gun wouldn't fire like that and the lead shell jammed half in and half out of the chamber.

A cool-headed man would have cleared the mechanism, slammed home the clip, and shot me. Slider wasn't cool or fast enough. I strode across the room and knocked the gun out of his hand. I pistol-whipped him back onto the bed.

He resembled his mother more than any of his brothers. Dead crab eyes, one brown, the other blue, graying unkempt hair, lank smell, a broken nose. He was thin, but the skin was hanging off him. With a haircut he could have passed for Iggy Pop on a bad day but that wouldn't get him on my good side.

He put his hands up, and keeping the gun on him, I patted down his dirty jeans and a suede sweatshirt that was covered with food stains.

"Are you going to turn me in?" he asked.

"I'm going to fucking kill you if you don't tell me everything you know," I said.

"About what?"

I shot him in the left kneecap, the noise sounding dissonant and terrible in the wee room. He screamed and tumbled off the bed. The kneecap is a nasty place to take a bullet because of the conjunction of bone, muscle, and nerve endings. Especially at close range with a .38.

"You fucker, you shot me, I'm dying, I'm fucking dying," he gurgled, writhing in agony.

I knelt beside him.

"No one ever died because of a bullet in the kneecap. One time, many years ago, I shot a man in the kneecaps, the ankles, and the elbows. Christ, you should have seen the state of him. Well, that's what I'll do for you. To begin with."

"Why, why, you bastard?" he said.

"Now listen to me, Slider. I'm not fucking around here. I'll torture you and I'll kill you unless you tell me where she is."

A sudden burst of pain rode through him.

Tears were running down his face.

"What do you want to know?" he managed.

"Do you know what's going to happen tonight at the exchange?"

"I know a bit."

"Well, talk then."

"Bridget Callaghan's getting a phone call at the Albert Clock in Belfast," he said, every word an effort.

"I know that. What happens after that?"

He groaned and shat himself. He was in agony. Goddammit. I looked around the room and saw that there was a bottle of Johnnie Walker next to the dead man who'd been reading the *Belfast Telegraph*. I went across the floor, grabbed the bottle, poured a full measure into a coffee mug, handed it to him.

"Drink the whisky," I said.

He sipped and then gulped it. I let it bubble through him for a minute. He started doing a wee bit better.

I spoke softer.

"Ok, Slider, what happens tonight? Tell me everything."

"They're supposed to make her drive to a couple of different call boxes over the city," he muttered.

"Go on."

"And then there's the swap. We're supposed to wait here. We couldn't all go, but we're rendezvousing back here with the money, after Bridget and the girl are dead."

"What are you talking about? After you swap the girl for the money, you mean?"

"Nah, I don't think the boss wants to do it that way. I think he wants to kill the pair of them or something. Maybe for security reasons. But we get the money anyway." Slider groaned again and I forced him to drink another mug of whisky. He sobbed a little.

"Get that down your neck, mate, go on," I said.

He drank gratefully, looking at me as if I were an old friend.

"Tell me about this boss. Who is he?" I asked.

"I don't know, he's from Dagoland, probably the Mafia or something, for all I know. Dead good English, though."

"Ok, Slider, you're doing great, now where's the girl?" I asked.

But the whisky was working too well. Slider recovered some of his bravado. He looked at me suspiciously.

"Who are you?" he asked, his eyes still filled with tears.

"I'm asking the questions. Where the's girl?"

"She's gone, she's not here," he said.

"So I see. Listen, mate, my finger's getting awful itchy, so you better keep talking."

"I don't know anything more," he said.

"Slider, I want to know where the exchange is going to be."

"We're not in on that. The boss comes back here. He didn't want to tell us the place. You know how it is, some things you have to keep secret. It was on a need-to-know basis," he said, thinking he was pretty smart wasting time like this.

"Slider, listen. Your mate outside already told me that you know where they're doing the fucking swap. If you don't tell me, I'll fucking kill you," I said.

"You wouldn't kill me in cold blood," he said with a half-drunken smile and closed his eyes.

I smacked him across the face with the barrel of the gun, opened his eyes with my fingers, and made sure he saw me standing over him pointing the gun at his head. I had to end this little chitchat right now. I mean, for Pete's sake, I was only bluffing about the torture. There was no time to torture the information out of him. I didn't have all bloody night.

"Slider, you're taxing my patience, so I'll tell you what I'll do. Are you a reader? I'm a big reader. Have you ever read Zeno? He's the Greek guy that says an arrow can't move, because it has to cross an infinite number of slices in the air between the shooter and the destination. So let's do an experiment. You keep your head there and I'll keep the gun here and I'll pull the goddamn trigger and we'll see what happens with the bullet. Fingers crossed for Zeno, huh?"

I began squeezing the trigger.

"Wait, wait, wait, oh God, wait," he screamed. He was shaking and the terror was locked in his eyes.

"You don't want to do the experiment?"

"No."

"Ok. Talk. Where's the rendezvous?"

"The boss asked Jackie to ask the boys if they knew any out-of-the-way places, you know, discreet. Well, I came up with somewhere. I used to go fishing at—"

"Not the whole goddamn story, just the place."

"On Islandmagee, there's a path called Black Head Cliff Path; it splits, the top path goes to Black Head Lighthouse, the bottom path works its way round to the Witches' Cave. They scouted it out yesterday. Boss really liked it. Single route in and out. Bump Bridget over Belfast and bring her down to Islandmagee. I think that's what he's going to do."

"Islandmagee, Black Head Cliff Path, lower path to a cave," I repeated.

"Exactly."

"Whereabouts is Islandmagee?"

"About ten miles or so from here," he said, his face more relaxed now.

"Quickest route?" I asked.

"Drive down to the lough, go through Carrickfergus and White-head."

"How will I find this path?"

"Ask anybody in Whitehead, you can't fucking miss it. Right under the lighthouse, you'll see it," he said.

"You better not be lying, Slider," I said.

"I'm not fucking lying, it's the honest truth, I swear it."

I had a million more questions. What was the girl doped with? What were the goons carrying? Tell me everything about the boss. How many in the team? What was the backup plan? But there was no time. I stepped away from him.

What I was going to do next was going to hurt.

Cold blood was cold blood.

But time was the operative word. I didn't have the time to be smart, to make the right call.

"Well, Slider, you've been very helpful and I'll be honest with you, I thought about not killing you. It's very good the way you look after your wee brother and everything but I don't have the time to tie you up."

"What are you saying?"

"Slider, I can't have the possibility of you escaping on me and alerting your boss that I'm on my way to stop him," I said.

I was trying to convince myself as well as him. What was the less wrong thing to do? Was it less wrong to leave him and risk it? Or was it better to shoot him and rule out any possibility of him screwing with me? My watch said five minutes to eleven. I didn't have the luxury of thinking it through.

"Y-you're going to kill me? But I helped you. You can't kill me."

"I have to kill you, I'm close now. Can't afford interference. And after all, you did assault the wee lass."

"You're not serious. I'm a good guy. You know I have a kid brother, I look after him."

"I am serious. Like I say, I was in two minds about it, but this is the only prudent course of action. I'll do something for your wee brother, I promise."

"You fucker, you fucker, you can't. I'll fucking see you in hell," Slider sobbed.

"Nah, with all your good deeds, Slider, you'll be going to the other place," I said and shot him in the chest and then in his stunned, half-open auburn-colored eye.

On the tabletop there was a box of shotgun shells and assorted ammo for a handgun. I grabbed what I could, picked up the shotgun, and went outside.

Raining again.

I slipped in the mud, dropped all the weapons, picked them up, walked over to the body of old-knife-in-the-neck, removed the blade, and pocketed it.

I wanted to run to the car. I had to run to the car. Time was of the essence.

But I walked.

It's never easy.

I don't care what anybody says.

It's never easy.

I avoided the puddles and the mud.

Alone now, save for the hawks.

And sparrowhawks.

Rain.

A breath of wind.

One foot followed another down the Knockagh lane to where the road curved and the woods came and the path wound its way back to the other millions of souls huddled in this green lifeboat of an island in the western sea.

The taxicab.

The key.

I threw the guns in the trunk.

I started the car.

Drove.

I'll come on the halo. I'll come on the white water. I'll come from the cinder sky.

Yes.

Greenisland, Carrickfergus, the small town of Whitehead.

A lighthouse above the cliff.

A storm barreling in from the North Atlantic.

I ditched the Toyota in a seafront parking lot. I popped the trunk, quickly checked the mechanism on the shotgun. It was so filthy with mud I knew I couldn't rely on it. My pistol, however, was clean.

Slider had said that the boss had several men with him. If there was going to be a shoot-out, I'd have to be ready to be outgunned.

Outgunned, outnumbered, outflanked.

Exhausted, wounded, done.

I smiled.

What else was new?

I loaded six more rounds in the .38 and went to get Siobhan.

12: ITHACA
(ISLANDMAGEE—JUNE 16, MIDNIGHT)

Wild horizon. Black sea. Prisoner path to the trapdoor floor. A banshee wind. The storm throwing water up the cliff. Thick clouds concealing the full moon and innumerable stars. Arctic waves. Heavy weather. The cliffs the anvil, the waves the hammer.

It had been raining all day on the high bog. Slurry and muck had sluiced down from the lighthouse hill and seaweed and kelp had been cast up from the lough.

The way was treacherous, and it wasn't helped by a murderous gale escaped from its holding cell near the pole.

It was midnight.

Somewhere it's always midnight.

The now distilled to basics: Cold. Pain. Fear.

Darkness, except in the eastern sky, where those pinpricks of lights were the meteors of the June Lyrids.

I was poised at the very edge of Ulster, the dominating feature no longer earth or grass but rather the jet-colored vacuum that was the Irish Sea. And here, in the cauldron, at the meeting point of island and ocean, all land seemed impermanent, fragile, existing on a knife edge.

"Jesus, Mary, and Joseph," I muttered as I slipped and nearly went down onto the rocks.

A big breaker could carry me out into Belfast Lough and the Atlantic. I'm no swimmer, but the cold would stop my heart in any case.

I took a second to steady myself. Thunder rumbling over from Scotland. Foghorns, bell buoys. A canopy of porter-colored clouds. The pistol sweetening in my sweat.

The front not even an orchestra tuning, but rather one loud, continuous, shrieking note.

Have to go carefully. Unlikely that they would be here already. But you never knew. I checked my watch, tapped it, something wrong. I examined it but it had stopped at eleven o'clock. I shook it, goaded it, but the rain had finally spoiled the action. I'd bought it for a half a sol in a market in Lima, so I couldn't really complain.

Sheep loomed out of the murk in front of me, coming down from one of the upper fields. Bedraggled, waterlogged. Even an older, more experienced ewe drenched with muck, staring at me with desperation in her dead eyes.

"Go on, scoot," I told her, and she and the other sheep scrambled away into the heather. I stopped for a second.

Unnerved.

I found the path again. A concrete-and-gravel job. "The path to the future," I muttered. Soaked, slippery, unseen—the adjectives working for both literal and metaphoric journey.

I followed it farther around to Black Head. Slider had been right. It split here. The upper path wound up to the lighthouse at the top of the cliff, the lower made its way down almost to the water.

"This way," I said to myself, and found my place along the lower route. The direction of the cave.

I hoped my information was correct. But it had to be. I had frightened the truth out of that son of a bitch. And if he was lying, if he had pulled this wee hidey-hole out of his arse, he was a more impressive individual than I gave him credit for.

The path worked down to the bottom of the cliff. Spray hitting me every time a wave broke.

Lightning had transformed the sea between Ireland and Scotland into a landscape spectral and fantastic. Splintered light showing the hills in Galloway and their mirrors in the Glens of Antrim. And for a moment, if you were so inclined, you could almost imagine that the boiling waters between Ireland and Britain were, in fact, a silent valley of writhing souls in Hades.

I shivered.

The wind howling up to thirty or forty miles an hour now, ringing in my ears. I cursed, but I couldn't hear my own voice.

I walked a little farther, turned a corner, looked up, the lighthouse suddenly seventy-five feet above on the clifftop. A spectacular sight. The large white structure silhouetted against the storm clouds and the big mirrored bulb radiating powerful beams across the water—visible from Scotland and the Isle of Man. I stood transfixed. I had never seen anything like it. Great sheets of light above me, rotating and hypnotic. Millions of candlepower warning ships about the coast of Ireland from as far away as the Earth's curve would allow.

And all of it coming together.

Like I knew it would.

The crescendo.

The climax.

The lighthouse. The lightning. The storm. The night. The frothing sea and rain. It was a coda from Götterdämmerung and enough to make you scrap your disbelief in the sympathetic fallacy.

"A hell of a night," I said to no one.

I walked farther along the lower path. The tide was high and the sea was only a few vertical feet beneath me. And, Jesus, of all places to meet, why this one? I was hard pressed to think of a more desolate spot in the whole of Ireland. You certainly couldn't make a quick getaway from here and you couldn't count the money and you couldn't wait in comfort. The only advantage would be the certitude with which you could verify Bridget's adherence to the plans. You'd see her coming from a mile off. She'd have to be alone. No cops and no goons could possibly follow her without being seen. If she approached from the south, from the direction I was taking, you'd come from the north, over the fields. You'd do the exchange at the cave and both parties would go home the way they came.

I turned another corner as a deck of cold water smashed into the bottom of the cliff, the initial break missing me but the bounce off the cliff catching me full on the back.

Bugger.

The path had a safety rail here now. But I wasn't going near it. Rusted and warped by wind, rain, and spray, it didn't look at all safe. I hoped Bridget wouldn't put her trust in it. Christ, it would give and she'd be in the Atlantic, doomed, drowned, dead.

I shook my head.

There it was again.

A contradiction of emotions. For wouldn't that be in my best interests, if Bridget did somehow end up in the sea? Wouldn't things be much easier for me if Bridget was erased from my life forever? No more vendetta, no more blood feud? No more waking in the middle of night, my heart pounding, reaching for the Glock under my pillow?

A dead Bridget would be my chance for a normal existence. The first chance in twelve years.

I turned the final corner and the sound of the sea changed. A hollow, booming noise echoing off the walls. A black void in the cliff face.

I took out my revolver.

This was the cave. The Witches' Cave. The name an unwelcome dose of melodrama in a spot that was bloody tight enough.

Why hadn't I thought to bring a flashlight? I walked over the slime-covered rocks into the cave mouth. I clutched the revolver. Maybe the girl was here already. Maybe she was tied up and I'd rescue her and save the day and Bridget's eternal love would shine down from on high. Maybe all would be forgiven and I'd live happily ever after.

Aye.

I crouched and hunched farther into the pristine darkness. The cave went back a good bit into the cliff, but sea spray could still make it this far and on the seventh wave it smacked into the walls and drenched me again. I crouched lower and moved forward a little. How deep did this bastard go?

I stooped almost horizontal and inched ahead even more slowly. I was being careful, but despite my caution I still managed to slip on the rocks and cut myself badly on the left hand. Fortunately, the revolver was in my right, but I didn't want to lose it now, so I put it back in my jacket pocket.

I kept still for a moment and got on my haunches.

My eyes adjusted, and from the ambient light and odd lightning flash, I could see for certain that the cave was empty. No girl, no kidnapper, no Bridget.

Garbage, seaweed, beer cans, sodden paper, some luminous graffiti but nothing that looked as if anyone had even been here recently.

Shit. Had Slider stroked me after all? This was no place for an exchange. Jesus, this was no place at all.

"Is there anybody here?" I called out.

Not a sound. Not even a goddamn echo.

I looked at my watch. 11:00, it said. Oh, yeah. Broken. But it was bound to be after midnight now. Bridget would be on the move. Juking from phone box to phone box and car to car. Probably heading for Dublin or Donegal or the hill of Tara. Anywhere but here. What a waste of time.

"Ya did it to me, Slider. Conned me. Stroked me," I said.

Well, I was committed to this place now in any case. The only course would be to wait. If they didn't show up at midnight, I'd have no option but to head for the nearest ferry port or air terminal. Get out of Ireland as soon as possible. Bob's brother had been very clear. If Bridget gets the girl or the girl dies, all bets are off. He and the whole organization would be coming to kill me and with the full wrath of Bridget and her men I wouldn't last a day in this country.

I shivered and sat down on a rock. I could have done with a cigarette. A nice wee ciggy to warm me up. I tapped my watch and wound it, listened, took it off, and threw it behind me into the stinking, moving pile of flotsam and jetsam.

Seawater was coming in along the bottom of the cave now. Maybe McFerrin was even smarter than I thought. He tells me about this cave in the middle of bloody nowhere. He figures I'll go wait inside it like a complete eejit. He knows that at high tide the cave is completely submerged and by the time I realize this, I'll be goddamn drowned.

Great.

Nice plan. I suppose you thought you'd be waiting for me in hell with a big grin on your face. That right, Slider? I looked at the water level. Was it rising? I tried to see if there were high-tide marks on the walls, but you couldn't tell.

Sometimes it was the wrong thing to kill a man. Maybe I should have brought the son of a bitch with me. Someone to talk to while we waited. And then I could have popped him. Then again, no. Too many difficulties.

The water was licking around my boots.

Jesus Christ. Well, I'd shoot myself before I let the sea drown me. Awful way to go. Especially on a night like this.

But wait a minute.

McFerrin wasn't that clever. And not with a gun pointed at his head. And offhand, who would even know the high-tide tables except fishermen and lobstermen?

"Nah, you couldn't have thought of a plan like that, could you, mate?" I said to the walls. McFerrin's hell-bound grin faded, like the cat from the book.

But where the hell was everybody? I suddenly remembered there was a clock on my cell phone. I took it out, hit the back light. 4:59, it said. It was a second-rate phone and still locked in on Peru time.

And, oh boy, South America, that seemed like a million miles away. The mere thought of the journey and all that had happened in between made me yawn. God Almighty, I hadn't slept for more than a couple of hours in the last two days. As soon as the adrenaline stopped pumping, I'd be in for a serious crash.

I looked at the phone. Worked out the time zones. Aye. Nearly twelve o'clock British Summer Time. I blinked down the fuzziness in my head, the flashes before my eyes, dialed Bridget's number and got no answer. Of course, they told her to leave her phone.

I pulled out a sodden piece of paper and dialed the other number. Earlier on top of the mountain, I couldn't get a signal, but now, of course, despite being a troglodyte deep within a cave system, the phone worked just fine.

Moran answered.

"Yeah?"

"It's Forsythe."

"What do you want?"

"Did they call her?"

"Yeah, they did, gave her instructions; we were on her tail to the bridge but then we lost her."

"You followed her?"

"Yeah, tried to."

"What happened?"

"He had her drive down a road that we thought was a dead-end street. It wasn't. It was a fake sign, so we waited at the end of the street for her to come out and of course she didn't. We waited and waited and then we went down there and her car was empty and she was gone."

"What do you think happened?"

"I think they had another car waiting down there. Norris thought he saw a Ford Escort drive off, but we had to hang back, so we couldn't really tell," Moran said bitterly.

"Was she in the Ford?" I asked.

"We couldn't tell. Smart that they had her change vehicles in case we'd bugged her car. Which, of course, we had."

"So what does that mean?" I asked.

"It means we've fucking lost her."

"The cops lost her too?"

"Bridget told the cops not to tail her, she told me, too, but I couldn't resist. In any case, we're both out of the picture now. I'm sorry to say it, but she's on her own."

"Shite."

"What have you come up with?" Moran asked.

"I might have a good lead."

"Where are you?"

"Islandmagee."

"Where the fuck is that?"

"North of Belfast, it's a peninsula, not an island but—"

"You're in County Antrim?" Moran asked, surprised.

"That's right."

"She went over the Lagan Bridge into County Down. We lost her over there. You're not even in the right fucking county."

Dead air. We both knew what it meant.

"It looks like my informant lied to me," I said with resignation.

"Well, Forsythe, you can't say you haven't had fair warning."

"I know."

"Goodbye."

Click and the dial tone.

I put my head in my hands. Laughed. Well, he was right about one thing, I'd been warned. Couldn't fault him on that score. And on the surface he seemed like a decent enough bloke. Still, it bugged me. It was amazing that he'd let her go on alone. I would never have done that, no matter what the kidnappers said. Maybe he was half hoping it would all fuck up and Bridget would take a hit. This whole thing had already made her look weak. If Siobhan died or Bridget got hurt, perhaps it would be Moran's turn to step up to the plate. He was no instigator. He didn't have the bottle for that. But he'd certainly be there to pick up the pieces. Step into her shoes. First order of business, kill me.

The time on the phone said five o'clock now.

Midnight in the Emerald Isle. The time for the exchange. And here I was in a deserted cave, miles from the action, miles from anywhere.

At least I'd been vague. I'd told Moran I was on Islandmagee, but that's all I'd told him. He'd be hard pressed to find me. The morning papers would let me know what happened with Bridget and her daughter, and I'd take a ferry to Scotland and maybe a flight from Glasgow to New York. Dan would let me back in the WPP. He was a good guy too. They were all goddamn good guys.

I was tired.

Stupid.

Wet.

I stood up. Stretched. At least you couldn't say I hadn't given it my best shot. One bloody Bloomsday I wouldn't bloody forget in a hurry.

I walked back to the cave mouth.

And then I heard it.

A voice.

No.

Voices.

Closer.

I got down.

"She's late."

"Aye, well, she'll be coming."

"And if she doesn't?"

"She will."

Something familiar about that second voice. It was barely more than a croak, it sounded like someone who had terminal throat cancer or had just sung a marathon rock show or had worked in a powdered-glass factory for fifty years. I knew no one with a voice like that. And yet there was something in it that I did know. A shiver went down my spine. I couldn't place it, but I felt it, and it wasn't right. No. It was all fucking wrong.

I lay down on the cave floor, nudged myself forward, crawling over the barnacle-covered rocks and the retreating tide.

There were four figures in the mouth sheltering from the rain. They'd only just arrived. Three men and a girl. The girl had a hood up over most of her head, but you could tell it was her. Siobhan. Bridget's girl. She was tiny. Wearing blue jeans and a clear plastic coat.

She turned her head slightly. Red golden hair dangling over wet cheeks. But the Polaroid I had didn't do her justice. Her face had an odd, faraway loveliness—stolen child, elf child, but more than that. Yes. In a box somewhere I've got a sepia picture of my grandmother at a similar age. The resemblance was uncanny. Unmistakable, in fact.

And then I knew the whole story.

And then I knew the stakes were much higher than before.

The three men were in black Bear jackets, carrying flashlights and huge Pecheneg machine guns.

"Ten million, boss, be a nice wee bonus," one of them said.

"This isn't about the money," the boss croaked.

He could barely speak at all, you could tell that every word was painful and his accent was all over the place. Sometimes it sounded Spanish, sometimes American, sometimes Irish. But I recognized a part of it. I'd talked to this man before. Years ago. I knew him. If only I could—

"What about the wean?" one of the men asked.

"You know fucking full well. You know what we have to fucking do. Don't mention it again," the boss said ominously.

The girl didn't move. Didn't react. What had they done to her?

"Where's your fags?" the boss asked.

They handed him a cigarette. He lit it and smoked it. So if the cancer theory was correct, it certainly wasn't deterring the bastard.

"How long do we wait here?" an underling asked.

"Go on out and check. Harry should be seeing her real soon," the boss said.

One of the men put his hood up and stepped outside the cave.

270 / Adrian McKinty

The boss drew in the tobacco smoke with relish. A cheap brand, an American brand, I could smell it from here. What did that tell me? It told me something. I recognized his tobacco.

A walkie-talkie crackled.

"Aye?" the boss said.

"She's coming."

The man outside came running back. He passed across a pair of binoculars with a night scope on them. The boss took them greedily.

"I heard Harry on the walkie-talkie and I seen her, too, she's on her own," the man said.

The boss stood. He limped over to Siobhan.

"Your ma is fucking coming for ya, love," he said, and poked at the girl.

Siobhan whimpered and retreated back into the wall. Her hands were tied in front of her, but if anything, she had underreacted to the poke. They'd obviously done something to her. McFerrin had said something about drugs.

"She's alone, nobody for fucking miles," the other man said, coming in from outside, brandishing the binoculars in triumph.

"Call Harry up at the lighthouse and get him to double-check for anybody following her or fucking boats or helicopters or anything," the boss said, and again I noticed that agony with his speech, every word difficult, painful. Did I know any chain-smokers? Or someone scheduled for a larynx removal?

One of the men picked up the walkie-talkie, spoke, got his answer, turned to the boss. He was excited.

"Dave says the coast is clear. She's coming alone and he says she's definitely carrying a briefcase."

"The money," the other goon said happily, forgetting the boss's admonition that this wasn't about the cash. Which made me think, well, if not dough, what was it about?

The boss threw away one fag and lit another. The smoke drifted back, and now I recognized it. Tareyton. Only one person I ever knew smoked Tareyton, and he was dead.

"Game faces on," the boss said, and the two others took off their coats. Put on black baseball caps. But with their coats off and hoods down I could see them quite clearly in the lightning flashes. I didn't recognize either of them. Just a couple of low-level gangsters, of the type you'd find in any bar in Belfast or Derry or Dublin.

The boss took off his coat and the lightning flashed and I saw his horribly disfigured face.

I recognized him instantly.

And of course I knew immediately what this whole thing was about.

Slider hadn't misspoken. He *was* going to kill Bridget and he *was* going to kill the girl and he was going to take the money in compensation for what Darkey White had done to him all those terrible years ago.

For the man standing there with the Pecheneg and the scarred throat and mangled mouth and patchy red hair and cadaverous cheeks was none other than my old long-deceased mate Scotchy Finn.

❖ ❖ ❖

The last time I had been with Scotchy he was on the razor-wire perimeter fence of the prison in Valladolid, Mexico. Bridget's fiancé, Darkey White, had set us up on a drugs buy so that the whole crew, but especially me, would get arrested and I'd be bunged inside some Mexican hellhole in order that he and Bridget could marry and Bridget would forget me forever. But Scotchy was a resourceful wee fuck. A nasty annoying pain in the ass but a resourceful wee fuck nonetheless. He had broken us out of the nick and he'd gotten as far as the razor wire before an M16 rifle round had hit him in the back. He'd fallen onto a big loop of razor wire and from my angle the wire had nearly decapitated him. It had certainly killed him. Even if the M16 bullet hadn't topped him, there was no way anybody could have survived a fall like that onto a loop of sharp tensile steel.

But let's say, by some fucking miracle, you had survived and your head wasn't taken clean off, well, then you'd die anyway when the prison guards ripped you down. They wouldn't be careful about it. Why would they? They'd rip you down and that would tear you up and kill you.

But for the sake of argument, let's imagine that Mother Teresa and the pope and Saint Nicholas of Myra (the patron saint of thieves) are, at that precise moment, thinking about the destiny of redheaded fuckup scumbags from Crossmaglen and they intervene personally with the Angel of Death to save you on the wire. So you live through that. But how in the name of God and all that's holy do you survive the medical treatment that you'll get in a Mexican prison hospital, especially when the guards were less than inclined to save our old pal Andy when he got near beaten to death?

They wouldn't have surgeons that could save your life.

They wouldn't give you a blood transfusion, and if they did, it would probably be the wrong blood type or contaminated with the AIDS virus.

Nah. To survive the bullet, the wire, the ripping down, the Mexican hospital, you'd have to have ninety-nine lives, be born on Christmas, find a shamrock in your crib, and do Lourdes in advance for thirteen summers.

None of which Scotchy did. And he was an unlucky son of a bitch to begin with. Stupid, quick tempered, and a bad penny with a capital *P*. There is no way Scotchy could have survived what I saw happen to him.

Not a fucking chance.

And yet.

And yet.

Scarred, bent over, scorched, nasty looking.

The motherfucker himself.

Scotchy.

My old nemesis.

My old pal.

The way he stood, the way he looked, the way he talked, the way he smoked.

Oh my God.

It is definitely him.

I want to get up and run over and hug the dumbass bastard. I want to shake him by the hand. Scotchy, oh my God.

I killed Sunshine for you. I killed Bob for you. I killed Darkey White for you. All for you, mate. Because you made me promise. And now what?

Now I want your blessing.

I want to kneel down before you and I want you to put your bony hand on my head and say "You done good, son. You done good."

I need that, Scotchy.

I need to know that I did the right thing. That you approve. And I want to look you in the eye, talk to you, have a pint. I want to get in a fight with you and make up and have more pints and have you fucking steal from my wallet while I go to the bathroom.

I want to see your ugly fangs break into a grin.

I want you to call me Bruce.

Scotchy, I am so happy to see you.

My world overthrown.

You are my brother. You are the closest thing to flesh and blood I have in this world.

Well, *second* closest. (Tonight it was getting to be like the season finale of a Spanish soap opera.)

But, oh Scotchy, I want to go over and hug you and shake your hand.

I want to.

I need to.

But I don't.

I sit there in the dark.

Like a rat.

Waiting.

Not the time. The time will come. But not now.

You're going to kill her. You're going to kill both of them. I know you, Scotchy. I know what you were capable of before. God knows what you can do now. After what you've been through.

And I have only a six-shot revolver.

And they have assault rifles.

And this is Scotchy fucking Finn, no mean hand in a gun battle. No mean hand.

The walkie-talkie crackles.

"She's coming, she's right on you," Steve says.

"Ok, ya fucks, drop your cocks, grab your fucking guns, if wee Siobhan does anything stupid fucking shoot the bitch. I want my words with Bridget, but if there's any fucking funny stuff, shoot her without my say-so. Safety fucking first, lads. Understood?"

The two men nod and I grin. Aye, that's my Scotchy, no doubt about it.

His hair has been ripped out in chunks. There's a massive scar across his throat and obviously his voice box has been badly damaged. His face has been pummeled, his nose repeatedly broken, and it looks like he's lost an eye. I've seen a dozen better-looking corpses, and that's just today.

But he's alive.

He hadn't been decapitated and he hadn't died from blood loss and the Third World doctors had saved his fucking life. And then what?

What happened to you, Scotchy?

Ten years in some hellhole in Mexico. All the tortures of the world. But if nothing else, Scotchy is a wee rat-faced survivor. I know how he'd get through. Sell out his mates, his pals; he'd turn informer, dealer, pimp. He'd shank someone, kill his way out, lie his way out. And now this. Back to Ireland, rebuilding a life. Where would he go? Belfast? Dublin? South Armagh? He'd work his way up. Maybe he'd stay in Mexico until he had the dough and clout to come home.

Well, he's got at least partway up the ladder. Those boys called him boss, didn't they?

All this time hungering for revenge. I don't have a monopoly on that. There's enough out there for both of us. Hate has a big reservoir. He finds out that Bridget and Siobhan are in town and he grabs her wean. Where did he see her? Was he watching the hotel? How did he do it? How many men?

Certainly a good scheme.

A way to make his fortune and take revenge on Bridget at the same time. Kill two birds.

Literally.

Jesus, maybe he planned the whole thing from the start, years ago, back in Mexico, in the dog years of a jail cell, although maybe not. Scotchy's an opportunist, not a planner. I like that about him. There's a lot I like about him.

Scotchy . . .

One of the men lit a hurricane lamp. It was powerful and cast a good glow over the walls. I hugged the floor of the cave and slunk as far backward as I could.

Scotchy cocked his Pecheneg and stood. His mates tensed. They were both in their early twenties, kids. The type that Scotchy always liked to surround himself with, easily influenced, easily impressed.

"Marty, you go, meet her at the path. Check one final time she's not being followed. I'm sure we would have fucking seen somebody by now, but you never know. Search her, search her fucking well, bring her in to see me. We'll do this fast, but I want to have my fucking word," Scotchy talking as fast as he could with his condition. You could tell that every time he spoke he was biting back pain. No, you could tell that he was in continuous pain, speaking just made it worse. Twelve years of that.

"Ok, boss," Marty said and went outside.

"Cassidy, you stand way back there in the cave, like I say, any sudden move fucking shoot her, and don't shoot me by mistake, you'll regret it, I'm a hard fucking man to kill, easy man to piss off," Scotchy said.

"Sure, boss."

Cassidy made his way back toward me. If he turned around and had a good look, he was bound to see me hiding here against the wall. But Scotchy hadn't ordered them to check out the cave first. I would have. I would have had a man here all fucking day. But Scotchy was Scotchy. Brilliant at some things, half-assed at others.

We waited. Not long.

Marty appeared with Bridget. He had stripped her of her coat. She was standing there in a white turtleneck and jeans. Her red hair matted, soaked, plastered against her face and neck.

"Siobhan," she gasped as she saw her baby hooded and tied.

Siobhan didn't say anything. She was breathing shallowly and they'd clearly doped her. Bridget dropped the briefcase and made a dash for the girl.

"Don't fucking move, Bridget," Scotchy said, pointing the big Russian machine gun at her.

"What have you done to her?" Bridget demanded.

"A wee bit of Valium, she's fine. For now," Scotchy said.

"You've got your money. Now let us go," Bridget said.

Scotchy laughed. Bridget's eyes narrowed. She looked at him in fury, but she was trying to conceal her fear. Her hands were trembling. She hid them behind her back.

"You don't recognize me, do you?" Scotchy said.

Bridget shook her head.

"Take a seat, Bridget. Something I have to tell you. Something we have to discuss," Scotchy said.

"I want to see my daughter," Bridget insisted.

Scotchy fired the Pecheneg into the ground, a short two-second burst, but the noise and ricochets were terrifying. Any of us could have caught a bullet in an enclosed space like this. Miracle that we didn't. Bloody maniac.

"Take a fucking seat, bitch," Scotchy screamed. Cassidy and Marty looked as shocked and as shit-scared as I felt.

Bridget sat down on a rock as close as she could to Siobhan.

"I'm going to speak and you are going to listen," Scotchy began. "Every word is an effort. So every word is precious. I've had four operations on my throat in two years and what you hear now is the best they can come up with. The ten years I was in jail, I could barely grunt. You know what they called me? *El Americano Quieto*. It's a joke, see. A famous book. You probably seen the fucking picture."

"I don't see what your problems have to do with me or my daughter. I've given you your money, count it and let us go and you can have all the surgeries you need," Bridget said.

"Did I ask you to speak? Your job is to fucking listen, bitch. That's all. You just fucking listen and you'll understand. I want you to understand before I kill you. I want you to know what it's been like. Darkey White, your beloved, sent us to Mexico, he left us there, the fucking deal went sour, and he left us there to fucking die. Only two of us didn't die. Fucking young Michael Forsythe, he managed to get out. Aye, you remember him, don't ya. I heard what he did. He killed Darkey and Sunshine and Big Bob. Proud of him for that. Fucking disappeared into the WPP after that. Some say he was a fucking quisling, ratting out the whole organization to save his hide. But I don't blame him. He did right. Only thing, though, he didn't finish the job."

Bridget was stunned with recognition. Her hand went to her mouth. Her eyes widened, first in amazement and then horror.

"Scotchy, is it you? Is it really you?" she whispered.

Scotchy smiled.

"It's me. *Me llamo Señor Finn* . . . what I mean is, you can call me Mr. Finn, the name Scotchy is only for mates," Scotchy said.

"Everybody said you were dead. Even Michael said you were dead," Bridget said, horrified.

"Oh aye, but it takes more than a few fucking dagos to kill oul Scotchy boy. *Estoy vacunado* against death."

Scotchy shook his head.

"No more of that. Making me angry, Bridget, slipping back. But you're right, everybody did think I was topped. Me and Bruce tried to break out, I didn't make it. I was nearly killed dead, so I was. But somehow they fixed me up and after near a year in hospital they transferred me to a sweat-box jail in Baja. You know what it's like there? Fucking desert. Hundred degrees on the chilly days. Hundred and thirty wasn't so unusual. Nine years there until the amnesty under President Fox. I won't even begin to describe the horrors I went through, love. Every day of my life. Dreaming of you and Darkey and Big Bob. Dreaming of the moment when I'd get to see you all again."

Scotchy started to cough. Marty came over to help him. Scotchy waved him away.

Marty looked at the briefcase full of money.

Bridget looked at it too, in a different sort of way.

My heart skipped a beat.

Oh-ho, she had something up her sleeve.

Scotchy caught his breath, pulled a flask out of his jacket pocket, and drank from it. He continued with his diatribe.

"Aye, President Fox pardoned a couple of hundred of us foreigners. Fucking good man. And when I got out, I learned that Bruce had gone on a killing spree back in 1992. He had robbed me of some of it, but not all. Not my piece. Hadn't done a thing to you, had he? Oh aye, and Darkey had a daughter, didn't he? Well, well, well."

"You better not have hurt her," Bridget snarled.

"Not a pretty hair on her pretty head. Yet. Oh yeah. Coming to you, love. Fucking surprised when I heard Bridget was the boss now. Aye. Well, she inherits the empire as well as its fucking debts. And that's why you're here, love, to repay your debts."

"Ten million will go a long way," Bridget said, still not understanding what Scotchy meant to do. But I did. Bridget and the girl. The girl first to show Bridget the meaning of pain. Then her.

It was clever on Scotchy's part, it would establish him as a bad lad, the one who topped Bridget and her wee girl. Nobody would fuck with him after that. And ten million quid. Nearly eighteen million dollars with the weak greenback. Scotchy could return to America and ride out any storm he wanted. Or stay here. Belfast was on the up and up. If there was prosperity he could move into drugs and protection. And if it went the other way . . . Maybe by the 2011 census, certainly in the five years after it, the Catholics would have a majority in Northern Ireland. And any fool could see what that would mean. A Catholic majority in Ulster would mean a vote for union with the south and a million Protestants, many of whom had served in the armed forces, would suddenly find themselves in a foreign country. Think Bosnia, Rwanda, Kosovo. Oh, for a player like Scotchy, the possibilities would be endless.

Kill Bridget, kill Siobhan, establish his kudos, rise, rise, rise.

He could go far, that boy, especially with a smart consigliere like me beside him. His old mate. He'd take me back. I know he would.

Reveal myself, hugs, tears, slaps on the back, and then ride with Scotchy into the good times. He'd provide protection from Moran, from the peelers, from everybody. He was destined for great things.

Aye, you could say that that was the right and only move. Just close your eyes, Michael. Stick your fingers in your ears. All be over in a moment. The smart play. Crouch down and let it happen.

But no.

Siobhan had changed everything. Even if she'd only been Darkey's kid I wouldn't have let him do it.

And certainly not after what I knew now.

"Well, it's painful for me to talk. And it's the end of my story, bitch. You're going to pay without further fucking ado. Say goodbye to your wee girl," Scotchy said and stood back from her. He pointed the machine gun at Siobhan.

"The money, you have to count the money," Bridget said desperately.

"Fuck the money," Scotchy said, raised the gun.

I stood.

"Scotchy," I said.

Scotchy looked like he been electrocuted. He shook, froze, turned. His jaw opened. His good eye bulged in its socket. Cassidy almost shot me on the spot but reacted just in time.

"Bruce. You fucker," Scotchy said and the delight on his face would have curdled milk from fifty paces.

He ran to the back of the cave and embraced me.

"What the fuck are you doing here?" he screamed, literally jumping for joy.

"Scotchy, I—"

"Boys, boys, this is me old mate Bruce," he said to the other two, who were looking at me with a mixture of suspicion, horror, and disbelief. This whole scene was tense enough already without some ghost from Scotchy's past appearing like a magician at the back of cave. I mean, what the fuck else was back there? The Heavenly Choir, the FBI, the Irish Guards Pipe Band?

Cassidy kept one gun on me, Marty kept his on Bridget.

At least, it appeared that I was unarmed.

Scotchy grinned at me with false teeth, a pockmarked face, a reconstructed nose, a jaw that could never close properly, a white left eye.

"What the fuck are *you* doing here? You're dead," I said in amazement.

Scotchy smiled.

"How did you find this place?" he asked.

"I found your boy McFerrin. I asked him. He told me," I said.

Scotchy laughed.

"Bruce, Bruce, Bruce, you have no fucking idea. You have no idea how badly I've been trying to get you. Fucking hell, Bruce. I have moved heaven and earth. And I even sent a couple of guys to Australia. You were in Australia for a while, right?"

"No, Scotchy, I was never in Australia. But what about you, how the fuck are you still alive? When did you get out?" I asked, slapping him on the back.

"Two years, Bruce. Two years."

I hugged Scotchy and looked at Bridget behind him. I looked at her to get her attention. She saw my glance and it helped. She was a tiny bit less afraid, a wee bit reassured. I gave her the slightest inclination of my head, a hint to get as near to Siobhan as she possibly could. If bullets were going to fly, I needed them together and out of my kill box. I let go the hug and held Scotchy at arms' length. I punched him on the shoulder. He was fighting it, but the tears were welling up.

"Scotchy, I saw you fall on the razor wire, it nearly took your fucking head right off," I said.

"Aye," Scotchy said and his scarred and hideous face broke into a leer. "I was lucky. More lucky than I deserved to be, and the fucking wogs, they did me right considering everything, the fuckers. Those fucking bastards."

Scotchy sagged, his body almost tumbling into mine with the memory of it.

"It must have been terrible," I said.

"Bruce, I'll never tell you, we'll chat about old times, but I'll never talk about that with you because it'll break your heart," he said sadly.

I believed him. He wouldn't tell me and wouldn't blame me. He'd protect me from what I couldn't know. He'd look after me.

Scotchy clipped me around the top of the head.

"I heard about you in Mexico, killed Darkey White," he said, grinning.

"I finished it," I said.

Scotchy shook his head. He wasn't having that. He wanted his piece and he wasn't going to be denied. It would be pointless trying to talk him out of it. But I had to try.

"You survived, Scotchy, you're a tough son of a bitch, and now you've got some dough, a wee crew. It's great," I said.

He nodded, stretched, held his gun tight, turned around to look at Bridget.

"Bruce, wee bit of business to take care of, then we'll talk," he said.

"Aye, boss, we should head," Marty said.

"Wait a minute. You said you were looking for me?" I asked.

"Aye," Scotchy said.

"You didn't send a couple of guys to Dublin to pick me up, by any chance?" I asked him.

"Fuck aye, Bruce, I've been desperate, you are my right-hand man missing these twelve fucking years. Tell ya, half the reason I snatched the bairn in Belfast was the fucking hope that Bridget would send for you. Who did she know that knew Belfast? I knew she could get a message to you through the FBI. Maybe she'd promise you immunity or a couple of million. Christ, it couldn't have worked out better. Bridget and Siobhan, the money, and now you, Michael. It's like fucking Christmas," Scotchy said, laughing.

He leaned against an outcrop of rock.

"I think this is even better than the day I got out," he whispered to me with an affectionate smile.

I looked at Bridget and she began slowly moving next to Siobhan.

"So you sent a couple of clowns to get me in Dublin?" I asked.

Scotchy laughed.

"Aye, I had a couple of blokes try and pick you up in Dub. Put a local crew on it. Said just keep an eye out at the airport, pass the word around. Had a wee crew at Belfast airport too. Told them both: bring him to me. Don't hurt him, but make sure he bloody comes," Scotchy said.

"They were too heavy, Scotchy," I said.

"Aye, well, I allowed them a wee bit of leniency; I had to get you, Bruce, if you were coming, I couldn't allow you to see Bridget, knowing your weakness and all," he said, laughing.

"Aye, Scotch," I said.

"'Course, forgot who I was dealing with, not bloody Bruce at all, Michael fucking Forsythe, the man who killed Darkey White," he said with a laugh that became a cough. A whole series of long speeches for Scotchy. He was done in. His finger slipped off the safety on the Pecheneg and he leaned on me.

A big new shiny gun, the Pecheneg. The successor to the most successful rifle ever made—the AK-47. Anybody could fire an AK. We all knew its strengths and weaknesses. The AK was not a weapon of finesse. No sniper ever used an AK. You only have to look at that video of Osama bin Laden sighting his AK like it's a .303 Lee Enfield to know that he's a clueless rich boy. A good gun, though, reliable and easy to handle. The Pecheneg was the new Russian heavy machine gun. The Russians were touting it as an even better weapon. But there was a difference between the two guns. In an emergency you could shoot an AK from the hip. But the Pecheneg was much more powerful. You had to lift it up and aim it. And it would take a second for the lads to get the guns to their shoulders.

That one-second window was enough to give me the hint of a plan.

I'd pull out my pistol, I'd shoot Scotchy in the head. As he fell, I'd shoot Cassidy and after that—if all this has only taken that one second—I'd have at least a fifty-fifty chance of killing Marty before he managed to throw any fire near me.

"Scotchy, I am so happy to see you. I can't believe you're alive, ya big fucking girl, ya. I can't believe it," I said, and got ready.

"Here in the flesh," Scotchy said.

"You're right, it all worked out perfect. I'm just sorry about those players in Dublin, that's the only fuckup," I said.

"Aye, you killed one of them, Bruce, sent the other to the fucking hospital," Scotchy said.

"You sure they weren't there to kill me?" I asked.

"What for, Bruce? I owe you. I wouldn't kill you. Listen, I would have been more explicit, but I couldn't have my name bandied about, not with Bridget's people everywhere. I'd thought they'd lift you easy, bring you to me. I swear, Bruce, I wasn't trying to top you. Jesus, why would I?"

"You might have thought I'd abandoned you in Mexico, Scotchy," I said with genuine guilt.

"Fuck no. You did good getting out and killing that fucker Darkey White and his fucking evil apprentices. I wouldn't hurt you, Bruce. I was proud of you. I am proud of you. You're my kid brother," Scotchy said.

That was all I needed to hear.

The blessing. I was redeemed. The debt paid. I could end it now.

"I did it for you, Scotchy. I did it all for you."

He smiled.

"I know," he replied.

For you, Scotchy.

Forgive me.

I took the revolver out of my pocket.

"Bruce, we have to hurry on. Just glad you're here to see this, can't have all the revenge to your fucking self. The line has to end. Top the wean, top the lass. It's rough, Bruce, but I have to do it. Getting off light, really."

"Bridget didn't have anything to do with it, Scotch. Believe me, I know."

Scotchy snarled.

"She's the inheritor, Bruce. She's the fucking boss. And she was fucking engaged to that evil son of a bitch. I'm sure you're not saying nobody was responsible for all my fucking years of pain."

I nodded.

"Both of them, Scotchy? The wean, too?" I asked just to make sure.

"Aye, both of them."

"But I know you told your boys not to touch the wee girl," I said, giving him a last chance to recant.

"Aye, only me that does it. Only me. I have to kill them both, Bruce. Justice demands it," he said regretfully.

"That's what I thought, Scotchy," I said, raised the revolver to his temple, pulled the trigger.

It clicked. I pulled the trigger again. The chamber rotated, the hammer came down. No bullet came out. Goddamn misfire. What do you expect with half the Atlantic in your pocket? I smacked the pistol butt into the side of Scotchy's head and screamed at Bridget: "Hit the fucking deck."

She dived on top of Siobhan. I smacked Scotchy again as hard as I could and ripped the Pecheneg out of his grip. He fell to the ground. Bullets tore up the inside of the cave. Marty fired at me and Scotchy. I shot the Pecheneg for a count of two full seconds at Marty's chest. It tore a hole the size of a volleyball in his abdomen and as he fell backward, his intestines were flung into the air like silly spray from a joke can. Aghast, he scrambled to put his bloody guts back inside and died doing it.

Cassidy was too afraid of hitting Scotchy to shoot at me. Standing there paralyzed.

I aimed the Pecheneg high and gave him a burst that ripped his head apart.

Scotchy was on his feet. He had a handgun. He was pointing it at me. He was pulling the trigger.

Bridget leaped on top of him.

Fire in the barrel of the revolver. Scotchy pulling the trigger, rage contorting his face into even more hideous postures.

I dived for cover but thumped immediately into the cave wall. I couldn't hear. Lights. Blood. Silence. Blackness coming down like the fucking guillotine.

One second, two seconds, three seconds. Trade seconds for years, I wouldn't have known.

Bridget shaking me. Her face bruised, her lip bleeding.

"What the fuck?" I moaned.

I sat up. Two dead bodies in the cave. Marty and Cassidy.

"Scotchy?" I asked.

"Gone, grabbed Siobhan, I shot him in the back. Come on."

She pulled me up.

"What happened?"

"I jumped him, he punched me, I grabbed the gun and he grabbed Siobhan, I shot him, he ran, come on."

I sat up. The briefcase was gone too. He'd taken the time to lift that, too. And so, despite his words, this was a little bit about the money.

Bridget hauled me to my feet. I lifted one of the Pechenegs from the floor.

We ran to the cave mouth and I saw Scotchy running up the steps to the top of the cliff, dragging the girl after him. Not a bad feat for a skinny motherfucker like Scotchy.

"Are you sure you hit him?" I asked Bridget.

"I hit him."

The rain was easing, but the steps carved into the cliff face were slick with water, seaweed, and spray.

Rifle fire from the lighthouse sparked across the rocks. The tracer helping the shooter to get a bead on us. Bullets ricocheting on the path dead ahead.

"Harry," I said. Gang member number four.

And I saw that once Scotchy got to the top of the cliff, we were fucked. He could shoot us from a dozen high-angled positions around the lighthouse. And Jesus, if he couldn't get Bridget he could still throw Bridget's daughter off the cliff. Bridget's daughter? Mine own precious darling girl.

Yes, I'll move the Earth.

I ran the steps two at a time.

Pecheneg rounds smacking off the steps in front of and behind me.

I ran faster, slipped, got up.

But it was too late. Scotchy made it to the top. Harry passed him a revolver, they pushed the girl to the ground, and they both began to shoot. I stumbled and fell, dropped the machine gun. The only sensible policy now was to retreat back to the cave. But I kept fucking going. I sprinted the last of the bastard stairs.

Twenty feet from the top. Scotchy shooting a 9mm semi, Harry shooting the machine gun. I probably would have lasted a heroic two or three seconds more had not the briefcase in Scotchy's left hand, at that exact moment, exploded in a huge ball of fire and white light.

A thunderflash, she'd fucking booby-trapped it with an army-issue thunderflash.

That's my lass.

Scotchy screamed as his arm caught fire. Harry pushed him to the dirt and tried to roll him out. I made it to the top of the stairs just as Scotchy was getting to his feet.

"Bruce, what the fuck do you think you're doing?" Scotchy yelled in a confusion of betrayal, rage, and disappointment. But there's a time for talking and a time for not talking. Instead of giving him an answer, I jumped the fucker, threw him into Harry, rolled to the side, got to my feet.

Harry recovered, raised his Pecheneg. Bridget got to the top of the stairs and shot at him twice.

"Michael," she screamed.

Harry turned to fire at her. I charged him, barreled him to the ground, knocked his rifle away, stabbed a finger in his eye, punched him in the throat, threw him over on his face, put my arm around his fat neck and my knee on his spine, and twisted his neck hard backward until it snapped and the life instantly went out of him.

Scotchy's right hand was burned. But with his trembling left he found his gun, fired the rest of his clip at Bridget, every shot missing by miles. He slotted another clip, but I was on him. I head-butted him on the nose, breaking it. I grabbed his weapon hand and bit him on the thumb.

"Traitor, you traitor, Bruce," he snarled, spitting the words out, kicking me.

"My name's not Bruce," I said and bit through his thumb, right to the bone. He screamed, dropped the weapon. I fell on him and we scrambled for the gun. I kicked it away from him and kneed him in the head. Somehow he rolled to one side and got to his feet. His skull cracked, his face covered with blood. He ran at me screaming with incandescent rage. I let him run, and I moved to the side like a fucking matador, grabbed him, threw him.

The poor bastard never had a chance.

His feet scrambled for purchase in the cold sea air and then he fell. Down, down, a hundred feet, into the sea, his body smashing to pieces on the razor-sharp rocks. There would be no resurrection this time, my old mate.

I sank to my knees.

I slumped forward, wavered for a moment, and cried. . . .

A minute passed.

Bridget stroking my face.

Holding me.

Siobhan, dazed, looking at her ma. The spit of her mother. Right down to the crimson hair and the eyes like a forest glade. Still under, drugged, baffled, wondering what was going on. She wouldn't remember a lot of this.

"It's going to be ok, it's going to be ok," Bridget was saying.

"Mommy," Siobhan said.

Bridget crawled next to me and all three of us held one another on the clifftop in the wind and rain.

"Michael, there's something I have to tell you," she said. "I lied about Siobhan. I didn't tell you the whole story. I didn't want it to be true. Oh God, I didn't want it to be true. But it is."

I nodded.

"Michael. It's you. You're her father," Bridget said softly.

And as my fingertips reached for her fingertips and the blood dripped from my hand to her hand, I turned to her and said: "I know."

✧ ✧ ✧

The cliff path under the lighthouse. The sea had receded and the rain had ceased and turned to mist. The wind had slunk back to its box in Iceland. The scene was done and the sympathetic fallacy was back in force. Stars. I looked for the Southern Cross, but it wasn't there. That was another hemisphere. Another time.

The girl was sleeping now. My daughter. Sleeping after all this. How could you not love her? I carried her wrapped in both our jackets. Behind us, shrouded in fog, the lighthouse keeping ghost time in broad beams across the sea.

We walked and Siobhan slept and we stopped at the first house we saw. A white timber frame with palm trees up the drive. Palm trees in Ireland. A thing that always made me smile. I carried Siobhan between the trees and up the gravel path. Bridget knocked on the door.

A kid answered. Big guy in jeans and Metallica T-shirt. He looked at me, Bridget, and then Siobhan.

"Has there been an accident?" he asked.

I nodded.

"You better come in. Do youse need an ambulance?" he asked calmly.

"We're ok. The girl's shaken up, she's sleeping, but she'll need a doctor," I said.

"In to the left, have a seat, I'll dial 999."

We went in. The kid phoned for the authorities and a few minutes later brought towels and chocolate biscuits. He told us his name was Patrick. He was about nineteen, alone here tonight as his parents were at a Handel concert in Belfast.

I nodded, unable to speak. That adrenaline crash was coming. Exhausted, I could have slept right there on the couch.

Four of us sitting there.

"Do you want a blanket or anything for the girl?" he asked.

"Aye," I said and gave him a wee look. The sort of look only a gunman can give. He took the hint.

"I'll bring that tea, get you towels, youse just relax now, the ambulance might be a while getting down the path; but it'll get here."

He got up, gave me a nod to show that he understood my wish to be left alone.

"Cheers, thanks," I said.

And when he had gone, Bridget sighed, leaned back on the sofa, began to cry. We sat in silence, listening to the waves retreating on the stony beach.

Siobhan woke, looked at her mother and father, whimpered for a moment, and with a single caress from Bridget fell back into a doze.

Bridget turned to me.

"A week ago I would have given anything to see you dead," she said.

"Aye, and a week ago I would have given anything just to see you," I said.

"So what happens next? After tomorrow we wake up like Cinderella and try to murder each other again? Or does this change everything?" she asked.

This changes everything, I thought.

I looked at her.

"You want to know what happens next?" I asked in a whisper.

"I do."

"Well, I'll tell you. The first thing we do is get out of Ireland. Your man Moran wants me dead, so you'll either have to talk to him, or we'll have to kill him. Or we'll have to give him the slip."

"We?"

"We."

She stared at me and mused the word over in her mind. Her tired eyes processing the information.

"We," she said, really considering the possibility for the first time.

"We," I insisted. "And then you'll retire and I'll retire and we'll move to Peru."

"Peru, are you kidding?"

"It's got a bad rap, but I really like it there. We'll move there and we'll have more kids and we'll watch the sun set over the Pacific, and with your dough we can buy a big house with stables and trails up into the mountains and a Lima pied-à-terre in the Calle de las Siete Revueltas. And we'll be done with the life. Done with it. And Siobhan will go to school and she'll speak Spanish and English and be smart and beautiful and content; as will her brothers and sisters, and we'll ride horses, and surf, and eat steak, and all live happily ever after."

And Bridget thought about it.

She thought about me and retirement and what that would mean. And she thought about Siobhan. And she lived with the past too.

That Christmas night in 1992. Me cutting her fiancé's throat.

She thought about that.

I could read her. I always could, or at least I imagined I could. Her emotions like ripples on the lough, or a sidewinder on the desert floor. What was owed and what was paid. And who deserved to die and who deserved to live. And how easy it would be to kill me tonight and be done with it all. Except that you're never done. Never.

That was one universe of possibilities.

But there was another. An escape from the blood feud and the vendetta and the law of honor. The alternative, a new life in a new world. I knew she had picked up Scotchy's gun and I knew she could use it. And if it was going to happen, it was going to happen now, before the cops showed, with the witness out of the room, with her girl back safe and sound. "After all this we had a terrible accident with the gun, officer."

I waited, flinched. Dan's troika arguing it out. The general, the killer, the mother. The strong, the vengeful, the weak.

Her hand reached inside her coat.

The lids closed on those big emerald eyes.

Opened again.

She produced a gun, Scotchy's gun.

She set it on the sofa.

I looked at Bridget and I looked at the gun. Neither of us moved. Then Bridget reached in her coat again and found the thing she'd really been searching for: a brush. She began taking the knots out of Siobhan's hair. She tried to say something, coughed. Her throat was hoarse from crying and she couldn't speak, but her head bobbed the affirmative, and finally, in that husky, tired New York whisper, she said simply:

"Yes."

ABOUT THE AUTHOR

Adrian McKinty was born and grew up in Carrickfergus, Northern Ireland, when terrorism in Ulster was at its height. Educated at Oxford University, he then immigrated to New York City, where he lived in Harlem for five years, working in bars and on construction crews. He lives in Colorado with his wife and daughters. When not writing crime fiction, he teaches high school English, plays rugby at the weekend, and gives much joy to his neighbors as he attempts to learn the accordion.